Deemed 'the father of the scientif[...] **Austin Freeman** had a long and di[...] a writer of detective fiction. He was born in London, the son of a tailor who went on to train as a pharmacist. After graduating as a surgeon at the Middlesex Hospital Medical College, Freeman taught for a while and joined the colonial service, offering his skills as an assistant surgeon along the Gold Coast of Africa. He became embroiled in a diplomatic mission when a British expeditionary party was sent to investigate the activities of the French. Through his tact and formidable intelligence, a massacre was narrowly avoided. His future was assured in the colonial service. However, after becoming ill with blackwater fever, Freeman was sent back to England to recover and, finding his finances precarious, embarked on a career as acting physician in Holloway Prison. In desperation, he turned to writing and went on to dominate the world of British detective fiction, taking pride in testing different criminal techniques. So keen were his powers as a writer that part of one of his best novels was written in a bomb shelter.

BY THE SAME AUTHOR
ALL PUBLISHED BY HOUSE OF STRATUS

Helen Vardon's Confession

R Austin Freeman

HOUSE OF
STRATUS

This edition published in 2001 by House of Stratus, an imprint of
Stratus Books Ltd., 21 Beeching Park, Kelly Bray,
Cornwall, PL17 8QS, UK.
www.houseofstratus.com

Typeset, printed and bound by House of Stratus.

A catalogue record for this book is available from the British Library
and the Library of Congress.

ISBN 0-7551-0363-7

CONTENTS

CONTENTS CONTD.

Prologue

To every woman there comes a day (and that all too soon) when she receives the first hint that Time, the harvester, has not passed her by unnoticed. The waning of actual youth may have passed with but the faintest regret, if any regret for the lost bud being merged in the triumph at the glory of the opening blossom. But the waning of womanhood is another matter. Old age has no compensations to offer for those delights that it steals away. At least, that is what I understand from those who know, for I must still speak on the subject from hearsay, having received from Father Time but the very faintest and most delicate hint on the subject.

I was sitting at my dressing-table brushing out my hair, which is of a docile habit though a thought bulky, when amidst the black tress – blacker than it used to be when I was a girl – I noticed a single white hair. It was the first that I had seen, and I looked at it dubiously, picking it out from its fellows to see if it were all white, and noticing how like it was to a thread of glass. Should I pluck it out and pretend that it was never there? Or should I, more thriftily – for a hair is a hair after all, and enough of them will make a wig – should I dye it and hush up its treason?

I smiled at the foolish thought. What a to-do about a single white hair! I have seen girls in their twenties with snow-white hair and looking as sweet as lavender. As to this one, I would think of it as a souvenir from the troubled past rather than a harbinger of approaching age; and with this I swept my brush over it and buried it even as I had buried those sorrows and those dreadful experiences which might have left me white-headed years before.

But that glassy thread, buried once more amid the black, left a legacy of suggestion. Those hideous days were long past now. I could look back on them unmoved – nay with a certain serene interest. Suppose I should write the history of them? Why not? To write is not necessarily to publish. And if, perchance, no eye but mine shall see these lines until the little taper of my life has burned down into its socket, then what matters it to me whether praise or blame, sympathy or condemnation, be my portion. Posterity has no gifts to offer that I need court its suffrages.

BOOK ONE
TRAGEDY

CHAPTER ONE

The Crack of Doom

There is no difficulty whatever in deciding upon the exact moment at which to open this history. Into some lives the fateful and significant creep by degrees, unnoticed till by the development of their consequences the mind is aroused and memory is set, like a sleuth-hound, to retrace the course of events and track the present to its origin in the past. Not so has it been with mine. Serene, eventless its quiet years had slipped away unnumbered, from childhood to youth, from youth to womanhood, when, at the appointed moment the voice of Destiny rang out, trumpet-tongued; and behold! in the twinkling of an eye all was changed.

"Happy," it has been said, "is the nation which has no history!" And surely the same may be said with equal truth of individuals. So, at any rate, experience teaches me; for the very moment wherein I may be said to have begun to have a history saw a life-long peace shattered into a chaos of misery and disaster.

How well I remember the day – yea and the very moment – when the blow fell, like a thunderbolt crashing down out of a cloudless sky. I had been sitting in my little room upstairs reading very studiously and pausing now and again to think over what I had read. The book was Lecky's "History of England in the Eighteenth Century," and the period on which I was engaged was that of Queen Anne. And here, coming presently upon a footnote containing a short quotation from "The Spectator," it occurred to

3

me that I should like to look over the original letter. Accordingly, laying aside my book, I began to descend the stairs – very softly, because I knew that my father had a visitor – possibly a client – with him in his study. And when I came to the turn of the stair and saw that the study door was ajar, I stepped more lightly still, though I stole down quickly lest I should overhear what was being said.

The library, or book-room as we called it, was next to the study, and to reach it I had to pass the half-opened door, which I did swiftly on tiptoe, without hearing more than the vague murmur of conversation from within. "The Spectators" stood on a shelf close to the door; a goodly row clothed in rusty calf to which the worn gilt tooling imparted a certain sumptuousness that had always seemed very pleasant to my eye. My hand was on the third volume when I heard my father say: "So that's how the matter stands."

I plucked the volume from the shelf, and, tucking it under my arm, stole out of the book-room, intending to dart up the stairs before there should be time for anything more to be said; but I had hardly crossed the threshold, and was, in fact, exactly opposite the study door, when a voice said very distinctly, though not at all loudly: "Do you realise, Vardon, that this renders you liable to seven years' penal servitude?"

At those terrible words I stopped as though I had been, in a moment, turned into stone: stopped with my lips parted, my very breathing arrested, clutching at the book under my arm, with no sign of life or movement save the tumultuous thumping of my heart. There was what seemed an interminable pause, and then my father replied: "Hardly, I think, Otway. Technically, perhaps, it amounts to a misdemeanour – "

"Technically!" repeated Mr Otway.

"Yes, technically. The absence of any intent to defraud modifies the position considerably. Still, for the purpose of argument, we may admit that it amounts to a misdemeanour."

"And," said Mr Otway, "the maximum punishment of that misdemeanour is seven years' penal servitude. As to your plea of absence of fraudulent intent, you, as a lawyer of experience, must know well that judges are not apt to be very sympathetic with trustees who misappropriate property placed in their custody."

"Misappropriate!" my father exclaimed.

"Yes," replied Mr Otway, "I say misappropriate. What other word could you apply? Here is a sum of money which has been placed in your custody. I come to you with authority to receive that money from you on behalf of the trustees, and you tell me that you haven't got it. You are not only unable to produce it, but you are unable to give any date on which you could produce it. And meanwhile it seems that you have applied it to your own uses."

"I haven't spent it," my father objected. "The money is locked up for the present, but it isn't lost."

"What is the use of saying that?" demanded Mr Otway. "You haven't got the money and you can't give any satisfactory account of it. The plain English of it is that you have used this trust money for your own private purposes, and that when the trustors ask to have it restored to them, you are unable to produce it."

To this my father made no immediate reply; and in the silence that ensued I could hear my heart throbbing and the blood humming in the veins of my neck. At length my father asked: "Well, Otway, what are you going to do?"

"Do!" repeated Mr Otway. "What can I do. As a trustee, it is my duty to get this money from you. I have to protect the interests of those whom I represent. And if you have misapplied these funds – well, you must see for yourself that I have no choice."

"You mean that you'll prosecute?"

"What else can I do? I can't introduce personal considerations into the business of a trust; and even if I should decline to move in the matter, the trustors themselves would undoubtedly take action."

Here there followed a silence which seemed to me of endless duration; then Mr Otway said, in a somewhat different tone: "There is just one way for you out of this mess, Vardon,"

"Indeed!" said my father.

"Yes. I am going to make you a proposal, and I may as well put it quite bluntly. It is this. I am prepared to take over your liabilities for the time being, on condition that I marry your daughter. If you agree, then on the day on which the marriage takes place, I pay into your bank the sum of five thousand pounds, you giving me an undertaking to repay the loan if and when you can."

"Have you any reason to suppose that my daughter wishes to marry you?" my father asked.

"Not the slightest," replied Mr Otway; "but I think it probable that, if the case were put to her – "

"It is not going to be," my father interrupted. "I would rather go to jail than connive at the sacrifice of my daughter's happiness."

"You might have thought of her happiness a little sooner, Vardon," Mr Otway remarked. "We are not quite of an age, but she might easily find it more agreeable to be the wife of an elderly man than the daughter of a convict. At any rate, it would be only fair to give her the choice."

"It would be entirely unfair," my father retorted. "In effect, it would be asking her to make the sacrifice, and she might be fool enough to consent. And please bear in mind, Otway, that I am not a convict yet, and possibly may never be one. There are certain conceivable alternatives, you know."

"Oh," said Mr Otway, "if you have resources that you have not mentioned, that is quite another matter. I understood that you had none. And as to sacrifice, there is no need to harp on that string so persistently. Your daughter might be happy enough as my wife."

"What infernal nonsense you are talking!" my father exclaimed, impatiently. "Do you suppose that Helen is a fool?"

"No, I certainly do not," Mr Otway replied.

"Very well then: what do you mean by her being happy as your wife? Here am I, standing over a mine – "

"Of your own laying," interrupted Mr Otway.

"Quite so; of my own laying. And here you come with a lighted match and say to my daughter, in effect: 'My dear young lady, I am your devoted lover. Be my wife – consent this very instant or I fire this mine and blow you and your father to smithereens.' And then, you think, she would settle down with you and live happy ever after. By the Lord, Otway, you must be a devilish poor judge of character."

"I am quite willing to take the risk," said Mr Otway.

"So you may be," my father retorted angrily, "but I'm not. I would rather see the poor girl in her grave than know that she was chained for life to a cold-blooded, blackmailing scoundrel – "

"Softly, Vardon!" Mr Otway interrupted. "There is no need for that sort of language. And perhaps we had better shut the door."

Here, as I drew back hastily into the book-room, quick footsteps crossed the study floor and I heard the door close. The interruption brought me back to some sense of my position; though, to be sure, what I had overheard concerned me as much as it concerned anyone. Quickly slipping the book back on the shelf, I ran on tiptoe past the study door and up the stairs; and even then I was none too soon; for, as I halted on the threshold of my room, the study door opened again and the two men strode across the hall.

"You are taking a ridiculously wrong-headed view of the whole affair," I heard Mr Otway declare.

"Possibly," my father replied, stiffly. "And if I do, I am prepared to take the consequences."

"Only the consequences won't fall on you alone," said Mr Otway.

"Good afternoon" was the dry and final response. Then the hall door slammed, and I heard my father walk slowly back to the study.

CHAPTER TWO

Atra Cura

As the study door closed, I sank into my easy chair with a sudden feeling of faintness and bodily exhaustion. The momentary shock of horror and amazement had passed, giving place to a numb and chilly dread that made me feel sick and weak. Scraps of the astounding conversation that I had heard came back to me incoherently and yet with hideous distinctness, like the whisperings of some malignant spirit. Disjointed words and phrases repeated themselves again and again, almost meaninglessly, but still with a vague undertone of menace.

And then by degrees, as I sat gazing at the blurred pages of the book that still lay open on the reading-stand, my thoughts grew less chaotic; the words of that dreadful dialogue arranged themselves anew, and I began with more distinctness to gather their meaning.

"Seven years penal servitude!"

That was the dreadful refrain of this song of doom that was being chanted in my ear by the Spirit of Misfortune. And ruin – black, hideous ruin – for my father and me was the burden of that refrain; no mere loss, no paltry plunge into endurable poverty, but a descent into the bottomless pit of social degradation, from which there could be no hope of resurrection.

Nor was this the worst. For, gradually, as my thoughts began to arrange themselves into a coherent sequence, I realised that it was not the implied poverty and social disgrace that gave to that sentence its dreadful import. Poverty might be overcome, and disgrace could be endured; but when I thought of my father dragged away from me to be cast into jail; when, in my mind's eye, I saw him clothed in the horrible livery of shame, wearing out his life within the prison walls and behind the fast-bolted prison doors; the thought and the imagined sight were unendurable. It was death – for him at least; for he was not a strong man. And for me?

Here, of a sudden, there came back to me the rather enigmatical speech of my father's, which I had heard without at the moment fully comprehending, but which I now recalled with a shock of alarm.

"Please bear in mind, Otway, that I am not a convict yet, and possibly may never be one. There are certain conceivable alternatives, you know."

The cryptic utterance had evidently puzzled Mr Otway, who had clearly misunderstood it as referring to some unknown resources. To me, no such misunderstanding was possible. More than once my father had discussed with me the ethics of suicide, on which subject he held somewhat unorthodox opinions; and I now recalled with terrible distinctness the very definite statement that he had made on the occasion of our last talk. "For my part," he had said, "if I should ever find myself in such a position that the continuance of life was less desirable than its termination, I should not hesitate to take the appropriate measures for exchanging the less desirable state for the more desirable."

In the face of such a statement, made, as I felt sure, in all sincerity and with sober judgment, how could I entertain any doubt as to the interpretation of that reference to "certain conceivable alternatives." To a man of culture and some position and none too robust in health, what would be the aspect of life with its immediate future occupied by a criminal prosecution ending in an inevitable conviction and a term of penal servitude?

Could the continuance of such a life be conceived as desirable? Assuredly not.

And then imagination began to torture me by filling in with hideous ingenuity the dreadful details. Now it was a pistol shot heard in the night, and a group of terrified servants huddled together in the corridor. But no; that was not like my poor father. Such crude and bloody methods appertain rather to the terror-stricken fugitive than to one who is executing a considered and orderly retreat. Then I saw myself, in the grey of the morning, tapping at his bedroom door: tapping – tapping – and at last opening the door, or perhaps bursting it open. I saw the dim room – Oh! How horribly plain and vivid it was! With the cold light of the dawn glimmering through the blind, the curtained bed, the half-seen figure, still and silent in the shadow. Horrible! Horrible!

And then, in an instant, the scene changed. I saw a man in our hall. A man in uniform: a railway porter or inspector. I heard him tell, in a hushed, embarrassed voice, of a strange and dreadful accident down on the line…And yet again this awful phantasmagoria shifted the scene and showed me a new picture: a search party, prowling with lantern around a chalk pit; and anon a group of four men, treading softly and carrying something on a hurdle.

"Dear God!" I gasped with my hands pressed to my forehead, "must it be – this awful thing! Is there no other way?"

And with that there fell on me a great calm. A chilly calm, bringing no comfort, and yet, in a manner, a relief. For, perhaps, after all, there *was* another way. It was true that my father had rejected Mr Otway's proposal, and such was my habit of implicit obedience that, with his definite rejection of it, the alternative had, for me, ceased to exist. But now, with the horror of this dreadful menace upon me, I recalled the words that had been spoken, and asked myself if that avenue of escape were really closed. As to my father, I had no doubt; he would never consent; and even to raise the question might only be to precipitate the catastrophe. But with regard to Mr Otway, the manner in which my father had met and rejected his proposal seemed to close the subject finally. He had called him a blackmailing scoundrel and used other injurious expressions, which might make it difficult or, at least, uncomfortable to re-open the question. Still that was a small matter. When one is walking to the gallows, one does not boggle at an uncomfortable shoe.

As to my own inclinations, they were beside the mark. My father's life and good name must be saved if it were possible; and it seemed that it might be possible – at a price. Whether it were possible or not depended on Mr Otway.

I recalled what I knew of this man who had thus in a moment become the arbiter of my father's fate and mine. My acquaintance with him was but slight, though I had met him pretty frequently and had sometimes wondered what his profession was, if he had any. I had assumed, from his evident acquaintance with legal matters, that he was a lawyer. But he was not in ordinary practice; and his business, whatever it was, seemed to involve a good deal of travelling. That was all I knew about him. As to his appearance, he was a huge, unwieldy man of a somewhat Jewish cast of face, some years older, I should think, than my father; pleasant spoken and genial in a somewhat heavy fashion but quite uninteresting. Hitherto I had neither liked nor disliked him. Now, it need hardly be said, I regarded him with decided aversion; for if he were not, as my father had said, "a blackmailing scoundrel," he had, at any rate, taken the meanest, the most ungenerous advantage of my father's difficulties, to say nothing of the callous, cynical indifference that he had shown in regard to me and my wishes and interests.

It may seem a little odd that I found myself attaching no blame to my father. Yet so it was. To me he appeared merely as the victim of circumstances. No doubt he had done something indiscreet – perhaps incorrect. But discretion and correctness are not qualities that appeal strongly to a woman: whereas generosity – and my father was generous almost to a fault – makes the most powerful appeal to feminine sympathies. As to his honesty and good faith, I never doubted them for an instant; besides, he had plainly said that no fraudulent intent could be ascribed to him.

11

What he had done I had not the least idea. Nor did I particularly care. It was not the act, but its consequences with which I was concerned.

My meditations were interrupted at length by an apologetic tap at the door, followed by the appearance of our housemaid.

"If you please, Miss Helen, shall I take Mr Vardon's tea to the study, or is he going to have it with you?"

The question brought me back from the region of tragedy and disaster in which my thoughts had been straying, to the homely commonplaces of everyday life.

"I'll just run down and ask him, Jessie," I answered; "and you needn't wait. I'll come and tell you what he says."

I ran quickly down the stairs, but at the study door I paused with a sudden revival of those terrors that had so lately assailed me. Suppose he should open the subject and have something dreadful to tell me? Or suppose that, even now, already –

At the half-formed thought, I raised a trembling hand, and, tapping lightly at the door, opened it and entered. He was sitting at the table with a small pile of sealed and stamped letters before him, and, as I stood, steadying my hand on the doorknob, he looked up with his customary smile of friendly welcome.

"Hail! O Dame of the azure hosen," said he, swinging round on his revolving chair, "and how fares it with our liege lady, Queen Anne?"

"She is quite well, thank you," I replied.

"The Lord be praised!" he rejoined. "I seemed to have heard some rumour of her untimely decease. A mere canard, it would seem; a fiction of these confounded newspapermen. Or perchance I have been misled by the jocose and boisterous Lecky."

The whimsical playfulness of speech, habitual as it was to him, impressed me – perhaps for that very reason – with a vague uneasiness. It was not what I had expected after that terrible conversation. The anticlimax to my own tragic thoughts was too sudden; the descent to the ordinary too uncomfortably steep. I perched myself on his knee, as I often did, despite my rather excessive size and passed my hand over his thin, grey hair.

"Do you know," I said, clinging desperately to the common-place "that you are going bald? I can see the skin of your head quite plainly."

"And why not?" he demanded. "Did you think my hair grew out of my cranium? But you won't see it long. I've heard of an infallible hair-restorer."

"Indeed!"

"Yes, indeed! Guaranteed to grow a crop of ringlets on a bladder of lard. We'll get a bottle and try it on the carpet broom; and if the result is satisfactory – well, we'll just put Esau in his place in the second row."

"You are a very frivolous old person, Mr Pater," said I. "Do you know that?"

"I hope so," he replied. "And again I say, why not? When a man is too old to play the fool, it is time to carry him to the bone-yard. Am I going to have any tea?"

"Of course you are. Will you have it here alone or shall we have tea together?"

"What a question!" he exclaimed. "Am I in my dotage? Should I drink tea in musty solitude when I might bask in the smiles of a lovely maiden? Avaunt! No, I'll tell you what we'll do, Jimmy. I'll just telephone down to the office and see if there is any silly nonsense there that may distract me from serious pursuits, and, if there isn't we'll have tea in the workroom and then we'll polish off that coal scuttle."

"Finish it! But there's quite a lot to do."

"Then we'll do the lot."

"But why this hurry? There's no particular reason for getting it finished tonight, is there?"

"I don't know that there is; but we've had the thing hanging about long enough. Better get it finished and start on something else. Now you trot off and see about tea while I ring up Jackson."

As he turned to the telephone, I hurried away to give instructions to the maid and to set the workshop in order so that we might start without delay on our evening's task, concerning which a few words of explanation would seem to be called for.

My father was by nature designed to be a craftsman. He was never so happy as when he was making something or in some way working with his hands; and remarkably skilful hands they were, with an inborn capacity for the dexterous manipulation of every kind of material, tool or appliance. And to his natural skill he had added a vast amount of knowledge of methods and processes. He was an excellent woodworker, an admirable mechanic, and a quite passable potter. Our house abounded in the products of his industry; stools, cupboards, clocks, fenders, earthenware jars; even our bicycles had been built, or, at least, "assembled" by him, and a bronze knocker on our door had been finished by him from castings made in our workshop. If his powers of design had been equal to his manual skill, he would have been a first-class art craftsman. Unfortunately they were not. Left to himself, his tendency was to aim at a neat trade finish, at smooth surfaces and mechanical precision. But he knew his limitations, and had been at great pains to have me instructed in the arts of design; and, as I apparently had some natural aptitude in that direction, I was able to help him by making sketches and working drawings and by criticising the work as it progressed. But my duties did not stop at that. In our happy, united life, I was his apprentice, his journeyman, his assistant – or foreman, as he pleased to call me – and his constant companion, in the house, in the workshop, and in our walks abroad.

As our maid, Jessie, laid the tea tray on a vacant corner of the workbench, I examined our latest joint-production, a bronze coal scuttle, the design of which was based on a Roman helmet that I had seen in the British Museum. There was a good deal more than an ordinary evening's work to be done before it could be finished. A portion of the embossed ornament on the foot required touching up, the foot itself had to be brazed to the body and the handle had to be riveted to the lugs, to say nothing of the "pickling," scouring, and oxidising. It was a colossal evening's work.

But it was not the magnitude of the task that troubled me, for I shared my father's love of manual work. What had instantly impressed me with a vague discomfort was the urgency of my father's desire to get this piece of work finished and done with. That was not like him at all. Not only had he the genuine craftsman's inexhaustible patience, but he had a habit of keeping an apparently finished work on hand, that he might tinker at it lovingly, smooth and polish it, and bring it to a state of even greater completeness and finish.

Why, then, this strange urgency and impatience? And, as I asked myself the question, all my fears came crowding back on me. Again there came that dreadful sinking at the heart, that strangling terror of the storm-cloud that hung over us, unseen but ready to burst and overwhelm us in ruin at any moment.

But I had little time for these gloomy and disquieting thoughts. The tinkling of the telephone bell in the study told me that my father had finished his talk with his managing clerk, and a few moments later he strode into the workshop and began taking off his coat.

"Where's your apron, Jimmy?" he asked (the pet name "Jimmy" had been evolved out of an ancient fiction that my name was Jemima).

"There's no hurry, Pater, dear," said I. "Let a person have her tea in peace. And do sit down like a Christian man."

He obediently perched himself on a stool as I handed him his tea, but in less than a minute he was on his feet again, prowling, cup in hand, around the end of the bench where the work lay.

"Wonder if I'd better anneal it a bit," he mused, picking up the bronze foot and examining the unfinished space. "Mustn't make it too soft. Think I will, though. We can hammer it up a little on the stake after it's brazed on. That will harden it enough."

He laid the foot down, but only that he might apply a match to the great gas blowpipe; and I watched him with a sinking heart as he stood with his teacup in one hand, while with the other he held the foot, gripped in a pair of tongs, in the roaring purple flame. What did it mean, this strange, restless haste to finish what was, after all, but a work of pleasure? Did it portend some change that he saw more clearly than I? Was he, impelled by the craftsman's instinct, turning in this fashion a page of the book of life? Or was it – Oh! dreadful thought! – was it that he was deliberately writing "Finis" before closing the volume?

But whatever was in his secret mind, he chatted cheerfully as he worked, and submitted to be fed with scraps of bread and butter and to have cups of tea administered at intervals; yet still I noted that the chasing hammer flew at unwonted speed, and the depth of the punch-marks on the work that rested on the sand-bag told of an unusual weight in the blows.

"What a pity it is," he remarked, "that social prejudices prevent a middle-class man from earning a livelihood with his hands. Now, here I am, a third-rate solicitor perforce, whereas, if I followed my bent, I should be a first-rate coppersmith. Shouldn't I?"

"Quite first-rate," I replied.

"Or even a silversmith," he continued, "if I could have my mate, Jim, to do the art with a capital A while I did the work with a capital W. Hm?"

He looked up at me with a twinkle, and I took the opportunity to pop a piece of bread and butter into his mouth, which occasioned a pause in the conversation.

I had entertained faint – very faint – hopes that he might say something to me about his difficulties. Not that I was inquisitive on the subject; but, in view of a resolution that was slowly forming in my mind, I should have liked to have some idea what his position really was. It seemed pretty plain, however, that he did not intend to take me into his confidence; notwithstanding which I decided in a tentative way to give him an opening.

"Wasn't that Mr Otway who was with you this afternoon?" I asked.

"Yes," he replied. "How did you know?"

"I heard his voice in the hall as you let him out," I answered, with something of a gulp at the implied untruth.

The chasing hammer was arrested for a moment in mid-air, and, as my father's eye fixed itself reflectively on the punch that he held, I could see that he was trying to remember what Mr Otway had said in the hall.

"Yes," he replied, after a brief pause, "it was Mr Otway. I should hardly have thought you would have known his voice. Queer fellow, Otway. No brains to speak of, but yet an excellent man of business in his way."

"What does he do – by way of profession, I mean?"

"The Lord knows. He was originally a solicitor, but he hasn't practised for years. Now he is what is called a financier, which is a little vague, but apparently profitable. And I think he does something in the way of precious stones."

"Do you mean that he deals in them?"

"Yes, occasionally; at least, so I have heard. I know that he is something of a connoisseur in stones, and that he had a collection which he sold some time ago. I have also heard – and I believe it is a fact – that his name was originally Levy, and that he is one of the Chosen. But why he changed his name I have no notion, unless it was an undesirable one to present to the financial world."

I was half disposed to pursue my enquiries further, but as he finished speaking, he once more began to ply the hammer with such furious energy that I became quite uneasy.

"You mustn't exert yourself so much, Pater," I remarked. "Remember what Dr Sharpe said."

"Bah!" he replied. "Sharpe is an old woman. My heart is sound enough. At any rate, it will last as long as the rest of me. An old fellow like me cannot expect to go in for sprinting or high jumping, but there's no need for him to live in splints and cotton wool."

"Nor to endanger his health by perfectly unnecessary exertion. Why on earth are you in such a fever to get this thing finished?"

"I'm not in a fever, my dear," he answered; "I'm only tired of seeing this thing lying about unfinished. You see, as it stands it is only so many pounds of old bronze, whereas a couple of hours' work turns it into a valuable piece of furniture, fit to take a dignified place in the catalogue when we are sold up. Just consider how finely it would read: 'Handsome bronze scuttle, in form of Roman helmet, the work of the late owner and his charming and talented daughter, capable of serving either as a convenient receptacle for coal or as a becoming head-dress for a person with a suitable cranium.' Don't you think that would sound rather alluring?"

"Very," I replied; "but as we are not going to be sold up – "

The rest of my sentence was drowned in the din of the beaten metal as my father returned to his hammering, and I only watched in mute discomfort until this part of the work was done and the great brazing jet was once more set a-roaring.

The work progressed apace, for my father was not only skilful and neat, but could be very quick on occasion; and as I watched the completion of stage after stage, I was conscious of a growing uneasiness, a vague fear of seeing the work actually finished; as if this mere toy – for it was little more – held some deep and tragic symbolism. I felt like one looking on at the slow wasting of one of those waxen effigies which the sorceresses of old prepared with magical rites for the destruction of some victim, whose life should slowly wane and flicker away with the wasting of the wax.

And meanwhile, above the roar of the blowpipe flame, my father's voice sounded now in a cheerful stave of song, and now in lively jest or playful badinage. But yet he did not deceive me. Behind all this show of high spirits was a sombre background that was never quite hidden. For the eye of love is very keen and can see plainly despite quip or joke or jovial carol, when "Black Care rides behind the horseman."

What a miserable affair it was, this pitiful acting of two poor, leaden-hearted mortals, each hiding from each the desperate resolve with smiles and jests that were more bitter than tears! For I, too, had now my secret, and must needs preserve it with such a show of gaiety as I could muster by sheer effort of will. The resolution of which I have spoken was growing – growing, even as the toy that we were making was growing towards completion, and as I seemed to see, as if symbolised by it, the sands of destiny trickling out before my eyes. So I, too, had my part to play in this harrowing comedy.

Works which have consumed much time in the doing have a way of coming to an end with disconcerting suddenness. When I mixed the acid for the "pickle" in the great earthenware pan, it seemed that a great deal still remained to be done, in spite of my father's feverish energy and swift dexterity. And then, but a few minutes later, as it appeared to me, behold the finished piece standing on the bench its embossed ornament telling boldly against the sulphur-browned background, and my father stretching himself and wiping the blackened oil from his hands; and it was borne in on me that, with the final touch, his interest in the thing had fallen dead.

"Nunc dimittis!" he murmured. "It's finished at last. 'Now lettest Thou Thy servant depart in peace.' And that reminds me, Jim; don't the shops keep open late tonight?"

"Some of them do," I replied.

"Good," said he. "Tell Jessie to bring up the supper while I'm washing. I've got to make a business call tonight, and I want to get some things, so we won't make it a ceremonious meal. Not that I want to put you on short allowance, for I expect you are hungry after your Titanic labours. You mustn't take any notice of me."

As he hurried away, I rang the bell, and, when I had given the necessary instructions, I went up to my bedroom to remove the traces of the evening's work and make myself presentable.

At the supper table my father preserved the same quiet gaiety of manner – his usual manner, in fact; for he was always cheerful and companionable – though, on this occasion, the speed with which he disposed of his food gave little opportunity for conversation. After a very hurried meal, he rose, and, pushing back his chair, glanced at his watch.

"You mustn't mind my running away," said he. "Time, tide and the shopkeeper wait for no man."

He moved away toward the door, but before he reached it he paused and then came back and stood beside my chair.

"You needn't sit up for me," he said. "I may possibly be rather late. So I'd better say 'goodnight' now." He took my head in his hands and, looking earnestly into my eyes, murmured: "Dear little Jim; best and most loyal of apprentices." Then he kissed me very tenderly and passed his hands over my hair.

"Goodnight, sweetheart," said he. "Don't sit up reading, but go to bed early like a sensible girlie – if you will pardon my dropping into Weggish poetry without notice."

He turned away and walked quickly to the door, where he stood for a moment to wave his hand. I heard him go to the study, and sat stiffly in my chair listening. In a few moments he came out and stepped quietly across the hall; there was a brief pause, and then the outer door closed.

He was gone.

At the sound of the closing door, I sprang to my feet with all my terrors revived. Whither had he gone? It was unusual for him to leave his home at night. What was it that had taken him abroad on this night of all others? And what was it that he wanted to buy? And wanted so urgently that he could not wait until the morrow? And why had he wished me "goodnight" with such tender earnestness? A foolish question, this, for he was a loving father, and never sought to veil his affection. But tonight I was unstrung; haunted by nameless fears that gave a dreadful significance to every passing incident. And as the chill of mortal terror crept round my heart, the resolution that had been growing – growing, came to its final completion.

It had to be. Horrible, loathsome as, even then, I felt it to be, it was the only alternative to that other nameless and unthinkable. The sacrifice must be made by us both for both our sakes – if it were not too late already!

Too late? Even as the dreadful thought smote like a hammer on my heart, I ran from the room and sped up the stairs on the wings of terror. With trembling fingers I took my hat and cloak from the wardrobe and hurried downstairs, putting them on as I went. At the dining-room door I called out a hasty message to the maid, and then, snatching up my gloves from the hall table, I opened the door and ran out into darkness.

CHAPTER THREE

The Covenant

As I sped swiftly along the quiet roads on the outskirts of the town the confusion and sense of helplessness began to subside under the influence of action and a definite purpose; by degrees my thoughts clarified, and I found myself shaping out, with surprising deliberation and judgment, the course that I intended to pursue. Mr Otway's house was about a mile distant from ours, somewhat farther out of town, though on a frequented road; a short distance and quickly covered by my flying feet. Yet, short as it was, and traversed with a phantom of terror in close pursuit, it gave me time to collect my faculties, so that, when I opened the gate and walked up the little drive, I had already to a large extent recovered my self-possession, though I was still trembling with the fear of what might be happening elsewhere at this very moment.

The door was opened by a small frail-looking woman of about fifty who did not look quite like an ordinary servant and whose appearance instantly impressed me disagreeably. She stood with her face slightly averted, looking at me out of the corners of her eyes, and holding the door open as she asked, with a slight Scotch accent: "Who would you be wanting?"

"I wish to see Mr Otway, if he is at home?" I replied.

"If ye'll come in and give me your name, I'll tell him," said she; and with this she showed me into a small room that opened out of the hall, where, when I had told her my name, she left me. In less than a minute Mr Otway entered, and having carefully closed the door, shook hands gravely and offered me a chair.

"This is quite an unexpected pleasure, Miss Vardon," said he. "Oddly enough, I was just thinking about you. I called on your father only this afternoon."

"I know," said I. "It was about that that I came to see you."

"Your father, then," said Mr Otway, "has mentioned to you the subject of our not entirely pleasant interview?"

"No, he has not," I replied. "Nothing has passed between us on the subject, and he is not aware that I have come here. The fact is, I overheard a part of your conversation and made it my business to hear as much of the rest as I could."

"Ha! Indeed!" He gave me a quick glance, half enquiring, half suspicious and added: "Perhaps, Miss Vardon, you had better tell me what you heard."

"There is no need for me to repeat it in detail," said I; "but, from what I heard, I gathered that my father had rendered himself liable to a prosecution. Is that correct?"

"Yes," said Mr Otway, "that is unfortunately – most unfortunately – the case."

"And that the proceedings will be taken by you, and that you have the power to stay them if you choose?"

"I wouldn't put it that way, Miss Vardon. That hardly states the position fairly. Do you know nothing of the circumstances at all? Has your father not told you anything about this unfortunate affair?"

"He has not spoken a word to me on the subject, and he has no idea that I know anything about it."

"H'm," Mr Otway grunted, reflectively. "Yes. Well, Miss Vardon, if you wish to talk the matter over with me, perhaps I had better just let you know how the land lies although, really, your father is the proper person to tell you."

"I think you had better tell me, if you don't mind," said I.

"Very well, Miss Vardon," he agreed. "Then the position is this: A sum of money – five thousand pounds, to be exact – was handed to your father by the trustees of a certain estate, to be invested by him on behalf of the trust; and the manner of its disposal – into which we need not enter – was quite clearly specified. But your father, instead of disposing of the money as directed, chose to make over the whole of it as a loan to a friend of his who was in temporary difficulties; a manufacturer, as I understand, who had suffered an unexpected loss and was on the verge of bankruptcy. There was no proper security, nor even, as I understand, any satisfactory arrangement as to the payment of interest. The whole affair was most improper; a gross violation of trust. In effect, your father converted this money and made use of it for his own purposes."

"Is the money lost?" I enquired.

Mr Otway shrugged his shoulders. "Who can say? It may be recoverable some day, or it may not. But that is very little to the point. The position is that it is now demanded of your father and that he can't produce it."

"And so you are going to prosecute him?"

"Oh, please don't put it that way, Miss Vardon. I am a quite involuntary agent. My position is that I am instructed to get this money from your father and dispose of it in a particular way. But I can't get it; and when I report that fact I shall, of course, be urged – in fact, compelled – to take criminal proceedings. I shall have no choice. It isn't my money, you know."

"But why criminal proceedings?" I asked. "It seems to me that a civil action to recover the money would be the natural course."

Again Mr Otway shrugged his shoulders. "I don't see that it makes much difference," said he. "The money has been made away with. Even if the trustees took no criminal action, there is the Public Prosecutor and there is the Incorporated Law Society. A prosecution is inevitable."

"And supposing my father is convicted?"

"It is hardly necessary to suppose," said Mr Otway. "He will be. There is no defence. As to the sentence, I don't imagine that the maximum punishment of seven years penal servitude is likely to be inflicted. Still, your father is a solicitor, and the law is, quite properly, very severe in the case of solicitors who misappropriate their clients' property. He is almost certain to get a term of imprisonment."

To this I made no reply. There was nothing to say. It was only too clear that every avenue of escape was closed – save one; and realising more fully every moment where that one led, I could not bring myself to make the fateful move. So for a while, we sat in a hideous silence through which the ticking of a clock penetrated noisily and seemed to keep pace with the thumping of my heart.

As I sat, bracing myself for the effort that had to be made, my eyes travelled, half unconsciously, over the person of my companion. His appearance was not prepossessing. Huge unwieldy and shapeless although by no means grossly fat, his great size carried no dignity; nor did his very marked and prominent features impart to his face anything of distinction or nobility. He was of a distinctly oriental type, with black and rather curly hair, oiled and combed over a slightly bald head, a large aquiline nose, a wide mouth rather full and fleshy, and very dark eyes, under which were baggy folds of skin creased by innumerable tiny wrinkles. As I looked at him with growing distaste, I found myself comparing him to a gigantic spider.

Suddenly it was borne in on me – perhaps by the measured ticking of the clock – that time was passing: time which might be infinitely precious. To delay further were mere cowardice. Nevertheless, when I spoke, it was in a voice so husky that I had to stop and begin again.

"You spoke, Mr Otway – I heard you mention to my father that – that on certain conditions, you would – would be prepared to abandon your intention of prosecuting – or, at least – "

I could get no farther. Fear and shame and loathing of this thing that I was going to do, overpowered me utterly. It was only by the most strenuous effort that I choked down the sob that was rising in my throat. But I had said enough, for Mr Otway now came to my assistance.

"I told your father that I was prepared to take over his liabilities, for the time being, at least, on condition that you became my wife. He refused, as perhaps you know refused very definitely, I may say."

"And rather rudely, I am afraid."

"He was not at any great pains to wrap his refusal up delicately. But we may let that pass. Is it in respect of this proposal of mine that you have done me the very great honour of calling on me, Miss Vardon?"

I felt myself turn scarlet, but nevertheless I answered, resolutely: "Yes. I came to ask if my father's very blunt refusal had closed the matter finally, or whether you were prepared to – to re-open it."

"We won't talk about re-opening it. It was never closed, by me. The proposal that I made to your father I now make to you; and if you should see your way to accepting it, I believe you would never have occasion to regret your decision."

He spoke in a dry, commercial tone, as if he were trying to sell me something at a rather high price; as, in fact, he was. And meanwhile I found myself wondering dimly why on earth he wanted to marry me.

"May I ask," he continued, after a pause, "if you are disposed to entertain my proposal?"

"I would do anything to save my father," I replied.

"That," said he, "is what I thought, judging from my previous knowledge of you; and it was the knowledge of your devotion to your father that encouraged me to make the proposal. For it seemed to me that a young lady of your attractions who could so completely devote herself to an elderly father might find it possible to devote herself to an elderly husband."

His reasoning did not impress me as very sound, seeing that it took no account of the respective personalities of the father and the proposed husband. But I made no reply, and, after a further pause, he asked: "Am I to understand that you – that you regard my proposal favourably?"

"I can't say that" I replied. "But I came here tonight prepared to accept your conditions, and I am ready to accept them now. But, of course, you understand that I do so under compulsion and not of my own free choice."

"I quite realise that," said he; "but I take it that you will carry out fairly any covenant into which you may enter."

"Certainly I shall," was my reply.

"Then may I take it that you are willing to marry me, on the conditions that I named?"

"Yes, Mr Otway. I consent to marry you on those conditions and on certain others that I will propose."

"Let us hear the other conditions," said he.

"The first is that you give me a promise in writing that, in consideration of my consent to marry you, you will do what is necessary to get my father out of his present difficulties."

"That is quite fair, though it is rather unnecessary. I shouldn't want a convict for a father-in-law, you know. But, anyhow, I agree, as soon as the marriage is over, to pay into your father's bank a cheque for five thousand pounds, or, if he prefers it, to give him a full discharge for that amount. And I will give you an undertaking in writing to that effect before you leave here tonight. Will that do?"

"It will do quite well," I answered. "But I wish you also to add to that undertaking a proviso to the effect that, if at any time before the marriage takes place, any circumstances shall arise by which your pecuniary help shall become unnecessary, then this agreement between you and me shall not take effect, and you shall have no claim of any kind on me."

Mr Otway looked at me in some surprise, and, indeed, I was somewhat surprised myself at the completeness with which my judgment and self-possession had revived as soon as it came to making terms; though I had considered the matter very carefully on my way to Mr Otway's house.

"You are a true lawyer's daughter, Miss Vardon," said he, with a somewhat wry smile. "You are not going to give yourself away gratis. No play, no pay, h'm? However, you are quite right. You agree to marry me for a certain consideration. If you don't receive the consideration, you don't marry me. Very well. That is a perfectly businesslike proposition, and I agree to it. You think that perhaps your father may be able to meet his liabilities, after all?"

"I do not think anything of the kind." The proviso was introduced by me in view of a very different contingency. I was making this sacrifice to save my father's life. If I failed in that, the sacrifice would be useless. But I did not think it necessary to mention this to Mr Otway. I therefore replied that, as I knew very little about my father's affairs, I thought it wise to provide even against the improbable.

"Quite so, Miss Vardon, quite so," he agreed. "One should always make provision for the unexpected. Well, I have said that I accept your first two conditions. What is the next one?"

"I want you to write my father a letter which shall relieve him of all present anxieties, and I want you to give me that letter so that it may be delivered tonight."

At this Mr Otway's countenance fell somewhat. He pursed up his lips disapprovingly, and, after some moments of reflection, said gravely: "That, you know Miss Vardon really anticipates the fulfilment of the contract on my side. Such a letter would commit me to a withdrawal of my demand for immediate payment of this money."

"But," said I, "you have my promise, which I am willing to give you in writing, if you wish me to."

"Well," he replied, dubiously, "that would seem to meet the difficulty, not that I am suspecting you of trying to evade fulfilment. But, you see, your father has refused his consent and will probably continue to refuse, so that one would rather not raise the question. By the way, I suppose you are over twenty-one?"

"I was twenty-three last birthday."

"Then, of course, his consent is not necessary. Still, one doesn't want a fuss; and if you delivered this letter to him, he would be in possession of the facts, and then there would be trouble."

"I was not proposing to deliver it to him. I should drop it in the letter box and let him think that you had sent or left it. He would know nothing of my visit to you or of the arrangement we have come to."

"I see. That alters the position somewhat. But is it really necessary? I can understand your wish to relieve his anxiety; but still, it need be only a day or two. Do you really think it is essential?"

"I do, Mr Otway. I think it absolutely essential. If I had not, I should not have come here tonight. My father is in a desperate position, and one never knows what a desperate man may do."

Mr Otway gave me a quick glance, and I could see that he was considerably startled. The possibility at which I had hinted would have consequences for him as well as for me, and I saw that he fully realised this. But he did not answer hastily. Perhaps he saw more in my suggestion than I did myself. At any rate, he pondered for some seconds before he finally replied: "Perhaps you are right, Miss Vardon. I'm sure I shall be very glad to put an end to his suspense. Yes, I'll write the letter and give it to you. Are there any more conditions?"

"No; that is all. So if you will write the letter and the agreement and draft out what you want me to say, we shall have finished. And please make as much haste as you can. It is rather late, and I am anxious to get home before my father if possible."

My anxiety apparently communicated itself to Mr Otway, for he immediately swung his chair round to his desk, and, taking one or two sheets of paper from the rack, began to write rapidly. In two or three minutes he turned, and, handing me what he had written, together with a blank sheet of paper and a pen and ink-bottle, took a fresh sheet himself, and, without a word, began once more to write. The draft which he had handed me was simply and concisely worded as follows:

"I, Helen Vardon, of Stonebury, Maidstone, in the county of Kent, spinster, hereby promise to marry Lewis Otway, of The

Beeches, Maidstone, in the county of Kent, attorney-at-law, within fourteen days from this present date, in consideration of his assuming the present liabilities of my father, William Henry Vardon, in respect of the estate of James Collis-Hardy deceased, this promise to be subject to the conditions set forth in a letter written to me by the said Lewis Otway and dated the 21st of April, 1908.

"(signed) Helen Vardon.
"Maidstone, Kent.
"21st April, 1908."

I read the draft through carefully, noting that it was not only quite simple and lucid, but that it embodied the terms of our agreement with scrupulous fairness and took over my father's liabilities without any limit as to time; then I dipped the pen in the ink and made a fair copy on the blank sheet which I signed, and laid on the corner of the desk.

By the time I had finished my copy, Mr Otway had completed the first of the documents, which he now handed to me; and as I read it he took up the paper that I had written, and, having glanced through it, placed it in a drawer and began once more to write. The paper that he had given to me was in the form of a letter, and read thus:

"Dear Miss Vardon,

"At your request I put on record the terms of the arrangement which has been made between us today, and which are:

"1. That in consideration of my taking over your father's liabilities in respect of the Collis-Hardy Estate, you agree to marry me within fourteen days of this present date.

"2. That on the completion of the marriage ceremony, or at such time thereafter as you may decide upon, I shall pay into your father's bank the sum of five thousand pounds, or, if he prefers it give him a full discharge of all liabilities in respect of the Collis-Hardy Estate aforesaid.

"3. Provided that if at any time prior to the said marriage your father shall discharge the said liabilities, or any circumstances shall arise by which the said payment or discharge by me shall become unnecessary, then the agreement between you and me which is herein recorded shall become void, and neither of us, the contracting parties, shall have any claim upon the other.

"I am, dear Miss Vardon,

"Your obedient servant,

"Lewis Otway.
"Maidstone, Kent.
"21st April, 1908."

Mr Otway glanced up from his desk as I folded the paper and bestowed it in my purse, and asked: "Will that do? I think it covers the terms of our arrangement."

"Thank you," I answered; "it will do quite well."

He made no rejoinder, but went on with the letter that he was writing; and meanwhile I sat and watched him, with a strong distaste of his appearance, dimly wondering at this strange interview and at my own curious self-possession and mental alertness. But behind these hazy reflections was a background of haunting terror that had never quite faded even when I was putting the utmost strain upon my wits; terror lest all this bargaining should be useless after all; lest I should arrive home to find that my help had come too late.

These disquieting thoughts were presently interrupted by Mr Otway, who, laying down his pen and swinging round in his revolving chair, took up the letter that he had just written.

"This is what I have said to your father, Miss Vardon. I think it will make his mind quite easy for the present, which is all we want.

" 'Dear Vardon,

" 'Since my talk with you this afternoon, I have been thinking over matters and considering whether it is not possible to give you more time. On looking into the affairs of the trust more closely, I think it can be done; in fact, I am sure it can with some careful management on my part. So you may take it from me that the demand, which I felt compelled to make, is withdrawn for the time being. When you are in a position to surrender the money, you had better notify me; and in the meantime you have my assurance that no further demand will be made without reasonable notice.

" 'I hope this will relieve your natural anxiety, concerning which I have been a little uncomfortable since I left you.

" 'Yours sincerely,

" 'Lewis Otway.
" 'The Beeches.
" '21st April, 1908.' "

He handed me the letter when he had finished reading, and I glanced through it quickly before returning it to him.

"I think that ought to relieve him of all anxiety," said he.

"Yes," I answered. "It will do admirably. And if you will kindly seal it and let me have it, I will go at once and drop it in the letter box. It is most important that it should be in his hands as soon as possible."

"Quite so," he agreed; "and I won't detain you further excepting to point out that, by giving you this letter, I am putting myself entirely in your hands. You will observe that this amounts to a surrender of my claim on your father for the time being. He will, of course, keep the letter, and could produce it in answer to any sudden demand for the restitution of the money. So I am really carrying out my part of the agreement in advance."

"Yes, I see that," I replied, "and I thank you most sincerely; but," I added, rising and holding out my hand for the letter, "you have my solemn promise to carry out my part. If you were better acquainted with me, you would consider that enough."

"But I do, Miss Vardon," he rejoined, hastily; "I do. If I did not trust you implicitly, I should not have written this letter. However, I mustn't delay you. I will make all the necessary arrangements and let you know when everything is ready. Will next Thursday be too soon?"

At the mention of an actual date, and one so near, too, something like a complete realisation of what I was doing flashed into my mind and set my heart thumping painfully. But it had to be, so why haggle for terms? Nor, indeed, since it must be, was there any use in trying to put off the evil day. The urgent need of the moment was to get this letter into my father's hands, if it were not already too late.

"I must leave the arrangement of the affair to you, Mr Otway," I murmured, shakily. "Do as you think best. And now I must really go."

He shook my hand in a drily, courteous fashion and let me out accompanying me down the drive to the outer gate, which he opened for me with a ceremonious bow. I wished him a hurried "goodnight," and, as soon as I was outside the gate ran off in the direction of home holding the precious letter in the little pocket of my cloak.

CHAPTER FOUR

The Eleventh Hour

As I drew near the neighbourhood of our house my fears grew so that I was compelled by sheer breathlessness and the trembling of my limbs to slacken my pace. I was sick with terror. In my mind, pictures, vague and nebulous but unspeakably dreadful, rose like the visions of a nightmare. I clutched the precious order of release in my pocket and set my teeth, trying not to think of what I might find at my journey's end.

At last I came in sight of the house. It was all dark save two of the upper windows – those of the servants' bedrooms. The servants, then, were going to bed as usual, for ours was an early household. This seemed reassuring, but only to a slight degree; for even if –

I opened the gate softly – I do not know why, but somehow I instinctively avoided noise of any kind – and running up the garden path, let myself in quietly with my latchkey. With one quick and fearful glance around the darkened hall, I stole up to the hat-stand. Apparently my father had not yet come home, for his stick was not in the stand, and one of his hats was missing. I looked at the tall clock and noted that it was not yet half past ten; I peered out through the open doorway, down the dark road, and listened awhile for the sound of footsteps; then, slipping the letter into the letter box – which I could see contained no other missives – I lit one of the candles from the hall table, and, having peeped into the study, the book-room and the workshop, stole silently up the stairs.

First, I went to my father's bedroom, and, by the glimmer of gas that the maid had left burning, and the light of my candle, inspected it narrowly. I looked over the trifles on the mantelpiece and on the dressing-table, and even opened the little medicine-cupboard to run my eye over the collection of bottles and boxes, pausing from time to time that I might listen for footsteps, strange or familiar, as Fate might decree. But pry as I would, there was nothing unusual, nothing on which the most eager suspicion might fasten. All the details of that room were familiar to me, for it had been my daily task since my girlhood to look them over and see that my father's orderly arrangements were not disturbed by the servants; and everything was in its place, and nothing new or strange or sinister had made its appearance.

When I had finished my inspection, I stole softly along the corridor to my own bedroom, which was at the head of the stairs, and, turning up the gas, but leaving the door ajar, began slowly to undress, listening intently the while for any sounds that might confirm or dispel my fears. The house was very quiet and still; so quiet that the tinkle of the water, as I poured it out from the ewer, struck with disturbing harshness on my ear, and even the ticking of the little clock and my own slippered footfalls seemed an impertinent intrusion into that expectant silence.

It was a few minutes past eleven when the sound of a latchkey and the gentle closing of the hall door sent the blood tingling to my very fingertips. No footsteps had been audible on the garden path, but this, in itself, was characteristic; for my father and I were alike in that we both disliked noise and habitually moved about softly, avoiding the slamming of doors or the production in any way of jarring sounds.

I crept on tiptoe to the door and listened. A stick was carefully put down in the hallstand, and then I thought – but was not quite sure – that I heard my father unlock the letter box. A few seconds later I caught a faint creak, which I recognised as proceeding from the study door, and, after a short interval, the creak was repeated and the door closed. Then the hall gas was turned out and soft footfalls began to ascend the stairs.

"Is that you, Pater, dear?" I asked.

"Is it I, indeed, O! wicked and disobedient child and likewise minx!" was the welcome answer. "Didn't I tell you to go to bed?"

"Yes, you did; and I am going. But I thought I would like to see you safely home from your roisterings."

"*Mures ratti!*" he exclaimed, as he came into the light from my open door. "It is poor old Queen Anne who has been keeping you out of your little nest. I know you."

Here he gave a gentle tug at one of the tails into which I had plaited my hair, and, having kissed me on the tip of my nose; continued: "And you look as tired as the proverbial dog – which is the only kind of dog that ever does get tired. Now go to bed and sleep like a young dormouse. Goodnight, Jimmy, dear."

With the aid of the convenient tail, he drew my face to his and kissed me again; then he went off along the corridor singing very softly, but just audibly to me:

"Her father he makes cabbage nets
And in the streets does cry 'em;
Her mother she sells laces long – "

Here a rapid diminuendo indicated the closing of the door, and the silence that had been so agreeably broken once again settled down upon the house. Still, I stood at the open door, looking out into the darkness. Had my father seen the letter? He had seemed very cheerful. But then, he would have seemed very cheerful if he had been walking to the scaffold or the stake. That was his nature. Yet his gaiety had appeared to me more genuine than that which he had exhibited earlier in the evening. However, there was no need to speculate; the question could easily be set at rest. Taking the matchbox from my candlestick, I stole silently down the stairs, steadying myself by the handrail, and groped my way across the hall until I reached the door. Then I struck a match and by its light, peered through the wire grating into the letter box.

It was empty. The letter had been taken out.

I blew out the match, and, having dropped it into the salver on the table crept back up the stairs to my room. Closing the door silently, I made my final preparations, turned out the light and crept into bed, feeling in the sudden ecstasy of relief that I could now shake off all care and bury the anxieties and alarms of this dreadful day in slumber.

My father was saved! No haunting fear of imminent tragedy, no dread of impending ruin and disgrace, remained to murder sleep or mingle it with frightful visions. My father was saved. At the eleventh hour I had made my bid for his life and liberty; and the eleventh hour had not been too late.

But it was long – very long before sleep came to shut out for a time the realities of life. The blessed feeling of escape from this appalling peril, the sense of restored security, was presently followed by the chill of reaction. For the end was not yet. I had bid for my father's life and had bought it in; but the price remained to be paid. And only now, when I could consider it undisturbed by terror for my father's safety, did I begin to realise fully how bitter a price it was. Not that I would have gone back on my bargain, for I had made it with my eyes open; and would have made it over again if the need had been. But it was a terrible price. I had sold my birthright – my precious woman's birthright to choose my own mate – for a mess of pottage. It was a price that I should have to pay, and go on paying as long as life lasted.

Hour after hour did I lie, gazing wide-eyed into the darkness, letting my thoughts flit hither and thither, now into the quiet, untroubled past, now into the dim and desolate future, whence they would come hurrying back affrighted. But always, whithersoever they wandered, behind them rose, now vague and remote, now horribly distinct, that unwieldy figure with the impassive oriental face; even, as to the eyes of the fisherman in the Arabian tale, the smoke from the magic jar shaped itself into the menacing form of the gigantic Jinn.

I tried to consider dispassionately the character of Mr Otway. It was very difficult. For had he not come into our life like some malignant spirit, to dispel with a word and in the twinkling of an eye, all the peace and happiness of our quiet home? To snap off short my serene companionship with my father? To turn into dust and ashes all the vaguely-sweet dreams of my maidenhood? To shut out the warm and hazy sunshine from my future and fill the firmament with unrelieved, leaden greyness? Still, I tried to consider him fairly. Callously, cynically, he had driven his Juggernaut car over my father and me, his eyes fixed upon his own desires and seeing nothing else. He was an absolute egoist. That was undeniable. For some reason he wished to marry me; and to achieve that wish he had been willing to put us both on the rack, and, with passionless composure to turn the screw until we yielded. It was not a pleasant thing to think of.

On the other hand he seemed, in his way, to be a just man. By no hair's breadth had he sought to modify the terms that he had first proposed; indeed, in his letter to me he had treated the loan to my father as an almost unconditional gift, and the other details of our agreement he had expressed in writing fully and fairly with no attempt at evasion. Nor was he niggardly. Five thousand pounds is a large sum to pay for the privilege of marrying an unwilling bride. Under other circumstances I might have appreciated the implied compliment. Now, I could only admit that, according to his lights, he seemed not ungenerous.

But when I considered him as the companion with whom I must share the remainder of my life – or, at least, that part of it which mattered – the thought was almost unendurable. To live day after day and year after year, under the same roof with this huge, dull, uncomely man; to sit at table with him, to walk abroad by his side, to spend interminable evenings alone with him: it was appalling. I could hardly bear to think of it. And yet the horrible reality would be upon me in the course of a few swiftly-passing days.

Nor was it a question of mere companionship – but from this aspect I hurriedly averted my thoughts in sheer cowardice. I dared not let myself think even for a moment of what marriage actually meant. Under normal conditions it may be permitted to the modesty of an unwedded girl to cast an occasional glance, half-shy and not wholly unpleasurable, at the more intimate relations of married life: but to me, if the thought would rise unbidden, it could call up nought but the quick flush of shame and loathing whereat I would bury my face in the pillow with a moan of shuddering disgust.

It was a relief to turn from the distressful present and the unthinkable future to the past, or even to the future that might have been. For, like most other girls, I had had my daydreams. The companionship with my father had been happy and full of interest; but it had never seemed final. I had looked on it as no more than the prologue to the real life, which lay, for the moment, hidden behind the near horizon of my maidenhood. And as to that reality, though it offered but a vague picture, yet it had a certain definiteness. To many modern girls, ambition seems to connect itself with the academy and the laboratory, with the platform and the forum. They appear to hanker after fame, or even mere notoriety, and would contend with men – who have nothing better to do – for the high places in politics, in science or in literature. I had read the impassioned demands of some of these women for political and economic equality with men, and had looked at them with a certain dim surprise to see them so eager to gather this Dead Sea fruit and turn their backs upon the Tree of Life, with its golden burden of love and blessed motherhood. Ambition of that kind had no message for me. So far my mind was perfectly clear. As to the terms in which I conceived the final realities, the blossom and fructification of a woman's life, I am less clear. A home of my own like the pleasant, peaceful home that my father had made; a man of my own in whom I could feel pride and by whom I could be linked to the greater world outside; and a sweet brood of little people in whom my youth could be renewed and for whom I could even cherish wider ambitions: this was probably what my rambling thoughts would have pictured if they could have been gathered up and brought to a definite focus. But they never had been, The necessary refracting medium had been absent. For what the burning-glass is to the sunbeam, the actual love of some particular man is to the opening mind of a young girl, bringing the scattered rays of thought to a single bright spot in which the wished-for future becomes sharp and distinct. And this influence, in its completeness had never come into my life. The undoubted liking that I had for the society of men was due, chiefly, to their larger interests and wider knowledge. Of experiences sentimental or romantic there had been none.

And yet the little god had not entirely forgotten me. Indeed, his winged shaft had missed me so narrowly that I could hardly yet be certain that I had passed quite unscathed. That little episode – tame enough in all conscience – had occurred two years ago, when a Mr Davenant had come from Oxford with a small party of fellow-undergraduates, to spend a more or less studious vacation in our neighbourhood. I had met him, in all, three times on the footing of a casual acquaintance, and we had talked "high philosophy" with the eager interest of the very young. That was all. He had been a bird of passage, alighting for a moment on the very outskirts of my life, only to soar away into the unknown and vanish for ever.

It seemed an insignificant affair. A score of other men had come and gone in the same way. But there was a difference – to me. Those other men, too, had talked "high philosophy," but I had forgotten utterly what it was that they had said. Not so had it been in the case of Mr Davenant. Again and again had I found myself thinking over his talks with me, not, I suspect, for the sake of the matter – which, to speak the truth, was neither weighty nor brilliantly original – but rather because I had enjoyed talking to him. And sometimes I had been surprised to notice how clearly I remembered those talks even to the very words that he had used and the tones of his pleasant, manly voice. Two years had passed since then – a long time in a girl's life; but still Mr Davenant – his name, by the way, was Jasper, a pleasant-sounding name I had thought it – remained the one figure that had separated itself from the nebulous mass of humanity that had peopled my short existence. And tonight – on this night of misery and despair, when all that was worth living for seemed to be passing away, as I lay staring up into the darkness, the memory of him came back to me again. Once more I heard his voice – how strangely familiar it sounded! – framing those quaintly – abstruse sentences, I recalled the look in his eyes – clear, hazel eyes, they were, that sparkled with vivacity and the fresh interest of youth – and his smile, as he uttered some mild joke – a queer, humorous smile that drew his mouth just a little to one side and seemed to give an added piquancy to the jest by its own trifling oddity. I remembered it all, clearly, vividly, with the freshness of yesterday; the words of wisdom, the humorous turn of speech, the earnest, almost eager tone, the easy manner, friendly yet deferential – all came back to me as it had done a hundred times before, though it was two years ago.

He had been but a stranger – a mere passing stranger who had come and gone – who had sailed across the rim of my horizon and vanished. But even in that swift passage some virtue had exhaled from him by which it had been given to me to look beyond the present into a world hitherto invisible to me. He was my one little romance; a very little one, but all that I had; and, to me, he stood for all those things that might have been and now could never be. And so it happened that, on this night, when I seemed to be bidding farewell to my youth and all its dimly-cherished hopes, the memory of him lingered in my thoughts and was with me still when, at last, sleep – the sleep of utter weariness and exhaustion – closed my eyelids and shut out for a time the realities of that life on which I would have been well content never to look again.

CHAPTER FIVE

On the Brink

Of the four days that followed, I do not, even now, like to think. The dreadful change that was coming into my life loomed up every moment more distinct, more threatening, more terrible. The hideous realities of what was about to happen to me refused to be ignored. They thrust themselves upon me and filled my thoughts every instant of the day and haunted my dreams at night. There were times when I turned a wistful eye upon that solution of the hopeless difficulties of life at which my father had hinted; but alas! even that was no solution as matters stood. Death, which would have released me from this bondage into which I had sold myself, would have left my father unemancipated; and to attain it by my own act would have been a grossly dishonest evasion of the covenant into which I had entered with Mr Otway. Expediency and honour both demanded that I should carry out the terms of my agreement.

But it was a terrible burden that I bore during those four days, and bore, of necessity, with a cheerful face and as little change as might be from my usual manner. That was the most difficult part of all. To keep up the appearance of quiet gaiety, which was the tone of our house; to smile, to jest, to discuss projected work and to talk over the history which I was supposed still to be reading; and all the time to feel the day of doom creeping upon me, nearer and nearer with every beat of my aching heart. That was the hardest part. But it had to be done and done with thoroughness; for my father's watchful and sympathetic eye would have detected at once the smallest flutter of a signal of distress. And it was imperative that he should be kept in the dark.

And that, perhaps, was the bitterest drop in this bitter potion. For the first time in my life I had a secret from my father. I was systematically deceiving him. And the secret that I withheld from him and shared with a mere stranger – with an enemy, in fact – was one that concerned him profoundly. And yet that, too, had to be. It was of the essence of the transaction. For, if he had suspected, for one instant what I proposed to do, he would certainly have interfered; and I knew him well enough to feel sure that his interference would not have taken the form of mere persuasion. He was a quiet man, suave and gentle in manner; even-tempered, patient, forbearing – up to a certain point; but when that point was passed, a change occurred which was apt to surprise those who knew him but slightly. Like a heavy body, he was difficult to move and difficult to stop when moved. If he had suspected Mr Otway of putting unfair pressure on me – which he would certainly have done – then I would not have answered for the consequences to Mr Otway.

But strive as I would to keep my secret, the intolerable strain of those days of misery must have made itself visible in some change in my appearance. Once or twice I caught my father looking at me narrowly with something of anxiety in his expression and hastened to put on a little extra spurt of gaiety and to divert his attention from myself. Still, he was not entirely deceived by my assumed cheerfulness, though he made no remark until the very last evening when, I suppose, my efforts to conceal the grief and wretchedness that were gnawing at my heart were less successful than usual. Then it was that he took me quite seriously to task.

"I wonder what is the matter with my little girl," he said, looking at me reflectively as we sat at the supper table. "She has been getting a little pale of late, and looks tired and worn. Is it too much Queen Anne and not enough sleep, think you?"

"I am feeling quite well," I replied.

"That is an evasion, my dear, and a tarradiddle to boot, I suspect. You are looking quite well. What is it, Jimmy?"

"I don't think it is anything, Pater, dear," I answered, not without a qualm of conscience at the direct untruth. "I haven't been sleeping so very well lately, but that is not due to my sitting up reading. Perhaps it's the weather."

"H'm!" he grunted; "perhaps it is – and perhaps it isn't. Are you sure there is nothing troubling you? No – what shall we say? Well, to put it bluntly, no young man, for instance, competing with the good Queen Anne for your attention?"

I laughed a little, bitterly. If only there had been!

But, alas! I was only too well secured against any troubles of that sort. So I was able to reply with a moderately clear conscience.

"No, of course there isn't. You know that perfectly well. How could there be when you keep me so securely in my little hutch?"

"That's true, Jimmy," he answered. "I certainly haven't noticed any buck rabbit sniffing around. But perhaps it is the hutch itself that is the trouble. It is a dull life for a girl, to be shut up with an old fellow like me. Coal-scuttles and suchlike are all very well for an ancient fossil who has sucked all the juice out of life and must needs content himself with a modest nibble at the rind that's left. But it's not the sort of thing for a girl. Your orange is still unsucked, Jimmy, dear, and we mustn't leave it to get over-ripe."

"I've always been very happy with you, dear old Pater," I said; and a lump rose in my throat as I spoke. How happy I had been! And oh, how thankfully would I have gone on with that serene, peaceful life and never asked for anything different, if only it might have been so!

"I know you have, my dear," he rejoined; "always contented and cheerful and kind to your old father. But still – well, we mustn't get too groovy. We must have a little change now and again. I have been rather preoccupied these last few days, but I shall be more free now. What do you say to a few days in London? It's quite a long time since we've been to town. Shall we take a week off and dissipate a little? Just spread a thin wash of carmine – quite a thin and delicate one – over the metropolis, and incidentally see for ourselves if the population of the great world doesn't still contain a few presentable human males. What do you say?"

I don't know what I said, or how I controlled the almost irresistible impulse to fling myself on his neck and sob my secret into his ear. It was terrible to listen to him making these plans for one of those blissful little holidays that we had enjoyed together from time to time, and to know that the morrow would see my own life spoiled irrevocably and his home made desolate. Some vague answer I murmured, and then managed to lead the conversation into a less distressing channel. But once or twice during the evening he reverted to the subject, and when, at a rather early hour, I wished him "goodnight," he said, as he held my hands and looked me over-critically: "Yes; the blossom is undoubtedly a little faded. We must see to it, Jimmy. Think over my proposal and consider whether there is any particular kind of jaunt that you would like; whether, for instance, you would rather go to the sea than to London."

"Very well, Pater, dear," I replied; "I'll think about it," and with this only too easily fulfilled promise I turned away and went upstairs.

It was my last night at home; the last night of my girlhood and of freedom. Virtually and to all intents, I had said farewell to my father for ever; for though, hereafter, we should meet, I should be his daughter, in the old sense – no more. I should be the chattel of another man, and that man no friend of his.

For long after I went to my room I sat thinking these thoughts and gazing with scared bewildered eyes into the dark future on whose threshold I already stood. What that future held for me, beyond the certainty of misery and degradation, who could tell? I dared not try to pierce that dread obscurity. From what might lie beyond that threshold my thoughts shrank back, appalled. The whole thing seemed like some hideous dream from which I should presently awaken, trembling, but with a sigh of relief. And yet it was not. Unbelievable as was this awful thing that had descended upon me in a moment, it was yet but too real for any hope of awakening.

And what of my father? For him, too, the old pleasant life was at an end. The quiet gaiety, the serene happiness of his home was gone for ever. Henceforth he would be a lonely man, mourning the loss of his companion and cherishing a bitter resentment against the man who had stolen her away. But what would he feel about this shipwreck of my life – for so he would certainly regard it? What portion of the wretchedness and degradation into which I had sold myself would have to be borne by him? It was a question which I had hardly asked myself before; but now, when I thought of his devotion to me, of his sympathy with me and his self-forgetfulness, a sudden misgiving crept into my mind. Was it worthwhile, after all? If my father and I were both to be made wretched for life, what good had I done by this sacrifice?

I thought of him as he had been this evening and for the last day or two. All his light-heartedness had come back. He was quite himself again. Since I had delivered Mr Otway's letter, all signs of care had vanished. That letter had apparently put him entirely at his ease; naturally enough, since it had put an end to his immediate difficulties, and since he knew nothing of the price at which it had been purchased. And though I knew better, yet his ease and confidence were not without their effect on me. Under the clear sky and in the sunshine, it was hard to believe that the thunderbolt was still ready to fall. And so it was that, more than once on that night, I found myself asking if it were possible that I had done the wrong thing? Had been too precipitate.

But it was of no use to think of that now. The bargain had been made, and payment accepted in advance. Nor if it had been possible for me to go back on a promise voluntarily given – which it obviously was not – could Mr Otway have been held to his. The original situation would have been created afresh.

Before undressing, I sat down at my little bureau and wrote a letter to my father in case there should be no time on the morrow. For the arrangements – which Mr Otway had communicated to me in a letter addressed in a feminine handwriting – were necessarily of a somewhat clandestine character. Mr Otway had obtained a special license and had given notice to the clergyman of a small church on the outskirts of the town, and on the by-road leading to the church I was to meet him on Thursday morning as near as possible to eleven o'clock. There was not likely to be any difficulty in carrying out my part of the arrangement, but nevertheless, it was as well to leave nothing to be done on the morrow.

The letter that I wrote to my father was quite short. There was no need for a long one, since the facts to be communicated were of the simplest and I should probably see him in the course of the day. What I wrote was as follows:

"My dearest Father,

"I am writing to tell you that I am about to do a thing of which I fear you will disapprove. I am going to marry Mr Otway; and by the time you get this, the marriage will have taken place.

"You will understand why I have done this when I tell you that I accidentally became aware of your difficulties and of the claim which he had on you, and you will understand, too, why I have kept my intention secret from you. It was the only way out for us; and you are not to think that I have done it for you only. I was equally concerned, and have acted in my own interests as well as yours.

"Please, dearest, try to forgive me for taking this step without your sanction. You would never have consented, and yet it had to be.

"Your loving daughter,

"Helen."

I sealed the letter, and, having addressed it, placed it in my bureau in readiness for the morning. Then I made various little arrangements of my possessions, tidying up my bureau and wardrobe, tearing up letters that had been answered and packing a small trunk with necessary articles of dress, to be sent for on the morrow; and all this I did with a curious stony calm and the sense of setting my affairs in order as if preparing to bid farewell to life. And this calm – a calm like that which persons of character often exhibit in the face of unavoidable death, or on the eve of a dangerous operation, continued even after I went to bed, so that, in contrast to the perturbed nights that I had passed since my interview with Mr Otway, I presently fell into a sound sleep and slept late into the morning.

CHAPTER SIX

A Meeting and a Parting

It turned out to be easier than I had expected to keep my appointment with Mr Otway, for my father had business that took him abroad early, and, when I came down to breakfast, he had already left the house; which was a profound relief to me, since it saved me the added misery of a last farewell and the necessity of further deception.

It was half past ten when, after placing my letter in the salver on the hall table, I set forth from the house. The most direct way to the church was across the town, but the fear of meeting my father or any of my acquaintances led me to take the roads that led out from the environs towards the country, and thus skirt the circumference of the town. I walked at a good pace, unconsciously threading my way through the rather complicated maze of by-roads, and still pervaded by the curious, half-dreamy calm that had possessed me on the preceding evening.

As I approached the vicinity of the little church – which was a kind of mission-chapel, in charge of a supernumerary curate – I glanced at my watch and saw that it was five minutes to eleven; and almost at the same moment, on turning a corner, I came in sight of a figure the very first glance at which so completely shattered my self-possession that I felt ready to sink down upon the pavement. There was no mistaking it, though the back was towards me; a huge, ponderous figure that walked away from me with the peculiar gait of the heavy and unathletic man; a silent, deliberate gait that recalls the action of the hind legs of an elephant.

I followed him breathlessly up the rather sordid-looking street, noting that, from time to time, a thin cloud of blue smoke floated over his shoulder. At length, at the corner of an intersecting road, he turned and saw me; upon which he flung away a cigar, and, retracing his steps towards me, saluted me with a flourish of his hat and held out his hand.

"This is good of you, Miss Vardon," he said, "to be so punctual. I hardly hoped that you would be able to be here so – er – so punctually."

I took his hand limply, but made no reply. The shock of the sudden encounter was slowly passing off and giving place to a sort of benumbed indifference mingled with vague curiosity. I felt as if I had been drugged or were walking abroad in a hypnotic trance, half conscious and waiting with dull expectancy to see what would happen next. I walked at Mr Otway's side up the mean little street with a feeling somewhat like that with which one would walk in a dream beside some historical or mythical personage, accepting the incongruous situation from mere mental inertia.

Mr Otway, too, seemed subdued by the strangeness of the position, or perhaps he was embarrassed by my silence. At any rate, although he occasionally cleared his throat as if about to make a remark, he did not actually speak again until we turned a corner, when there appeared, embedded in a row of mean houses, a small brick building which, in general shape and design, resembled a large dog-kennel.

"That," said he, "is the church, Miss Vardon – or perhaps I should say, Helen. It is a little difficult to – ah – get used to these – these intimacies, I may say, at so short a notice. No doubt you find it so?"

"Yes," I answered.

"I am sure you do. Naturally. My own name, you may remember, is Lewis. My Christian name, I mean," he added, shying slightly at the word "Christian."

"I remember," said I.

"Quite so. I had no doubt you would. Ahem." He cleared his throat once or twice in an embarrassed manner, and then, as we crossed over towards the church, he continued: "I think we shall find the doors open. The law, I believe, requires it. And we shall find my housekeeper, Mrs Gregg, inside. She will be one of the witnesses, you know. The other will be the sexton."

The outer door was on the latch, as he had said, and, when he had admitted me, he closed and re-latched it. From the dark vestibule, I stepped into the bare, comfortless building, from the white-washed wall of which a great, emblazoned text grinned at me, as if in derision, with the words: "I was glad when they said unto me, 'Let us go into the House of the Lord.' "

Near the door, on one of the deal benches, the little, frail-looking woman whom I had seen at Mr Otway's house was seated, conversing with a very bald and rather seedy elderly man; but, as we entered, the man hurried away towards the vestry and the woman rose and came forward a few paces to meet us.

"This is Miss Vardon, Mrs Gregg," said Mr Otway, introducing me in a heavy, embarrassed manner.

Mrs. Gregg stared at me with undisguised curiosity and something of hostility in her expression, as she replied: "Ah've seen her before."

"Yes," said Mr Otway, "I believe you have. Yes. To be sure. Of course. And I – er – hope in fact, I may say that I – ah – "

What he was going to say I have no idea, and I suspect that he was not very clear himself; but at this moment the man – who was apparently the sexton – emerged from the vestry in company with a young clergyman, vested already in his surplice and carrying a book in his hand.

Apparently everything had been explained and arranged beforehand by Mr Otway, for, as we advanced up the nave the curate took his place before the communion table and opened his book. I noticed that he gave me one quick and intense look, full

51

of surprise and curiosity, and thereafter seemed, as far as possible, to avoid even glancing in my direction.

The ceremony began abruptly and without preamble. With dim surprise, I became aware that the clergyman was speaking, or rather reading aloud, in a rapid and indistinct undertone. I listened with but slight attention, and failed, for the most part, to distinguish the words which, I think, was what the curate intended; his half-apologetic mumble being, I believe, designed to mitigate the effect of those coarsely-phrased impertinences with which the service is besprinkled, and which have survived so inappropriately into this age of decent and reticent speech. I tried to fix my thoughts on the ceremony in which I was taking part, but found them constantly wandering away to my father, busying themselves with his present whereabouts and occupation. Was he still at his office? Or had he perchance called in at our house, as he sometimes did, and already seen my letter?

I was brought back to the happenings of the moment by a question addressed to me by name in more distinct tones, and followed by the murmured instruction: "Say I will." I obeyed the gently-spoken command and then, with my right hand enveloped in a large and flabby grasp, I heard Mr Otway repeat after the curate the solemn form of words that should mean so much and that was, as now spoken, so empty a mockery; of which the phrase "to have and to hold from this day forward" seemed to separate itself as the only part truly applicable.

Still passive, and conscious only of a certain, dull discomfort and surprise at the incongruity of the whole affair, I permitted our hands to be separated and re-joined, and obediently repeated the form of words as the curate dictated.

"I, Helen Vardon, take thee Lewis Otway to my wedded husband, to have and to hold from this day forward, for richer for poorer, in sickness and in health, to love, cherish, and to obey, till death us do part, according to God's holy ordinance; and thereto I give thee my troth."

It was amazing! These burning words, so charged with love, with utter devotion and self-abandonment I was actually addressing to a mere stranger, to a man who, even now, was but a name attached to an unfamiliar, ungracious personality; upon whose corpse, if he had fallen dead at my feet in the very moment of my speaking, I could have looked with no emotion but relief.

It was an astounding situation. The wonder, the incredibility of it filled my mind to the exclusion of all else until, as Mr Otway began once more to speak at the curate's dictation, and I became aware that a ring had been slipped on my finger, I realised dimly that the ceremony was complete and that the irrevocable change had occurred.

But even then my thoughts quickly flitted away from this significant scene to others that seemed more deeply to concern me. As I knelt at Mr Otway's side and the monotonous mumble recommenced, I began once more to wonder where my father was and what he was doing. Had he come in and seen my letter, or had the maid noticed it and taken it to the office? And would he be angry or only grieved? Would he think that I had acted rightly? Or would he condemn my action as ill-considered or even unnecessary? And lastly, was it just barely possible that I had done the wrong thing? Had I sacrificed myself – and him – without sufficient cause?

Thus my thoughts wandered to and fro to the mumbled accompaniment of the interminable prayers and exhortations that rolled past me in an unheeded stream. At last the ceremony came to an end. Rising from our knees, we trooped after the curate to the vestry, where, as I signed the familiar name in the register, the first clear realisation of my changed condition came upon me. But even then the vivid flash of perception was but transient. Hardly had I shaken hands with the clergyman and passed out into the street, when my thoughts sped away once more to my home – my real home – and my father.

For some time after leaving the church Mr Otway and I walked in silence. He hemmed once or twice and seemed on the point of speaking, but either he could find nothing appropriate to say or he found some difficulty in opening the subject of his thoughts. And meanwhile I pursued my own reflections. At length, however, after one or two preliminary hems, he managed to make a beginning.

"I am afraid, Helen, you may think that I have put rather unfair pressure on you to marry me."

I roused myself to consider what he had said, and replied, after a slight pause: "Whatever I may think, I am not complaining. I don't forget that I accepted your proposal of my own free will; and I intend to try to carry out honestly my part of the bargain."

"I am glad to hear you say that, Helen," he said eagerly. "I was afraid you might feel resentful – might think I had driven a rather hard bargain."

"Perhaps I do," I replied. "But that doesn't affect the terms of the bargain. My feelings towards you were no part of the agreement."

"No; that's true," he agreed hastily; but he was visibly crestfallen, and walked by my side for some time without speaking. My thoughts began to wander again; and then, suddenly, there occurred to me a question that I had already asked myself over and over again without finding any answer. Now, moved by a fresh impulse of curiosity, I put it into words.

"Would you mind telling me, Mr Otway, why you wished to marry me?"

He looked at me in some surprise and a little confusion.

"Why, my dear Helen," he replied hesitatingly, "there is nothing remarkable about it, is there? I wished to marry you for the same reason that any other man would; because you are a handsome girl – a beautiful girl, I may say – and clever and bright, and, as far as I could judge from your manner to your father, a good, affectionate girl. I have admired you ever since I first met you, a year and a half ago."

I suppose I looked surprised – I certainly felt so, seeing that he had made no effort to cultivate our acquaintance – for he continued: "Yes, Helen, I admired you; but as I had nothing to offer in the way of personal attractions, and I did not suppose that my means would be a sufficient set-off for my – ah – personal disadvantages, I kept my admiration to myself. In fact, I suppose, if it had not been for this lucky chance – lucky for me, I mean – a little unfortunate perhaps for you – though not so unfortunate as it might – er – at least I venture to hope that things may turn out – "

He paused awkwardly, as if expecting me to help him. But I made no comment. My momentary curiosity was satisfied. I had heard his explanation, and a very insufficient one it seemed to be. So the sentence remained unfinished, and, in the silence that ensued, my thoughts went back once more to my father.

When would he get my letter? And what would be his feelings when he realised that his daughter – his companion and playmate, his beloved apprentice – was lost to him for ever? And what would be his attitude to Mr Otway? Deeply resentful, beyond a doubt. His scornful rejection of the proposal had shown that clearly enough. Yes, he would be angry – furiously angry; for quiet and gentle as his manners were, he was a passionate man. He could even be violent, as I knew from one or two experiences. And our doctor, Dr Sharpe, knew it, too, and had warned him to be careful, had cautioned him not only to avoid overexertion, but excessive excitement of any kind. The doctor's words came back to me now with a qualm of uneasiness. I had not thought of that before. His distress, his grief, his anger against the man who had exacted this price from me – all that I had thought of and fretted over. But the actual physical shock that my letter would inflict on him, utterly unprepared as he was – that I had somehow overlooked. And yet it was palpable enough. He would come home expecting to find me waiting for him as usual; and then, without an instant's warning, in the very twinkling of an eye, he would learn that I had been spirited away out of his life for ever. It would be a terrible blow.

The more I thought of it the more uneasy I became. Supposing he should become seriously ill on receiving my letter. It was quite possible it was even very probable. And if he should have got my letter already! If he should be, at this very moment lying prostrated by the shock, with none but the servants to tend him! As I thought of this dreadful possibility, my anxiety grew, moment by moment; and I was beginning to consider how soon I could contrive to escape to him, to satisfy myself that all was well, when the voice of Mr Otway broke in on my thoughts. I did not at first gather clearly what he was saying until, by an effort, I detached my attention from the agitating subject of my reflections.

"Of course," he was saying as I endeavoured to catch up the thread of his remarks, "it answered my purpose as a solitary bachelor; but it won't do now. We shall have to get quite a different class of house. And we shall want some other servants. I shall keep Mrs Gregg, if you don't object, as she has been with me so long and knows my ways, but we shall want a couple of maids in addition, I suppose."

"Is Mrs Gregg your only servant?" I asked, rather absently.

"Yes," he replied; "that is to say, the only resident servant. She has a girl to help her in the mornings with the housework and to mind the place when she goes out shopping. That is how she was able to attend at the church this morning."

As he was speaking, we turned into the quiet, countrified road in which he lived, and a few more steps brought us to the house. Mrs Gregg, who had apparently hurried on in advance by a different route, was standing at the open door talking to a girl of about sixteen, and, as we ascended the steps, she addressed Mr Otway.

"I've got to see to some things in the town. D'ye want Lizzie to stay or will ye open the door yourself if anyone comes?"

"Oh, she needn't stay, Mrs Gregg," was the reply. "I shan't be going out. But don't be any longer than you can help."

On this Mrs Gregg dismissed the girl, and followed her out, shutting the door after her. Mr Otway hung his hat on a peg in the hall, and placing his umbrella in the stand, remarked apologetically: "Mrs Gregg's manner is not all that might be desired in a servant; but she is a capable woman and absolutely trustworthy. She comes from the North, you know, where manners run a little more blunt than with us. Shall I show you your room?"

Without waiting for a reply, he preceded me up the stairs to the first floor, where he ushered me into a bedroom and stood by the door with an embarrassed and rather deprecating air, casting a glance of obvious disparagement over its somewhat meagre appointments.

"It's a poor place to bring you to, Helen," he remarked, "but that can be mended. It was good enough for a bachelor. You'll find the wardrobe and chest of drawers empty when you send for your things. Mine are in the dressing-room – that little room to the right. And now I'll leave you in possession for the present."

With this he went out, closing the door behind him, and I heard his soft, heavy tread descending the stairs.

For some time after he had gone I stood looking about me in absolute dismay. The room was mean almost to sordidness – surprisingly mean for the habitation of an admittedly wealthy man. But it was not that which filled me with consternation. Delicately as I had been brought up, the mere surroundings of life were of no great consideration to me. What appalled me utterly was the feeling, now brought home to me with overwhelming force, that I was no more my own; that I had surrendered myself to the possession of another person, a strange man, towards whom I felt a growing repugnance. This was not my room: it was our room. No longer had I any rights of privacy or of personal reticence. I was his, "to have and to hold from this day forward," with no power of escape or protest against the most repulsive familiarities. I had voluntarily surrendered, not only my liberty, but even the appearance of security from the most outrageous intrusions.

Of course I had known all this before. But in the hurry and rush, the alarms and agitations of the events that had forced me to my hasty decision, perception had been partly obscured. I had known what I was doing, but had only dimly realised. It had needed the sight of that mean room, with its significant contents and the presence of that man who stood at my side as joint occupier, to light up the vague perception into realisation of the most horrid vividness.

Presently I began, with the dull curiosity of a prisoner introduced to a new cell, to explore the room, opening the empty wardrobe and pulling out the ill-fitting drawers of the plain pine chest. Then I peeped into the dressing-room – a bare little closet, furnished with a wash-stand, a dressing-table and a chest of drawers – and even stepped in to glance over the half-blind down into the garden and street beyond. I was about to turn away when I noticed a man approaching the house at a rapid pace; and in an instant my heart leaped with mingled joy and alarm.

It was my father.

I watched him nervously as he strode towards the house, and my fears rose with each step that he took. Every movement was expressive of excitement and anger; the swift stride, the forward-thrust chin, the very set of the shoulders; the way in which he grasped his stick by the middle, as if aiming a blow, was full of menace. As he drew nearer I shrank behind the curtain, but still watched him; watched him with growing alarm, for now I could see that his eyes were wild under the frowning brows his mouth was set and his face was of a strange, blotchy, purple colour. He looked as if he had been drinking, but I knew he had not.

As he reached the gate, he wrenched it open violently, and, entering, slammed it behind him; a thing I had never before known him to do. He strode up the path, without a glance upwards, and disappeared from my sight, and a moment later there came a wild jangling of the bell, followed by a thundering knock at the door.

I hesitated, undecided what I should do. Should I go down and meet him with appeasing words, or should I wait until the first explosion of his wrath had subsided? I crept out of the bedroom to the landing and stood with my hand on the baluster rail, listening. I heard Mr Otway walk along the hall, softly and rather slowly. I heard him open the door, and then my father's voice rose, loud and fierce.

"Where is my daughter, Otway? Is she here?"

"Yes," Mr Otway replied; "she is upstairs. We have just returned from the church."

"Do you mean to say," my father demanded, "that the marriage has actually taken place."

"Yes," Mr Otway answered. "We were married half an hour ago."

"What!" roared my father. "After my letter! Did you tell her about that letter? You didn't, you damned scoundrel! You've tricked her! You've swindled her!"

"As to your letter, Mr Vardon," I heard Mr Otway reply, "I haven't seen it myself, yet. The morning's correspondence is still – "

Here a door closed, and his voice became inaudible. They had gone into one of the rooms. I staggered back into the bedroom and sank on to a chair, trembling from head to foot. In the name of God, what did my father mean? Tricked! Swindled! Could it be true? Was it actually possible that I had been lured into the arms of this ungainly lout by a false pretence? It was incredible. And yet –

As the first shock of this amazing statement began to pass off, a storm of anger and indignation arose in my breast; and I was on the point of rising to go down and confront Mr Otway, when the house shook to a heavy concussion. I sprang from the chair, and flying on the wings of terror down the stairs, opened the first door that I came to.

Years have rolled by since that unforgettable moment, but even now, as I write, the tableau that met my eyes as I opened the door rises before me vivid and distinct as the dreadful reality. I saw it even then but for a single instant, as I darted into the room; but it has remained with me and will remain till my dying day.

My father lay motionless on the floor near the fireplace; his face an awful, livid grey, his eyes staring fixedly at the ceiling; and from a small wound on the right side of his forehead a few drops of dark blood trickled down his temple. Beside him, and stooping over him, stood Mr Otway, with ashen face and dropped jaw, the very picture of horror and mortal fear; and in Mr Otway's right hand was grasped my father's stick, a stout Malacca, with a heavily-loaded silver knob.

I flew past him and sank on my knees by my father's side; and in that moment I knew that my father was dead. I had never seen a dead person before. But it was unmistakable. I spoke to him; I called to him in an agonised whisper; I patted his head and touched his face. But all the while I knew that he was dead; that he was gone from me for ever. Even as I looked at him, the livid grey of his face faded to a dead white; the staring eyes relaxed and seemed to sink into their sockets; and the mouth slowly fell open. It was death. I knew it. Dazed, stricken almost bereft of consciousness and the power of thought, I knew it, with the dull certainty of despair.

As I had entered the room, Mr Otway had started up with a look of terror, and when I sank at my father's side, I had heard him move away softly towards the writing-table. He was now back and once more stooping over my father's body. I felt that he was there, although my eyes were fixed on that pallid face that gave back no answering glance. Presently he spoke, in a hushed, awe-stricken whisper.

"This is terrible, Helen! Can't we do anything?"

I looked up at him with a sudden flush of loathing and detestation; and as I looked, I noticed that he no longer held the stick. I rose slowly to my feet and faced him.

"No," I answered. "He is dead. He is dead. Mr Otway, you have killed my father."

As I faced him, he shrank away from me, staring at me as if I had been some horrid apparition. His face, blanched to a horrible white and shiny with sweat, was dreadful to look upon; the face of abject mortal terror.

"Helen!" he gasped. "Helen! For God's sake don't look at me like that! It was not I who killed him. I swear to God it was not. He fainted. I was trying to take the stick from him – I had to, or he would have killed me – and his head struck the mantelpiece.

Then he fainted and fell. I am telling you the truth, Helen. I am, before God!"

To this I made no reply. Whether I believed him or not, I cannot say. Stunned as I was by this frightful thing that had befallen, I could only look at him with utter loathing as the cause of it all.

"Helen!" he continued, imploringly, "say you believe me! I swear I never touched him. And don't look at me like that! Helen! Why do you look at me in that awful way?"

He clasped his hands, and, casting a fearful glance at my poor father's corpse, moaned: "My God! my God! but this is horrible! Horrible! Do you think he is really dead? Don't you think – can't we do anything? If a doctor were here – if we only had someone to send – Shall I go and fetch a doctor, Helen?"

"Yes," I answered, "you had better."

"I will," he said. "But you do believe me, don't you? I swear – "

"You had better go at once, Mr Otway," I interrupted.

He gave me one pitiful glance of appeal, and then, with a despairing moan, turned and left the room. I heard him hurry along the hall and a moment later the outer door closed.

Once more I sank on my knees beside my father, and, taking the passive hand in mine, looked into the pallid face, dimly surprised to find something new and unfamiliar creeping into it. I did not weep. The blow was too crushing, too overwhelming to call forth common emotion. Nor did I think coherently; but knelt, looking dumbly into the face that was my father's, and yet was not, wrapped in a sort of dreadful trance, conscious only of bitter pain and a sense of unutterable loss.

After a time – I do not know how long – I became aware of sounds of movement in the house, and presently soft footsteps approached the room. The door, which Mr Otway had left ajar, opened with a faint creak, and the voice of Mrs Gregg ejaculated: "Sakes! What's this?"

She stole on tiptoe into the room until she stood beside me, looking down with a scared expression at my father's corpse.

"Why!" she exclaimed, "the man's dead! Who is he?"

"He is my father, Mrs Gregg," I replied.

She stood for some time in silence, apparently considering the import of my answer. Then she walked round and looked down curiously at the wound on the forehead.

"Where is Mr Otway?" she asked.

"He has gone to fetch a doctor," I answered.

"A doctor!" she repeated. "And what might be the good of a doctor when the man is dead? D'ye know how it happened?"

Before I had time to reply to her question, there came the sound of a latchkey inserted into the hall door. She turned quickly and made as if she would leave the room, but, as she reached the threshold, Mr Otway entered, followed by the doctor, and she fell back to let them pass. I rose to my feet, and the doctor – a hard-faced, middle-aged man whom I knew by sight – knelt down in my place. He lifted the limp hand and laid his finger on the wrist; he raised the eyelid and touched the glazing eyeball; then drawing out his stethoscope he listened for some time at the chest over the region of the heart. And meanwhile we all stood watching him in a profound silence through which the ticking of the clock broke noisily, as it had done on that fateful night when I had sat in this very room unconsciously preparing the elements of this tragedy.

At length the doctor rose, and, folding his stethoscope, deliberately slipped it into his pocket and turned to Mr Otway.

"I am sorry to say that it is as you feared," said he. "He is quite dead. From what you have told me, I should say it was a case of heart failure from over-excitement. Have there been any previous attacks?"

"No," I answered. "But I think Dr Sharpe considered that his heart was weak."

"Ah! He did, did he? Well, I had better call on Dr Sharpe and hear what he knows about the case." He walked round, and, stooping down, examined the wound attentively. Then, without looking at Mr Otway, he asked: "You say he struck his head against the corner of the mantelpiece? This corner, I suppose?"

He touched the right hand corner of the marble shelf, and, as Mr Otway assented, I saw him place his shoulder against it as if to measure its height.

"Was that when he was in the act of falling?" he asked, with his eyes fixed on the wound.

"Yes," replied Mr Otway. "At least, I think so – I should say yes, certainly – that is, to the best of my belief. Of course, Dr Bury, you will understand that I am a little confused in my recollection. The – ah – the circumstances were very agitating and – ah – confusing. Is the point of any importance?"

"Well, you see," the doctor replied a little drily, "when a man dies suddenly and only one person is present – as I understand was the case in this instance – every point is of importance."

"Yes, of course. It would be, naturally."

Mr Otway spoke these words in a low, husky voice, and, as I looked at him, I saw that he had turned as pale as death and that his face had again broken out into a greasy sweat. Nor was I the only observer. Mrs Gregg, who had been standing in the corner by the door, quietly attentive to all that passed, was now watching her employer narrowly and with a very curious expression. There was a brief interval of silence, and then Mr Otway having cleared his throat once or twice, asked, in the same husky, unsteady voice: "I suppose, when you have talked the matter over with Dr Sharpe, you will be able to certify the death in the usual way?"

"In the usual way?" Dr Bury repeated. "Yes: in the way that is usual in cases of sudden death. Of course, I shan't be able to give an ordinary certificate. I shall write to the coroner, giving him the facts, and he will decide whether an inquest is necessary or whether he can issue a certificate on my statement."

"I see," said Mr Otway. "You will report the fact – and, I suppose, you will state what your own views on the case are?"

"I shall make any comments that seem to be called for, but, of course, the facts are what the coroner wants."

"And would you consider that, in a case like this, an inquiry is necessary?"

"I don't know that I should," was the reply; "but it doesn't rest with me. Would you like me to help you to move him? You can't leave him lying here, and you can hardly have him carried to his own house by daylight."

"No," Mr Otway agreed, "we could not. If you will kindly help me to carry him to the drawing-room, we can lay him on the sofa."

The two men raised my poor father, and, while I supported his head, they carried him to the drawing-room and laid him on the sofa, when Dr Bury, having taken an embroidered cover from a table and spread it over him, drew down the blinds.

"Perhaps," said he, "you had better leave him here until we know what the coroner intends to do. In case he should decide – "

Here he glanced a little uncomfortably at me, and I realised that he would rather speak of the grim details unembarrassed by my presence. Accordingly, I stole from the room and returned to the one from which we had just come. The door was open as we had left it, and, as I came opposite to it, treading softly, as was my habit, I saw Mrs Gregg standing by the roll-top table with my father's stick in her hand, apparently testing the weight of the heavy lead loading that the silver knob concealed. She started as she suddenly became aware of my presence, but, quickly recovering her self-possession, asked: "Will this be your father's stick?"

I answered that it was, whereupon she remarked, as she stood it in the corner behind the writing-table, whence, I suppose, she had taken it: "I thought 'twas a stranger to me. A fine stick it is, too, and a trusty companion 'twould be on a dark night and a lonely road."

To this I made no reply; and when she had glanced at the clock and peered curiously into my father's hat, which stood on the table, she turned abruptly and left the room.

CHAPTER SEVEN

The Terms of Release

When Mrs Gregg had gone, I shut the door, and, sinking on to the chair by the writing-table, tried to collect my thoughts. But though I was vaguely conscious that this dreadful disaster vitally affected my position, and must in some way affect my actions, overwhelming grief and a sense of irreparable loss rendered coherent thought impossible. My father was dead. That was all I could think of. My one perfect friend, who had absorbed all my affection and given me all of his, had gone out of my life. Henceforward I was alone in the world.

Presently I heard Dr Bury leave the house, and then the door opened and Mr Otway came into the room, looking like a man who had risen prematurely after a severe illness. He dropped limply on a chair, and sat, with his hands on his knees, looking at me with a pitiable expression of misery and consternation.

"This is a terrible affair, Helen," he said in a broken voice. "Terrible! Terrible!"

I made no reply, but looked at him, half-curiously and resentfully. In the extremity of my grief I had no pity to spare for him who was the cause of this dreadful calamity.

"Won't you speak to me, Helen?" he said, imploringly. "Won't you try to give me some comfort? Think of the awful position I am in."

At his miserable egotism, my grief blazed up into sudden wrath.

"You!" I exclaimed, scornfully. "And what of me? You have robbed me of my father – of all that matters to me in life – and now you ask me to comfort you!"

He stretched out his hands to me with a gesture of entreaty.

"Don't say that, Helen!" he implored. "Don't say I robbed you of him. It was an accident that no one could foresee. And after all, you know, Helen," he added, persuasively "if you have lost a father, you have gained a devoted husband."

At these words I gazed at him in utter amazement; and quite suddenly the confusion of my thoughts began to clear up. I began to realise that some action was called for, though what that action was I could not clearly see at the moment. But what I did see quite clearly was that the thing he was suggesting was utterly unthinkable.

"Do you suppose, Mr Otway," I demanded, "that I could possibly live with you as your wife after what has happened?"

"But you are my wife, Helen," he protested.

"I agreed to marry you, Mr Otway, in order to save my father. My father has not been saved."

"That was, no doubt, your motive, Helen," he answered. "I don't deny that. But, actually, you agreed to be my wife on certain specific conditions, which I carried out – or at least, was prepared – "

He hesitated with sudden embarrassment; and the embarrassment, with the statement, in the midst of which he had broken off, gave me my cue.

"Mr Otway," I said, "you had a letter from my father. What was in that letter?"

At this question his self-possession broke down completely.

"I have had no letter," he stammered; "at least, that is to say, I haven't seen – he spoke of a letter, but – but the fact is, in my excitement this morning I forgot to look at my correspondence. If there was a letter, it must be in the box still."

"Let us go and see if it is there," said I. My confusion of mind was fast clearing up, and as my wits returned, I found myself shaping a definite course of action. I rose and accompanied him to the hall door and stood by while he unlocked the letter box. As he opened the trap, I perceived that the box contained a single letter; and even in that agitating moment, the significance of the fact struck me. It was strange, indeed, that the morning's delivery should bring to a man of business no more than a single letter.

He picked the missive out, and, having glanced at it, handed it to me. I looked at it, and, perceiving that it was in my father's handwriting, tore open the envelope and drew out the letter, which I read aloud. It ran thus:

> "Stonebury, Maidstone.
> "25th April, 1908.

"Dear Otway,

"You will, no doubt, be glad to learn that our little difficulty is at an end. The unexpected has happened. My friend has been able to raise the wherewith to repay the loan that I made to him, and has sent a cheque for the full amount. I have paid it into my bank, but, as a measure of security, in view of the magnitude of the sum, I am waiting until the cheque is cleared before sending you mine. However, you may expect to receive payment in full in the course of three clear days from this date.

"With many thanks for your forbearance,

> "I am, yours very truly,

> "W H Vardon."

As I finished reading, I looked Mr Otway sternly in the face.

"You realise," I said, "that this letter makes our agreement void?"

He did not reply immediately, but stood with his eyes averted from me and his fingers working nervously.

"Do you realise that?" I demanded.

"Well, in a way, yes," he replied, hesitatingly. "If it had reached me sooner – that is to say, if I had seen it – "

"If you had seen it!" I interrupted, angrily. "What has that to do with the question? The letter was delivered to you, as the postmark shows, before you left the house. It came by the first post. If you chose to leave it unopened, that is your affair. When you met me this morning, the agreement was already at an end."

He glanced nervously along the hall towards the kitchen stairs.

"We needn't stand here," he said. "Let us go into the study and talk this affair over quietly."

He led the way back to the room we had left, and, having shut the door, turned to me deprecatingly.

"It's an unfortunate business, Helen," he said. "Very unfortunate. Of course, I ought to have looked over the morning's post, but, in my natural excitement, I overlooked it; and now I don't see that there is anything for us to do but make the best of it."

I looked at him in amazement. "But," I exclaimed, "you don't seem to realise that our agreement was at an end before the marriage took place."

"No I don't," he replied. "You see this letter is only a notification – a conditional promise to pay. It doesn't discharge the debt."

At this my patience gave out completely. "Let us have no evasions or quibbles Mr Otway," I said. "Our agreement was at an end before the marriage took place, and I have no doubt that you knew it. You obtained my consent by fraud."

"I don't admit that," said he. "But even if it were so, what would you propose?"

"I propose to have the marriage annulled," I replied.

He shook his head. "That is impossible, Helen," he said. "The marriage is not voidable. An action for nullity can be sustained only on certain conditions, none of which exist in our case."

"But," I exclaimed, "my consent was obtained on a fraudulent pretence! Surely that is a sufficient ground for claiming to have the marriage annulled!"

"I deny the fraud," he replied, doggedly. "But in any case it is not material. The marriage was perfectly regular, you are of full adult age, you gave your consent without compulsion, and there are none of those impediments which the law recognises. I assure you, Helen, that our marriage is not voidable – that it cannot be annulled by ordinary process."

Little as I trusted to his truth or honour, I suspected that what he was now saying was true. But yet the position was unthinkable.

"Do you mean to tell me," I demanded, "that the law would uphold a marriage between a woman and the murderer of her father?"

He winced as if I had struck him a blow, and his face grew sensibly paler.

"For the love of God, Helen," he entreated, "don't talk like that! You don't believe it. I can see you don't. You know I did not kill your father."

"I know nothing," I replied, "but this: that when I came into the room my father was lying dead with a wound on his forehead and that you were standing over him with a formidable weapon in your hand."

I thought he would have fainted. He sank into a chair with a gasp that was almost a sob, and the sweat streamed down his pallid face. He was a pitiable spectacle; but yet I felt no pity for him. I was bent only on escaping from the net in which he had caught me.

"I swear I never touched him, Helen," he protested breathlessly. "I swear it. But you know I did not. You are only saying this to torture me. You don't believe it. I know you don't."

"It is of little importance what I believe, Mr Otway," I replied, coldly. "The decision will not rest with me. You will be judged by others on the facts which I have stated."

He made no immediate reply. He seemed absolutely paralysed by terror, and sat, breathing quickly and staring at me, as if he expected me to kill him then and there. At length he spoke in a husky, indistinct voice.

"Helen. What is it you want of me?"

"I want this marriage set aside," I answered.

"But," he protested, "I have told you that is impossible. It cannot be annulled in the ordinary sense. Be reasonable, Helen. Let us talk the matter over and see if we can't come to terms."

"What do you mean?" I asked.

"Well," he said, persuasively, "I should like to meet your wishes if I can. I am not unreasonable. I can see that, as things are, you would not wish to live with me as my wife. We can't get the marriage annulled, but we can arrange a separation – a temporary separation, say, without prejudice to any future arrangements – by mutual consent. What do you say to that?"

"If the marriage cannot be set aside, I suppose a separation would be the next best thing. Do I understand that you are willing to agree to a separation?"

"Yes," he replied; "on certain conditions I am willing to agree to a separation – a temporary separation, you know."

"What are your conditions?" I asked.

He cleared his throat once or twice, as if in doubt how best to put the matter. Then, avoiding my eye, he began, hesitatingly, but with an obsequiously persuasive manner.

"The exact circumstances of your father's most lamentable death, Helen, are known to you and to me and to no one else. As I have told you, and I am convinced that you believe, the heart attack which killed him came as we were struggling for possession of his stick. It was due to the excitement and the violent exertion. Perhaps the blow on the head from the corner of the mantelpiece may have had something to do with it, for the fainting attack came on almost directly afterwards. He relaxed his hold on the stick and fell, leaving it in my hands. There was no violence on my part. I never struck him or did anything that could in any way make me responsible for his death. That is the truth, Helen, and I am convinced that you believe it, in spite of what you have said."

"I have only your word that it is the truth," said I.

"Exactly," he agreed. "But you believe me. You know what your father's state of health was, and you know that he was liable, on occasions, to be – er – somewhat violent. So you believe me. But others, who have not the knowledge that you have – ah – might – ah – might not believe me."

"I haven't said that I do," I interposed. "However, we will let that pass. Go on, please."

He paused to wipe his face with his handkerchief, and then proceeded: "You said just now that when you entered the room you saw me standing over your father with a weapon in my hand."

"So I did."

"I know you did, Helen. You saw me holding your father's loaded stick. It is quite true. But – it would – ah – greatly simplify matters if – well, if that circumstance were not communicated to – ah – to anyone else."

"You mean to say," said I, "that you want me to suppress the fact that I saw you standing over my father's dead body holding a loaded stick?"

"I wouldn't use the word 'suppress,' Helen," he replied, passing his handkerchief once more over his haggard face. "I only ask you to refrain – in the interests of justice and – ah – of common humanity – from mentioning a circumstance that – ah – mentioned, might mislead the hearers, and might, conceivably, lead them to quite erroneous conclusions. It is a reasonable thing to ask. No doubt you blame me; you look upon me as the cause of this dreadful trouble – which, in a certain sense, I admit I am. But you would not be vindictive, Helen, or unjust. You would not wish to see me placed in the dock – perhaps even convicted – think of that; Helen! Convicted and sentenced when I am absolutely innocent! My God! It would be an awful thing! You wouldn't wish to have such a frightful miscarriage of justice as that on your conscience, I am sure."

"It wouldn't be on my conscience," I replied, coldly. "The verdict would not be mine; and besides, I have only your word that you are innocent. You have made the statement to me, and you could make it to others, who would take it for what it is worth."

He clasped his hands passionately and leaned forward towards me with an imploring gesture.

"Helen!" he exclaimed. "Don't be so hard, so cold! Have you no pity for me? Think of my awful position – an innocent man, but yet with appearances so horribly against me. And the whole issue is in your hands. You were not present when – when it happened. You have only to say so and to refrain from making any unnecessary additions to that statement, and no miscarriage of justice can occur. I am not asking you to say anything that is not true; I am only asking you to keep irrelevant and misleading matter out of the inquiry. Do this, Helen, and I promise to execute a deed surrendering all claims on you – at least for a time."

I made no immediate answer. Mr Otway was perfectly right on one point. I did not believe that he had killed my father. I think I only half believed it, even, at the awful moment of the discovery; for the alarming appearance that my father had presented as he strode up the garden path, with his wild eyes and his strange, blotchy colour, had made me fear a catastrophe; and when the catastrophe had almost immediately followed, it was natural that my mind should refer it to a cause already considered rather than to one totally unexpected. Moreover, Mr Otway's account of the tragedy was intrinsically probable; it fitted the facts that were known to me; whereas the supposition that he had killed my father was wildly improbable.

It is not to be supposed, however, that, in my present agitated state, I reasoned the matter out consciously in this methodical fashion. But unconsciously, and perhaps vaguely, my mind had worked along these lines to a conclusion; and that conclusion was that Mr Otway's account of what had happened was substantially correct. Nevertheless, I was not prepared to admit this at the moment; indeed, my whole desire was to be rid of the man's irksome presence – to be alone with my grief.

"I can't give you an answer now, Mr Otway," I said. "I am not in a condition to discuss anything. I want to go home and be quiet."

He acquiesced with surprising readiness, no doubt encouraged by my tacit abandonment of the accusation.

"Of course you do," he agreed. "It has been a fearful shock for you. Go home and keep yourself quiet. I shall hear from Dr Bury, in the course of the day, what the coroner intends to do, and I will call and let you know. And I will bring a draft of the deed for you to look at. The sooner we arrive at a settlement, the better. And, Helen, let me beg you not to say anything to anyone about – anything that might complicate matters. You understand what I mean."

I nodded wearily and moved towards the door. I was still wearing my outdoor clothes, so I had no preparations to make. Mr Otway opened the door for me and I passed out into the hall; but before leaving the house, I turned back into the darkened drawing-room, and, raising the cover from my father's face, kissed his already cold cheek.

"Goodbye, dearest! Goodbye!" I whispered, passionately; and then, feeling the tears rushing to my eyes, I kissed him again, and, replacing the cover, hurried from the room. Mr Otway was standing at the hall door to let me out, and timidly offered his hand; but I walked quickly past him, and, running down the steps, made my way out through the gate that had admitted me to my ruin and my father to his death.

CHAPTER EIGHT

"Whom God Hath Joined – "

Our states of mind in certain unforeseen circumstances are sometimes surprising, even, to ourselves. As I walked away from Mr Otway's house, I think I was dimly surprised at my own self-possession. The worst had happened. The calamity which I had feared, and which I had made such sacrifices to avert, had befallen; and yet I was comparatively calm. My heart ached, it is true, with a grief such as I had never known before; with a sense of irreparable loss and a feeling of utter loneliness and desolation; but yet, under it all was a certain indefinable peace.

Looking back with more natural knowledge and experience, this state of mind is not difficult to understand. My father's sudden death was a crushing calamity; but, in the very moment of its happening, the incubus of my relation to Mr Otway was lifted. For, though I was not at the time conscious of the fact, I now see clearly that, even as I passed out of the house of the man whom the law regarded as my husband, my mind was made up that I had done with Mr Otway.

Moreover, my new trouble was in other ways more easy to bear than the misery of the last few days. My marriage had seemed, in a manner, to put an end to my life. It had offered nothing but an unending vista of wretchedness, an unending submission to a state of things that was intolerable even to think of. But this new catastrophe was sudden and final. The blow had fallen, once for all;

shattering, indeed, my present, but calling upon me instantly to make provision for the future. And in action, the necessity of which forced itself upon me even before I reached home, I found, if not relief from my sorrow, at least some temporary distraction.

As I let myself in with my latchkey, our housemaid met me in the hall to announce that lunch had been waiting for some time, and to ask me if I knew at what time my father would come in.

"My father is dead, Jessie," I replied. "He died suddenly at Mr Otway's house about an hour ago. I can't tell you any more just now."

I walked past her and ascended the stairs to my room, leaving her standing in the hall as if petrified; but, before I reached the landing, I heard her rush away towards the kitchen, making the house resound with her hysterical shrieks and lamentations. It was very dreadful and distressing, but yet it had a steadying effect on me, reminding me of my isolated position and of the need for firmness and self-control. In a few minutes I came down, and disregarding Jessie's sobs and tears sat out the simple formalities of lunch as a matter of discipline and example, and even compelled myself to take a certain amount of food.

As I sat at my silent and solitary meal, my thoughts were busy with the many things that had to be done. Not willingly, indeed; for I longed to be quiet and nurse my grief – to forget everything but my sorrow and my great bereavement. But that was impossible. I was practically alone in the world, for I had no near relatives, and all that had to be done must be done, or at least directed, by me. There was my father's funeral to be arranged, the business to be transferred or wound up, the property to be realised – and there was Mr Otway.

Naturally enough, my thoughts constantly came back to him. As to his moral claim on me, it was null and void. Whether he had, as I suspected, seen my father's latter and deliberately left it unopened, or whether he had simply neglected to look for it, made no difference. It had been delivered to him, and thereupon our agreement had ceased to exist. But if he had no moral claim, he had, apparently, a legal hold on me which would have to be considered. If he could be induced to surrender that, the position would be greatly simplified. And he was ready to surrender it on a certain condition.

To Mr Otway's proposal my thoughts came back again and again. The condition that he had made was not an unreasonable one, or, at least, it did not appear so to me. My father had died when they were alone together: they had admittedly been quarrelling; my father bore the mark of a heavy blow; and Mr Otway had been found standing over the body with a loaded stick in his hand. The appearances suggested that he had killed my father. And yet I was convinced that he had not. Profoundly loathing him as the cause of all my misfortunes, I still felt that he was, in this respect, an innocent man; and common justice demanded that he should not be made to suffer for a crime that he had not committed.

Now what was my position in the affair? Practically I held the scales of justice. The one absolutely damning fact was in my sole possession; and I alone, in all probability, would appreciate the misleading appearances which that fact created. That was my dilemma. I could make known the fact itself to those who should judge him, but could I make them understand how little it was worth? It seemed very doubtful. *I* had trembled for my father's safety and had seen him come in at the gate, already in a dangerous condition. *They* had not. They might easily fail to weigh his state of health against that one, apparently, sinister fact of the loaded stick. In short, it came to this: that if I mentioned what I had seen, Mr Otway ran a serious risk of being punished for a crime which he had not committed, whereas if I refrained from mentioning it, justice would take its proper course.

That, I think, is, in effect, how I argued. Neither the logician nor the jurist will commend me. But women have their own ways of looking at things, and one of those ways is somewhat to confuse conviction with knowledge. A thing firmly believed is apt to present itself as a thing known. I had come to the conclusion that

Mr Otway was innocent of my father's death, and having done so, had unconsciously treated his innocence as a fact that was within my knowledge.

After lunch, I telephoned to the office, asking. Mr Jackson, my father's managing clerk to come and see me; and while I was waiting for him, I took down from the study shelves a treatise of the Law of Husband and Wife, and turned over those of its unsavoury pages which dealt with suits for nullity. Apparently Mr Otway was right. So far as I could make out, the circumstances of our marriage afforded no grounds for such a suit. I was married irrevocably. My complete freedom was gone beyond recall; I should have to be content with such incomplete freedom as is conferred by a deed of separation.

I had just returned the book to the shelf when Mr Jackson arrived and entered the room looking very flurried and uncomfortable.

"What a dreadful thing this is, Miss Vardon!" he exclaimed. "Shocking! Shocking! So unexpected! I need not say how much we all sympathise with you."

"It is very kind of you," I said, offering him a chair.

"Not at all," he rejoined. "It is a terrible misfortune for all of us. Would it distress you very much to tell me how it happened?"

"It was for that purpose that I sent for you, Mr Jackson; to tell you exactly what has happened and to ask your advice" and here I gave him a brief account of the events of the morning.

At the mention of my marriage he looked profoundly surprised, but also, I thought, distinctly relieved; but he did not make any comment until I had finished the whole tragic story, when he remarked: "I am very glad to hear that you are married, Miss Vardon – or rather, I should say, Mrs Otway – to a man of such very substantial means, if I am rightly informed."

"Why are you glad?" I asked.

"Because," he replied, "it disposes of rather a difficulty. Your father was a man of great abilities and an excellent lawyer, but he was somewhat inattentive to the financial side of his profession. I am afraid you would have been left rather badly provided for."

"I am sorry to hear that," said I, "because I am not proposing to live with Mr Otway. I have asked him to agree to a separation."

Mr Jackson raised his eyebrows. "May I ask why?" he enquired.

"I don't want to go into details just now," I answered, "but I may say that the marriage was an affair of accommodation; I supposed my father to be in a position of embarrassment, and I made the arrangement with Mr Otway without his knowledge. It turns out that I was mistaken. He was not embarrassed. When the marriage took place, I was under a misapprehension and I was misled by Mr Otway. Accordingly, I have asked to have a separation deed drawn up."

"Does he agree to the separation?"

"He has not yet, but I think he will; so I shall have to consider my resources, after all."

"But," Mr Jackson objected, "he will have to make you an allowance."

"That," I said, "is impossible. If I repudiate the marriage, I could not, of course, allow him to support me."

"Why not?" demanded Mr Jackson. "He is legally bound to. You are his wife. While the marriage stands, you can't marry anybody else. Besides, he is not likely to raise any objection. He is a lawyer, you know."

"I am not thinking of him: I am thinking of myself. I wish to be under no obligations to Mr Otway, and I shall not accept any assistance from him."

"I am sorry to hear you say that," Mr Jackson said, gloomily; "because I am afraid you will be rather badly off. The business is a very personal one, and is worth practically nothing to sell. If I were a qualified solicitor, I might be able to carry it on. But I'm not; and I doubt if anyone would care to buy the goodwill at any price. Still, I'll see what can be done. As to your father's will, I happen to know that you are the residuary legatee – practically the sole legatee –

but what that amounts to, I shouldn't like to say. Mighty little, I fear. However, it's of no use to worry you with these matters now. If you will authorise me to look into your father's affairs, I will let you know exactly how things stand; and if I could be of service to you in any way, I hope you'll let me know. There's the funeral, for instance – "

He paused suddenly, and ran an uncomfortable eye along the rows of law books on the shelves.

"You are very kind, Mr Jackson," I said, "and your help will be invaluable. As my father's friend, I should like you to take charge of the funeral arrangements, if you would be so good."

The rest of our conversation was concerned with the various things which had to be done during the next day or two, and it left with a feeling of the warmest gratitude to this quiet and rather dry man of business, whose sympathy took such a practical and acceptable form.

It was past six o'clock when the red-eyed Jessie came to the study to announce that Mr Otway was waiting in the drawing-room; and there I found him wandering restlessly round by the walls and making a show of examining the pictures. He was still very pale and looked haggard and weary, but yet he held out his hand to me with a certain confidence.

"I think, Helen," said he, "that you will be a little relieved at my news. I have seen Dr Bury, and he tells me that the coroner will be satisfied with his evidence and Dr Sharpe's."

"Do you mean that there is to be no inquest?" I demanded, with sudden suspicion.

"No, no," he replied. "Of course, there will be an inquest. But the coroner thinks that the circumstances do not call for a post-mortem. I thought you would be glad to know that. The – er – body will remain where it is until the jury have viewed it, and then it can be brought here for the – ah – the funeral."

I nodded but made no comment on this statement, and he continued after a brief pause: "I suppose Helen, you would like me to act for you in regard to the funeral arrangements."

"Thank you, Mr Otway," I replied, "but Mr Jackson has very kindly undertaken that for me."

He looked somewhat crestfallen at this, and said, deprecatingly: "I am sorry you did not leave the arrangements to me. It would have looked better." Which it undeniably, would – from his point of view.

As I made no rejoinder, there followed a slightly uncomfortable pause, during which he was evidently bracing himself up for what was the real object of his visit. At length he began nervously: "Have you been able to give any more consideration to my proposal, Helen."

"Yes," I answered; "I have thought about it a good deal. Perhaps we had better go into the study, which is more out of the way of the servants than this."

We crossed the hall and, when we had entered the study and closed the door, I resumed: "I may as well say, Mr Otway, that I am prepared to accept your statement. On reflection, I believe that your account of what happened is true."

"Thank God for that!" he ejaculated. "I felt sure you believed me, Helen; but it is an unspeakable relief to hear you say so. And I am sure you will agree with me that the – the apparently incriminating circumstance need not be mentioned."

"I might even agree to that," I replied; "but there must be a clear understanding. I am not going to say anything that is not strictly true."

"Oh, certainly not!" he agreed. "All that I ask is that you refrain from volunteering a perfectly unnecessary and misleading statement. Will you promise to do that?"

"I am not sure that I have any right to make such a promise, Mr Otway; but still, on the conditions that you mentioned, I am prepared to do so."

His relief was really pathetic. Its intensity made me understand what torments of terror he had been suffering. He flung out his hands as if he would have embraced me, but drew back, as I said, coldly: "You are prepared on your side, Mr Otway, to carry out your part? You agree to execute a deed of separation, as I asked?"

"If you insist," he replied. "It's a hard bargain, but if you hold me to it, I have no choice. Would not a short, informal separation do?"

"No, Mr Otway," I replied firmly, "it would not. I am acting somewhat against my conscience in agreeing to suppress this fact, and I want full compensation for doing so. I must have a legally-valid deed of separation."

"Very well, Helen," said he; "if it must be, it must. I hope that, later, you will take a kinder view of our relations, but meanwhile I will do exactly as you wish. I have drafted out a deed, in a simple form, with as little legal verbiage as possible. If its terms satisfy you, I will copy it out and sign it."

He handed me a sheet of paper on which the deed was drafted, and I read it through carefully. Like the other documents that he had drawn up, it was lucid, simple and concise, and set forth quite fairly the conditions to which he had agreed, with one exception. It determined automatically at the end of three months.

"I can't agree to that," I said. "There must be no specified time; it is to be just a separation."

"But," he exclaimed, "you don't propose that the separation should last for ever, do you?"

That was precisely what I did propose, but I thought it politic not to express myself too definitely.

"It is impossible," I replied, "to say what may happen in the future; but if you make the separation determinable by mutual consent, that will provide for all eventualities."

He agreed, with a somewhat wry smile, that this was so and then asked how soon I should like to have the deed executed.

"As it must be signed before I give my evidence," I replied, "it had better be done now. If you will make two copies, I will go and fetch the maids to witness the signatures."

"Dear me, Helen!" he exclaimed. "What an extraordinarily businesslike young lady you are! But I suppose you are right; only

I would suggest that you do not acquaint the witnesses with the nature of the document. We don't want to take the world into our confidence, especially just now."

This was reasonable enough, though it would obviously be impossible to keep the world in the dark as to our position, particularly after what I had said to Mr Jackson. However, I agreed to maintain a discreet reticence, and when he had made the two copies – which I carefully read through – I went out and called Jessie and the cook.

"I want you," said I, "to witness my signature and Mr Otway's to a couple of documents. You have just to see us sign our names and then sign your own underneath."

The two women came into the study with an air of mystery and awe, gazing furtively from me to Mr Otway. The two documents lay on the table, each with a sheet of blotting paper spread over it, exposing only the blank spaces which were to receive the signatures, on each of which a red wafer seal had been stuck. Mr Otway signed first, and then, indicating to the cook the place where she was to write her name, placed the pen in her hand.

"That's right," said he, when she had painfully and with protruded tongue, executed the signature of "Ivy Stokes." "Now you will do the same with the other paper as soon as Mrs Otway has signed."

The cook gazed curiously at me as I signed the second document, and then, in the same strained and laborious fashion, traced the scrawling characters over the name that I had lightly pencilled in for her guidance. Having watched with feverish interest while I marked the next space, she drew back and made way for Jessie, who, by watching her colleague, had learned what was required of her.

When the formalities were completed and the two maids dismissed – to discuss these strange proceedings, doubtless, in the kitchen – Mr Otway handed me the copy, bearing his signature, and, taking the other, rose to depart.

"Before I go, Helen," he said, "there is one matter to settle. In the document I thought it best to say nothing about an allowance – "

"You were quite right," I interrupted. "Of course, I should not ask for, or accept, any allowance under the circumstances."

"You won't need one at present," said he. "We know there are five thousand pounds lying to your father's credit at his bank – "

"That money was not his," I said, "and it is not mine. As soon as the will is proved it will be paid to you on behalf of your clients."

"But that is quite unnecessary, Helen," said he. "The use, for an unspecified time, of that sum of money was the consideration in respect of which you agreed to marry me. As the marriage has taken place, it is only fair and reasonable that you should receive the consideration. In effect, that five thousand is yours by the terms of our agreement."

I was on the point of replying that our agreement was null and void, and that I had no intention of carrying out its conditions; but prudence whispered that I had better keep my intentions to myself, at least as to my ultimate conduct. Besides which, Mr Otway's statement was not entirely correct, as I proceeded to point out.

"The use of this money," I said, "was to relieve my father, who was assumed to be insolvent. But it appears that he was not insolvent; and it is my intention that all his debts shall be paid, in so far as there are funds to meet them. It is certainly what he would have wished."

"But," Mr Otway protested, "supposing the payment of these debts should consume all the available assets? How are you going to live?"

"I suppose I shall do as other women do when they have no independent means. I shall work for my living. But it is premature to discuss that until I have had Mr Jackson's report. I don't suppose I shall be absolutely penniless."

He shook his head gloomily. "You are Quixotic, Helen, and wrong-headed, too. There is no reason why you should work for your living. As a married woman, you are entitled to maintenance, and I am willing, and even anxious, to maintain you. But I won't press the matter now. If you want money, you know that you can have it, not as a favour but as a right. And now there is just one other matter that I want to speak about. In the deed of separation I said nothing about our relations other than was actually necessary. I made no stipulation as to your keeping me informed of your whereabouts; but I ask you now, if you should be leaving Maidstone, to let me have your address and to allow me to keep up communication with you. It is a reasonable request, Helen, and I am sure you will not hesitate to accede to it."

I did hesitate, however, for some time. In truth, I was not at all willing to agree to this proposal. My wish was to sponge Mr Otway, once and for all, out of my life and to make a fresh start. Still, the request was a reasonable one, and could, I suspected, have been enforced as a demand; and, in the end, though very reluctantly, I yielded.

"Thank you, Helen," said he, holding out his hand; "then I won't worry you any more just now. It is understood that I am not to lose sight of you, and that if you should want help, pecuniary or other, you will let me know. And I may rely on you to say no more at the inquest than is actually necessary?"

I gave him the required assurance on this point, and, having somewhat frigidly shaken his hand, accompanied him to the hall door and let him out.

As I stood in the open doorway, watching him walk away up the street in his heavy, elephantine fashion, a man entered at the gate, and, approaching with a deferential and rather uncomfortable air, took off his hat and offered me a small, blue envelope, which bore the superscription "Mrs Lewis Otway." I took it from him, and, closing the door, went back to the study, where I opened the envelope and extracted the little slip of blue paper that it enclosed; which turned out, as I had expected, to be the subpoena to the inquest. I glanced through the peremptory phrases of the summons, and, laying the slip of paper on the table, went up to my own room to be quiet and think upon all that lay before me.

But thought – orderly, useful thought – was impossible. Everything around me spoke of the life that had been so tragically broken off, rather than of the future that loomed so vague and empty before me. The open book on the reading-stand, the hastily scribbled notes upon the writing-block, the unanswered letters and a little pile of rough drawings on the table, all seemed to call to me to take up afresh the thread that had been dropped; seemed to interpose the unfinished past before the uncommenced future. Restlessly I wandered down to the workshop – where the coal scuttle still stood on the bench, a mute but eloquent memorial of that tragic final evening – only to gather a fresh sense of loss and desolation. And so, for the rest of the day I haunted the house like some unquiet spirit, watched with pity, not unmixed with fear, by the awe-stricken servants, tearless and outwardly calm, but inwardly torn by grief and a sense of bereavement that seemed to intensify moment by moment.

And yet, when, in the silence of the night, the tears came at last, and my sorrow, no longer mute, voiced itself in sobs and moans of pain, still, under the feeling of utter bereavement and desolation, was a half-felt sense of peace, of respite, and reprieve.

CHAPTER NINE

Testimony and Counsel

Those who are apt to refer in contemptuous terms to the artificiality of the plots of the novelist must have failed to observe the orderly way in which events arrange themselves in real life; how the circumstances of the vital and essential happenings of our lives may, if attentively considered, be separated out in a coherent group of causes and effects as closely knit and inevitably connected as the parts of the story-teller's plot.

The reflection is suggested to me by the distressing experiences of the inquest on my father's death. Clearly enough, indeed, did I realise at the time that this would never have been but for those fateful words so calamitously overheard by me, and for my ill-considered, though well-meant, efforts to avert the apparently impending catastrophe. But I realised not at all – as, indeed, how should I? – that this day of sorrow, of shame and humiliation, was not only the harvest of the irrevocable past but the seedtime of an even more momentous future.

As I approached the school-house in which the inquest was to be held, I observed Mr Otway pacing slowly up and down the little courtyard. He was pale and haggard, and though he preserved his usual ponderously reposeful manner, it was not difficult to see that he was in a state of intense, nervous excitement and suppressed anxiety.

He was evidently waiting for me, and turned to meet me as I entered the gate.

"I thought we had better go in together, Helen," he said, as we exchanged a formal greeting. "They know that we are married, and, of course, they don't know that our – ah – our arrangements are in – ah – in suspense. And it would perhaps be as well if no reference were made to – ah – to those –ahem– temporary modifications which – ah – in short, to our provisional agreement."

He looked at me deprecatingly and I nodded. There would be quite enough painful detail to be dragged into the light of day without this sordid addition. Besides, any reference to the deed of separation would start enquiries which neither of us desired, as was plainly evident to Mr Otway; for he continued in a husky undertone, as we approached the schoolroom door: "And you will fulfil your part of our covenant faithfully, Helen, I am sure."

"Most undoubtedly I shall," I replied. "But you will remember that our covenant does not include false evidence. I shall say as little as is possible, but if I am asked a direct question I must answer it, and answer it truthfully."

"Of course you must," he agreed: "but it is often possible to ward off an inconvenient question which may lead to others still more inconvenient."

"You make take it," I said, "that I shall carry out my part of our bargain in the spirit as well as in the letter."

With this assurance he appeared to be satisfied, and we now moved slowly towards the door of the school-house. While we had been talking, a party of men – the coroner and his jury – had filed past us and entered; and when we followed a minute later, we found them already in their places and the proceedings about to begin. We seated ourselves on the two chairs placed for us, which were next to those of the two medical witnesses, and as I glanced round the Court, I observed Mr Jackson sitting near the coroner, and by his side a gentleman whose face I seemed to recognise, but to whom I could not give a name. Some dim recollection connected the quiet, strong, intellectual face with my father and the happy past, but not until near the close of the inquiry was I able to bring my memory to a clear focus.

The attitude of the coroner and jury alike – they were all local men and most of them known to me – made my difficult task as easy as was possible. They were all anxious to spare me to the utmost and to make the best of what the coroner described as "a grievous and terrible calamity." Moreover, they restrained in the most delicate manner their evident curiosity as to the relations of Mr Otway and myself. But of course the facts had to be given, and very distressing and humiliating it was to me to have to confess to what must have looked like a mere sordid intrigue with the uncouth creature at my side.

As the only person present when the death occurred, Mr Otway was necessarily the first witness; and a very nervous, hesitating witness he was; and very fortunate was it for him that he had so sympathetic a court. As he stammered out his evidence I noted, again and again, the searching, grey eye of the strange gentleman fixed upon him, not indeed with any obvious distrust, but with the most concentrated attention.

"Do we understand," asked the coroner, "that Mr Vardon was angry and excited when he arrived at your house?"

"Yes, furiously angry."

"Do you know why he was angry and excited?"

Yes, the witness did know. And as he proceeded to relate, in husky, uncertain tones, the circumstances of the secret marriage, more than one of the jurymen glanced from him to me with hardly-concealed astonishment; and I felt my face burning and my eyes filling with humiliation.

"Was there any reason for this secrecy?" the coroner asked.

"Yes. The deceased had already refused his consent to the marriage."

"But that is hardly a reason for secrecy in the case of an adult. Could he have prevented the marriage from taking place?"

"No. But it seemed better to – ah – to avoid discussion and unpleasantness."

The coroner looked dissatisfied. He considered a few moments, and then asked: "Do you know why the deceased objected to the marriage?"

"I think he considered that the – ah – the inequality of age was undesirable," Mr Otway replied.

Still the coroner looked dissatisfied, and as he paused to reflect, and the jurymen looked at him expectantly, Mr Otway furtively wiped his forehead with his handkerchief. Evidently, he was profoundly disturbed, as well he might be; for if this line of inquiry were pursued much farther, it must inevitably lay bare the real nature of the transaction.

At length the coroner turned to the jury. "Well, gentlemen," said he, "I suppose the question is not very material. It is clear that the deceased was extremely excited and angry. The ultimate cause of his anger is, perhaps, not very relevant to the subject of our inquiry."

To this the foreman of the jury readily agreed, and I could almost see the sigh of relief with which Mr Otway hailed the passing of this perilous incident – a relief in which I participated to no small extent.

The narrative was now resumed, and as it proceeded, Mr Otway's voice became more and more husky and his speech more hesitating. He had a difficult course to steer, and his nerves were at their utmost tension. He had to tell a consistent story without telling the whole truth, and he had to bear in mind that my evidence was yet to be given. It was a position that might have shattered the nerve of a much bolder man than Mr Otway.

"You tell us that the deceased was violent and threatening in his manner. Do you mean that he was physically violent?"

"Yes – at least he threatened to use physical violence."

"He did not actually assault you?"

"Not actually. The blow that he aimed – at least that he was about to aim – ah – did not – er – did not take effect."

The coroner's brows puckered into a puzzled frown. "This is not quite clear," said he. "Did he or did he not aim a blow at you?"

"He did – at least, that is to say, he appeared –" – here Mr Otway mopped his streaming forehead – "well, I think he actually raised his – ah – his – ah – his clenched fist – "

"Did you have to restrain him?"

"No," replied Mr Otway, with rather unnecessary emphasis. "No, I did not. I stepped back, and – ah – the incident – ah – passed. In fact, it was at this moment that the fatal attack occurred."

"Tell us exactly what happened then."

"He suddenly turned very pale," said Mr Otway, speaking now with more fluency as he got back to the narration of the actual events, "and seemed to stand unsteadily. Then he staggered backwards and fell, striking his head on the corner of the mantelpiece."

"Did he appear to have fainted before he struck his head?"

"I should say, yes, but – ah – I would not – ah – I was very agitated and alarmed – and –ah – "

"Naturally. But you would say that the fainting attack preceded the blow on the head."

"There was no blow," Mr Otway exclaimed quickly; and then, perceiving his mistake, he added, hastily, "that is to say, you are referring to his striking the corner of the mantelpiece?"

"That is what you were telling us about."

"Yes. I should say that he struck – or rather that he fainted and staggered and that he struck his head in falling."

Once more the coroner paused and seemed to reflect; and in the intense silence and stillness that enveloped the court, my eye travelled from the huge, ungainly figure of the witness to the face of the tall stranger by Mr Jackson's side. And a very striking face it was: a handsome, symmetrical face, but strangely – almost unhumanly – reposeful and impassive. Yet, though it was as immobile as a mask of stone, it conveyed an impression of intense attention – almost of watchfulness; and the clear, grey eyes never moved from the face of the witness. To me there was something a little uncanny and disturbing in that immovable mask and that steady, unrelaxing gaze. I found myself hoping that those searching grey eyes would not be fixed on me in that relentless observation when my turn came to give my evidence. And even as this thought flitted through my mind, I remembered who this stranger was. He was a Dr Thorndyke, an old, though not very intimate, friend of my father's, a famous criminal lawyer and a great authority on medical jurisprudence. I had met him only once, when he had dined, many years ago, at our house; but I had often heard my father speak of him in terms of the highest admiration.

When the coroner resumed his interrogation, it seemed that the crisis was past, so far as Mr Otway was concerned, for his first question was: "What did you do when the deceased fell down?"

"For a moment or two," was the reply, "I was too bewildered to do anything. Then his daughter – my wife – came into the room, and, as he appeared to be dying or dead, I went off to fetch a doctor."

This virtually concluded his evidence, and the next name called was my own, which, in its new form – Helen Otway – I heard with a start of surprise and something like disgust. As I rose to approach the table, I caught an instantaneous glance – a terrified imploring glance – from Mr Otway; and as my eye lighted immediately afterwards on Dr Thorndyke's face, I felt that this momentary look, too, had been noted by that inexorably attentive grey eye. But I was relieved to observe that he did not look at me, but, as I gave my evidence, fixed a steady, introspective gaze upon a spot upon the opposite wall.

My task turned out to be easier than I had hoped, though perhaps it might have been less easy if I had had more time to reflect on the significance of the questions. The coroner began by expressing the sympathy of the court with my bereavement and apologising for imposing on me the painful duty of attending the inquiry. Then he asked: "You have heard the evidence of Mr

Otway with reference to your marriage and your father's attitude in regard to it. Do you confirm what he has said?"

"I do," I replied.

"You were not present at the interview of Mr Otway with the deceased?"

"No, I was not. When I entered the room my father was lying on the floor and appeared to be already dead."

"Had you seen your father since the solemnisation of the marriage?"

"I saw him from the window as he entered Mr Otway's garden."

"Did you notice anything unusual in his appearance?"

"Yes; his appearance alarmed me very much. He seemed excessively excited, and his face was deeply flushed and of a strange, purplish colour."

"Had you any special reason to be alarmed?"

"Yes. I knew that his doctor had warned him to avoid all excitement and exertion on account of the weak state of his heart."

"You did not hear what passed between your father and Mr Otway?"

"I heard my father ask where I was, and I heard Mr Otway tell him that the marriage had taken place."

"Did you hear anything more?"

"My father then called Mr Otway a scoundrel, and was still speaking loudly and angrily when the study door closed and I heard no more."

"What made you go to the study?"

"I heard and felt the shock when my father fell."

"Would you mind telling us again in what condition you found your father?"

"He appeared to be dead. His face was at first a livid grey, but it faded to marble whiteness as I looked at him. There was a small wound on the right side of his forehead and a drop of blood had run down on to his cheek and on his temple."

The coroner glanced at the jurymen. "I think, gentlemen," he said, "that is all we need ask Mrs Otway?" And when the foreman had acquiesced, and he had thanked me for "the very clear and lucid manner" in which I had given my evidence, I was permitted to resume my seat.

"I can never thank you enough, Helen," whispered Mr Otway, as I sat down. "You managed admirably – admirably."

To this I made no reply; for now that the ordeal was over I began to be assailed by certain doubts as to whether I had been quite candid. I had told all that was really material to the inquiry; but – however, at this point Dr Sharpe approached the table and picked up the Testament.

His evidence practically settled the verdict. He testified that my father had suffered for some years from a dilated heart and arterial degeneration. "I warned him frequently to avoid excitement and undue exertion, for he was inclined to be careless and take liberties with himself."

"You considered his state of health precarious?"

"I thought he might fall down dead at any moment."

"You have heard the evidence of the two previous witnesses. Does that evidence contain any suggestion to you as to the cause of death?"

"It suggests to me that the deceased hurried to Mr Otway's house in a towering rage, and that, during the interview, he worked himself up into a fury. I should say that the combined exertion and excitement brought on a fatal attack of syncope."

"You think that death was caused by heart failure?"

"I have no doubt of it."

Dr Bury's evidence was much to the same effect, though less positive.

"The deceased had apparently been dead about half an hour when I arrived. The cause of death was not obvious, but the appearances were consistent with the account given by Mr Otway. There was a small, contused wound at the junction of the forehead and right temple, apparently caused by the violent impact of some hard and blunt body. Judging by the small amount of bleeding, the wound had been sustained immediately before death. A single drop of blood had trickled down on to the cheek, and one or two drops on to the temple."

"You have heard Mr Otway's account of the way in which that wound was occasioned. Do you consider that the appearances are in agreement with that account?"

"There is no disagreement. The appearance of the wound was consistent with its production in the manner described."

"Would you say that it was probably so produced?"

"That" replied Dr Bury, "is a question for the jury. It might have been. I can't go beyond the appearances."

"No, of course you can't. And is that all that you have to tell us?"

"That is all," was the reply; and this virtually brought the inquiry to an end. After a brief summing-up by the coroner, the jury held an equally brief consultation and then unanimously returned a verdict of "Death from natural causes."

On the announcement of the verdict everyone rose, including myself and Mr Otway, and the latter, turning to me, said in a low voice: "I think I won't wait. I want to get home and be quiet; but I shall call on you tomorrow, if I may, to make – ah – any – ah – arrangements that – ah – in fact, to speak to you about the – ah – the funeral."

"Very well," I said, reluctantly – for, deeply as I loathed him, I could not exclude him even from that sacred ceremony without creating an open scandal. "You had better come early in the forenoon"; and with this I dismissed him with a stiff bow, and made my way to where Mr Jackson and Dr Thorndyke were standing. As I held out my hand to the latter and recalled to him our meeting years ago, Mr Jackson said: "Dr Thorndyke happened to be in Maidstone today and to call at our office, so I prevailed on him to come here and watch the proceedings on our behalf in case any complications should arise. But everything has gone off quite smoothly."

"Very smoothly indeed," Dr Thorndyke agreed, with, as it seemed to me, a certain degree of emphasis.

"Both the coroner and the jury were most considerate," pursued Mr Jackson.

"Most considerate," assented Dr Thorndyke; and again I seemed to detect a note of emphasis, as also, I think, did Mr Jackson, for he glanced quickly at our companion, though he made no remark.

"I wonder," said I, "if you two gentlemen would care to come and take a cup of tea with me?"

Mr Jackson had an engagement at the office, and as Dr Thorndyke appeared to hesitate, I added quickly: "I should be very glad if you could, though I don't wish to take up your time if you are busy."

"My time is my own for the next three hours," said Dr Thorndyke, "and if I should really not be an inopportune visitor, I should like very much to have tea with you."

"Let us go, then," said I. "Mr Jackson will accompany us as far as Gabriel's Hill, won't you?" And as my old friend assented with a prim, little bow, we set forth.

"I have offered no condolences, Mrs Otway," said Dr Thorndyke. "I knew your father, I saw you and him together, and I realise what this loss must mean to you. There is nothing to say except that you have my most real sympathy."

"Thank you," I said, and for a time we walked on in silence. And as we walked I found myself recalling, with a strong, speculative interest, that curious, subtle emphasis which Dr Thorndyke had conveyed into his agreement with Mr Jackson. At length, when we had dropped the latter near the Town Hall, I summoned up courage to raise the question.

"I have an impression, Dr Thorndyke, which may be quite a mistaken one, that you were not completely satisfied with the way in which the inquest was conducted. Am I mistaken?"

"Well," he replied, slowly, "the coroner's methods were not what one would call rigorous."

"I suppose they were not. But in what respect are you disposed to find fault with them?"

"Principally," he replied, "in his failure to elicit a really conclusive verdict. The verdict of the jury was based upon Dr Sharpe's opinion as to the cause of death. That opinion was probably correct, but it was based upon reasoning which was not sound. His position was this: If certain circumstances – excitement or exertion – should arise, there would be a great probability of their causing sudden death. But those circumstances had actually arisen and sudden death had actually followed. Therefore the death was due to the factors of the said circumstances. But this conclusion is fallacious. It does not prove a fact: it merely indicates a probability."

"But are not all verdicts statements of probability?"

"Too often they are. But it is a coroner's business to bring the conclusions of his court, as far as possible, into the region of ascertained fact. The immediate cause of death can usually be demonstrated by scientific methods, and the inquiry can then be built up on a foundation of certainty. Opinion should never be accepted where knowledge is obtainable."

"Do you think, then, that the verdict was not a proper one?"

"I am not criticising the verdict," he replied, "but the methods by which it was arrived at. I think that the cause of death should have been established beyond all doubt before any contributory circumstances were inquired into."

"But otherwise; apart from that one point?"

"I thought the examination of the witnesses rather easygoing. No doubt it elicited all the relevant facts. But that is impossible to decide on. One cannot judge of the relevancy of a fact until one has got the fact. I think, for instance, that most counsel would have pressed your husband a good deal more closely. The coroner appeared to decide that the matter was not relevant without being quite clear as to what matter he was dealing with."

This, I must confess, had been my own impression, but I had been so relieved at the easy manner in which the difficult passages had been allowed to pass that I had been little disposed to criticise the considerate and sympathetic coroner. Nor did it seem quite safe to pursue the present discussion much farther, for it was tending in a rather dangerous direction. My own reservations began to weigh on me somewhat – and Dr Thorndyke was not quite the same type of listener as the coroner. Nevertheless, the conversation pleased me, though I could not but be struck by the oddity of this detached discussion of a matter which was of such vital moment to me. But that very oddity was itself an element of gratification; for a woman is naturally flattered when an intellectual man appears to credit her with the power of impartial judgment of her own conduct and affairs – that faculty not being one by which our sex is peculiarly distinguished.

But at this point, our discussion was brought naturally to an end by our arrival at my house – as I must now call it; and here a quick glance of surprised recognition on my companion's part gave me a new note of warning and prepared me for the inevitable question.

"You are living at your father's house, I see."

"*I* am, for the present. Mr Otway remains in his own house."

"Yes. I suppose it will be more convenient to settle everything up here before joining your husband."

I was on the point of temporising by a vague assent; but my lips refused to frame the implied falsehood. It may have been my natural dislike of secrecy and concealment it may be that my womanly pride resented the very idea of association with that unwieldy human spider. At any rate, an irresistible impulse drove me to say: "I am not going to join my husband at all, Dr Thorndyke. I am not going to live with Mr Otway."

I did not look at Dr Thorndyke as I made this statement and he made no comment beyond a matter-of-fact "Indeed." But I had the feeling that, in the silence that followed, he was fitting this new fact into its place in some ordered scheme; that he was docketing it as an appendix to Mr Otway's evidence.

Nothing more was said until we had entered the house and I had given instructions for tea to be brought to the study. But in that interval I was aware of a growing impulse to have done with this miserable secrecy – this sordid fencing and dodging, which must come, in the end, to downright lying – and tell this strong, wise man the whole wretched story. Besides, I wanted counsel and guidance: and who was so fit to give them as he?

Accordingly, when the tray had been laid on the study table, I re-opened the subject.

"I did not mention this matter in my evidence," I said. "It had no bearing on the inquiry."

"I am not clear," he replied, "that you were entitled to make any reservations. A witness's duty is to state the whole truth. The question of relevancy is for the court to consider."

"But unfortunately there were other reservations that had to be made. Dr Thorndyke, I want to tell you the whole story – in confidence – and to ask your advice."

"I counsel you to make no confidences," he said, gravely, "unless you really wish to consult me in my professional capacity."

"That is what I wish to do," I said.

"Very well," said he. "That places us in the secure relation of lawyer and client; and I need not say that your father's daughter is very welcome to any help or advice that I can give."

With this encouragement, I poured forth the story that I have told in these pages and in almost as much detail. But still I held back one fact. I said nothing of my having found Mr Otway grasping my father's loaded stick. That single reservation had to be. Not only was I bound by a solemn promise; my silence on that point was the price of my release. The letter of the covenant, indeed, had reference only to my evidence at the inquest; but its spirit sealed my lips even in this my most intimate confidence.

And so, once again a secret guarded from a friendly eye remained, like a seed dropped in a summer's drought, to germinate and bring forth its fruit in its season.

CHAPTER TEN

The Turning of the Page

Dr Thorndyke listened to my recital of the history of the tragedy, not only with patience, but with close attention and apparently keen interest, interrupting me only at rare intervals to ask a question or elucidate some point that was not quite clear. When I had come to an end I was disposed to be apologetic, for I had told the story in the fullest detail, with only the single reservation that I have noted.

"I am afraid," I said, "that I have been rather victimising you and trespassing on your very great patience."

"By no means," he replied. "Men and men's actions and motives are my merchandise. If I could listen to a story like yours without the deepest interest I should not be in my present profession. But, now that I have heard it, I think I can guess the subject on which you wish to consult me. You would like to annul your marriage with Mr Otway."

"Yes; if it is possible."

"It is very natural that you should wish to recover your freedom. I sympathise with you entirely and I wish I could give you some encouragement. But I fear that you have no remedy."

"It seems rather hard," I said, "that I should be bound for life to this man whom I detest and who has done me such grievous injuries."

"It is very hard," he agreed, "and, humanly speaking there ought to be some remedy. But the law provides none; nor is it really possible for the law to make provision for every imaginable contingency. Yours is a very exceptional case."

"Yes, I see that; but it seems unreasonable to compel two people to maintain a relationship which is not only unsuitable but quite unreal."

"It does," he admitted. "But the law takes a very unsentimental view of these matters. It regards marriage as an institution concerned with the establishment of families and the orderly devolution of property, and its interference is, in the main, limited to circumstances connected with that assumed function. Of the human aspects of marriage it takes little account. In a purely legal sense – which is what we are considering – your position is this: You were competent to contract a marriage and you did contract one, of your own free will, without any compulsion or misrepresentation that the law would recognise. The circumstances that appeared to exist before the marriage still appear to exist. No new facts have come to light which would affect the competence of either party. It is a case in which one of the parties has disregarded the old legal maxim, *Caveat emptor* – buyer beware! You bought, at a high price, something which turns out to be of no value. You agreed to marry Mr Otway for a consideration – the release of your father from his embarrassments – which seemed to be valuable enough to justify the great sacrifice that you contemplated. But it turned out that your father needed no release; and the consideration thereupon ceased to have any value. As far as the law is concerned, you have simply made a very bad bargain."

"Does the law attach no importance to fraud?" I demanded.

"But has there been fraud?" he objected. "No representations true or false were made to you by Mr Otway. You acted on knowledge which you assumed that you possessed. You laid down the conditions; he accepted them. You demanded a certain consideration; he furnished the consideration demanded. Even with regard to the letter from your father, we may – and do – suspect that he knew that it was in the box, and probably guessed at its contents. But we have no proof. Moreover, if he did know that it was there – even if he had opened it and read it, he was under no obligation to communicate its contents to you. Your agreement made no such provision. It laid down specific conditions, and with these Mr Otway had fully complied. On the plea of fraud, I am afraid you would have no case."

"Apparently not," I agreed. "You are most horribly convincing, Dr Thorndyke."

"I am putting the case as a lawyer, and very much against my own feeling as a man. But my present office is rather like that of a Devil's Advocate in a theological council. I think that this marriage ought to be annulled, but I am sure that, in point of law, it is not voidable.

"But there is yet another aspect of the case, and you must forgive me if I put it rather bluntly. There are not many women to whom I should have spoken in as downright a fashion as I have to you, and I shall continue to pay you this rather unpleasant compliment. Mrs Otway, even if, legally speaking, you had a case, you could not take it into court."

"Why not?" I asked, more than a little startled

"Because of the incidents of the inquest. You have spoken of certain reservations in your evidence. But in the case of Mr Otway there was more than reservation. There was deliberate mis-statement, and that, too, in respect of a question that was highly material to the inquiry. He was asked the reason of your father's resentment of this marriage, and he stated it to be the disparity of age. But that was not the reason, and he knew it was not. Your father would have raised no obstacle if you had really wished to marry Mr Otway. He resented the marriage because it had been brought about by means which he regarded as – morally speaking – fraudulent. Mr Otway's evidence was false evidence, and it was deliberately given with the intention of misleading the jury."

"But it was a small point and of no importance. Besides Mr Otway's evidence is no concern of mine."

"Pardon me," Dr Thorndyke objected, gravely, "the point was of very great importance. It would have started a train of entirely new issues. And Mr Otway's evidence is very much your concern. You heard it given, you were asked if you confirmed it, and you did confirm it. There upon Mr Otway's evidence became your evidence.

"Now, if you were to embark on a suit for the annulment of your marriage, the plea of fraud, on which you would base your claim would have to be supported by evidence which would conflict with that given by you at the inquest. Your position would be a very uncomfortable one and it would be made more so by the fact that your evidence was in agreement with Mr Otway's. When two witnesses agree in a departure from the actual facts known to them, a suspicion of collusion is apt to be raised; and collusion again suggests purpose and motive. I am afraid, Mrs Otway, that the Devil's Advocate is making out a diabolically complete case. But that, you know, is his business. The conclusion is that a malignant fate has woven around you a mesh of circumstances from which there is no escape, and that the less you struggle the less irksome will be your bonds."

To this conclusion, unsatisfactory as it was, I assented with a readiness born not only of conviction but of a certain amount of alarm. I had heard my father speak with admiration of Dr Thorndyke's amazing power of analysing evidence and extracting its essentials, and I now began to wonder how much of the actual truth he had extracted from the evidence at the inquest, elucidated by my narrative. His warning as to a possible suspicion of collusion with "a purpose and a motive" in the background, set me speculating as to whether he, himself, entertained such a suspicion; and his next question was by no means reassuring on this point.

"You spoke," said he, "of having decided not to live with Mr Otway, and of having communicated your intention to him. Do I understand that he assents to a separation?"

"Yes. He sees that the position would be quite impossible."

"Is your arrangement with him merely a verbal one or has it been placed on a regular footing by a document of some kind?"

"Mr Otway has executed a deed of separation, which I think is quite regular. But I had better let you see it."

With some trepidation, I produced the deed and nervously watched him as he read it through, which he did with an inscrutable expression, and – as it seemed to me – a horrible appearance of seeing through it to the rather questionable circumstances that had brought it into existence.

"Yes," he said, as he handed it back to me; "it is quite regular. You may congratulate yourself on finding Mr Otway so compliant. It is more than one would have expected of him."

"He could hardly have done otherwise," I answered hastily. "We couldn't possibly have lived together after what had happened. Still, I am glad he took the reasonable view. It leaves me free to make my own arrangements for my future."

"And what arrangements do you propose – if your legal adviser is not too inquisitive."

"Not at all. I was going to ask you to advise me. I don't think there will be enough to support me, and of course, I can't accept any help from Mr Otway. I shall have to earn my living in some way."

"You could compel Mr Otway to support you, but I appreciate your unwillingness to accept an allowance and thereby recognise the relationship. Have you any means of livelihood in your mind?"

I hesitated a little shyly. For I had; but my plan might sound rather an odd one, at least to a stranger.

"I thought," said I, at length, "of trying to get a living by doing what I have been accustomed to do as a hobby – by making simple jewellery and small ornamental metal objects. I am afraid you will look on it as rather a wild scheme."

"No," he answered. "It is an unconventional scheme but not in any way a wild one. I think we often appreciate insufficiently the wisdom of the artist's choice of his profession. In choosing a means of livelihood we are choosing the way in which we shall spend the greater part of our lives. We have something to sell – the bulk of our waking lives; and we are apt to think too much of its selling price – its value to the purchaser – and not enough of its value to ourselves. A man, such as a navvy, a miner, a bank clerk or a factory hand, barters for the means of subsistence so many hours a day spent in doing something that he does not want to do. He sells the best part of his life. But the artist or craftsman makes a much better bargain, for he contrives to obtain a subsistence by doing what he enjoys doing and what he would elect to do for his own satisfaction. He sells only the by-products of his life; the whole of that life he retains for his own use, to be spent as he would in any case, wish to spend it. But there is an inevitable proviso; his acceptable occupation must really yield a subsistence. His wares must be of value to the purchaser, and he must be able to find a market. Do you think you could satisfy those conditions?"

"I think I could make the things pretty well, but, as to selling them, that is a different matter. I have to find that out. May I show you some of my work?"

"I should like very much to see some of it," he replied.

"I will fetch a few pieces. And meanwhile, that clock on the mantelpiece is partly my work. My father made the clock, itself; but I made the dial, the hands and the case."

Dr Thorndyke rose, and, stepping over to the mantelpiece, looked at the work with keen interest. It was a little bracket-clock with a bronze dial, a silver circle for the figures, silver-gilt hands and a simple wooden case decorated with gesso. Leaving my visitor to inspect it, I went away and collected a few samples of my work in metal; a bronze candlestick, an enamelled silver belt-buckle, a gold pendant set with opals and one or two silver spoons; all of which Dr Thorndyke examined with that friendly interest – unmistakable to the artist or craftsman – that evinces some knowledge of and liking for the thing examined.

"Well" he said, as he laid down the last of the spoons, "these things answer the first question. They are quite workmanlike, and they are attractive and tastefully designed. The next question is the economic one. Could you sell them? and if so, would they realise a price that would furnish a reasonable livelihood? You would have to compete with commercial products made in large numbers by cheap processes. Your hammered, embossed and chased work would compete with work stamped from steel dies or with comparatively rough castings. Of course, your work is infinitely better value; but this is a commercial age, and buyers are bad judges. And then you would have to sell to dealers who would demand not less than fifty per cent profit, which, I am afraid, would leave you a pitiable, small return for your labour and skill."

"Yes," I agreed. "That is all quite true. But still I think I will try. The work would be interesting and pleasant, and, as you implied just now, an artist cannot expect to be paid as much for doing what he likes doing as another man receives for doing what he dislikes. Pleasant work is, to some extent at least, its own reward; and if my work doesn't yield enough to live on, I shall have to try something else. But I don't suppose I shall be absolutely without means when my father's estate has been wound up."

"Do you think of continuing to live here?" Dr Thorndyke asked.

"No. As soon as everything is settled, I propose to go to London. It will be much easier – or, at least, less difficult – to dispose of my work there."

"Undoubtedly. And have you any definite arrangements in your mind – where and how you are going to live, for instance?"

"None whatever, at present."

"I ask because I happen to know of a place where you could put up, at least temporarily; where you would be comfortably lodged well fed and cared for, and where you could pursue your labours under good working conditions and at small expense. There is only one drawback, but you may consider that a fatal one.

It is in the immediate neighbourhood of Ratcliff Highway – or, as it has been renamed St George's Street."

"Is that a very dreadful place?"

"It is far from being an aristocratic locality. But let me describe the establishment. It is conducted by a Miss Polton, who is the sister of my laboratory assistant – a most expert and talented mechanician. Miss Polton was at one time a nurse; but when her brother entered my employment, he was able to help her to set up in Wellclose Square, Ratcliff, a boarding-house for mercantile marine officers. At the same time, she, being like her brother, a highly-capable, ingenious person, got herself a hand-loom and took up weaving as a hobby. But since then times have changed. Sailing ships have to a great extent disappeared, and Miss Polton's clients with them, while the hobby of making excellent cloth has turned out quite a profitable one. So Miss Polton plies her shuttle industriously, and, in the place of the merchant seamen, has collected a little family of women who also work at handicrafts for their living. I believe they form quite a happy little community, and, of course, they are able to assist one another in disposing of their wares. So that is the position. I know that Miss Polton has room for another boarder, for it is quite a large house – Wellclose Square was once the abode of well-to-do shipowners and retired sea-captains – and I am sure she would welcome another novice to her community. The drawback, as I have said, is the neighbourhood, which is to put it bluntly – just a trifle squalid."

"I don't see that the neighbourhood matters," said I; "and in every other respect it sounds like the very thing I want."

"I think you would be quite well-advised to give it a trial. You would be among friends and fellow-workers, and, if you found that the neighbourhood was too much for you, you would be in London and could seek a new residence at your leisure. I will write the address on one of my cards, and if on reflection you decide to give Ratcliff a trial, you can write to Miss Polton and me at the same time."

He wrote the address, and, handing me the card, stood up and glanced at his watch.

"How long will it take me to walk to the station?" he asked.

"Less than twenty minutes."

"I have half an hour, so I can walk easily. Goodbye, Mrs Otway. I wish I could have given you a better account of your position. But I can only advise you to make the best of a bad bargain and keep your own counsel."

"You have been most kind, Dr Thorndyke," I said, earnestly, "in giving me so much time and patient attention. I don't know how I can thank you."

"I will tell you," said he. "By keeping a good heart and letting me know how your affairs progress."

He shook my hand heartily, and, when I had let him out, strode down the garden path, the very personification of manly dignity, alertness and vigour. At the gate he turned to raise his hat, with a smile of friendly farewell; and I closed the door and turned back into the house, feeling, for the first time since my father's death, that I was not alone in the world, but that, if the need should arise, the strength of this strong, commanding man was at my call.

The short remainder of my life at Maidstone I shall pass over briefly. It comes back to me in scenes like those of a play, separate but related. I see the interior of the parish church, noble, spacious, cathedral-like; I hear the voice of the clergyman reciting reverently those flowers of ancient poetry rendered into perfect English speech that usher the departed into the realms of silence with so gracious a dignity; I see the flower-strewn coffin sink into the grave wherein sleeps my unremembered mother, while the russet-sailed barges glide past the churchyard on the placid river below towards the mills at Tovil. And so farewell for ever to the best of fathers and the kindest, most lovable of friends.

These closing weeks, in which I wound up my old life and made ready for the new, were full of bustle and unrest. I had written to Miss Polton and Dr Thorndyke, and from the former had received a kindly letter assuring me of the warmest welcome:

and now I was busily collecting my tools and workshop appliances and packing them into travelling boxes to be dispatched with my heavier luggage. There was the furniture to be stored or set aside for sale, the servants to be placed in new situations, and various business to be transacted with Mr Jackson, who, indeed, relieved me of all that lay within his powers.

Then there was Mr Otway, from whom I received an abject letter and with whom I must needs have a rather distressing interview. He was really horrified at my proposed mode of life (I suspect he had never done a stroke of manual work in his life), and even more so at my proposed place of residence; and was, I believe, sincerely distressed at my firm refusal to permit him to make me an allowance. Indeed, the devotion which he professed for me, little as I wanted it, seemed to be as real as was possible in the case of a man so self-centred and so callously egoistic. But the very sight of him hardened my heart and lighted up afresh my indignation at the havoc that he had wrought in my life. What I had agreed to do, I did; but I made no hair's breadth of concession. I gave him my future address, and agreed to his addressing letters there; but I refused resolutely to receive any visits from him, or even to enter into any correspondence other than that which circumstances might render necessary.

And now the last day has come; the day of final parting. I see myself wandering through the empty house, stripped of all but the barest necessaries and filled with new and strange echoes; the van drawn up at the gate to take away the last of the furniture, and the tearful Jessie carrying my two little portmanteaux down the path to the porter's barrow. I see her return, wiping her eyes and gazing at me in dumb appeal, and, with a sudden impulse of tenderness, I kiss her and stroke her hair; whereupon she bursts into tears and throws herself sobbing on to my breast.

It was hard to close the old life, which had been so sweet and peaceful, so full and satisfying; to bid farewell to the beautiful old town which was the only place I had known and which I had loved so well. As I took my way through the streets, attaché case in hand, all my old friends seemed to look on me reproachfully and call on me to stay. The quaint plaster-fronted house in Week Street, the venerable medieval pile at the corner of Gabriel's Hill, the grinning masks on the corbels of the old house-fronts of Middle Row; all the old familiar landmarks, had suddenly grown dear and precious, and each exacted its twinge of regret as I looked my last on it. On the bridge I halted to survey the upper river, with the church and the Old Palace, "both embowered in trees and brooding over the quiet water. Often as I had looked upon that view, it had never seemed to me so pleasant and desirable as now. And with this last impression – to be recalled how often in the troubled future! – I turned away and headed resolutely for the station.

BOOK TWO

ROMANCE

CHAPTER ELEVEN

A Harbour of Refuge

It was the cabman who first made it clear to me that my town address was somewhat out of the common. He had stowed my two portmanteaux on the roof (it was a four-wheeled cab), and, descending to hold the door open for me to enter, shut it after me with a bang and waited while I stated my destination.

"I beg your pardon, Miss," he said, incredulously; "did you say Wellclose Square?"

"Yes. Number sixty-nine."

Again he regarded me with wrinkled brows. "That won't be Wellclose Square down by the Docks?" he suggested.

"I don't know if it's near the Docks," I replied, "but it isn't far from Ratcliff Highway."

"That's the place, sure enough," said he. "Number sixty-nine. Well, I'm jiggered." With this he turned and slowly climbed to the box, looking in at me through the front window as he mounted; and even when he had taken his seat and gathered up the reins, he took yet another confirmatory glance over his shoulder before starting.

These mysterious proceedings occasioned me some surprise not entirely unmixed with anxiety. Dr Thorndyke had admitted that the neighbourhood was squalid, and the question arose, How squalid was it? The first part of the journey, through Eastcheap and Great Tower Street, was rather reassuring; and as we crossed Tower

Hill and the grey pile of ancient buildings loomed up above the trees, I was quite pleasantly impressed. But then came a change for the worse. Long streets of characterless houses, all of a dingy, grey colour – the colour of all-pervading dirt – and growing greyer and dingier as we proceeded; populated by men and women, and especially children, of the same cobwebby tint, with something foreign and unfamiliar in their aspect and manners – a deficiency of artificial head-covering with a remarkable profusion of the natural, and a tendency to sit about on doorsteps; these, with a general outbreak on the shop signs of Wowskys, Minskys, Stems and Popoffs, were the features of the neighbourhood that chiefly attracted my attention as the cab rattled eastward. But there was not much time for extended observation, for I had barely noted these appearances when we turned into a short side-street and emerged into a square, the dinginess of which was somewhat relieved by a group of faded trees in the central enclosure.

Round the square the cab trundled slowly until it drew up opposite a tall house of the Georgian type, with white window frames and a green door. As the cab stopped, the green door opened and a small elderly lady came forth, while three younger women lurked in the background. Escaping from the cab, I advanced to meet the elderly lady, who received me with a singularly pleasant smile and a few quietly-spoken words of welcome; a proceeding that was observed with furtive interest by the cabman as he transferred my portmanteaux from the cab-roof to the pavement and thence to the hall; nor did his curious observation of me cease until it was brought to an end by actual invisibility, for, as the cab moved out of the square I saw his face still turned towards me over the roof, with the same expression of puzzled surprise.

"You would like to see your room, I expect," said the elderly lady whom I had correctly assumed to be Miss Polton; "then we will have tea and talk over your arrangements." She moved towards the stairs (up which I had just seen one of the young women hopping with surprising agility, with one of my portmanteaux in either hand), and conducted me to a room on the second floor, where the portmanteaux had been duly deposited, though the bearer had vanished.

"It's rather bare," said Miss Polton, "but you can have some pictures and ornaments if you like. My young ladies usually prefer to have their own things and arrange them in their own way. Your workroom is downstairs. I consulted my brother about it, and he said he thought you would like a room with a stone floor if you were going to do hammered work and use a furnace. So, as I had one with quite a good light, I have kept it for you – that is, of course, if you like it."

"I expect I shall," I replied. "A wooden floor is dreadfully noisy when one is hammering on a stake, and not very safe when there are red-hot crucibles about."

"Yes," she agreed, "and you can have a mat for your feet when you are sitting at the bench. And now I will leave you and go and see about the tea."

Left to myself, I looked around at my new home. The room, though spacious, was undeniably bare, but yet it gave me an impression of comfort. For its bareness was due merely to the absence of superfluities. The empty walls, distempered a pale cream colour, were severe to baldness; but how much better than the usual boarding-house walls, covered with staring flowered paper and disfigured with horrible prints or illuminated texts! They, like the empty book-shelves, were ready to receive the personal touches and to become friendly and sympathetic. Of actual necessaries there were more than in many an over-furnished room; a small wardrobe, a good-sized, firm table, a chest of drawers with a looking-glass on it, a small writing chair, a comfortable folding arm-chair, a washing-stand and a sponge bath, besides the book-shelves aforesaid and a daintily-furnished bed, gave me a foundation of material comfort and convenience on which it would be easy to build and make additions. As I concluded my survey and refreshed myself with a wash, I decided that, whatever the surroundings of the house might be like, its interior seemed to have the makings of a home.

Nor was I less favourably impressed when I went downstairs. The dining-room, in which I found the ladies assembled, was pervaded by an air of spotless cleanliness with a severity approaching bareness. The absence of superfluous furniture and useless ornaments and bric-a-brac struck me, indeed, as rather odd in a household composed – so far as I knew – entirely of women.

"I must introduce you to the family," said Miss Polton, with a pleasant wrinkly smile, "at least those who are at home. There are three more who will come in to dinner. This is Miss Blake, and these ladies are Miss Barnard and Miss Finch."

I shook hands with my new comrades – the last being the little lady who had skipped up the stairs so actively with my luggage – and then we sat down to the table, at the head of which Miss Polton presided, and made the tea in a delightful Delft teapot from a brass kettle on which I cast an expert and somewhat disapproving eye, for it was of a blatantly commercial type and quite unworthy of the teapot.

At first conversation was spasmodic and punctuated by considerable pauses. Miss Polton was evidently a silent, self-contained woman, though genial in a quiet, restful way. Miss Finch, too, who sat by me, was quiet and a little shy, speaking rarely but silently plying me with food. Miss Blake on the other hand, had a restless manner, and, though she spoke little at first, was undisguisedly interested in me, for whenever I looked at her I caught her wide-open, blue eyes fixed on me with an intensity that was almost embarrassing. She was a rather remarkable-looking girl, with a wealth of red-gold hair, a white and pink complexion, and a profile which, with its sharp, projecting chin and retroussé nose, might have been taken direct from one of Burne-Jones's allegories; indeed, my first glance at her had made me think of the "Briar Rose" and the "Golden Stairs." And now, as I caught her intense gaze again and again, I had the feeling that she was wanting to say something to me; and the more so since I thought I detected a certain expectancy in the expression of her neighbour, Miss Barnard. Nor was I mistaken; for, after one of the periodic pauses in the conversation, she leaned over the table towards me and said in low, portentous tones: "Mrs Otway, I want to ask you a question, if you won't think me too inquisitive." Here she paused – and Miss Barnard also paused in the conveyance to her mouth of a large piece of bread and marmalade.

"I don't suppose your question would be too inquisitive," I said, guardedly.

"It isn't really," said she. "You know, I have been looking at your face, and I've been wondering – it's an extraordinary psychic face, do you know?"

"Is it?" said I, noting that Miss Barnard had broken out into a slow smile, which she was trying to obliterate with the lump of bread and marmalade.

"Oh, very. Intensely so. It is a face, you know, in which the workings of the subconscious appear, as it were, like an undercurrent moving beneath the surface of the conscious. I have been watching it with deep interest, and I have been wondering if you are, as I am, a dweller in the larger world beyond that inhabited by the conscious self, beyond the mere material universe. Is it not so, Mrs Otway?"

Now this was a "facer." As my dear father would have expressed it in his playful fashion, it "knocked me sideways." I cast a bewildered glance round the table, and was aware of a very extensive outbreak of the subconscious, Miss Polton was blandly indulgent, her face transformed into a network of amiable wrinkles; Miss Finch was engaged in an intense scrutiny of the bowl of a jam spoon; while Miss Barnard's feats, with the bread and marmalade, were becoming positively dangerous.

"I am not sure that I quite understand your question," said I.

"You generally don't," murmured Miss Finch as Miss Polton explained that "Miss Blake was somewhat of a mystic."

"Like her famous namesake," said I.

117

"And ancestor," Miss Blake added, eagerly.

"Really!" I exclaimed, clutching at this straw; "you are actually a descendant of William Blake? And I daresay you are a great admirer of his works?"

"I should think she is!" exclaimed Miss Barnard. "You should just see her fashion plates."

Recalling Blake's usual rendering of the human figure and its unadaptability to the conditions of our climate, I secretly resolved to take an early opportunity of examining those fashion plates. Meanwhile, I remarked, "I was thinking of his poems rather than the drawings."

"Yes" said Miss Blake; "though the drawings are very spiritual, too. But to return to my question. You see, I had been looking at your intensely psychical face, and hoping that, at last, I had met with a kindred spirit. And I do hope – I feel convinced – that I have. Perhaps I did not put my question very clearly – it is difficult to be very definite when one is speaking of the psychic life; but I was wondering if you had ever had experiences that had made you aware of that larger world beyond the world of mere matter and sense-perception; if you had sometimes felt the thoughts of other minds stealing into your own without the aid of speech or bodily presence and even perhaps, held converse with those dear to you who, while they have passed out of this little, material world, still share with you the greater world in which soul speaks to soul unhampered by the limitations – "

The humorous wrinkles had suddenly faded from Miss Polton's face, leaving it grave and quiet; and now, in a quiet, grave voice, she interposed: "I think, Lilith, dear, that Mrs Otway's griefs are too new and too real – "

"I know!" Miss Blake exclaimed, impulsively. "I am an egotistical wretch. It was horrid of me to be so wrapped up in my own interests. I am so sorry; so very, very sorry. Please forgive me, dear Mrs Otway! Let us talk of something else."

"I don't think we must talk of anything much longer," said Miss Polton. "We have finished tea and we ought to get on with our work. Besides, Mrs Otway will want to unpack her things and set her room in order."

On this there was a general up-rising. Miss Finch immediately fell to work gathering up the debris and returning the cups and saucers to the tray, while Miss Blake renewed her apologies and expressions of sympathy. Then Miss Polton took possession of me and, having shown me my workshop – a smallish, well-lighted room, with a paved floor and a large window looking on an unexpectedly pleasant garden – took me upstairs to a box-room in which my personal luggage had been deposited.

"Supper is at eight o'clock," said she. "We have made it rather late so that everyone may have a good, long day's work and all the wanderers may have come home. It is the social event of the day. And now I will leave you to your unpacking."

She tripped away up a narrow flight of stairs that opened from the landing, towards what I took to be the attics; from whence presently came a rhythmical "click-clack" that I associated with the loom of which Dr Thorndyke had spoken. Meanwhile, I fell to work on my trunks with a view to transferring their contents to my room; but I had hardly got them open when Miss Finch appeared at the open door.

"Can I help you?" she asked. "If I carry some of the things down you won't have so many journeys."

"But aren't you busy?" I asked in return.

"Do I look like it? No, I'm lazy this afternoon, but I should like to help you if you will let me."

Of course I was only too glad, and forthwith loaded her with an armful of books, following her with a second consignment. For some time we continued our journeys up and down the stairs with very little said on either side, and gradually my room began to lose its emptiness and severity, and to take on the friendly aspect of an inhabited apartment.

"It doesn't look so bad," said Miss Finch, surveying it critically. "Looks as if someone lived in it. Do you like the wash-stand?"

"I've been admiring it. It's so simple and so tasteful and unusual."

"Yes; and yet it is only stained deal with a few touches of gesso. Phillibar made it – Phyllis Barton, you know. You'll meet her at supper."

"Is she a carpenter?"

"No; she makes frames for mirrors and pictures; wooden frames decorated with gesso, or compo, or else carved. But she's very thorough. Does it all herself. Makes up the frames from the plank, makes the compo and the moulds and does the gilding. And she is quite a good wood-worker and carves beautifully."

"And does she make a pretty good living?" I asked, bearing Dr Thorndyke's observations in mind.

"She does quite well now, though she had a hard struggle at first. But now she works direct for the artists and gets as much as she can do. You will often see her frames in the exhibitions. The floor-cloth is rather nice, too, isn't it, though it is only stencilled sacking. You'd be surprised to see how durable it is. The more it is worn, the better it looks – if it is properly done. This is stencilled with a stain. Lilith did it."

"Lilith? Is that Miss Blake?"

"Yes. Her name is really Winifred, but we call her Lilith because she looks as if she had come out of a stained-glass window. You might think that she was a little – well, a little barmy. But she's awfully clever."

"She does fashion-plates, doesn't she?"

"Yes, poor Lilith! She hates them, but she does them rippingly all the same. She would rather paint pictures or mural decorations or design tapestries, but you've got to do what you can sell, you know, if you want to make a living; and Lilith has a little brother whom she keeps at school – an awfully nice little kiddie. She's a really good sort, you know, though frightfully spooky – planchette, crystal ball and all that sort of tosh; and she thinks she has found a fellow-spook, so you will have to look out."

As Miss Finch paused to take another survey, her eye and mine fell upon the wash-stand, or rather on what it supported.

"I think," I remarked, "that I shall have to treat myself to some new crockery. That jug and basin are hardly worthy of Miss Barton's masterpiece."

"No; they're horrid, aren't they? Regular Whitechapel china-shop stuff. But I believe I've got some – I'll just run up and see."

She tripped away up the stairs and presently returned, bearing a basin and pitcher of simple, reddish-buff earthenware glazed internally with a fine green glaze.

"They are frightfully crude and coarse," she said apologetically (and with cheeks several shades redder than the ware), "but they aren't vulgar. Would you like to have them until you can get something better?"

"I shall have them a long time, then," said I. "They are charming – delightful, and they suit the wash-stand perfectly. What a house this is for pottery! I noticed the teapot and the beautiful cups and plates, all so interesting and uncommon. And now you produce these wonderful things like some benevolent enchantress. How do you do it? Do you keep a crystal ball, too?"

Miss Finch laughed and blushed very prettily. "We all do our little bit towards making the home presentable and saving expense. Miss Polton distempered these walls, and Joan Allen painted the woodwork – you'll like Joan, I think; she paints portraits when she can get them, and fills in her time by doing magazine covers and book-wrappers. We shall expect a diploma work from you, too. You're a goldsmith, aren't you?"

It was my turn to laugh and blush as this magnificent title was applied to me. "Not exactly a goldsmith," I protested. "Say, rather, a very elementary jeweller and metal-worker, or perhaps a coppersmith. And, as we have finished with this room for the present, I had better begin to get my workshop in going order."

"And you'll let me help you with that, too, won't you?" said Miss Finch, with a wheedling air; and as I gladly accepted her help, she linked her arm in mine and we descended together to the scene of my future labours.

My experience of various workers has led me to observe that manual skill is a much more generalised quality than is commonly realised. The old saw of the "Jack of all trades and master of none" is entirely misleading; for manual skill acquired in the practice of one art is largely transferable to others. The acquirement of a particular kind of skill results in the establishment of a generally increased manual faculty, so that a person who has completely learned one handicraft is already more than halfway towards the attainment of skill in any other. This fact was impressed upon me as I watched little Miss Finch and noted her extraordinary handiness with probably unfamiliar appliances and her instant comprehension of the uses of things that she had probably never seen before. My two benches – the jeweller's and the general bench – had fortunately been made in a portable form, and now had to be joined up with their screw-bolts. But my little assistant took this in at a glance, and, before I had half finished unpacking the tool cases, she had the bench-tops up-ended, had sorted out the legs, struts and the appropriate bolts, and was hard at work with the spanner. Yet, as she worked, she kept an alert and interested eye on the tools and appliances that came forth from the cases.

"What a jolly little muffle!" she exclaimed, as I deposited the small enamel furnace on the floor, pending the erection of its stand; "but won't it eat up the gas. You'll have to have your own meter – and watch it, too, to see that your earnings don't all go to the gas company. And what a little duck of an anvil! But what on earth are those things?" pointing to a bundle of body-tools and snarling-irons.

I explained the use of these mysterious appliances and of sundry others and so, with a good deal of gossip, partly personal and partly technical, we worked on until the sound of the first supper-bell sent us to our rooms to make ourselves presentable; by which time the fitting out of the workshop was so far advanced as to make it possible for me to begin work on the morrow.

The great social function of supper introduced me to the rest of my comrades; Phyllis Barton, who turned out, to my surprise, to be a tiny, frail-looking middle-aged woman of meek aspect – I had pictured her as a large, muscular, boisterous young woman; Joan Allen, who really corresponded somewhat to this description, and whom I detected more than once in the act of inspecting me with one eye closed; and a tall, rather shy girl, by name Edith Palgrave, a scrivener and calligrapher, who, I learned from Miss Finch, wrote, by choice, Church service books and illuminated addresses, but, by necessity, gained her principal livelihood by writing shop-tickets.

It was a pleasant genial gathering: homely, informal, and yet quite regardful of the indispensable social amenities. What the social class of my companions might have been I could hardly guess. They were all educated women, of good intelligence and pleasant manners, all keenly interested in one another's doings, but each fully occupied with her own activities. The agreeable impression was conveyed that, in this little human hive, the companionship arising from the community of domestic life tended in no way to hinder a self-contained person like myself from living her own life and pursuing her own interests and satisfactions.

And so, when, somewhat early, I retired to my room to spend an hour with my books before going to bed, my thoughts turned gratefully to Dr Thorndyke, and I congratulated myself not a little on having found this quiet anchorage in which to rest after the stormy passages of my troubled life.

CHAPTER TWELVE

The Hidden Hand

I had been settled in my new home about a month when I received a letter from Mr Jackson. It was principally devoted to a report on business matters concerned with the disposal of my father's practice and the sale of the surplus furniture and effects, but it contained one passage that gave me considerable food for thought. The passage in question had been added as a postscript, and ran thus:

"You have probably heard that Mr Otway has left Maidstone. I fancy things had become rather uncomfortable for him. From what transpired at the inquest, an impression got abroad that he was, to a great extent, responsible for your father's death, and there was consequently a rather strong feeling against him. I don't know where he has gone, but rumour has it that he has migrated to London."

This was, in more than one respect, somewhat disquieting news. I turned it over again and again as I sat at my bench and tried to estimate its significance. The inquest had "gone off quite smoothly," as Mr Jackson had expressed it, but it was clear that some, at least, of the persons present had read a meaning into the evidence which the coroner and his jury seemed to have missed. Dr Thorndyke was one of these; but, as no rumour could be traceable to him, there were evidently others. What did this portend. To Mr Jackson it meant no more than a local prejudice. To me, conscious of a secret covenant which I had not dared to confide even to Dr Thorndyke, it conveyed an uneasy feeling that suspicion was abroad, that it might become cumulative, and that, even yet, that covenant might be dragged into the light of day which it would bear so ill. Ever since my talk with Dr Thorndyke, my conscience had been somewhat ill at ease. I felt that, as a witness giving testimony on oath, I had been at least uncandid, if not positively untruthful; and the word "collusion" had acquired an unpleasantly personal quality.

And then, what of Mr Otway? Had he slipped away out of my life to hide himself where suspicion would not reach him? Or had he really migrated to London, and would his sinister shadow presently fall upon my new life as it had done upon the old? My hopes pictured him driven by his fears – for he was a timorous man – far afield, perhaps beyond the seas; but a presentiment whispered that I had not heard or seen the last of him.

And the presentiment was right. Less than a week after the arrival of Mr Jackson's letter came one from Mr Otway; and its contents were even more disquieting than those of the former. It was headed "Lyon's Inn Chambers, W.C.," and its contents were as follows:

"My dear Helen,
"As you will see by the above address, I have moved to London. You will, no doubt, easily understand that, after the late distressing events, the neighbourhood of Maidstone was intolerable to me, and I am writing this to give you my new address. But, also, I have two other matters on which I want to speak to you. One is to recommend to you a dealer to whom I think you may be able to dispose of your work, which you might otherwise have to sell at a great disadvantage. His name is Campbell, and his premises are in Wardour Street, near the Oxford Street end on the west side. Mr

Campbell deals in pictures and works of ancient and modern art, jewellery, goldsmith's work, etc.; and, as he is personally known to me, I have taken the liberty of writing to him to the effect that you may possibly call on him, and describing you as a relative of mine without mentioning the nature of the relationship.

"And now I come to a rather difficult matter, which I hope you will not misunderstand. I am going to ask you to meet me, either here or in any other place that you may choose, to talk over something that has happened recently. I have, in fact, received a letter the contents of which have greatly disturbed me. I will not go into details now, but when I say that the matter is of importance to you as well as to me, I think you will understand what I mean and what the letter refers to. I beg you very earnestly not to refuse this request. The letter in question has caused me deep anxiety, and, in fact, some alarm, and I think you ought to be put into possession of its contents.

"Trusting that you will not withhold your help and support in these new and harassing circumstances.

"Believe me,

"Your devoted husband,

"Lewis Otway."

It would have been wiser of Mr Otway to adopt some other mode of ending his letter. The disgust and repulsion that the phrase "your devoted husband" occasioned me had nearly determined my refusal. But on reflection, not only reason, charity and a certain reluctantly admitted sense of duty, but curiosity, not unmixed with anxiety, counselled compliance. His letter was vague enough, yet it made pretty clear to me that trouble of some kind was brewing, and I was not in the position of a disinterested spectator; that, in short, my forebodings of the last few days were, perhaps, already receiving some justification.

Accordingly, I decided to agree to the meeting, and the question arose, where was it to take place? His own rooms were out of the question; for the fact of my having visited him there would greatly weaken my position if I should have to resist a claim to end the separation. Finally, I selected the Tower Wharf as a place sufficiently public and yet unfrequented enough to allow of a confidential talk secure from eavesdroppers. It had, of late, become a favourite resort of mine, for it was a pleasant place, with the trees and the old Tower on one side and the broad river on the other, and was but ten minutes' walk from Wellclose Square. I wrote by return, naming six o'clock on the following evening; and at half past five on that evening I set forth by way of Ship Alley and Upper East Smithfield.

Although I had walked slowly, it wanted yet ten minutes to six when I passed under the side span of the Tower Bridge and came out on to the gravelled walk overlooking the river. But already Mr Otway was there, pacing up and down a sort of bay at the east end, with his hands behind him grasping a stout cane; and though he made a pretence of inspecting the old guns that, on their side, make a pretence of defending the fortress, he was evidently watchful and expectant, for he saw me almost as soon as I saw him, and quickened his pace to meet me.

His appearance impressed me deeply, even before we met. When I had seen him last he had been looking anxious and worried. But now he was positively haggard, and he had a furtive, hunted look that, little as I was disposed to be sympathetic, made me glad that I had not refused to meet him.

"This is really very good of you, Helen," he exclaimed, with obvious sincerity. "But I felt sure that you would – er – respond to my appeal. It is strange," he added, "considering what our relations are and what your feelings are towards me, that I seem to look to you, and to you alone, for support and counsel in this – er – this unexpected trouble."

"I don't suppose," said I, "that any counsel of mine will be of much value to a man of your experience. But perhaps you had better tell me what the trouble is – Shall we sit down here? You spoke of having received a letter."

"Yes," he replied, as we sat down on a seat near the bridge. "It is an anonymous letter and its purport is – ah – very singular, and is – ah – to the effect that – er – in fact – "

"Is there any objection to your repeating the actual wording of the letter?" I asked.

"Well, no. Certainly not. Perhaps it would be better. You are really remarkably businesslike and clear-headed. I suppose it is your up-bringing and being so much with your father. No, there is no objection. In fact"– here he produced from his pocket, with evident reluctance, a leather wallet, from which he extracted a folded paper –"in fact, you may as well see the letter for yourself."

I took the paper from him, and opening it found it to be a quite short letter, typewritten upon ordinary typist's paper, without any address or other heading, and undated save for Mr Otway's written and signed endorsement. There was no signature, but in place of one was written in typed characters, "A Well Wisher," and this is what it said:

"Mr Lewis Otway,

"The undersigned is writing to put you on your guard because Somebody knows something about how Mr Vardon came by his death, and that somebody is not a friend, so you had better keep a sharp look out for your enemy and see what they mean to do. I can't tell you any more at present.

"A Well Wisher."

I read it through twice, noting, the second time, the peculiar construction, the faulty grammar and punctuation, and especially the confusion in the pronouns which is so characteristic of the writing of an uneducated person. Of course, these peculiarities might have been assumed as a disguise; but they established a probability that the writer was a person of indifferent education;

to which class, indeed, the bulk of anonymous letter-writers belong.

I handed the document back to Mr Otway, and asked: "Does this letter convey anything to you?"

"Nothing," he replied. "Absolutely nothing. It speaks of somebody knowing something. But that is impossible. There was no one in the house but you and I and – er – your father. Besides, there is nothing to know – excepting what you know."

"Have you any idea or suspicion as to who the writer of this letter may be?"

"None whatever. I have not the faintest clue. You see, there is nobody in the world who has any – er – any special knowledge of the – ah – the exact circumstances but yourself." He paused for a few moments, and then, in a lower tone, asked hesitatingly: "I suppose, Helen, you cannot – er – guess or – ah – surmise who might have – "

I looked up quickly and caught a furtive glance which was instantly averted; and in a moment it was borne in on me that he suspected me of either being the writer or concerned in the writing of this letter.

"Mr Otway," said I, speaking slowly and quietly, the better to command my temper, "if you have any idea that I know anything of this wretched production, dismiss it. If you have any idea that there lurks in my mind any suspicion that your account of my father's death was untrue, dismiss that, too. If I had known, or even had the smallest grounds for suspecting, that my father met with foul play, you would not have had to wait till now to hear from me; nor would my communication have reached you in this form or through these channels."

As I said this, looking at him, I do not doubt, sternly and forbiddingly enough he turned horribly pale and seemed to shrink visibly. He was completely cowed; so much so that, cordially as I detested him, I felt really sorry for him.

"You mistake me, Helen. You misjudge me," he protested, huskily; "you do, indeed. I had no intention – I never, for one moment, suspected – but why do I say this? Of course, you must know I did not. I merely thought it possible that you might be able to guess – that you might know of some person – "

"I do not, Mr Otway," said I. "No one connected with me has any knowledge that is not public knowledge. Nor do I believe that anyone else has. I should say that this person – apparently a person of the lower class – is just a common blackmailer, who was present at, or has read the report of, the inquest, and is trying to make you believe that some suspicion attaches to you."

Mr Otway drew a deep breath and reflected gloomily. Perhaps my suggestion was not a very comforting one, for a blackmailer is a rather formidable enemy to a man who is concealing an incriminating fact.

"Probably you are right, Helen. But you notice that there is no threat – no direct threat, at least – and that there is no suggestion of any attempt to obtain money from me."

"Perhaps that will come later," said I.

Again he drew a long breath and cast a furtive glance at me. "Perhaps it will," he agreed. "This may be the preliminary move, the laying of ground-bait, so to speak. It's a harassing business Helen. What do you think I had better do? You see, I rely on you for counsel, although I am so much older. But you have your father's gift of clear judgment and perfect coolness in emergencies."

It was rather a tactless observation, for it recalled vividly my dear father's coolness in that last, fatal emergency; his composure and unruffled cheerfulness when the menace of ruin and disgrace – set up by Mr Otway – had seemed poised over his head, ready to fall at any moment; and the recollection did not tend to increase my present sympathy.

"For my part," I said, coldly, "I should do nothing at present. I should ignore this letter and wait for the writer to show his hand more clearly. If he should make any threats or demands for hush-money, I should at once put the matter in the hands of the police."

I could see that this advice – particularly the latter part of it – did not greatly commend itself to Mr Otway. Nor did it to me. But circumstances offered no choice. Any risk is better than that of life-long subjection to a blackmailer.

"It would be very unsafe," said Mr Otway, "to have any dealings with the police. They are pretty severe on blackmailers, but they are naturally ready to listen to anyone who professes to have information to give them. And a blackmailer may be very dangerous if he is brought to bay. We couldn't afford to have any enquiries made that might seem to establish what they would call collusion to suppress evidence. We know that the facts that we withheld were not material. Other people would not."

I could not but admire the adroitness with which Mr Otway made me a participator in his own difficulties and secured me as an ally against his unseen enemy. And the uncomfortable aspect of the case was that he was right. We were partners in an unlawful act. That, I had already recognised; and the different significance of that act in our respective cases did not so very much affect our position in the present circumstances. I had nothing further to say, but to repeat that I should ignore the letter; and for a time we sat silent, looking out on the river.

"Well," said Mr Otway, at length, "so be it. We will wait and see what happens. And now let us put this miserable affair away and talk about your future. I have seen some of your work, and I am sure that you could get good prices for it if it were placed in the proper quarter. But the ordinary shops would be of no use to you. The common retailer does not know or care anything about individual work. He just buys from the wholesaler or the manufacturer, and sells to the public. He would probably not look at your work, or if he were willing to buy it, he would pay no more than he pays to the manufacturer who rattles off his goods by the thousand, with the aid of cheap labour and machinery. But there are people who know the difference between artists' works and manufactured goods, and are willing to pay for the better things. And there are dealers who supply them. Mr Campbell is one. I have known him for many years, and I can assure you that he is an excellent judge of works of art and very anxious to get the best for his customers, who are mostly good judges, too. He is well known in artistic circles, and, as he is able to dispose of things of real value, he can afford to pay the artist a fair price. I strongly advise you to give him a trial. Of course, I would infinitely rather that you accepted an allowance from me, but, if you really – "

"It is very good of you, Mr Otway, but I assure you that it is out of the question."

"Very well, then. If you are quite resolved, I can only advise you to make the most profitable use of your talents. Go to Mr Campbell, and I am sure that you will be treated fairly."

I thanked him for his advice and promised to act on it; and very shortly after this I brought the interview to an end.

As I took my way slowly back to Wellclose Square, I reflected on the new developments that my meeting with Mr Otway had disclosed. That some mischief was brewing there could hardly be a doubt. The disguise of the "Well Wisher" was too thin to create any illusion. As to the somebody who knew something, he was an obvious myth, for, as Mr Otway had said, the circumstances did not admit of anyone knowing even what was known to me. My own explanation was that some person, who had been present at the inquest, had observed Mr Otway's excessive nervousness and had marked him as a likely subject for blackmailing operations. It was a chance shot and nothing more.

But Mr Otway's evident alarm was not difficult to account for. He was a naturally timorous man; he had been subjected to a great and prolonged strain, and he had an incriminating secret. His position was, in fact, one of appreciable danger, as he fully realised. If the details of my father's death had been fully disclosed at the inquest, Mr Otway's statement and explanation would probably have been accepted without demur. But the suppression of certain material facts put a different complexion on the matter. If the inquiry were now revived, he would have to explain, not only the original circumstances, but his motives for suppressing them. He had very good reason for alarm.

And yet his abject terror produced an uncomfortable impression on me. I could not disguise from myself that the whole tragedy of my father's death was due to an error of judgment on my part. The secret marriage was the outcome of a mistake. Woman-like, I had acted on a strong conviction; and that conviction had been wrong. What if I had once again acted on an erroneous belief? I had assumed that Mr Otway's account of my dear father's death was correct. There had seemed to be excellent reasons for the assumption. But what if I had been wrong, after all? If I had actually misled a Court of Justice to shield the murderer of my dearly loved father? It was undeniably possible. I had formed my opinion on mere probabilities, backed by a statement that, however plausible, was manifestly worthless as evidence. And that opinion might have been utterly wrong. It was a dreadful thought. So dreadful that, though I tried to put it away and remind myself that I did not entertain and never had entertained it, it haunted me during the whole of my walk home, even to the exclusion of the menace to myself that lurked in this blackmailer's letter.

CHAPTER THIRTEEN

A Crystal-Gazer and Other Matters

The cheerful atmosphere of the old house in Wellclose Square soon dissipated my gloomy thoughts. It was nearing supper-time when I arrived and an agreeable clink of china proceeded from the dining-room, accompanied by a faint aroma suggestive of curry. On my landing I found Lilith and Miss Finch engaged in earnest discussion, and both greeted me as if I had returned after a long absence.

"We have been wondering," said the former, "what had become of our Sibyl" (she had bestowed this title on me, presumably, by reason of my peculiarly "psychic" cast of countenance). "As for the poor Titmouse" (this was Miss Finch's pet name), "she has been wandering about like a cat that has lost its kitten."

"Or like a kitten that has lost its cat," I suggested, bestowing an affectionate pinch on my little comrade's ear. "Well I haven't been far afield, but I have done quite an important stroke of business."

"You don't mean to say you've sold something!" the Titmouse exclaimed, incredulously.

"Not actually sold. But I have discovered a market. I have tidings of a benevolent person – of the Scottish persuasion, I believe – who traffics in works of art and other productions of the human hand."

134

"A Scotchman!" exclaimed Miss Finch. "I thought all art dealers were Jews. When are you going to call on the Laird?"

"It is hardly worth while to call on him until I have a fair collection of work to show him," said I.

"I don't agree with you, Sibyl," said Lilith. "The first thing to do is to catch your dealer. To do that, you must find out what he wants. He is sure to have his own personal fancies, and he knows what he can sell most easily. Take him all that you have ready. He will be able to see from that what you can do, and he will tell you what kind of work he will take from you. And don't lose any time. I should go tomorrow if I were you."

"Does an artist have to work to order, then, like salaried journeymen?" I asked.

"Practically, yes," replied Lilith. "And why not? He makes things that he wants people to buy. Surely it is only reasonable that he should consider the needs and the wishes of the buyers. And all good craftsmen do. Chippendale's chairs were not only good to look at; they were comfortable to sit on and serviceable in use. The only difference between an artist craftsman and a commercial producer is that the artist always does his best, for his own satisfaction apart from the question of payment; whereas the commercial producer thinks of the profit only, and turns out the worst stuff that the buyer will put up with."

"But surely an artist may choose what he will make," said I.

"Of course he may," replied Lilith, "if he is willing to keep the thing when he has made it. Not if he is going to ask someone to pay him money for it."

I was inwardly somewhat taken aback by this exhibition of hard-headed reasonableness on the part of the mystical Lilith; so much so that, when she had gone to her room, I remarked on it to Miss Finch.

"Yes," she agreed; "Lilith is an extraordinary girl. In fact, there seem to be two Liliths; one is as cranky as a March hare, and the other is perfectly sane and really very shrewd. I sometimes wonder whether she really believes in all that crystal-gazing tosh and telepathic bunkum. But she practices what she has just been preaching. She does her fashion-plates according to orders – but ever so much better than she need – and does other work to please herself and is content to keep it. You should look in at her studio and see her at work; then you'd understand."

"And you think I had better take her advice?"

"I do. First catch your dealer; and if he wants to keep you turning out the same things over and over again, try to catch another dealer who wants something different. The great thing is to get a market. It's frightfully disheartening to keep on doing good work and having it all left on your hands."

Impressed by this wise counsel, I betook myself after supper to my workshop and reviewed my stock. A month's work had produced no great accumulation, for I was still a slow worker though the continuous practice was improving that. On the other hand, I had brought with me a certain number of unfinished pieces as well as some of my finished work so that I had enough to give Mr Campbell the means of judging my capabilities. When I had looked over the collection and withdrawn one or two pieces that were not up to my present standard, I packed the approved specimens in a hand-bag which I took up with me in readiness for the morrow. I was just opening the door of my room when Lilith came running up the stairs.

"You see," I said, holding up the hand-bag. "I am acting on your advice. I have packed up a selection from my stock to take to the dealer tomorrow morning."

"I am glad of that," said she. "The business side of art is tedious and disagreeable, but you have got to sell if you are to live by your work. Would you mind giving me a private view of your masterpieces?"

"I shall be proud to show them to you" I replied, conducting her into my room and placing the armchair by the table, "Let us put out the whole collection."

I emptied the bag of its contents, which I set out on the table to the best advantage, and she examined the pieces one by one.

"They *are* charming," she exclaimed, enthusiastically. "I can't judge the work, though it looks most expert to my inexpert eye, but the design is delightful. They are all so individual and full of character, and so simple and restrained. You have a fine colour-sense, too. I think your use of enamel quite masterly, and I like your employment of bronze in place of the precious metals. It is fortunate that your dealer is a Scotchman, for the Jews, from Solomon downwards, have always had a leaning towards gold."

"Yes," said I; "bronze is my favourite material, even for personal ornaments. And it is capable of great variety in the patina, especially if one uses the Japanese methods of surface treatment. I wish it took the enamel better."

"You seem to have overcome the difficulties pretty completely," said Lilith. "This pendant, for instance, is beautiful, and so is the belt-clasp. Do you know, Sibyl, I think we might collaborate. Some of my designs might very well include metal ornaments – clasps, buckles, and buttons forming part of the decorative scheme. We must talk it over. And now, my dear Sibyl, I want to say something to you – something quite serious – and I want you to listen without prejudice."

I looked at her, and was instantly aware of a change that had come over her. The shrewd, businesslike, capable Lilith had suddenly become transformed into the mystic – ; wide-eyed, dreamy, yet intense.

"I have avoided talking to you about the things that are to me the great things of life" she said in low earnest tones. "I have wished to, but I have been fearful of intruding on your strongly individual, self-contained, personality. But I have felt that you have great gifts – great psychic gifts. You are a woman of power. The common herd live their little lives locked up in the prison of the visible and the conscious. If they would convey their thoughts to other minds they must use the unwieldy means of speech and visible signs. What they know of their fellow-immortals reaches them crudely through the organs of sense; and through those primitive and inadequate media they must needs communicate with others, bound by the limitations of time and space and mere material contact – at least, so long as they are prisoned within a material body. But there are others for whom no such limitations exist; specially gifted souls who can see without mere material eyes, who can hear without ears, who can speak their thoughts across the gulfs of time and space; who can look into the remote past, and even into the future; who can make their will-power operate at limitless distances and without the aid of gross bodily action. And you are one of these, Sibyl. I am convinced that you are endowed with these powers. But they are latent, unsuspected, because you have never tried to exercise them; because you have never sought to bring the subconscious within the domain of the conscious, or rather to make a contact between the two."

To this strange and rather wild harangue (which the matter-of-fact Titmouse would have called "barmy") I listened with grave attention, though with little enough conviction – for I could not but recall my ignorance and my mistaken judgment in the greatest crisis of my life – noting how like a prophetess the picturesque Lilith looked, with her golden aureole of auburn hair and her great, blue eyes and parted lips. But I made no reply – there was, indeed, nothing to say – and after a short pause she continued: "Don't think I am saying this with any impertinent intention of trying to force my own views on you. I have a definite practical purpose. You are going tomorrow to make your first essay in a vitally important branch of an artist's calling. On your success depends the possibility of your following art as a profession – that is, if you have not enough to live without work."

"I have not," said I.

"Then artistic success is not sufficient. You must achieve industrial success; you must get a livelihood out of your work. As far as the creation of beautiful things is concerned you are quite competent and will become more so with more practice. Now you have to learn how to dispose of those works profitably; how to make people buy them."

"But surely that will be decided by the suitability of the things themselves."

"Partly, no doubt. But you mustn't leave it at that. You must learn to exercise the power of silent willing combined with suggestion."

"I don't think I quite understand," said I.

"We must talk about this more fully some other time," said Lilith "and go into the theory and the results of experiments. For the present you must try to take my word for the fact that silent willing and suggestion are real powers. I don't ask you to believe it without proof – I will give you the proof later – but I do beg you, dear Sibyl, to give the method a trial. If it fails in your hands you will be none the worse; but it won't fail if you make up your mind to succeed."

"What do you want me to do, Lilith?" I asked, not a little bit bewildered by her mysterious and rather vague expressions.

"I will tell you what I do myself," she replied. " When I take a batch of drawings to a publisher, I stand outside the office for five minutes and silently will that he shall accept them. Sometimes I write on a piece of paper a command to the publisher to accept my work, and while I am waiting for the interview I keep my eyes fixed on the writing and mentally endorse the command. The writing, you see, helps me to concentrate my will-power. Then, at the interview, I use the method of suggestion. Whatever the editor or publisher may say, whatever objections he may make to my work, I continue steadily to impress on him that he is going to accept it, that, in fact, he has accepted it. If he refuses it, I ignore the refusal and go on talking as if he had accepted it – not rudely, of course; one must do these things tactfully – and all the time that he is talking I continue silently to concentrate my will-power on him."

"And what is the result?" I asked.

"The result, my dear Sibyl, is that I sell all the drawings that I offer for sale."

This sounded convincing enough, and would have been more so if I had not happened to know that Lilith's drawings were of the very best of their kind, and that she submitted them to the most rigorous criticism before letting anyone see them. Still, the fact that she sold her work was undeniable, and it was impossible to say how many excellent drawings had failed to gain acceptance. Certainly every capable artist is not a successful one.

"And what is it exactly that you want me to do?" I asked.

"I want you," she replied "to do just what I do, myself. I want you to stand outside the shop for five minutes and silently will that this dealer shall buy your work. It would probably help you if you were to write down the command and keep your eyes fixed on the writing while you are willing; but if the dealer himself should happen to be visible it would be well to fix your eyes on him so as to direct the will-force with more precision. And when you go into the shop, keep on willing with the greatest concentration that you can command, and when you are talking to the dealer, talk as if he had bought your work; keep on impressing on him that he *has* bought it, and don't take any notice of contrary statements on his part. If he seems to think that he has refused it, you must correct his mistake and guide his thoughts into the proper channels."

I suppose I must have looked somewhat dismayed at this rather startling programme, for Lilith continued eagerly: "Now, don't raise objections, Sibyl, dear. It will be quite easy if you will only make up your mind. You have abundant will-power, and I am certain that you have the gift of projecting your mental states into the minds of others. And I am so anxious that you should succeed and that your great gifts should not be wasted. Say you will try, Sibyl, if only to please your friend."

What could I do? Utterly as my mind refused to accept the connection between the alleged cause and effect, I could not say that no such connection existed. I was completely unconvinced; but my unconviction might conceivably be less rational than Lilith's whole-hearted belief. For she declared herself able to support her belief with proof, whereas I had to admit that my scepticism was largely a matter of temperament. And she was so eager, and it was so sweet of her to be so full of anxiety on my behalf, that it would have seemed ungracious to make difficulties. The end of it was that I agreed to carry out her plan of conquest, on which she further inducted me into the arts of silent willing and suggestion and even supervised me while I wrote out, at her dictation, a peremptory command to the dealer, which I promised to use, as directed, for the reinforcement of my will-power at the appropriate time.

On the following morning, after a careful study of my father's atlas of London, which I had brought with me from Maidstone, I set forth, hand-bag in hand and encouraged by the good wishes of my comrades and of Lilith in particular. Entering the Underground Railway at Mark Lane, I came to the surface at Charing Cross Station and bore away northwards across Leicester Square. During the journey, I had turned over in my mind the plan of attack to which I stood committed, with increasing distaste, I must admit, as the time for its execution drew nearer. And as my dislike grew, so also did my scepticism. I found myself recalling the fact that Lilith, successful as she claimed to be, was yet a fashion-plate artist very much against her own wishes, and reflecting that, if her silent willing were as efficacious as she believed it to be she might surely compel the purchase of the kind of work that she enjoyed doing, instead of being herself compelled to follow a distasteful occupation. However, it was useless to think about it now. I had promised to give the method a trial and must carry out my promise.

These reflections brought me to the bottom of Wardour Street, and my attention was now fully occupied by the search for Mr Campbell's shop. Mr Otway had omitted to give me the number of the house, but I remembered his saying that it was on the west side near the Oxford Street end; so I walked slowly up the east side and scanned the shop-fronts across the road. Near the top of the street my eye lighted on a smallish shop, above the window of which was inscribed in faded gold lettering "Donald Campbell," and I immediately crossed the road, becoming aware as I did so of a sudden access of nervousness. For this was a new experience to me. Hitherto all my transactions with shopkeepers had been in the character of a purchaser; and my transformation into a vendor was accompanied by a diffidence and shyness that I had not expected or foreseen. Indeed, in the course of that short journey across the road, my bashfulness increased so much that I had nearly forgotten my promise to Lilith and was on the point of entering the shop when it flashed into my mind.

But even when I recalled Lilith's instructions, they were not easy to carry out. I swerved from the shop door to the side of the window and stood there trying to concentrate my will-power. But it would not be concentrated. In the window was displayed a fascinating array of base metal spoons which instantly riveted my attention; particularly a set, of the late seventeenth century, wrought in a fine-coloured latten, and exhibiting in a most charming manner the combined effect of delicate workmanship, with the patina of age and the softening of outlines from use and wear. Unconsciously, I had begun to compare them with my own cruder productions before I realised that my will-power had escaped control. Then I jerked myself back from the spoons to my present task, and, hastily drawing the paper from my pocket, fixed my eyes on the written command and struggled to concentrate my thoughts on it and to suppress a growing consciousness of the absurdity of the whole proceeding. Presently I raised my eyes from the paper, and as they sought to dodge the spoons, they encountered another object equally disturbing. "It was only a face at the window," as the ridiculous song has it, but it instantly engrossed my attention and transported me in spirit, not to any Highland glen, but straightaway to the banks of the Jordan; a fattish face, framed with glossy, black hair that broke out at the temples into rows of little crisp curls like a barrister's wig; a face with small, grey eyes, full under the lids, and surmounted by strong, black eyebrows, with full, red lips and a rather sketchy nose of the general form of a William pear with the stalk uppermost. It was clearly not Mr Campbell's face, but it appertained to the establishment; and, recalling Lilith's instructions to direct my will-power with more precision by fixing my eyes on the dealer, I directed a stony stare at the face and willed silently. But here I was countered again; for the owner of the face was also apparently possessed of psychic gifts, and fixed on me a gaze of such intensity that I was covered with confusion. On this I straightway forgot all about will-power, and, hastily pocketing the paper, walked nervously and guiltily into the shop.

The proprietor of the face confronted me impassively across the counter; and such was my trepidation that, although he obviously was not Mr Campbell, I could think of nothing better than to ask him if he was; whereupon he completed my discomfiture by replying in the affirmative.

"I am Mrs Otway," said I; at which he suddenly grew keenly attentive, and I continued: "I understand that Mr Otway – Mr Lewis Otway – has written to you about me. I had a letter from him to that effect."

"Yes," said Mr Campbell, "he has; and, if I remember rightly, he suggested that I might be able to dispose of some of your work. I think he said you did some repoussé or something of the kind."

Apparently Mr Campbell was preparing to treat me as an amateur, and my work as the product of a hobby. This would not do at all. Before saying anything further, I opened my bag and handed out the pieces one by one, setting them on the counter before him.

"Oh!" said he. "Yes; ha–hum; this isn't exactly what I expected." He picked up a teaspoon, turned it over between his fingers, closely examined the joining of the shank and bowl and the little bust that formed the knob, and then held it at arm's length with his head on one side. There was something in the action and the facial expression that accompanied it which encouraged me even before he spoke.

"Nithe thpoon that" was his comment as he laid it down (I observed that he tended to develop a lisp when preoccupied or off his guard); "well made, well designed; quite original, too. Spoons

143

are my fancy – you saw that set in the window. If I could afford it, I would specialise in them more than I do. Not but what I'm fond of all goldsmith's work if it's good – or any other art work, for that matter; but I do love a good spoon."

This was pleasant hearing, for I had a weakness for spoons myself. They are useful objects, they admit of infinite variety in design, and their small size adapted them peculiarly to my rather limited resources.

"But there is one thing that you must bear in mind" continued Mr Campbell. "Single spoons are not very saleable unless they are antique or collectors' pieces. Modern spoons are bought for use as well as ornament, and buyers like them in sets; not all alike, of course, but with a general design running through the set. Twelve spoons, all different, but all brothers; that's what they want."

"Like the apostle sets," said I.

"Yes," he replied, "but we don't want any more apostles. Too many on the market already. The apostles are done. They're a back number. Everybody does them because they can't think of anything else connected with the number twelve. But there is an opening for something original. If you can do me a set with a good striking design, I think I know where I can place them at a liberal price."

I made a note of this proposal, and Mr Campbell proceeded with his examination of my samples, accompanying the process with shrewd comments and useful hints. "Now, I'm rather doubtful about this," said he picking up a bronze paperweight on which was a little figure with an open book; "it's pretty and might take the fancy of a bookish man, but I question whether you'll get paid for the work that you've put into it. People don't always realise the value of a bronze casting. You must have done this by the *cire perdue* process."

"I did."

"Well, I should save that for more important pieces. Simple modelling and sand-casting is good enough for paperweights. And you are too lavish with your silver. Just feel this candlestick. You could have done it with half the silver and got paid just as much. The extra cost of the unnecessary silver will have to come off the workmanship – at least, that is the tendency although it is nominally sold by weight."

As Mr Campbell was speaking, a woman came out of an inner room and advanced to the counter. I glanced at her casually and then looked again more attentively, for I had instantly the feeling of having seen her before, though I could not recollect where. She was a Jewess of the dark and sallow type, about my own age, and of a sombre and rather forbidding aspect; and the glance that she cast on my samples, though impassive, was faintly disparaging.

"This is Mrs Otway, me dear," said Mr Campbell. "You remember the letter I showed you about her. And these pretty things are her work."

Mrs Campbell – as I assumed her to be – raised her eyes and bestowed on me a quietly insolent stare, but made no remark. Then she cast another disparaging glance at my wares and said coldly: "They are all right of their kind; but you don't want to fill the place up with modern stuff."

Disagreeable as the remark was, its matter impressed me less than its manner. For again I was sensible of a certain vague familiarity in the voice, the intonation and the accent. She gave me, however, no opportunity for studying either, for, with the curt observation that "she supposed he knew his own business," she retired to the inner room without taking any further notice of me.

"Well," said Mr Campbell, "there's some truth in what my wife says. I can't afford to lock up my capital in things that I can't sell. But I like your work. It is good work, and you'll improve. I am willing to buy this lot of pieces – at a price. But it will have to be a low price, because I don't know how they will go. If you take my advice, you'll leave them with me and let me try the market with them. When I have sold one or two I shall know what I can do with them, and then I can offer you a fair price based on what they fetch. How will that thoot you?"

It seemed, on the whole, the most satisfactory arrangement, though I should have liked to have some definite idea as to the value of my work. I mentioned this, pointing out that I wanted to know if it would be worth my while to continue this kind of occupation.

"Well," said Mr Campbell, "you leave the things with me, and I will look them over carefully and weigh the silver. Then I will make you the best offer I can for the lot, and you can either accept it or refuse it, or wait and see what the things fetch. Give me your address and I will write you out a receipt for what you leave. Will that do?"

I replied that it would do admirably, whereupon he supplied me with a slip of paper and pen and ink, and retired to the desk with my collection to write out the receipt. I had taken off my glove and was beginning to write when somebody entered the shop with a quick, light step, suggesting a young and active man. Just behind me the footsteps shopped short, and a pleasant, masculine voice addressed the dealer.

"All right, Mr Campbell; don't let me disturb you. I'm in no hurry."

"I'm afraid, sir, your things are not quite ready, but if you don't mind waiting a moment I'll make sure."

"I suspected," the voice rejoined, "that I might be a little over-punctual. However, you finish what you are doing while I browse round the museum."

At the first sound of the voice my pen stopped short; and it seemed as if my heart stopped, too – though it soon began to make up for lost time. I was disconcerted and vaguely annoyed that a small surprise should set up such a disproportionate disturbance. Perhaps, too, I was a little startled to find a voice so long unheard elicit such instant and undoubting recognition. But I recovered immediately and resumed my writing, though, to be sure, the pen-point no longer traced the firm and steady lines of the first-written words. Meanwhile, Mr Campbell had completed his receipt, and we now exchanged our documents, I checking his list of my sample works, and he scanning my address with apparent surprise.

"Wellclose Square," he read out. "There is a Wellclose Square somewhere down Wapping way. It won't be that one?"

"Yes. But I think it is actually in Ratcliff. When shall I hear from you?"

"I will write and post the letter this evening."

"Thank you, Mr Campbell. Good morning."

As we exchanged bows, I turned and met the newcomer approaching the counter. He glanced at me, at first without recognition; then he looked again.

"Why, surely it is Miss Vardon!" he exclaimed.

"Wrong, Mr Davenant," said I. "It is Mrs Otway. But that is a mere quibble. I am the person whom you knew as Miss Vardon."

"Well, well," said he, "what a piece of luck to meet you – and here of all places!"

"Is this a peculiarly unlikely place, then?" I asked.

"Well, I suppose it isn't, really; at any rate, I mustn't let Mr Campbell hear me say that it is. Do you mind waiting a moment while I settle my little business with him? I want to hear all your news."

His little business amounted to no more than an arrangement that he should call in about three days for his "things," whatever they were, and when this had been settled, we left the shop together.

"Which way are you walking?" he asked.

"I really don't know," I answered. "I think I had some dim idea of seeing the town and taking a look at the shops."

"Then," said he, "as you are a country mouse, whereas I am a town sparrow of the deepest dye, perhaps I may be permitted to act as conductor and expositor of the wonders of the Metropolis, while you give me the news from Maidstone."

"There is little to tell you excepting that I have lost my father. He died quite suddenly, about two months ago, from heart failure."

"Ah!" said Mr Davenant, "I had a presentiment that it was so. Seeing you in mourning, I was afraid to ask after him; and I need not tell you how deeply I sympathise with you. I remember how much you were to one another. What a mercy it is that you were married!"

To this I made no reply, and for a time we walked on slowly without speaking. But though nothing was said, much was thought, at least by me. For I had to make up my mind now, and once for all, on a point that I felt to be of vital importance. Should I tell him how things were with me? Or should I let him think that all was well, and that I was a normal married woman? Something – I did not ask myself what – urged me to tell him everything. But caution, prudence, whispered – and that none too softly – that it were better not. The sudden wave of emotion that had surged over me at the sound of his voice was still a vivid and startling memory; and it counselled reticence.

Thus two opposing forces contended; on the one hand, an emotional impulse, on the other the admonitions of reason; and it is needless to say that reason played losing game. Swiftly I argued out the issues. Sooner or later, the inevitable question must come, and with it the choice of an evasion or a straightforward answer. If it was to be evasion, then must I put Jasper Davenant out of my life at once and for ever, for the evasion could never be maintained; must shut out this gleam of sunshine that came to me from the old, happy days as if to light up my sombre, lonely life, and wend on my pilgrimage without a friend save the companions of my working days.

And reason whispered again that it were better so.

CHAPTER FOURTEEN

Jasper Davenant

The silence that had fallen between me and my companion remained unbroken (with one exception, when he briefly drew my attention to the old stone name-tablet, inscribed "Wardour Street 1686") until we came opposite a church standing back from the road, and distinguished by a sort of tumour – containing a clock – on its spire. Here Mr Davenant halted, and looking up at the tower, remarked: "A quaint-looking church, this; odd and ugly, but yet not without a certain character and picturesqueness. Quite an aristocratic church, too, for it is the burial place of a king."

"Indeed," said I. "Which of the kings is buried there?"

"He was but a shabby little king – Theodore of Corsica – and he has the shabbiest little moralising monument. But he was a somewhat original monarch in his way, for, being in acute financial difficulties, he conceived the brilliant idea of making over his kingdom to his creditors. Would you care to see the monument?"

I assented, without enthusiasm, and we mounted the steps to the grimy churchyard, where presently, against the wall of the church, we found the monument. And still, as we deciphered the weathered inscription, I debated the question whether I should or should not tell him; and still I reached no conclusion.

"By the way," my companion said, suddenly, "I am acting the showman on the assumption that you are the complete and perfect country bumpkin. But perhaps you are, by now, a fully acclimatised Londoner. How long have you been living in town?"

"About a month."

"Then the hay-seed is still in your hair, so to speak. I still address a country cousin, and have not presumed unduly; though, no doubt, you are beginning to learn the rudiments. I heard Mr Campbell speak of Wellclose Square, for instance, as a region known to you."

"Yes. That is where I live."

As I caught his look of astonishment my heart began to race; for I knew that the inevitable question was coming.

"I suppose your husband is connected with the docks?"

"No," I replied. "And he doesn't live at Wellclose Square. I am not living with my husband, Mr Davenant. I never have lived with him, and it is not my intention ever to live with him."

The deed was done. The murder was out. And though I knew that I had taken the wrong course, I drew a deep breath of relief. As to Mr Davenant, he was, for a few moments too much taken aback to make any comment. At length he said, somewhat gloomily: "I am sorry to hear this, Mrs Otway. Very sorry. It sounds as if your domestic affairs were not very comfortable."

"They are not," I answered. "But, as I have told you so much, I should like to tell you what the position really is. Would you mind?"

"Mind!" he exclaimed. "Of course I want to know, if you are willing to tell me. Aren't we old friends? I am most concerned about you."

"Thank you, Mr Davenant. I *should* like to tell you how this extraordinary position has come about. Shall we sit down? This place is quieter than the street."

He dusted the wooden bench with his handkerchief, and we sat down just below the shabby monument of the poor, little, bankrupt king. And there I told once again that tragic story of cross-purposes and well-meant blundering. I had intended to give him but a bare outline of the catastrophe; but it could not be. For the bald fact was that I had sold myself to Mr Otway for money; and my womanly pride and self-respect would not be satisfied with anything short of a complete justification such as might be accepted by a scrupulous, high-minded man. And as I poured out my miserable history, glancing at him from time to time, I was surprised and almost alarmed at the change that came over him. He was a sunny-natured man, buoyant, high-spirited, playful and humorous, though all in a quiet way. But now, as he listened to my story, the genial face grew rigid, the humorous mouth set hard and stern, and the short, sharp questions that he put from time to time, came in a voice that was strange to me.

"So now," said I when I had come to the end of my recital, "you will understand why I refuse to recognise this marriage; and why I elect to live the life of a spinster, though without a spinster's privileges."

In a moment his face softened, and his clear, hazel eyes looked into mine with grave tenderness.

"Yes," he said; "I understand. I wish I could say more. I wish I could tell you adequately how I grieve for you – for all the sorrow that you have had to endure and for the maimed life that lies before you. But words are poor instruments." He laid his hand on mine for an instant, and added: "Yet I hope you will feel what I want to express in these threadbare phrases."

I thanked him for the sympathy, which he had indeed made very clearly evident, and for a time neither of us spoke. Nevertheless, I could see that he was cogitating something. Once or twice he seemed about to speak, for he looked at me, but then again bent his gaze reflectively on the ground. At length, with some hesitation, he said: "I hope you won't think me inquisitive or impertinent, but I feel rather anxious as to – as to how you are placed. I gather that this man Otway does not – er – contribute –"

"He is quite willing to. But I can't allow him to maintain me if I repudiate the marriage."

"No; at least I think you are quite wise not to. But – you don't mind my asking, do you? Are you properly provided for? I'm really not – "

"Of course, you're not," I interrupted, smiling at his diffidence. "As to my means – well, I don't quite know what they will be eventually, but at present I am living in a reasonable state of comfort. I am not anxious about the future."

My answer did not seem to satisfy him completely, for he continued to cogitate rather uneasily. But, now that I had the key, I could read pretty clearly, without the aid of any magic crystal, what was passing in his mind. He knew that I lived in a squalid east-end neighbourhood. He had seen me at the dealers, and evidently surmised that I was not there as a buyer; that I was in straitened circumstances – perhaps in a state of actual poverty – and that I was disposing of my jewellery and valuables to enable me to live. That, I had no doubt, was what he suspected; and the question that he was debating so earnestly was whether he could, without impertinence, extract any further information and whether our friendship was intimate enough to allow of his making any kind of offer of help.

I should have liked to set his mind at rest, but, in truth, I was none too confident about my future. That depended largely on the nature of Mr Campbell's offer; on my ability to earn a reasonable livelihood.

"Well," Mr Davenant said, at length, "I hope your confidence is justified. But in any case, I suppose you have friends?"

"There's no need for you to worry about me," I replied; evasively – for I had no near relatives from whom I could claim assistance. "I am in quite comfortable circumstances at present. And now let us put away my bothersome affairs and talk of something more pleasant."

"Very well," said he. "Let us choose an agreeable topic and discuss it in all its bearings as we used to do." He drew his watch from his pocket, and, glancing at it, continued: "It is now nearly one o'clock. What do you say to the question of lunch as an agreeable topic for our debate?"

I admitted that the subject was not without its attractions.

"Then," said he, "I will suggest that a club is an appropriate place in which to consume it, and that a mixed club satisfies the most extreme proprieties."

"I should hardly have suspected you of a mixed club."

"In strict confidence," he replied, "between you and me and our friend Theodore of insolvent memory, I have another − unmixed − for normal club purposes. This one is my lunch club. It is quite near to my chambers, and is quieter and more pleasant than a restaurant. And it has a special character of its own, as is indicated by its name. It is
called the 'Magpies' Club."

"That sounds rather ominous."

"Doesn't it? But it isn't a burglars' club. Its members are collectors and connoisseurs − furniture and china maniacs and so forth; and the main function of the club is to enable them to show their specimens to one another and to exchange or sell duplicate pieces. May I take it that you consent to honour the 'Magpies'?"

I accepted the invitation gladly, for a month's residence in the East End had made me decidedly appreciative of the amenities of the more civilised regions. We decided to walk to Essex Street, in which the club had its premises, and to go by way of the side streets for greater quiet and ease of conversation.

"You spoke just now of your chambers," said I. "Does that mean that you are in practice now?"

"Yes. But not in the law. I finished my legal studies and got called, but then I decided to give up the Bench and the Woolsack, though they shouted for me never so loudly, and return to an old love. I am now an architect."

"Is a barrister allowed to practice as an architect?"

"On that I am not quite clear; but it really doesn't matter to me. It is a question for the benchers or other authorities."

"Have you been in practice long?"

"Exactly three weeks today. And when I tell you that I have already received a commission to design and erect a greenhouse no less than twelve feet by eight in plan, you will realise that I am mounting the ladder of professional success, with the speed of an eagle with a balloon attachment. My client, by the way, is a member of the club."

Thus gossiping, we made our way by devious routes through the less frequented streets, by Garrick Street, Covent Garden and Drury Lane, until, by the Law Courts, we emerged into the Strand, crossed to Essex Street, and presently arrived at the roomy, old-fashioned house in which the Magpies had their meeting-place.

It was a pleasant, homely club, and certainly there could be no question as to its eminent respectability, for the aspect of the members − mostly middle-aged and many of them elderly − bordered on the frumpish. The room in which we selected our table was a large, oblong apartment, quietly furnished and decorated and provided with a glazed museum case, which occupied the centre; while a sort of dais at one end was devoted to the display of pieces of furniture exhibited by the members. I noticed, too, that the walls were occupied by pictures, each of which bore a written descriptive label.

"Are you interested in ancient ivories?" Mr Davenant asked, as we looked into the glass case, in which a collection of very brown and cracked specimens were exhibited by a Mr Udimore-Jones. "For my part, I find it difficult to develop great enthusiasm over the dental arrangements of superannuated elephants, carved into funny shapes by piously-facetious middle-agers. Look out! Here comes my client. Let us sneak off to our table. Aha! Too late! She's seen us."

"Which is your client?" I asked, looking round furtively.

"The elderly damsel with the smile − a Miss Tallboy-Smith. There! She has caught my eye now. Did you ever see such a set of teeth? She had better be careful or Udimore-Jones will have her."

We were edging away towards our table, with a feeble hope of escape, when she caught us.

"Now I don't believe you've seen my cup," she exclaimed with an engaging smile. "You must see it. It is not only genuine Nantgarw, but the roses on it are unquestionable Billingsleys."

"Observe," said Mr Davenant, "the pride of the inveterate collector. You'd think she had painted those roses herself."

"Indeed, you wouldn't" retorted Miss Tallboy-Smith; "not if you had seen them and knew anything about ceramic painting. And as to pride, isn't it something to be proud of? Nantgarw porcelain is rare, and roses painted by Billingsley are rare; and when you have them both in a single piece, why then you see, you – "

"Then," said Mr Davenant "you multiply the rarity of the one by the rarity of the other, and the product of the multiplication is the rarity of the piece as a whole."

"Isn't he absurd?" she simpered, treating me to a complete private view of the "ancient ivories." "Perfectly incorrigible. Don't you agree with me, Miss– Mrs – "

"Otway," said I.

"Oh really! Now I wonder – my brother knew a Mr – Oh, but he was a money-lender. That wouldn't be – but won't you come and look at my cup?"

We returned to the glass case, of which Miss Tallboy-Smith opened a door and lifted from its shelf a dainty porcelain teacup.

"Just feel how thin and light it is," she said, holding it out to me.

"I wouldn't if I were you," said Mr Davenant. "This Nantgarw stuff crumbles like a baked egg-shell; and it's hideously valuable."

"Don't take any notice of him," said Miss Tallboy-Smith. "Just feel it – it's positively delicious to touch; and look at the lovely roses; no one but William Billingsley could have painted those roses. And, if there could be any doubt, you have only to turn the piece up and look at the bottom. There is Billingsley's personal mark – the Number 7. That's infallible."

I took from her hand the delicate, translucent cup, and was admiring the freedom and softness of the flower-painting when she drew nearer and said in a warning whisper: "Here comes

Major Dewham-Brown. If he tries to sell you anything, don't buy it. He only brings his bad bargains here."

She had barely uttered her warning when a brassy voice behind me exclaimed: "How d'you do, Miss Tallboy-Smith? and how are you, Davenant?" and a tall, smart, rather stupid-looking man with a large nose – which seemed to have been produced at the expense of his eyes and chin – sailed into my field of vision.

"Ha!" said he. "Pretty cup, that. Worth a pot of money, too, I expect, though I don't know much about 'em. And that reminds me that I've got rather an interesting thing that I picked up the other day; bit of old church plate; seventeenth century, if not earlier. Like to see it?"

Without waiting for a reply, he fished out of a "poacher's" pocket a flat object wrapped in a silk handkerchief.

"Curious piece, this: interested me very much. The repoussé-work on it is remarkably fine." He unfolded the handkerchief as he spoke, and at length extracted, with a sort of conjuror's flourish, a small, circular, silver platter – apparently a paten, to judge by its size. This he handed to Miss Tallboy-Smith, who grinned at it indulgently and passed it to Mr Davenant, who, having looked it over without enthusiasm, handed it to me. A very brief inspection, with the piece in my hand, was enough to make Miss Tallboy-Smith's warning unnecessary; for, apart from the unsuitability of the ornament – if it was really meant for a paten – it was an obvious electrotype, which had, however, been pickled, polished and sulphured with intent to deceive. Having noted this fact, I returned the piece to its owner with a few words of polite and colourless commendation of the design; and the Major, chilled by the lack of enthusiasm, invested his treasure once more in its silken wrapping and went off in search of a more appreciative audience. Under cover of his parting courtesies to Miss Tallboy-Smith, Mr Davenant and I retreated to our table.

"That antique of the Major's looked to me rather like a fake," said my companion, when we had ordered our lunch. "It was so very venerable."

"It is an electrotype, sulphured to give an appearance of age," said I.

"Is it, by Jove? Now, how did you spot it as an electrotype?"

"It was the disagreement between the back and the face that first attracted my attention. The face was repoussé – pretty coarse too – but there was not a vestige of a toolmark on the back, where, of course, most of the punch-marks would be; nothing but the smooth surface of the deposited metal."

Mr Davenant chuckled. "I seem to have imported an expert Magpie. Oh! But I remember now that you and your father used to do all sorts of wonderful works in metal. Ha, ha! Poor old Dewham-Brown! He little suspected that he was dealing with a practical artificer."

Here the advent of food put a temporary stop to conversation, for we were both pretty sharp-set; but during the progress of the meal I looked about me and was vastly entertained by the proceedings of the Magpies. The glass case was the centre of interest, around which a small crowd of enthusiasts gathered, eagerly discussing the exhibits, which the proud owners expounded, with their noses flattened against the glass, or tenderly lifted out for closer inspection. And now and again a new exhibitor would arrive with a bag or attaché case, from which fresh treasures were disgorged into the glazed sanctuary.

"I suppose," said I, "your members will have nothing to do with any but antique works?"

"Not as a rule," Mr Davenant replied. "The collector is usually a lover of old things. But there are exceptions. A good many of the pictures shown here are modern; some, I suspect, are shown by the artists themselves. Then we have one member who collects modern pottery exclusively – not commercial stuff, of course, but the work of modern artist-potters, like De Morgan, the Martin Brothers and individual workers. Fine stuff it is, too. I have a few pieces myself. And, talk of the old gentleman – there he is. I'll fetch him over and make him show us what he has got in that bag."

He rose from the table, and crossed the room, and I saw him accost a very tall, pleasant-looking young man who was bearing down on the glass case with a good-sized hand-bag, but readily allowed himself to be led over our table.

"Now, Hawkesley," said Mr Davenant, "my guest wants to see what really high-class modern pottery is like. What have you got?"

"I have only three pieces with me," replied Mr Hawkesley, "and they are all of the same type; what I call 'mystery-ware.' "

"What is the mystery about it?" Mr Davenant asked.

"The mystery is, who makes it? As far as I know, there is only one dealer who has it, and he absolutely refuses to say where he gets it. I have never seen any of it exhibited – excepting here – and nobody can tell me the name of the potter or anything about it beyond the fact that it seems to be the exclusive monopoly of this one dealer, and that he has very little of it, and charges accordingly. But it is wonderful stuff." He lifted out of his bag a couple of jars and a bowl – handling them with that curious delicacy that one often notices in persons with large, strong, supple hands – and placed them carefully on the table.

"You see," he continued, "there are two methods of treatment, which are sometimes combined, as on this jar; and these two styles are based on two very different types, of old work – the old English slip-ware, such as the Wrotham and Staffordshire and Toft-ware, and the old French Henri Deux; or Oiron ware. In the one, the ornament is produced by laying on pipes or threads of coloured slip – that is, clay in the semi-liquid state; in the other by inlaying coloured paste or enamel in cavities in the body, which seems to be made with tools like those used by book-binders. This covered jar – which looks almost like a piece of fine Japanese cloisonné – and this bowl show the inlay method, and this other jar is an example of the slip decoration, but with one or two spots of enamel inlay."

"I think I prefer the pure inlay," said Mr Davenant.

"So do I" said Mr Hawkesley, "and so, I think, does the artist. All his finest work is done by the inlay method, though he uses the slip decoration with such skill and taste that it is virtually a new method. The old Wrotham and Toft-ware looks very primitive by the side of this scholarly, refined work."

I turned the three pieces of pottery over in my hands and warmly commended the judgment of the collector. No modern work that I had ever seen approached it for perfection of finish or grace of design; while the colour-scheme combined richness, delicacy and restraint in a truly marvellous manner. It seemed to unite the brilliancy of enamel to the sober beauty of old tapestry. And even the little blue bird, inlaid on the bottom of each piece to form the potter's mark, was finished with care and taste.

"May one enquire as to the local habitation and name of the dealer?" Mr Davenant asked.

"You may" was the reply. "His name is Maurice Goldstein, and he is to be found at Number 56, Hand Court, Holborn. And I should like to wring his neck."

We both laughed at the vindictive tone in which this benevolent wish was uttered, and at the sudden ferocity of aspect that swept over the usually good-humoured, kindly face.

"Why this homicidal craving?" Mr Davenant asked.

"Don't you see," the other demanded, indignantly, "that this infernal Goldswine – I beg your pardon – "

"You needn't," said I.

"That this miserable huckster is grinding the face of some poor artist; that he is not only devouring the earnings of this industrious, painstaking worker, but – for his own paltry profit – he is robbing that artist of the credit – of the fame – to which his genius and his enthusiasm entitle him. Look at this lovely jar! I gave that maw worm ten guineas for it. How much do you suppose he gave the potter?"

"Ten shillings, perhaps," suggested Mr Davenant.

"Probably not much more, though there is getting on for a week's work in it."

"Still," I said, with a mischievous desire to stir up his indignation afresh, "the potter probably enjoys making these beautiful things. The work is its own reward."

"I can't agree to that," Mr Hawkesley rejoined, warmly. "He doesn't enjoy being hard up and having to work for a pittance. Besides, it isn't just. This man makes a jar that is going to give me a life-long pleasure. I want to pay him for that pleasure. I want to know who he is, to shake his hand and thank him and tell him that he is the salt of the earth. And this Shylock hides him away and just feeds on him like the beastly parasite that he is."

He gathered up the treasured masterpieces, and having wished us adieu with a sudden return to his customary geniality, crossed to the glass case to find a vacant niche for his samples of "mystery ware."

"I like Jack Hawkesley," said my companion, as we watched him.

"So do I," I agreed warmly. "He takes a human interest in the artist. I wish more collectors were like him."

"Yes," said Mr Davenant. "He is a good type of rich man. Would that there were more Hawkesleys." He poured out the coffee which the waitress had just brought and then asked: "What do you think of this club – as a feeding and resting place, I mean?"

"It seems a comfortable, homely place, and the members and their exhibits are quite interesting."

"I find it so. You wouldn't care to join, I suppose? It is cheap, as clubs go: five guineas a year and no entrance fee. I should think you would find it a great convenience, living so far from the centre of town."

"It *would* be a great convenience. But should I be eligible? I am not a collector, you know."

"No, but you are something of an expert. At any rate, Hawkesley and I would manage the formalities. Think it over, and if you decide to honour us, drop me a line. This is my address – 56, Clifford's Inn."

He handed me his card, and when he had made a note of my address, I prepared to depart.

"I have wasted a fearful amount of your time, Mr Davenant," said I; "but it has been a very pleasant interlude for me."

"Has it really? I hope it has. For my part, I have enjoyed myself just as I did in the old days when you used to let me wag a philosophic chin at you, and I am reluctant to let you go so soon. Mayn't I see you to the station, or wherever you are going?"

"I thought of walking back to get myself acquainted with London."

"Then let me put you on the right road and show you some of the short cuts."

"But what about your work?"

He regarded me with that quaint, humorous smile that I had always found so attractive. "My work is, at present, of a somewhat intermittent type. This is one of the intermissions. Let us fare forth and study the architectural beauties of the Metropolis."

And we fared forth accordingly.

The short cuts discovered by my companion did not in the least conform to Euclid's definition of a straight line; and their brevity was relieved by sundry excursions into alleys and by-streets and incursions into churches and other ancient buildings. They led us by way of the Temple and its old round church, Mitre Court, Fetter Lane, Nevill's Court, Gough Square, and so to St Paul's Churchyard and into the Cathedral; thence by Paul's Alley, Paternoster Row, Cheapside and Lombard Street, dropping into one or two churches on our way, until we came out on Great Tower Hill, and drifted slowly down Royal Mint Street. And all the while we gossiped pleasantly of this wonderful city and its wonderful, inexhaustible past; and my guide expounded, with all his old gaiety and brightness – and with astonishing knowledge of his subject – until I had almost forgotten Wellclose Square and the sinister shadow that hung over my life, and seemed to be back in the untroubled days of my girlhood.

But not quite. For, even as I talked – or more often listened – with the liveliest interest and pleasure, a project was maturing in my mind. I had, in fact, conceived a brilliant idea. Mr Davenant's suggestion that I should join the club had started a train of thought that ran as an undercurrent – in the subconscious mind, perhaps, as Lilith would have said. It had begun vaguely when I saw the modern pictures on the walls, and the modern works in the glass case and the Major hawking round his little platter. Here was a place in which the work of the unknown artist could be shown and perhaps sold; my own work, Lilith's work, the Titmouse's, Philibar's, even Miss Polton's. For five guineas a year I could open this emporium, not only to myself, but to my fellow-workers; could slip past the dealer and secure his profits for us all. I say it was a brilliant idea – at least, it appeared so to me; and throughout that long peregrination, made delightful by the sympathetic companionship of my newly-recovered friend it germinated and grew until, as we halted to say goodbye at the corner of Cable Street, it had grown to full maturity.

"I have been thinking," said I, "of your suggestion – about joining the club, you know. It would be nice to have a place to go to for a rest or a meal, in the centre of town. And I shall often want such a place."

His face brightened perceptibly – perhaps at the implied assurance that I could afford to spend five guineas.

"Then, may I put your name up for election?"

"Will you be so kind?"

"Won't I? It will be jolly, and we shan't lose sight of one another again; though that was my fault for not writing. I was often on the point of sending you a letter, and then I felt a silly diffidence – thought that you might consider I was presuming on a mere acquaintanceship. However, I will propose you for membership at once, and in about a week's time you will be a full-blown Magpie. Then I will send you a line, though, of course, you will get the official notification."

He handed me my bag, and with a hearty handshake, we said "Goodbye," and went our respective ways.

It was but a few minutes' walk to Wellclose Square, and I took it slowly; for now that my companion was gone and I was bereft of his buoyancy and vitality, I was suddenly aware of intense bodily fatigue. Moreover, I felt a certain reluctance to bring to a definite close what had been an interval of quiet but perfect happiness. And so, in spite of my fatigue, I sauntered on, loitering awhile in St George's churchyard and stopping to look up at the quaint stone name-tablet at the corner of Chigwell Lane, until weariness and growing hunger drove me homewards. And even then, it was not without regret that I pulled the brass bell-knob and, as it were, wrote "Finis" to this pleasant and eventful chapter.

CHAPTER FIFTEEN

The Magic Pendulum

The weighty question whether my handicraft would yield me a livelihood was answered on the following morning by the arrival of a letter from Mr Campbell; and it was answered, though not very emphatically, in the affirmative. The prices that he offered, provisionally – and advised me not to accept – were appallingly low; very little above those of mere commercial goods. But even so, it would be possible, by hard work and spare living, to eke out a bare subsistence. And it was fair to assume that Mr Campbell's offer was, as indeed he explicitly stated, a minimum, on which an advance might be expected. Accordingly, I declined the offer and decided to await the results of actual sales to his customers.

I was turning these matters over at the breakfast table, when Lilith came and took a vacant chair by my side.

"Well, Sibyl," she said, in a low voice, "how did you fare yesterday? Did you have any success?"

"Yes. I came back with an empty bag."

"And a full purse?"

"Ah! That is another matter. The tide of handicraft doesn't seem exactly to lead on to fortune."

"I want to hear all about it," said Lilith. "But we can't discuss it here. Let us have a quiet talk up in my room after breakfast. If you will run up when you've finished, I will join you in a few minutes."

I assented gladly, for Lilith apart from what the irreverent Titmouse characterised as her "crystal-gazing tosh," was a sound adviser on business affairs; and a few minutes later I betook myself upstairs to her studio. I had scarcely seen this room before, for there was an unwritten law, sternly enforced by Miss Polton, forbidding the boarders to enter one another's workrooms except by invitation and on specific business, and I now looked about me with a good deal of curiosity.

It was a queer room. The two sides of Lilith's personality, like two separate persons, seemed to have parcelled it out into two distinct territories. There was the working territory, neat, precise, business-like, strangely free from the usual muddle and disorder of a woman-artist's studio; the big water-colour easel, the orderly painting cabinet, the papier-mâché lay figure, quaintly arrayed in a walking costume such as might have been seen in a Regent Street shop window (miraculously built up, as I observed, of draperies, pinned, tied or lightly stitched together), the charcoal studies from the figure, pinned up on the wall for reference, with careful pencil drawings of heads, hands and feet, and one or two casts of faces and hands. The working department was a model of matter-of-fact efficiency.

In curious contrast to this was the domain of Lilith, the mystic. In a well-lighted corner stood a small table supporting a black velvet cushion on which reposed a crystal globe of the size of a cricket ball. Above the table a couple of book-shelves exhibited a collection of volumes treating of Spiritualism, Telepathy, Apparitions, Psychical Research and other occult subjects. On the upper shelf stood a bowl filled with the letters of a dissected alphabet; while, hanging on the wall, was a small heart-shaped object with tiny castors, which I assumed to be Planchette, and by its side a single Egyptian bead suspended at the end of a silken thread.

Yet these two aspects of this strange girl's character were not without a connecting link. On the walls were several framed paintings signed "Winifred Blake," mystical figure subjects, recalling, but not imitating, the works of Burne Jones and Rosetti, exquisitely drawn and delicately painted in water-colour. The work on the easel was a similar drawing of a freize-like character, the figures nude but with lightly indicated draperies: and one of the nude figures had been traced on to a fashion-plate board and was already partly clothed in the walking costume.

My survey of the room and its contents was interrupted by the arrival of its occupant, who having seated me in the easy chair, perched herself on her painting-stool and opened the examination.

"Now," said she, "I don't want to be inquisitive, but I do want to know just how you got on. Did you carry out the methods that I proposed?"

"I did – at least as far as the silent willing was concerned – though not very thoroughly. I don't think I did much in the way of suggestion."

"And did you sell your work?"

"Yes, I think I may say I did," and here I gave her an account of Mr Campbell's two alternative offers.

"You have done admirably, Sibyl," she said enthusiastically. "Your first essay has been a perfect success. And now, tell me: are you convinced?"

As I could not truthfully say that I was, I took refuge in polite evasion, which, however, Lilith brushed aside with some impatience.

"I can never understand this kind of scepticism," said she. "You have the cause and effect before your eyes, but yet you refuse to recognise the connection. You take your work to this man. Outside the shop you will that he shall buy it. You go in and he does buy it. What more could you want?"

"But he might have bought the things if I hadn't willed, you know."

"Yes," she agreed; "he might. But that is not the way we reason about material things. I strike a match and apply it to a laid fire, and the fire burns. It might have burned if I had not applied the lighted match, but no one doubts the connection between the lighted match and the lighted fire. Physical causes and effects are accepted with unquestioning faith, but as soon as we come to spiritual or psychical phenomena, this extraordinary scepticism springs up – this curious refusal to admit and accept the obvious."

"I am not asserting that there was no connection between the silent willing and the purchase of my work," said I. "All I say is that I don't regard the connection as proved. I can't decide for or against because there doesn't seem to be enough evidence either way."

"Yes; I suppose you are right," she admitted, reluctantly. "But I should like to convince you, because I am sure you have very unusual powers."

She was silent for a short space, and then, suddenly, she asked: "Have you ever been to a seance, Sibyl?"

"Never," I replied.

"Well," said she, "you ought to go to one – not to any of those silly public shows conducted by mere mountebanks, but to a private seance, carried out by really earnest people who are seeking to extend our knowledge. Would you care to come to one with me?"

"It would be rather interesting," I replied, without much enthusiasm.

"It would," said she. "You were speaking of evidence just now. Well, at a genuine seance you would obtain evidence that I think would convince you of the reality of psychical phenomena. I have a friend – a Mr Quecks – who has given me some most remarkable demonstrations, and I have no doubt that he would be very pleased for you to accompany me to one of them."

"Is Mr Quecks a medium?" I asked.

"No; I shouldn't describe him as a medium, though he is very sensitive and has most extraordinary powers. But he is a profound student of super-normal phenomena and deeply interested in psychical research. May I ask him to show you some of his experiments?"

"Thank you Lilith; and I hope you will find me less disappointing than you have today. I am really quite curious about these things, although I admit a rather sceptical frame of mind. I was wondering, before you came up what you do with that bead on the string."

"That," replied Lilith, all agog at the question, "is the *pendule explorateur* – the magic pendulum. It is an instrument of the kind known in psychical science as an autoscope – an appliance for, as it were, bringing the subconscious into view."

"But how does it work?"

"It works by the influence of the subconscious mind upon the muscles. Let me show you – but you shall try it yourself because you are an unbeliever."

She removed the crystal ball and its cushion from the table, and taking the bowl of loose letters, turned out its contents and rapidly arranged the letters in a circle, forming a clockwise alphabet. Then she took the pendulum down from its hook.

"Now," said she, "what you have to do is this: you rest your elbow on the table to steady your hand, and you hold the string with the thumb and finger, letting the bead hang just clear of the table in the centre of the circle; and you must keep your hand perfectly still and steady."

"But if I do, the bead will remain still, too."

"No, it won't, excepting just at first. Presently it will begin to swing, apparently of its own accord, but really in accordance with your mental state. For instance, if you let it hang inside a glass and you will that it shall strike the hour, it will strike the hour. If you will – or I hold your other hand and will – that it shall swing round in a circle to the right or left, it will swing round in the direction willed. But that is an exercise of the conscious will. In the experiment that we are making now we tap the subconscious. If there is any thing or person occupying your subconscious mind, the pendulum will spell out the name of that thing or person by swinging towards the letters. Let me put the chair comfortably for you, so that you can keep quite still."

As I listened to Lilith's explanation I began to wish heartily that I had never embarked on this experiment. Of course, I did not believe for a moment that this absurd pendulum would develop the occult powers that Lilith claimed for it; but yet her confidence shook mine. And I had a very strong feeling that, on this day of all days, I should prefer to keep my subconscious mind to myself. However, there was no escape; so I seated myself and proceeded to carry out Lilith's directions.

For nearly half a minute the bead hung quite motionless from my steady hand. Then it began almost imperceptibly to oscillate. My eye had already taken in the positions of the letters which might be incriminating, and now I observed with uneasy surprise that the faint oscillations of the pendulum were taking a direction towards the letter J. I could detect no movement in my hand, but, nevertheless, the oscillations grew wider and wider until the bead, as if possessed by a private demon, swung briskly halfway across the circle.

"That is pretty definite," said Lilith. "It is swinging towards U – or is it J? The circle ought to have been bigger, so that the letters need not have been opposite to one another. But I'll write down both; U or J."

The swing of the pendulum now began to shorten; and then, almost abruptly, it changed its direction to one at right angles, and I observed with astonishment that it was pointing direct to A.

"It's either A or P," said Lilith. "I'll put them both down."

Once again the pendulum changed the direction of its swing, and Lilith noted down E or S; and so, to my growing consternation, it continued to take up quite distinct changes of direction until six variations had occurred, when the pendulum became stationary and then began to swing round in a circle.

"It has finished," said Lilith – whereupon I instantly dropped the pendulum. "It is a word of six letters: U or J, A or P, E or S, A or P, E or S, F or R. Let us see if we can make out what the word is. It is a pity the letters were opposite; it muddles it up so. They ought to be in a half-circle, but then they would be too close. But let us try a few combinations. U P E A S F; it can't be that. U P S A S F; it can't be that. We'll try it with J J A E P E F; that isn't it. J A S E S F; that can't be the word. Do the letters suggest anything to you, Sibyl? Is there any name that might be lurking in your subconscious mind, beginning with U or J? Try to think. What did you do in town yesterday?"

"Oh, various things. I went to the dealer, of course; and then I went to a private show of pottery and antiques."

"Pottery," mused Lilith, scanning the letters that she had written down. "Let me see: Upchurch? No, that won't do." She looked the letters through again and then asked eagerly: "There wasn't any Wedgwood there I suppose?"

Now it happened that while Mr Hawkesley was talking to us I had noticed an old gentleman tenderly placing a very fine green Wedgwood cup and saucer in the show case. So I could, and did, answer truthfully.

"Yes, there was; a beautiful green Jasper-ware cup and saucer."

"There!" Lilith exclaimed triumphantly. "Jasper! That is the word! And yet I don't suppose you have given that cup and saucer a thought since you saw it."

"I had forgotten its existence until you spoke of Wedgwood."

"Exactly," said Lilith. "And that is the mysterious peculiarity of the subconscious. You see a thing or a person perhaps only for a moment, and straightway forget it. It seems to be gone for ever. But it is not. It has sunk into the subconscious, to remain there unnoticed possibly for years until some chance association, or perhaps a dream, brings it to the surface. But all the time it has been there. And at any moment it can be brought into view by the use of some kind of autoscope such as the pendulum or the crystal."

"The crystal is an autoscope, too, is it?" I asked.

"Yes; but of quite a different kind. The pendulum acts by the effects of the subconscious mind upon the muscles; the crystal by the effects of the subconscious mind on the centres of visual perception."

"That sounds very learned; but tell me exactly what you do with the crystal."

"As to me, personally," replied Lilith, "I do very little with it. Crystal vision – or 'scrying,' to use the technical term – is a rather rare faculty. I am a very poor scryer. But in the case of a really gifted observer, the most astonishing results are obtained. The method of using the instrument is this: The scryer sits in a restful position with the crystal before her (all the best scryers, I think, are women) and gazes steadily at the bright lights in it, keeping the conscious mind in a passive state – thinking of nothing, in fact. After a time the lights in the crystal grow dim; a kind of cloud or mist seems to float before it, and in this cloud, and gradually taking its place, the picture or vision appears; sometimes dim and vague, but often quite clear and bright, like the little pictures that you see in a convex mirror or a silver ball."

"And what is this picture? I mean what is its subject?"

"That varies. It may be a scene from the past that had been forgotten by the conscious memory, or something that never happened at all – just a jumble of bits of memory like a dream. Or it may be the picture of some event that is going to take place in the near future."

"But," I objected, "how can an event which has not yet occurred be in your subconscious mind?"

"I know," said Lilith. "The whole subject of pre-recognition is a very difficult one. But there seems to be no doubt that prophetic visions do really occur. And then there is clairvoyance – seeing across space and through obstacles. A really gifted scryer, by concentrating her thought on a particular person or place as she looks into the crystal, can see that person or place, no matter how great the distance may be; can see exactly what the person is doing or what is happening at the place."

"Really!" I exclaimed. "That sounds like rather an undesirable faculty. Doesn't it strike you, Lilith, as a very great intrusion on the privacy and liberty of the subject to scry a person without his or her consent? Supposing the scryer should happen to discover the scryed one in the act of taking her – or his – morning tub. Wouldn't it be rather a liberty?"

Lilith laughed (but I could see that the idea was new to her): "You are dreadfully matter-of-fact, Sibyl. But, of course, you are quite right. We shouldn't misuse our powers. As for me, I have very little power of the kind to misuse, for I have never seen anything more than a sort of vague picture of unrecognisable figures in undistinguishable surroundings. But I think you might do better, for I am still convinced that you have special gifts. Would you like to try the crystal, Sibyl?"

"Not now, thank you, Lilith. We ought to get to work after all this gossip. And that reminds me that, before you came up, I was looking at your exquisite paintings and wondering if you are not, to some extent, wasting your great talents."

"In what way?" she asked.

"Of course," I said, "these designs would make magnificent tapestries or wall decorations. But if you can't get a wall, you might condescend to a smaller surface. Have you ever tried designing and painting a fan?"

"No," she replied.

"I wish you would," said I. "You would do it splendidly with your power of design and your delicate technique. And Phillibar could make the sticks and carve the guards, or I could do you a pair in silver repoussé, and a jewelled pin and loop. Will you think over the proposal?"

Lilith picked up the crystal on its cushion and, smiling at me, said: "I will make a bargain with you. If you will take the crystal to your room and give it a thorough trial whenever you have time, I will get out a design for a fan. Do you agree?"

I held out my hand for the crystal. Primarily, my desire was to introduce Lilith to Fame and Fortune through the medium of the Magpies Club; but the startling success of the magic pendulum had aroused my curiosity in regard to the other "autoscope," though I have to confess that, when I had borne it to my room, I concealed it guiltily in a locked drawer, where it should be secure from the prying eyes of the servant-maid, and above all from the observation of the sarcastic and sceptical Titmouse.

But there were other matters than crystals and magic pendulums to be thought of. There was, for instance, the set of twelve spoons which Mr Campbell had asked me to make and to which he had again referred in his letter. I knew now that I should be paid for them at a reasonably remunerative rate, and this, and the congenial nature of the task, encouraged me to get to work. But before I could begin there was the motive of the design to be considered; and since the apostles were ruled out as obsolete, I had to find some other group of twelve related objects. After a whole day's anxious thought, I fixed upon the Signs of the Zodiac as furnishing a picturesque and manageable motive, and with this scheme in my mind, I fell to work in earnest, first with the pencil and then with the wax and metal.

But busy as I was, and happy in the interest of my work I was yet aware of a change, of a something new that had come into my life. From the little workshop which had been my world, I found my thoughts straying out into the larger world, and particularly that part of it which is adjacent to Temple Bar; and if at times I viewed this change with some misgivings, I was more often conscious of a sense of exhilaration such as one feels when embarking on some new adventure.

In due course I received notice of my election as a member of the Magpies Club, and by the same post a letter from Mr Davenant asking me to celebrate the event by lunching with him there; and, as I had occasion to go into town to replenish my silver and some other materials, I accepted his invitation, intending to return to Wellclose Square in the afternoon. But it appeared that a loan collection of antique silver was being exhibited at the South Kensington Museum, and that he had hoped to have the pleasure of inspecting it under my expert guidance. Now, to a craftsman (or craftswoman) of small experience, there is no technical education to compare with the study of admitted masterpieces. I felt that strongly, and I felt that I needed that technical education;

furthermore, I felt that the attempt to explain the merits of the old work to an attentive and sympathetic listener would help me to concentrate my own attention. And perhaps it did. At any rate, I spent a long and pleasant afternoon at the museum, and we subsequently discussed the exhibits (and various other matters) very companionably over the dinner table at the club.

"It has been a jolly day for me, Mrs Otway," said Mr Davenant, as he wished me "goodbye" at the Underground Station. "I've learned no end about silver – you are a perfect encyclopaedia of knowledge in regard to goldsmith's work. And the delightful thing to think of is that we've only scratched the surface of the museum. The place is inexhaustible. Do you think I may hope for the pleasure of another visit there with you before long?"

I gave what I intended to be an ambiguous answer. But it was not ambiguous to me; and I suspect that Mr Davenant went on his way with a feeling that a precedent had been created.

When I arrived home, I found a letter awaiting me from Mr Otway. It was not entirely unexpected, for I had felt pretty certain that he would presently hear further from his mysterious correspondent. It now appeared that he had received one or two short letters, ostensibly of the nature of warnings, but actually threatening, though in vague, indefinite terms, and one more recently of a more explicitly menacing character. These he wished me to see and discuss with him, and he asked me to make an appointment, at my convenience, to meet him for that purpose. I replied, suggesting, as before, the Tower Wharf; and there, a couple of evenings later, I met him.

In appearance he had by no means improved. His pale face had a strained, wild expression, his eyelids were puffy and covered with curious, minute wrinkles. His hands were markedly tremulous, and his fingers bore the deep stains that mark the inveterate cigarette smoker. His dress was noticeably less neat than it had used to be; indeed, he presented a distinctly shabby and neglected appearance. Oddly enough, too, he seemed to have grown somewhat stouter.

I should have been less than human if these plain indications of sustained misery had awakened in me no feeling of pity. That his sufferings were the indirect result of his indifference to the happiness or misery of others, could not entirely stifle compassion, and I found myself speaking to him in a tone almost sympathetic.

"I am afraid, Mr Otway," said I, "you are letting these nonsensical letters worry you quite unnecessarily. You are not looking at all well."

"I am not at all well, Helen," he replied, dejectedly.

"And I think you are smoking too much."

"I am. And I am drinking too much – I, who have been a temperate man all my life. And I have to take drugs to get a decent night's rest. This worry is breaking me up."

"Oh, come, Mr Otway," I protested, "you mustn't give way in this manner. What is it all about, after all? Just a wretched blackmailer whom you know to be an imposter, whose threats you know to be mere empty vapourings."

"That is not quite true, Helen. The man is an impostor, no doubt. He doesn't really know anything. There is nothing for him to know. But he could create a great deal of trouble. He could, in fact, cause the – ah – the inquiry to be re-opened and –ah – "

"Exactly. And if it were re-opened? There would be unpleasant comment on the fact that a detail of the evidence had been withheld at the inquest. But that is the worst that could happen."

Mr Otway looked at me with a sort of dumb gratitude that was quite pathetic, but his gloom was in nowise dispelled by my optimism.

"It is very good of you, Helen," said he, "to speak in this cheerful, confident tone. But I assure you, you minimise the danger. There is no saying what construction might be put upon the suppression of that detail; what considerations of motive might be read into it – especially as there was what they would call collusion between us to suppress it. But let me show you the last letter – the others are of no consequence."

He produced his wallet, and, after some awkward fumbling, drew out the letter, which he held out to me with a hand that shook so that the paper rattled. Like the last, it was typewritten unskilfully, and characterised by the same semi-illiterate confusion in the wording, which ran thus:

"Mr Lewis Otway,
    "The writer of this warns you once more to look out for trouble. The person that I spoke of knows that something was held back at the inquest at least they say so and that they know why your wife won't live with you and that she knows all about it too and that someone knows more than you think anybody knows. This is a friendly warning.
                              "From a Well Wisher."

I returned the letter to Mr Otway after reading it through twice, and I must confess that my confidence was somewhat shaken. If the writer was merely guessing, he seemed to have an uncanny aptitude for guessing right. As to his claim to possess some further knowledge, I did not see how that could be possible. When the fatal interview took place between my father and Mr Otway, there were – to the best of my belief – only three persons in the house. Of those actually present at the interview there was only a single survivor – Mr Otway himself – and he alone knew with certainty what occurred. The claim was therefore almost certainly false. And yet, even as I dismissed it, there crept into my mind once again a vague discomfort, a doubt whether there might not be something that I was unaware of, and that Mr Otway knew; some dreadful secret that I, of all persons in the world, had been instrumental in guarding from discovery. And as I glanced at Mr Otway – haggard, wild, trembling, and terrified out of all proportion to the danger, so far as it was known to me – the horrid doubts seemed to deepen into something like suspicion.

    "Of course," said he, when he had returned the letter to the wallet, "I realise that you are right; that there is nothing to be done but to wait for this person to show his hand more plainly. It would be madness to apply to the police. They would immediately ask if there had been any evidence withheld and why you were not living with me. And if they succeeded in getting hold of the writer of this letter, we should have more to fear from them than from the writer himself. He may be, as you believe, a mere blackmailer who is preparing to extort money, but if he were brought to bay he would try to justify his threats."

With this I could not but agree. The implied allegations in this letter were, in point of fact, true; and any attempt to obtain help from the police would probably result in their truth being made manifest.

"Have you no idea whatever," I asked, "who might be the writer of this letter? He can hardly be a complete stranger. Have you no suspicion? Can you think of no one who might have written it?"

He looked at me furtively and cleared his throat once or twice before replying; and when he did answer, his manner was hesitating and even evasive.

"Suspicions," he said, "are – er – not very – ah – helpful. I have no facts. The mere – ah – conjecture that this person or that might possibly be concerned – if a motive could be supplied – and – ah – if one can think of no motive – "

He left the sentence uncompleted, giving me the vague impression that he was reserving something that he did not wish to discuss.

We were silent for some time, and I was beginning to consider bringing the interview to an end when he suddenly turned to me with a gesture of appeal.

"Helen," he said earnestly, "is it not possible for me to prevail on you to – ah – to reconsider your decision and – ah – to – to – to terminate this – er – this unhappy separation. Consider my loneliness, Helen, my broken health and this trouble – which is our joint trouble – and –ah – "

"Mr Otway," I answered, "it is not possible. I assure you it is not. I am deeply distressed to think of your unhappiness and to see you looking so ill, but I could not entertain what you suggest. You must remember that we are strangers. We have never been otherwise than separated. As we are so we must continue."

"You don't mean that we must always remain apart?" he exclaimed. "It was only meant to be a temporary separation."

"At any rate," I rejoined, "the time has not come to consider a change. But I shall be glad to hear how things go with you and to give you any help that I can."

I rose and held out my hand, which he took reluctantly (though it was the first time that I had ever offered to shake hands with him).

"I am driving you away, Helen," he said.

"No, indeed," I replied. "I had to go. You will write to me if anything fresh happens?"

He promised readily and we turned and walked away in opposite directions. When I had gone a little way I paused to look back at him; and as I noted his dejected droop and his air of something approaching physical decrepitude, I felt a pang – not of remorse, but of regret that I could not in some way lighten the burden of his evident misery. It is true that his unhappiness was of his own making, and that in wrecking his own life he had wrecked mine and my father's. But vindictiveness is a character alien to the civilised and developed mind. For what he had done I still loathed him; but it pained me to think of the haunting dread, the abiding fear that was his companion night and day.

CHAPTER SIXTEEN

The Sweated Artist

I had told Mr Otway that I had to go; but I did not tell him why. If I had, he would probably have been considerably startled. For the fact is that while we were talking I had formed a resolution which had rapidly matured – the resolution to go to Dr Thorndyke and make a clean breast of the whole affair. He had invited me to call on him and report from time to time, especially if I should be in need of advice or help, and I had been intending to write and propose a visit. Now, however, I decided to call on the chance of his being disengaged, and if he should be unable to see me, to make an appointment.

From the Tower Wharf I made my way quickly to Mark Lane, noting as I entered the station that it was a quarter to six; and as the train rumbled westward I turned over the situation and decided on what I should say. That some trouble was brewing I had little doubt, and though I did not share Mr Otway's alarm, I was more than a little uneasy. For, at the best, the re-opening of the inquiry into my father's death must entail a scandal and exhibit my conduct in a decidedly questionable light; and such a scandal would be a disaster. As a discredited witness, how could I face my comrades at Wellclose Square? And how should I stand with Jasper Davenant? These were unpleasant questions to reflect on. And underneath these reflections was the uneasy feeling that perhaps there was something more in Mr Otway's fear than was known to me; something of which I had hardly dared to think.

From the Temple Station I found my way without difficulty to Dr Thorndyke's chambers at Number 5A, King's Bench Walk, and was relieved to find the outer oak door open and a small brass knocker on the inner one tacitly accepting the possibility of visitors. I plied it modestly, and was immediately confronted by Mr Polton, whose countenance, at the sight of me, became covered with a network of benevolent and amicable wrinkles.

"The doctor is up in the laboratory looking over his apparatus, but I expect he has nearly finished. I'll go and tell him you are here. Have you had tea?"

I had not and admitted the fact, whereupon Mr Polton nodded meaningly, and having offered me an armchair, took his departure. In a minute or two Dr Thorndyke entered the room and greeted me with a cordiality that put me at my ease instantly.

"I have been wondering when you were coming to see me; in fact, I have seriously considered calling at Wellclose Square to see how you were getting on. Polton will bring you some tea in a moment, and then you must tell me all your news. I hope you are comfortable in your new home."

"I am very happy, indeed, Dr Thorndyke, and very grateful to you for finding me such a congenial home. And I have made quite a promising start in my new profession, too. But I have really come to ask your advice – and to make a confession."

"A confession," said Dr Thorndyke, looking at me gravely. "Is it necessary? and have you given it due consideration?"

"Yes, I think so. There is only one point. I should have told you this secret before, but as another person is involved in it, I felt that it would be a breach of confidence. But I now feel that my legal adviser should be told everything."

"That is so. Advice can only be based on known facts. And I may say that anything that you may tell me in my professional capacity is a privileged communication. A lawyer cannot be compelled to reveal anything that his client has told him, and is, in fact, forbidden to do so. You are, therefore, committing no breach of confidence in giving me any necessary information."

"I am glad to know that, because, when I last spoke to you about my affairs, I held back something that you may consider important."

"Something relating to the inquest?" he asked.

"Yes. Did you suspect that I had?"

"I suspected that Mr Otway was holding something back when he gave his evidence – but here is your tea, with all the little lady-like extras, just to show you what an old bachelor can do in the way of domestic miracles. I am ashamed of you, Polton. I call that embroidered tea-cloth sheer ostentation."

Mr Polton laid out the dainty service, beaming with satisfaction at the doctor's recognition of his efforts to maintain the credit of the establishment, and as he went out I heard him close the outer door.

"Polton evidently smells a conference," commented Dr Thorndyke. "The infallible way in which he always does the right thing without a word of instruction almost makes me believe in telepathy – which might be awkward if he were not as secret as an oyster. Now don't hurry, but tell me quietly what you want me to know."

Thus encouraged, I gave him the suppressed facts relating to the loaded stick that I had seen in Mr Otway's hand, and then told him about the mysterious letters. He listened very attentively, and seemed deeply interested, for he questioned me at some length about Mr Otway's establishment at Maidstone, his mode of life and such of his antecedents as were known to me.

"Is the stick in your possession or has Mr Otway got it?" he asked.

"I suppose he has it. At any rate, I have never seen it since that day."

"And you know nothing of any of his associates, other than the housekeeper?"

"Nothing whatever."

"Is Mrs Gregg still with him?"

"I believe so, but I am not sure."

"And you know nothing of his present mode of life excepting that he lives in Lyon's Inn Chambers?"

"No. I really know nothing about him."

"It is very satisfactory for you," Dr Thorndyke observed. "You are quite in the dark. These letters suggest an intention to extort money, but they may come from a personal enemy or from someone who has some design other than direct blackmail. And the question is, what cards does that person hold. Is he acting on a mere guess or has he any actual knowledge. The problem involves two questions: was there anyone in the house, that morning, besides you, your father and Mr Otway? and did anything occur on that occasion beyond what Mr Otway told you? The answer seems to be in the negative in both cases; but we cannot be certain on either point. Meanwhile, your position is very unpleasant, and Mr Otway's still more so, for his apprehensions, though perhaps exaggerated, are not entirely groundless. He has behaved with consummate folly. Whether his account of the tragedy be true or false, if he had had the courage to give it in full at the inquest, it must have been accepted in the absence of contrary evidence. But that is by no means the case now. If the inquiry were re-opened, a jury would tend to regard his suppression of certain facts as evidence of the importance of those facts.

"As to advice: there is nothing that you can do but try to forget these menacing letters. I will make a few cautious enquiries – though we have very little to go on; and you must let me know at once if there are any fresh developments."

This ended the conference, but not the conversation, for Dr Thorndyke insisted on a full account of my progress as a craftswoman, and even called down Mr Polton to give an expert opinion on Mr Campbell's prices; which opinion was to the effect that they were as good as could be expected.

"So," said Dr Thorndyke, as I rose to depart, "you have justified your rather bold choice of a profession. You have already made it an economic success, and with more experience on the commercial side, you will probably earn a very satisfactory livelihood."

This was encouraging enough, backed as it was by Mr Polton's practical experience. But with the other results of this conference I was much less satisfied. Indeed, my talk with Dr Thorndyke, though it had relieved me of the burden of concealment, so far from setting my apprehensions at rest, had rather increased them. Not only was it evident that he regarded these mysterious letters as indications of a real danger, but he clearly entertained the possibility that Mr Otway might have something more than I knew to conceal; in fact, I was by no means sure that he did not suspect Mr Otway of having killed my father.

Here, then, was abundant matter for reflection, and that none of the most pleasant; and during the next few days my mind was very full of these new complications of this dark cloud which had arisen over my brightening horizon. Again and again I recalled in detail the incidents of that terrible morning when my dear father was snatched from me, but no new light, either on the tragedy itself or on these sinister echoes of it, came to me. I even tried Lilith's crystal – having first locked my door – but either my faith was weak or I lacked those special psychical gifts with which its owner credited me. I did, indeed, get as far as the cloud, or mist, of which Lilith had spoken; which gathered before my eyes and blotted out the crystal. But that was all. When the mist cleared away, no picture emerged from it, but only the crystal ball with the diminutive image of my own head reflected on its bright surface.

But anxieties sit lightly on the young and healthy. As the days passed, the gloomy impressions faded and I became once more absorbed in my work. The Zodiac spoons were progressing apace, and were going to do me credit; and daily I became conscious of growing facility, of increasing skill, which not only lessened my labour but was itself a source of pleasure. To do a thing with ease is to do it with enjoyment; and, incidentally, added skill means added speed and greater earning power. Already I began to speculate on what Mr Campbell's idea of "a good price" would turn out to be.

Moreover, there were other distractions. Once or twice a week I looked in at the club, and these visits had a pleasant way of developing into impromptu jaunts – to picture galleries, exhibitions, museums, and even on one or two occasions a concert or a matinée. Of the relations which were growing up between Jasper Davenant and me I did not care to think much. Perhaps the ostrich is a wiser bird than we are apt to imagine, for it does, at least, avoid the pains of anticipation. Sooner or later, no doubt, some understanding would have to be arrived at; but meanwhile Mr Davenant was a delightful companion – gay, cheerful, buoyant, humorous, but withal a man of earnest purpose and a serious outlook on life. In all our junkettings there was little, real frivolity; the fun and gaiety were but the condiments to season the more solid and serious interests. In so far as a friendship between a young man and a young woman, which must necessarily stop at friendship, can be, our friendship was unexceptionable. But, of course, there was the qualification. However, as I have said, I let the future take care of itself and drifted pleasantly with the stream.

About this time, I made quite a startling discovery. It happened that in one of my journeys to town I had seen in a bookseller's window a book on studio pottery, and, thinking that it might be useful to Miss Finch, I had bought it, but had forgotten to give it to her. In the middle of my morning's work I suddenly remembered the book, which I had put in a cupboard in the workshop, and got up from my bench to take it to her. Her "works" were at the bottom of the garden, in an outhouse which had once been a shipsmith's shop; but, close neighbours as we were, and close friends, too, I had only once been in her workshop, when, on an off day, she had shown me her wheel, her lathe and her small glass kiln. About her work she was extraordinarily secretive; but then, she was a reticent girl in general, so far as her own affairs were concerned, though she showed a warm interest in her friends, and was, indeed, very affectionate and lovable.

As I came round the clump of bushes that hid her premises from the house, the silence and repose of the place gave me some qualms, and for a moment I hesitated to interrupt her work. However, I pocketed my scruples and rapped boldly on the door; whereupon the familiar voice at its highest pitch — several ledger lines above the stave — demanded who was there.

"It is I, Peggy; Helen Otway," I replied apologetically. There was a pause of nearly half a minute, and then she unlocked and opened the door, looking rather embarrassed and very pink.

"I always lock myself in when I am at work," she explained.

"Well, Peggy, don't let me disturb you. I've only brought you a book that I got for you in town."

"Oh, come in, Sibyl," said she. "Of course I don't mind you."

She took the volume from me, and quickly turning over the pages and glancing at the illustrations, exclaimed, "What a ripping book! I *shall* enjoy reading it. And how sweet of you to think of getting it for me!" She linked her arm affectionately in mine and conducted me into her domain, passing through the outer room, which was devoted to plaster work — the making of moulds and "bats" — to the clay room where the little gas engine and the mysterious wheel stood idle and a general tidying up appeared to have taken place. Here we stood chatting rather disjointedly, she still turning over the pages of the book with approving comments, and I looking about me with a craftsman's curiosity respecting the materials and appliances of an unfamiliar craft. And here I got my first surprise; for, on a side bench I noticed a collection of what were evidently bookbinder's tools. Was it possible that the secretive Titmouse was a bookbinder as well as a potter? I determined to enquire into this, but meanwhile my attention was attracted by the bench at which she had evidently been working, as suggested by the displaced stool. On this bench stood an object of some size — about twelve inches high — enveloped in a damp cloth. By its side were a spray-diffuser, a number of little spatulas and tiny bon modelling-tools and several little covered pots of a creamy, white earthenware delicately ornamented with floral decoration in a warm blue. Venturing to lift the cover of one, I found it to be filled with little rolls of brightly-tinted clay that looked like coloured crayons.

"You are mighty fastidious about your apparatus," I remarked, picking up the dainty little pot and wiping some smears of clay from its surface.

"And why not?" demanded Peggy. "Why shouldn't one have pretty things to work with? The old craftsmen did. I've seen some old planes and chisel-handles beautifully carved, and I am sure they did better work for having beautiful tools to work with. I would have pretty tools myself if I could make them."

"You shall, Peggy," said I. "You shall show me what you want and I will make them for you."

As I was speaking I absently turned the little pot upside down and glanced at the bottom. And then I really did get a shock. There was only a single spot of ornament on the base, but that spot was a revelation; for it was a little blue bird.

I smothered the exclamation that rose to my lips and put the pot down on the bench. What could be the meaning of this? Had Peggy, like Mr Hawkesley, been attracted by Mr Goldstein's wares? Or was it possible –

"Won't you show me what you were doing, Peggy?" I asked.

She turned scarlet at the question, and looked so distressed that I felt it a cruelty to press her. But cruel or not, I meant to get to the bottom of the mystery.

"I'd rather not, Sibyl, if you don't mind," she said, shyly.

"But why? What an extraordinary little person you are."

"Well," she said, doggedly, "if you must know, I am not allowed to show my work to anyone."

"Not allowed by whom?"

"By the dealer who takes all my work. For some reason, best known to himself, he makes a secret of it; won't allow anyone to know who makes it."

"But apart from the dealer, Peggy, you wouldn't mind my seeing your work?"

"Of course I shouldn't. I should like you to see it. But a promise is a promise, you know."

"Of course," I agreed; and then I stepped quickly up to the bench and very carefully picking up the damp cloth, lifted it clear of the object which it covered; which turned out to be a jar standing on a small turn-table. Peggy sprang forward with a gasp of consternation; but she was too late. The deed was done; moreover, the murder was out; for in the moment when my first glance fell on the jar, Mr Hawkesley's "mystery ware" had ceased to be a mystery so far as I was concerned.

The appearance of the jar was rather curious, but perfectly unmistakable. The clay, in its "green" state – unbaked and still somewhat plastic – was of a cool, grey colour, and the surface of the squat, octagonal body and the short neck and rim was covered with rich and intricate floral ornament, very minute, sharp and delicate. In the completed part this ornament was of dull blue and finished flush with the surface; in the unfinished part it was simply indented and had the appearance of what bookbinders call "blind tooling," but was somewhat deeper.

From the work, my eyes turned with a sort of respectful wonder to the creator, who stood by my side with an air partly embarrassed, partly defiant. To me there was something very impressive in the thought that this unassuming, little lady was actually a master craftsman (I am compelled to use the masculine form, there being no feminine equivalent); the creator of masterpieces which would live in the great collections of the future for the admiration of generations yet unborn. And in the first shock of surprised admiration and pride in my friend's achievement I had nearly blurted out all that I knew. But reflection suggested a better plan.

"My dear Peggy!" I exclaimed. "I never dreamed that you did work of this quality."

"There's nothing very wonderful about it," she replied, regarding the jar with a kind of affectionate disparagement. "It is only a poor imitation of the beautiful Oiron ware. That pottery has always interested me; partly because it is so lovely, and partly because, according to tradition, it was made by a woman – Helene de Hangest-Genlis. But my work isn't a patch of hers, and it isn't even as good as I could do."

"How is that?"

"Well, you see, it ought to have more modelled ornament than I put on. It ought to be more important. Her pieces were most elaborately modelled – many of them had figures in the full round. But I can't afford to carry my work as far as that. It would take too long. Besides, I have to work to order, to some extent, and my orders are to keep to moderately, simple pieces."

"Your orders! From the dealer, I suppose? Tell me about him, Peggy, and how it is that you are such a slave."

"I'm not a slave," she retorted doggedly. "But I have a contract with a dealer. He takes the whole of my work, and he makes it a condition that I shan't sell anything to anyone else or let anybody know what kind of work I do. I oughtn't to have let you in, but I know that I can trust you not to breathe a word to anyone of what you have seen here."

Mr Hawkesley was right, then; and I recalled with sympathetic vindictiveness his desire to wring the dealer's neck.

"Concerning this contract, Peggy," said I. "You say the dealer has the right to the whole of your work. Did he pay you anything for this privilege?"

"Yes. He paid five pounds when the agreement was signed; but he deducted it from the payment for the first lot of pieces."

"Then it was only payment on account, not payment for the exclusive right to all your work. And with regard to the prices, how are they fixed?"

"Oh, the dealer fixes the prices, of course. He knows more about it than I do."

"Evidently. But what sort of prices does he fix?"

"Oh, ordinary prices, I suppose. He will probably give me fifteen shillings for this jar."

"And how long will it take you to make it?"

"Let me see," she said, reflectively. "There is the throwing and turning; that doesn't take very long. Then this one had to be shaped after it was turned. Then there comes the decorating; of course that is what takes the time. Including the cover, I should say there is nearly a week's work in that jar. And then it has to be fired and glazed; but the firing and glazing are done in batches."

"And all this for fifteen shillings a week!" I exclaimed.

"Say a pound," said she. "That is about what I earn. It isn't much, is it? But I have a little money of my own, though I spent most of it on fitting up the workshop."

"And what period does this precious contract cover? When does it expire?"

"Expire?" she repeated, a little sheepishly. "I don't know that it expires at all. No period is mentioned in it."

"Peggy," I said, solemnly; "you should alter your potter's mark. Take out the little, blue finch and put in a little, green goose. But, seriously, we must see into this. I am a lawyer's daughter – not that I profess to have inherited a knowledge of law. But I am certain that this agreement is not binding. Will you let me show it to a friend of mine who is a lawyer? In strict confidence, of course."

"Yes, if you like, Sibyl. But I don't see that it matters. I like doing the work and I do make a living by it. What more would you have?"

"I thought you said you would like to do something more ambitious – the very best work of which you are capable. Wouldn't you?"

She was silent for a while, and a faraway, wistful look stole into her face. Suddenly she said: "Sibyl, I'm going to show you something; but you mustn't tell anyone." She led me to a large cupboard, the door of which she unlocked and threw open. On the single shelf was a model in red wax of a tall candlestick or lamp-holder of the most elaborate design, the shaft and capital-like socket enriched – though sparingly – with fine relief decoration, and the base occupied by a spirited and graceful group of figures, beautifully modelled and full of life and expression.

"That," she said, "is to be my *chef d'œuvre*, though it doesn't look much in the wax. You must think of it in ivory-white, with a rich coloured inlay and perhaps some under-glaze painting. It has taken me months, doing a bit whenever I have had time, or when I couldn't resist the temptation to go on with it. Now it is finished, as far as the modelling goes, and the next thing will be to mould it. But I shan't actually make the piece at present, because I don't mean *him* to have it – the dealer, you know. If I finished it now, it would be his, of course."

"Yes, by the contract it would. And it mustn't. This piece ought to give you a position in the front rank of artist potters. But I mustn't waste any more of your time. You will let me have that agreement, won't you?"

She promised that I should have it at lunch-time, and with this I went back to my workshop to consider a plan that had come into my mind for her enlightenment and emancipation. But it turned out that there was no need for scheming on my part, for chance or Providence offered me the opportunity ready-made. That very evening I received a short note from Mr Davenant informing me that Miss Tallboy-Smith had acquired a collection of English and French soft porcelain, and that she proposed to exhibit the whole of her new acquisition for a week at the club.

"She rather wants," he said, "to make the opening day something of a function, and has asked Hawkesley and me to be there to lunch. Can you come, too? It would please her if you could – and you know how delighted Hawkesley and I would be. Besides, I think it will really be a very interesting show."

Here was the very chance that I wanted. Forthwith, I swooped down on the unsuspecting Titmouse and secured her agreement to bear me company to a "pottery show," without giving too many particulars. Then I wrote to Mr Davenant telling him that I was bringing a guest who was deeply interested in pottery and porcelain, and suggesting that we might form a party of four at a small table.

By the same post I sent off Peggy's agreement to Dr Thorndyke, with the request that he would tell me whether it was or was not legally binding. And, having thus laid the train, as I hoped, for the discomfiture of Mr Goldstein, I felt at liberty to return to my own affairs.

CHAPTER SEVENTEEN

The Apotheosis of the Titmouse

The respective merits of hard and soft porcelain have been, from time to time, warmly debated by collectors and experts, but never, perhaps, have they been more earnestly discussed than on the occasion of the opening of Miss Tallboy-Smith's exhibition. During the half-hour which preceded lunch, the central glass case and the additional show-cases which had been set up for the occasion were surrounded by groups of eager connoisseurs, and the contrasting virtues of the *pâte tendre* and the more durable, if less beautiful, true porcelain were once more considered and expounded.

The attendance of the members and their friends must have been highly gratifying to Miss Tallboy-Smith, though it was no greater than was warranted by the importance of the exhibition; for the collection included representative pieces, not only of Chelsea, Bow, Nantgarw, Pinxton, and other English ware; but also of the old, French soft paste porcelain, including several early examples of Sevres. The preliminary glance at the collection had furnished material for conversation, as I could see by observing the occupants of the long central table, at the head of which sat the beaming hostess, supported by Major Dewham-Brown (who talked little, but consumed his food with intense concentration of purpose); and even our own small table tucked away inconspicuously in a corner, was not immune from the influence of soft porcelain, for Mr Hawkesley and my guest discussed the topic with a wealth of knowledge that reduced Mr Davenant and me to respectful and attentive silence.

Our two friends were evidently very pleased with one another; and not without reason. For Mr Hawkesley was much more than a mere collector; he was an enthusiastic and learned student of all kinds of ceramic work; while, as to my friend Peggy, her conversation revealed a familiarity with all kinds of materials and processes that made me feel quite shy as I thought of the artless handbook with which I had presented her.

But, indeed, Miss Peggy was quite transfigured. She had met with a kindred spirit. And under the influence of contagious enthusiasm, the usually silent and secretive Titmouse blossomed out in a manner that surprised me. As I listened to the animated duet of her chirping treble with Mr Hawkesley's robust baritone, I found it difficult to identify her with the quiet little potter who was wont to work behind locked doors in the old shipsmith's shop at Wellclose Square.

After lunch the siege of the showcases began again on a more portentous scale. Glass cases were opened for more complete inspection of their contents, and pieces were even handed out to be handled, stroked and smelled at by the more infatuated devotees. As neither Mr Davenant nor I could be included among the latter, we were satisfied by a comparatively brief inspection of the treasures, after which we retired to a sheltered seat to look on and talk.

"Just look at those two china-maniacs!" exclaimed Mr Davenant. "They are as thick as thieves already. And what is Miss Finch going to do with that *bieu de roi* vase? Is she going to kiss it? No; she has given it back to the Tallboy-Smith. Well, well; enthusiasm is a fine thing. By the way she is a nice little lady, this friend of yours; pretty and picturesque, too, and uncommonly well turned out. I'm beginning to have a new respect for Wellclose Square."

I looked at the Titmouse with a sort of motherly pride (though she was about my own age). The word picturesque described her admirably with her warm colour, her graceful hair, and the trim, petite figure that was so well set off by the simple, artistic dress – in which I seemed to trace the hand of Lilith. She was my importation to the Magpies, and I felt that she was doing me credit.

"I have often wondered," Mr Davenant said, after a reflective pause, "what made you choose such an unlikely locality as Wellclose Square for a residence, and, indeed, how you came to know of its existence. Very few middle-class people do. I hope Miss Vardon will not consider me unduly inquisitive."

"Mrs Otway will not," said I.

"Mrs Otway is a myth – a legal fiction. I refuse to recognise her existence. She is a mere creature of documents, of church registers. The real person is Miss Helen Vardon."

"That sounds rather like nonsense," said I, "but, of course, it can't be, because the speaker is Mr Davenant. Perhaps there is some hidden meaning in these cryptic observations."

"There isn't," he rejoined; "or, at any rate, it shan't remain hidden. I mean that I refuse to recognise your connection with this man, Otway, or to associate you with his beastly name."

"But it is my beastly name, too, according to law and custom."

"I don't care for law and custom," said he. "The name Otway is abhorrent to me, and it doesn't properly belong to you. I shall call you Miss Vardon, unless you let me call you, Helen; and I don't see why you shouldn't, considering that we are old and intimate friends."

"It would undoubtedly have the support of a well-established precedent. There was a certain bishop who was called Peter because that was his name. That precedent would apply to Helen, but it certainly would not to Miss Vardon."

"Then," he rejoined, "let us follow this excellent precedent. Let it be Helen. Is that agreed?"

"I don't seem to have much choice; for if 'Mrs Otway' is a legal fiction, 'Miss Vardon' is an illegal one."

"Well, don't let us have any fictions at all. Let us adhere to the actual baptismal facts."

"Very well, Mr Davenant."

"But why 'Mr Davenant'? My baptismal designation is 'Jasper.' "

"And a very pretty name, too," said I. "But the precedent does not apply in your case. You have not married Mr Otway."

"No, thank Heaven! If I had, there would be a case of petty treason. But neither have you, for that matter. You have only gone through a ridiculous ceremony which means nothing and signed a document which sets forth what is not true."

"It seems to me," I said, "that we are not adhering to our agreement to avoid fictions. My marriage unfortunately, is perfectly real and valid in the eyes of the law."

"The law!" he exclaimed, contemptuously. "Who cares for the law? Have we not the pronouncement of that illustrious legal luminary, Bumble C.J., that the law is a ass and a idiot? And, mark you, he was specially referring to matrimonial law. Now, who would base his actions and beliefs on the opinions of a ass and a idiot?"

"And to think," said I, "that you have abandoned the law for mere architecture! With your gift for casuistry, you ought to have been a Chancery lawyer or else a Jesuit. But here is Miss Tallboy-Smith. She thinks we are neglecting her treasures."

But our hostess had not come to utter reproaches. On the contrary, she was brimming over with pleasure and gratitude.

"My dear Mrs Otway," she exclaimed, beaming on me and grasping my hands affectionately, "I can't thank you enough for bringing that dear young lady Miss Finch, to see my porcelain. She is a *sweet* girl, and she simply knows *everything* about china. It is perfectly wonderful. She might be a potter herself. And her love of the beautiful things and her enjoyment in looking at them has given me, I can't tell you how much, pleasure. You must really bring her to see my whole collection. Will you? I shall love showing it to her."

I agreed joyfully, for this would mean another nail in the coffin of Mr Goldstein; and as Peggy and Mr Hawkesley joined us at this moment, I was able to complete the arrangement and fix a date.

As Miss Tallboy-Smith bustled away, Mr Hawkesley put in his claim.

"I don't see," said he, "why I should be left out in the cold. I've got a collection, too; and I think it would really interest Miss Finch, for she tells me she has seen very little modern pottery. Won't you bring her to see it, Mrs Otway?"

Again I accepted gladly, with Peggy's consent. My scheme was working rapidly towards a successful conclusion, and I felt that I could push it forward energetically; for that very morning I had received a letter from Dr Thorndyke returning the agreement and denouncing it as legally worthless and utterly opposed to public policy.

"As to fixing a date," said Mr Hawkesley, "I suggest that we all adjourn to my rooms now. Come and have a cup of tea with me and then we can look over the crockery. How will that do?"

It suited Peggy and me quite well, and we said so.

"And you Davenant?" asked Mr Hawkesley.

"Well, I had one or two cathedrals to finish," was the reply; "but they must wait. Art is long – deuced long, in my case. Yes, let us adjourn and combine crockery and tea – which, as Pepys reminds us is a 'China drink,' and therefore appropriate to the occasion."

On this, we sallied forth and made our way to the Strand, where we chartered a couple of hansoms to convey us to Dover Street, Piccadilly, where Mr Hawkesley had his abode in one of those fine, spacious, dignified houses that one finds in the hinterland of the West End of London. His rooms were on the first floor, and when we arrived there by way of a staircase which would have allowed us to walk up four abreast, we were received by a sedate and impassive gentleman, whose appearance and manner suggested a Foreign Office official of superior rank.

"Would you let us have some tea, please Taplow?" said Mr Hawkesley, addressing the official deferentially. Mr Taplow opened a door for us, and having signified a disposition to accede to the request, departed stealthily.

As we entered the large, lofty room, well lighted by its range of tall windows, I looked about me curiously, for I was instantly struck by the absence of pottery among its ornaments. The available wall-spaces were occupied by important pictures – all modern; the mantelpiece and other suitable surfaces supported statuettes of marble or bronze – again all modern. But of ceramic ware there was not a trace, with the single exception of a small framed cameo relief. Rather did the apartment suggest the abode of a furniture collector, for one side of the room, opposite the windows, was occupied by a range of armoires, or standing cupboards mostly old French or Flemish.

"You don't favour the glass case, I notice, Hawkesley," said Mr Davenant.

"No," was the reply. "They are well enough for public museums, but they are unlovely things. And one doesn't want to look at one's whole collection at once. I like to take the pieces out singly and enjoy them one at a time. You see, each piece is an individual work. It was the product of a separate creative effort, and ought to be enjoyed by a separate act of appreciation."

"You seem, Mr Hawkesley," said I, "to have a preference for modern work. Do you think it is as good as the old?"

"I think," he replied, "that the best modern work is as good as any that was ever done. Of course I am not speaking of commercial stuff. That is negligible in an artistic sense. I mean individual work, done under the same conditions and by the same class of men as the old craft work. That is quite good. The pity is that there is so little of it. But I am afraid the supply is equal to the demand."

"Don't you think," said Mr Davenant "that that is partly the fault of the modern craftsman? Of his tendency to confine himself to fine and elaborate, and therefore costly, productions? Of course the old work was not cheap in the modern factory sense of cheapness. The pottery and china that was made at the Etruria works or those of Bow or Chelsea was by no means given away.

But the prices were practicable for everyday purposes, whereas modern studio pottery is impossible for domestic use. And the same is true of other craftwork such as book-binding, fine printing, textiles, metal work, and so on. If the modern craftsman caters only for the collector and ignores the utilitarian consumer, he can't complain at being ousted by commercial production."

Here the arrival of Mr Taplow with the tea arrested what threatened to prove a too-interesting discussion. I should have liked to continue it – on another occasion; at present, my desire was rather to "cut the cackle and get to the hosses." Accordingly, while the tea was being consumed, I rather studiously obstructed any revival of the debate by keeping up a conversation of a general and somewhat discursive character; and as soon as we appeared to have finished I introduced the subject of Ceramics.

"Is that plaque on the wall a Wedgwood cameo?" I asked.

"Oh, no," Mr Hawkesley replied. "That is an example of Solon's wonderful *pâte-sur-pâte* work. It is done with white porcelain slip on a dark, coloured ground. Come and look at it."

We all rose and gathered round the plaque while Mr Hawkesley descanted on its beauties; which were, indeed, evident enough.

"It is lovely work," said he; "so free and spontaneous. The Wedgwood reliefs look quite stiff and hard compared with these of Solon's. I have some of his vases with the same kind of decoration, and we may as well look at those first."

He wheeled a travelling turn-table towards a fine Flemish armoire of carved oak, and opening the latter, displayed a range of pieces of this beautiful work, at the sight of which Peggy's eyes glistened. One after another they were carefully, placed on the turn-table, viewed from all points, admired, discussed and replaced. The other contents of the armoire were less important works – mostly French – but all received respectful attention. The next receptacle, a French armoire of carved walnut, was devoted to modern stoneware by the Martin Brothers, Wells and other individual workers, concerning which our host was specially enthusiastic.

"There," said he, placing on the turn-table a wonderful Toby jug of brown Martin ware, "Show me any old salt-glaze ware that is equal to that! Look at the modelling! Look at the beautiful surface and the quality of the actual potting! And then go and look at the stuff in the shop windows. Just good enough for the slavey to smash."

"Well," Mr Davenant remarked, "you can't say that she doesn't appreciate its qualities and do justice to them. If former generations had been as energetic smashers as the present, collectors of old stuff would have had to seek their treasures in ancient rubbish-heaps."

"Yes, that is a fact," agreed Mr Hawkesley, as we moved on to the next cupboard. "When domestic pottery was more valuable it got more respectful treatment. Now this cupboard is only partly filled. I keep it for the work of one artist whose name I don't know. I've shown you some of the ware, Mrs Otway, but it may be new to Miss Finch."

As he unlocked the door my heart began to thump, and I cast an anxious eye on Peggy. For I knew what was coming, but I didn't know how she would take it. At the moment she was looking at the closed door with pleased expectancy. Then the door swung open, and in a moment she turned pale as death. For one instant I thought she was going to faint, and so, apparently, did Mr Davenant, for he made a quick movement towards her. But the deadly pallor passed, and was succeeded as rapidly by a crimson flush; but her quick breathing and the trembling of her hand showed how great the shock had been.

Meanwhile, Mr Hawkesley, all unconscious, was glancing over the row of vases, jars and bowls, and expatiating on the peculiar beauties of the "mystery ware." The pieces were separated into two groups; the works in pure inlay and those combining the inlay with slip decoration and embossed ornament; and one of the latter he presently lifted from its shelf and placed on the turn-table.

"Now, isn't that a lovely jar, Miss Finch?" said he. "And doesn't it remind you of the beautiful St Porchaire, or Oiron ware?"

Peggy gazed at the jar with an inscrutable expression as she slowly rotated the turn-table. "It is somewhat like," she agreed; "at least, the method of work is similar."

"Oh don't give my favourites the cold shoulder, Miss Finch," said Mr Hawkesley.

"I think I prize my pieces of this ware more than anything that I have. It is so very charming and so interesting. For, you see, it is real pottery; I mean that, beautiful and precious as it is, it is quite serviceable for domestic purposes, whereas much of the studio pottery is made for the gallery or the cabinet."

"You haven't discovered yet where it is made, I suppose?" I asked.

"No," he replied. "Its origin is still a mystery and something of a romance – which may be one reason why I am so devoted to it. I often speculate about the potter, and invent all sorts of queer theories about him."

"As for instance?"

"Well, sometimes I fancy that he may be in debt to this dealer – that he may have had advances or loans and be unable to pay them off and get free. It is quite possible, you know. Then, sometimes I have thought that he may be one of those poor creatures who drink or take drugs, and that the dealer may keep him slaving in some cellar for his bare maintenance and his miserable luxuries. But I've given that idea up. This work is too sane and reasonable and painstaking for a drunkard or drug-taker. But, whoever and whatever he is, I wish I could find him out, and thank him for all the pleasure that he has given me, and help him to get a proper reward for his labour, which I am sure he does not."

"I don't know why you are so sure," said Mr Davenant. "This ware is pretty expensive, isn't it?"

"Not if you consider that each piece is an individual work on which a great deal of time and labour has been expended. The price that I paid Goldstein for this particular piece was seven guineas which wouldn't represent very high remuneration if the artist had the whole of it."

"Seven guineas, Mr Hawkesley!" exclaimed Peggy, incredulously.

"Yes, Miss Finch; and I should say very cheap at the price."

I glanced at Peggy with malicious satisfaction, for her cheeks were aflame with anger and the light of battle was in her eyes.

"What a shame!" she protested. "How perfectly scandalous! The grasping, avaricious wretch! To charge seven guineas for a piece that he bought for fifteen shillings!"

For a few seconds there was an awesome silence. Peggy's exclamation had fallen like a thunderbolt, and the two men gazed at her in speechless astonishment; while she, poor Titmouse, stood, covered with blushes and confusion, looking as if she had been convicted of pocketing the spoons.

"You actually know," Mr Hawkesley said, at length, "that Goldstein gave only fifteen shillings for that jar?"

"Yes," she stammered faintly, "I – I happen to have – to be aware – that – that was the amount paid – "

She broke off with an appealing glance at me, and I proceeded to "put in my oar."

"It's no use, Peggy. The cat is out of the bag – at least her head is, and we may as well let out the rest of her. The fact is, Mr Hawkesley, that this ware is Miss Finch's own work."

I now thought that Mr Hawkesley was going to faint. Never have I seen a man look so astonished. He was thunderstruck.

"Do you mean, Mrs Otway," he exclaimed, "that Miss Finch actually makes this ware herself?"

"I do. It is her work from beginning to end. She does the potting, the decorating, the firing and the glazing. And she does it without any assistance whatever."

Mr Hawkesley gazed at Peggy with such undissembled admiration and reverence that I was disposed to smile – though I liked him for his generous enthusiasm – and the unfortunate Titmouse was reduced to an agony of shyness.

"This is a red letter day for me, Miss Finch," said he. "It has been my dearest wish to meet the creator of that pottery that I admire so intensely; and now that wish is gratified, it is an extra pleasure to find the artist so much beyond – "

He paused to avoid the inevitable compliment, and Mr Davenant held up a warning finger.

"Now, Hawkesley," said he; "be careful."

"I know," said Mr Hawkesley. "It is difficult to steer clear of banal compliments and yet to say what one would like to say; but really the personality of the mysterious artist has furnished a very pleasant surprise."

"I can believe that," said Mr Davenant. "I can imagine, for instance, that you find Miss Finch a very agreeable substitute for the intoxicated gentleman in the cellar."

At this we all laughed, which cleared the air and put us at our ease.

"But," said Mr Davenant, "proud as we are to have made the acquaintance of a distinguished potter, we are haunted by the spectre of that fifteen shillings. We get the impression that Miss Finch's business arrangements want looking into."

"Yes," agreed Mr Hawkesley, "they do indeed. Why do you let this fellow have your work, at such ridiculous prices, too?"

"It isn't so ridiculous as it looks," replied Peggy. "When I began, I couldn't sell any of my work at all. It was frightfully discouraging. No one would have anything to do with it. My first work was simple earthenware, and even the cheap china shops wouldn't have it. Then I chanced upon Mr Goldstein, and he bought one or two simple, red earthenware jars and bowls for a few pence each. It didn't pay me, but still it was a start. Then I experimented on this pipe-clay body with slip decoration and coloured inlay and showed the pieces to Mr Goldstein; and he advised me to go on and offered to take the whole of my work if I signed an agreement. So I signed the agreement, and he has had all my work ever since."

"At his own prices?"

"Yes. I didn't know what the things were worth."

"Well," said Mr Davenant, "my law is a trifle rusty, but I should say that that agreement would not hold water."

"It won't," said I. "We have just had counsel's opinion on it, and our adviser assures us that it is worthless, and that we can disregard it."

"Then," said Mr Davenant, "you had better formally denounce it at once."

"Why trouble to denounce it?" demanded Mr Hawkesley. "Much better let me call on Goldstein and make him tear up the duplicate. He has got a fine, handy warming-pan hanging up in his shop. I saw it only this morning."

"The connection is not very clear to me," said I.

"It would be clear enough to him," was the grim reply.

Mr Davenant chuckled. "Your methods, Hawkesley, appeal to me strongly, I must admit; but they are not politic. Legal process is better than a warming-pan, even if it were filled with hot coals. Let us hand the agreement to a reputable solicitor, and let him write to Goldstein stating the position. Miss Finch won't hear any more of her benefactor after that."

After some discussion, in which I supported Mr Hawkesley's proposal, the less picturesque method of procedure was adopted, and Mr Davenant was commissioned to carry it out.

"And we will have a one woman show of Blue Bird Ware at the club," said Mr Hawkesley. "I will take my whole collection there and exhibit it with a big label giving the artist's name in block capitals. The pottery collectors will just tumble over one another to get specimens of the work when the artist is known."

The rest of Mr Hawkesley's collection received but a perfunctory consideration. Even the gorgeous De Morgan earthenware, glowing with the hues of the rainbow, came as something of an anticlimax; and we closed the last of the cabinets with almost an air of relief.

"And now," said Mr Hawkesley, as he pocketed his keys, "I suggest that we mark this joyful occasion by a modest festival – say, a homely little dinner at the club and an evening at the play. Who seconds my proposal?"

"We shall have to go as we are then," said I, "as we can't change."

"I think we can enjoy ourselves in morning dress," he rejoined; "and as we shall all be in the same shocking condition, we can keep one another in countenance."

The proposal was accordingly adopted with acclamation and carried into effect with triumphant success, and some slight disturbance of the orderly routine of the establishment in Wellclose Square; for it was on the stroke of midnight when Miss Polton, blinking owlishly, opened the green door to admit the two roisterers who had just emerged from a handsom-cab.

"It *has* been a jolly day!" Peggy exclaimed fervently as we said "goodnight" on our landing. "And it will be a jolly tomorrow, too."

"Yes; you will be able to get on with your masterpiece now; and when it is finished we can show it at the club and you will be able to sell it for a small fortune."

"I shan't want to sell it," she said. "If it is good enough and if it wouldn't seem too forward or improper, I should like to give it to Mr Hawkesley – as a sort of thank-offering, you know."

"Thank-offering for what?"

"For his appreciation of my work. I really feel very grateful to him, as well as to you, Sibyl, dear. You see, he not only liked the things, but he thought of the worker who made them.

"All the time that I was working alone, with the door locked, from morning to night to fill that cormorant's pockets, Mr Hawkesley was thinking of me, the unknown worker looking for me and wanting to help me. I don't forget that it is you who have got me out of Mr Goldstein's clutches. But I do feel very, very grateful to Mr Hawkesley.

"Don't you think it is quite natural that I should, Sibyl?"

"I think you are a little, green goose," said I, and kissed her; and so ended the day that saw the end of her servitude and the dawn of prosperity and success.

CHAPTER EIGHTEEN

Among the Breakers

My preoccupation with Peggy Finch's affairs had to some extent submerged my own, but now that my little friend had triumphantly emerged from the house of Bondage, I returned to my labours with a new zest. In spite of the various interruptions the Zodiac spoons had made steady progress and it was but a few days after our momentous visit to Mr Hawkesley's rooms that, almost regretfully, I put the finishing touches to the Fishes spoon – the last of the set.

It had been a pleasant labour, and as I laid out the completed set, I was not dissatisfied. True, there had been difficulties; but difficulties are the salt of craftsmanship. Some of the signs, such as Aries, Taurus, Leo, Virgo and Capricornus, had been quite simple, the head of the Ram, the Bull, or other symbolic creature furnishing an obvious and appropriate knop for the spoon. But others such as Gemini, Pisces, and especially Libra, had been less easy to manage. Indeed, the last had involved a slight evasion; for, since it seemed quite impossible to work a pair of scales into a presentable knop, I had relegated them to the shoulder of the bowl and formed the knop of a more or less appropriate head of Justice blindfolded. So all the difficulties had been met by a pleasant and interesting exercise of thought and ingenuity, and the work – my magnum opus, for the present – was finished. And it was rounded off by a very agreeable little addition; for Phyllis Barton, who had seen and greatly admired the set, had made a delightful little case to contain it – just a pair of walnut slab hinged together, the lower slab having twelve shaped recesses to hold the spoons and the lid ornamented with shallow carvings of a winged hour-glass and the phases of the moon.

I made up the spoons into a parcel and the case into another, so that they should not be treated together in a single transaction; and having advised Mr Campbell by a letter on the previous day, set forth one morning for Wardour Street. The silent willing which should have preceded my entry to the shop was inadvertently omitted, for as I crossed the street I observed Mr Campbell exchanging blandishments with a large Persian cat of the smoky persuasion, and, as he saw me at the same moment, I had no choice but to enter straightway.

He received me with the most encouraging affability – indeed, he even condescended to shake hands – and was evidently pleased to see me. And his reception of my work was still more encouraging. There was none of the buyer's proverbial disparagement. He was frankly enthusiastic. He held up each spoon separately at arm's length wagging his head from side to side; he inspected it through a watchmaker's lens; he stroked it with a peculiarly flexible thumb, and finally laid it down with a grunt of satisfaction. Then came the question of terms; and when he offered twenty-four guineas for the set, I was quite glad that the silent willing had been omitted. For I should probably have willed eighteen.

Having settled the price of my own work, I produced the wooden case. Phyllis had priced it at half a guinea, which was ridiculous. I boldly demanded a guinea for it.

"That's a long price," said Mr Campbell, pulling a face of proportionate length. But I watched his thumb travelling over the clean-cut carving, I saw him delicately fitting the spoons, one by one, into their little niches, and I knew that that guinea was as good as in Phillibar's pocket.

"It *is* a long price Mrs Otway," he repeated cocking his head on one side at the case. "But it's a pretty bit of work; and it's the right thing – that's what I like about it. Tho thootable; it would be a sin to put those spoons unto a velvet-lined case, as if they were common, stamped, trade-goods. Very well Mrs Otway, I'll spring a guinea for the case; and I should like to see some more work from the same hand."

This was highly satisfactory (though it was not without a pang of bereavement that I saw the little case closed and hidden from my sight for ever in a locked drawer); and when I had received the two cheques – I asked for a separate one for Phyllis – I tripped away down Wardour Street as buoyantly as if I had not a care in the world.

The association of ideas is a phenomenon that has received a good deal of attention. It was brought to my notice on this occasion when I found myself opposite St Anne's Church; for no sooner had my eye lighted on its quaint, warty spire than my thoughts turned to Mr Davenant – or rather, I should say, to Jasper. Perhaps he was in my mind already; possibly in the subconscious, as Lilith would have said, and the church spire may have acted as an autoscope – it would not have had to be an exceptionally powerful one. At any rate, my thoughts turned to him and to the Magpies Club and it was not unnatural that my steps should take a similar direction.

As I followed the well-remembered route, I reflected on the changes that a few short months had brought. In that brief space a new life had opened. The solitary, friendless orphan who had sought sanctuary in Miss Polton's house, how changed was her condition! Happy in her work, in her home, in her friends; for had she not her Lilith, her Phyllis, her Peggy – and Jasper? And here a still, small voice asked softly but insistently a question that had of late intruded itself from time to time. Whither was I drifting? My friendship with Jasper was ripening apace. But ripening to what? There could be but one answer; and that answer only raised a further question. In normal circumstances the love of a man and a woman finds a permanent satisfaction in marriage. But where marriage is impossible love is a mere disaster; a voyage with nothing but rocks and breakers at the end.

So whispered the still, small voice into ears but half attentive; and as I neared the bottom of Essex Street it became inaudible, for approaching the club-house from the opposite direction was Jasper himself.

"Well!" he exclaimed, "this is a piece of luck! And yet I had hoped that you might be coming into town today. Is it business or pleasure?"

"It has been business, and now I hope it is going to be pleasure. I am taking the rest of the day off."

"Now, what a very singular coincidence! I am actually taking the rest of the day off myself."

"Your coincidences," I remarked, "somehow remind me of the misadventures of the bread-and-butter fly; they always happen."

"Quite so," he agreed. "But then, you see, if they didn't happen they wouldn't be coincidences. Do we begin by fortifying ourselves with nourishment?"

"I don't know what you mean by 'begin,' but I came here to get some lunch."

"So did I – another coincidence, by the way. Shall we take our usual little table in the corner?"

We seated ourselves at the table, and as we waited for our lunch to be brought, I ventured on a few enquiries into Jasper's professional affairs.

"You seem to take a good many days off," I remarked.

"I do. There is, so to speak, a distinctly marked 'off side' to my practice."

"And when you are away, what happens? Do you keep a clerk?"

Jasper grinned. "You over-estimate the magnitude of my practice. No; I have a simpler and more economical arrangement. I let my little front office to a law writer, at a peppercorn rent, subject to the condition that he shall interview my clients in my absence, furnish evasive answers to their questions, and supply ambiguous and confusing information."

"But don't the clients get rather dissatisfied?"

Again Jasper smiled. "That question," said he, "involves an important philosophic principle. A famous philosopher has proved his own existence by the formula '*cogito, ergo sum*' – I think, therefore I am – implying that if he didn't exist he couldn't think. Now, that principle applies to my clients. Before they can be dissatisfied, they must exist. But they don't exist. Therefore they are not dissatisfied. Q.E.D."

"I don't believe you care whether they exist or not – but that is the worst of having an independent income."

"It is a misfortune, isn't it? But I bear up under it surprisingly. Will you have some of this stuff? It is called a *pelion*. I heard the waitress describing it as a pea-lion, apparently misled by the analogy of the pea-cock and the pea-hen. Evidently she is no zoologist."

At this moment Miss Tallboy-Smith entered the room and halted at our table to exchange greetings and remind me of my engagement.

"Tell Miss Finch not to forget," said she. "It's next Wednesday. I shall have my things back from here by then, and I understand that Mr Hawkesley has secured the cases for a special exhibition of studio pottery. You must bring Miss Finch to that, too."

Like Jasper's proxy, I gave an evasive answer to this, for I knew that wild horses would not drag Peggy to an exhibition of her own work. But evidently Mr Hawkesley had made no confidences so far.

"Have you ever seen the Diploma Gallery at the R.A.?" Jasper asked when Miss Tallboy-Smith had flitted away. "If you haven't, we might look in there for an hour this afternoon."

As I had never seen the diploma works, I fell in readily with the suggestion, and accordingly, when we had finished lunch, we strolled thither and spent a very pleasant hour examining and comparing the works of the different academicians, old and new.

From Burlington House we drifted into the Green Park, and presently took possession of a couple of isolated and lonely-looking chairs. For some time we gossiped about the pictures at which we had been looking in the gallery; then our talk turned on to the affairs of my friend Peggy.

"Hawkesley seems to have appointed himself Miss Finch's advertising agent," Jasper remarked. "And he'll do the job well. He is an energetic man, and he knows all the pottery connoisseurs. I met him yesterday, and had to listen to Blue Bird ware by the yard."

"I like him for his enthusiasm," said I.

"So do I," agreed Jasper. "And it is quite a little romance. His admiration of the pottery is perfectly genuine, as we know; but there is something in what he calls 'the personality of the artist.' I think he is distinctly 'taken' with your pretty little friend. How does she like him?"

"I think she is decidedly prepossessed. At any rate, she is profoundly grateful to him for discovering her work, and especially for the interest that he took in the unknown worker."

"There you are, then," said Jasper. "There are the ingredients of a life-size romance. Fervid admiration on the one side, gratitude on the other, and good looks and good nature on both. We shall see what we shall see, Helen; and I, for one, shall look on with the green eyes of envy."

"Why will you? Do you want Peggy Finch for yourself?"

"I want Hawkesley's good fortune. If he loves this little maid and thinks she cares for him, he can ask her to marry him. That is what makes me envious."

I made no reply; indeed, there was nothing to say; and already the sound of the breakers was in my ears.

"I suppose, Helen," he said, after a long pause, "you realise that I love you very dearly?"

"I know that we are the best of friends, and very deeply attached to one another."

"We are much more than friends, Helen," said he; "at least, there is much more than friendship on my side. You are my all – all that matters to me in the world. You live in my thoughts every moment of my life. When we are apart I yearn for the sight of you – I reckon the hours that must pass before I shall see you again, and when we are together the happy minutes slip away like grains of golden sand. But I need not tell you this. You must have seen that I love you."

"I have feared it, Jasper – and that I might presently lose the dearest friend that I have in the world."

"That you will never do, Helen, dearest, if I have the happiness to be that friend. Why should you?"

"It seems that it has to be. Our friendship has been a sweet friendship to me – too sweet to last, as I feared; and if some might cavil at it, it was innocent and wronged no one. But if it has grown into – into what I had feared it might, then it has become impossible. More than friends we can never be, and yet we cannot remain friends."

We were both silent for more than a minute, and both were very grave. Then Jasper asked, with a trace of hesitation: "Helen, if we were as those other two are – if you were free – would you be willing to marry me?"

It was a difficult question to answer, in the circumstances, and yet I felt it would be an unpardonable meanness to dissemble.

"Yes," I answered; "of course I should."

"Then," said he, "I don't see why we can never be more than friends."

"But, Jasper, how can we? I am a married woman."

"I don't admit that," said he. "Your marriage is a fiction. You are really a spinster with a technical impediment to the conventional form of marriage. Your so-called husband is a stranger to whom you have no ties. You don't like, or even respect him; and certainly you have no obligations of duty to him, seeing that he induced you by a mere fraudulent pretence to go through this form of marriage with him."

"I am not thinking of Mr Otway," said I. "He is nothing to me. I owe him no duty or consideration, and I would not sacrifice a single hair of my head for him. But the fact remains that I am, legally, his wife; and while he lives I can contract no other marriage."

"But is that quite true, Helen?" he objected.

"Certainly it is; unless you consider a bigamous marriage as an exception, which it is not."

"Of course I do not. Bigamy is a futile and fraudulent attempt to secure the appearance of a legal sanction. No one but a fool entertains bigamy."

"Then I don't see the meaning of your objection."

"What I mean," said he "is that a fictitious marriage does not exclude the possibility of a real marriage."

"Still I do not quite follow you. What do you mean by a real marriage?"

"A real marriage is a permanent, lifelong partnership between a man and a woman. Ordinarily, such a partnership receives the formal endorsement of the State for certain reasons of public policy. But it is the partnership which is the marriage. The legal endorsement is an extrinsic and inessential addition. Now, in your case the State has accepted and endorsed a marriage which does not exist – which is a pure fiction. The result is that if you contract a real marriage, the State will withhold its endorsement. That is all. It cannot hinder the marriage."

"This is all very ingenious, Jasper," said I, "and it does credit to your legal training. But it is mere sophistry. The position, as it would appear to a plain person of ordinary common sense, is that a woman who is legally married to one man and is living as the wife of another, is a married woman who is living with a man who is not her husband."

"That is the conventional view, I admit," said he. "But it is a mistaken view. It confuses the legal sanction – which is not essential – with the covenant of lifelong union, which is the essence of marriage – which, in fact, *is* the marriage."

"But what is the bearing of this, Jasper?" I asked. "We seem to be discussing a rather abstract question of public morals. Has it any application to our own affairs?"

"Yes, it has. At least, I think so, though I feel a little nervous about saying just what I mean."

"I don't think you need be. At any rate, there had better be a clear understanding between us. Tell me exactly what you do mean."

He considered awhile, apparently somewhat at a loss how to begin. At length, with evident embarrassment, he put his proposal before me.

"The position, Helen, is this: You and I have become deeply attached to one another; I may say – since you admit that you would be willing to marry me – that we love one another. It is no passing fancy, based on mere superficial attractions. We are both persons of character, and our love is founded on deep-seated sympathy. We have been friends for some years. We liked one another from the first, and as time has gone on we have liked one another better. Our friendship has grown. It has become more and more precious to both of us, and at last it has grown into love – on my side, into intense and passionate love. We are not likely to change. People of our type are not given to change. We love one another and we shall go on loving one another until the end.

"If our circumstances were normal, we should marry in the normal manner. That is to say, we should enter into a contract publicly with certain formalities which would confer a definite legal status and render our contract enforceable in a court of law. But our circumstances are not normal. We are willing to comply with the formalities, but we are not allowed to. We are not in the position of persons who, for their own purposes, lightly disregard the immemorial usages of society – who dispense with the formalities because they would avoid the responsibilities of formal marriage. We wish to enter into a lifelong partnership; we desire to undertake all responsibilities; we would welcome the formalities and the secure status. But the law refuses. There is a technical disability.

"We have, therefore, two alternatives. We may give up the marriage which we both desire, or we may marry and dispense with the formalities and the legal status. Supposing we give up the marriage. Just consider, Helen, what it is that we give up. It is the happiness of a whole lifetime. The abiding joy of the sweetest, the most sympathetic companionship that is possible to a man and a woman. For though we are lovers, we are still friends, and friends we shall remain until death parts us. Our tastes, our interests, our sympathies make us prefer one another as companions to all other human beings. Of how many married couples can this be said? To us has been given that perfect comradeship that makes married life an enduring delight, a state of happiness without a cloud or a blemish. And this is what we give up if we let this disability, this technical impediment, hinder us from marrying.

"On the other hand, supposing we marry and dispense with the formalities, what do we give up? Virtually nothing. The legal security is of no value to us, for each of us is secure in the constancy of the other. If we enter into a covenant, we shall abide by it, not by compulsion, but because we shall never wish to break it. As to the legal status and the social recognition, is it conceivable that two sane persons should give up a life's happiness for such trumpery? Surely it is not. No, Helen, let us boldly take our destiny into our own hands. Let us publicly denounce this sham marriage and cancel it for ever. I ask you, dearest, to give me the woman of my heart for my mate, my friend, my wife, for ever; to take me, unworthy as I am, for your husband, who will try, as long as he draws the breath of life, to make up to you by love and worship for what you have sacrificed to make him happy."

As I listened to Jasper's appeal – delivered with quiet but impressive earnestness – I think I was half disposed to yield. It was not only that I admired the skill with which he put his case and the virile, masterful way in which he trampled down the obstructing conventions; but deep down in my heart I felt that he was right – that his separation of the things that really mattered from those that were trivial and inessential and true and just. But there was this vital difference between us; that he was a man and I was a woman. Our estimates of the value of the conventions were not the same. Without the legal sanction I might be his wife in all that was real; but the world would call me his mistress.

"Jasper, dear," I said, "it is impossible. I admit the truth of all that you have said, and I wish – Oh! Jasper, *how* I wish, that I could accept the happiness that you offer me! You need not tell me that our companionship would be a delight for ever. I know it. But it cannot be. Even if I could accept it for myself, I could not accept it for you; I could not bear to think that, through me, you had been put outside the pale of decent society. For that is what it would mean. You – a gentleman of honour and reputation – would become a social outcast, a man who was living with another man's wife; who, if he were admitted at all to the society of his own class, would have to be introduced with explanations and excuses."

"I think you exaggerate the social consequences, Helen," said he. "I propose that we should write to Otway and formally repudiate the marriage. Then if we were boldly and openly to state our position and the exceptional circumstances that had driven us to it, I believe that we should receive sympathy rather than condemnation. I don't believe we should lose a friend; certainly not one whose loss would afflict us. And Otway could take his remedy, if he cared to."

"You mean he could divorce me," I said, with something like a shudder.

"Yes. But I am afraid he wouldn't."

"I don't think he would. But if he did, it would be an undefended suit, and the stigma of the Divorce Court would be on us for ever."

"It would be unpleasant, I admit," he replied. "But think of the compensations. Think of the joy of being together always, of having our own home, of going abroad and seeing the world together."

"Don't, Jasper!" I entreated. "It is too tantalising. And even all this would not compensate me for the knowledge that I had dragged you from your honourable estate to a condition of social infamy."

"You need not consider me," he rejoined. "I have thought the matter out and am satisfied that I should gain infinitely more than I should lose; for I should have you, who are much more to me than all the rest of the world."

"You haven't thought of everything, Jasper," said I. "You know of the folly I committed at the time of my father's death – in withholding facts at the inquest, I mean – and you have excused it and treated it lightly. But others would view it differently. And now there is this blackmailer of whom I have told you. At any moment, a serious scandal may arise; and in that scandal you would be implicated."

"It wouldn't matter to me," said he. "Nothing would matter to me if only I had you."

"So you think now. But, Jasper, think of the years to come. Think how it might be in those years when the social ostracism, the loss of position and reputation, had grown more and more irksome, if we should regret what we had done, if we should blame ourselves – even, perhaps, secretly blame one another – "

"We should never do that, Helen. We should always be loyal. And there wouldn't be any social ostracism. At any rate, I am quite clear as to my own position. I want you for my wife. To get you I would make any sacrifices and count them as nothing. But that is only my position. It isn't necessarily yours – or rather, I should say your sacrifices would be greater than mine. A woman's point of view is different from a man's."

"It is, Jasper. I realise fully how essentially reasonable your proposal is, and I am proud of, and grateful for, the love that has impelled you to make it. But to me the thing is impossible. That is the only answer I can give. What it costs me to give that answer – to refuse the happiness that you offer me, and that I crave for – I cannot tell you. But even if it breaks my heart to say 'no,' still, that must be my answer."

For a long time neither of us spoke. As I glanced furtively at Jasper, the dejection, the profound sadness that was written on his face wrung my heart and filled me with self-accusation. Why had I not foreseen this? Why had I, who had nothing to give in return, allowed his friendship to grow up into love under my eyes? Had I not acted towards this my dearest friend with the basest selfishness?

Presently he turned to me, and, speaking in quiet, even tones, said: "It would not be fair for me to make an appeal on my own behalf. I may not urge you to accept a relation which your feeling and judgment reject. But one thing I will ask. I have told you what I want; and you are to remember that I shall always want you. I will ask you to reflect upon what we have said today, and if perchance you should come to think differently, remember that I am still wanting you, that I am still asking you, and tell me if you can give me a different answer. Will you promise me this, Helen?"

"Yes;" I replied, "I promise you, Jasper."

"Thank you, Helen. And meanwhile we remain friends as we have been?"

"We can never be again as we have been," said I. "Friendship may turn to love, but love does not go back to friendship. That is as impossible as for the fruit to change back into blossom. No, dearest Jasper; this is the end of our friendship. When we part today it must be farewell."

"Must it be, Helen? Must we part for ever? Could we not go back to the old ways and try to forget today?"

"I shall never forget today, nor will you. For our own peace of mind we must remain apart and try to avoid meeting one another. It is the only way, Jasper, hard as it will be."

I think he agreed with me for he made no further protest.

"If you say it must be Helen, then I suppose it must," he said, dejectedly. "But it is a hard saying. I don't dare to think of what life will be without you."

"Nor I, Jasper. I know that when I say 'goodbye' to you, the sun will go out of my life and that I can look for no other dawn."

Again we fell silent for a while; and again I reproached myself for having let it come to this.

"Don't you think, Helen," he said at length, "that we might meet sometimes, say at fixed intervals — even long intervals, if it must be so — just that we might feel that we had not really lost one another completely?"

"But that is what I should wish to avoid. For we have lost one another. As to me, it has no significance. I have nothing to give and nothing to lose. I am shackled for life to Mr Otway. But you have your life before you, and it would only be fair that I should leave you free."

"Free!" he exclaimed. "I am not free and never shall be. Nor do I wish to be free. I am yours now and for ever. And so I would wish it to be. We may not be married in any outward form, but we are married in the most real sense. Our hearts are married. We belong to one another for ever while we live, and neither of us will ever wish to change. You know it is so, dearest, don't you?"

What could I say? He had spoken my own thoughts, had expressed the wish that I had not dared to acknowledge. Weak and unjust it may have been, but the thought that in the dark days of our coming separation we should still be linked, if only by an invisible thread, came as something like a reprieve. It left just a faint spark of light to relieve the gloom of the all too sombre future. In the end we agreed to a monthly letter and a meeting once a year. And so, having fixed the terms of our sentence, we tried to put our troubles away and make the best of the few hours that remained before the dreaded farewell.

But despite our efforts to get back to our wonted cheerful companionship, the swiftly-passing hours were filled with sadness and heartache. Instinctively we went and looked at things and places that recalled the pleasant jaunts that were to be no more; but ever Black Care rode behind. It was like the journey of two lovers in a tumbril that rolled its relentless way towards the guillotine; for at the end of the day was the parting that would leave us desolate.

And at last the parting was upon us. At the corner of Cable Street we halted and faced one another. For a few moments we stood in the gathering gloom, hand clasped in hand. I dared not speak, for my heart was bursting. Hardly did I dare to look at the man whom I loved so passionately. And Jasper could but press my hand and murmur huskily a few broken words of love. And so we parted. With a last pressure of the hand I turned away and hurried along Cable Street. I did not dare to look back though I knew that he was gazing after me; for the street swam before my eyes and I could barely hold back my sobs.

I did not go straight home. The tumult of emotion sent me hurrying forward – whither I have no recollection save that somewhere in Shadwell a pair of friendly policemen turned me back with the remark that it "was no place for the likes of me." At length, when the first storm of grief had passed, and I felt myself under control, I made my way to Wellclose Square, and pleading the conventional headache, retired at once to my room.

And there, in quiet and seclusion, with tears that no longer need be restrained, with solemn rites of grief, I buried my newborn happiness – the happiness that had died almost in the moment of its birth.

Chapter Nineteen

Illusions and Disillusions

It is a generally accepted belief that of all the remedies for an aching heart, the most effective is distraction of the mind from the subject of its affliction. And probably the belief is well founded. But it usually happens that the sufferer is the last to recognise the virtues of the remedy, preferring to nurse in solitude a secret grief and to savour again and yet again the bitterness of the Dead Sea fruit of sorrow.

So it was with me in these unhappy days. The seclusion of the workshop gave me the opportunity for long hours of meditation, in which I would trace and retrace the growth of my love for Jasper, would think with passionate regret of what might have been and speculate vaguely upon the future. So far from seeking distraction in these first days of my trouble, I kept aloof from my comrades, so far as I could; shut myself in the workshop, or in my room, or wandered abroad alone, following the great eastern thoroughfares where I was secure from the chance of meeting a friend.

But the distractions which I would have avoided came unsought. First, there was the visit with Peggy to Miss Tallboy-Smith. It was due but a day or two after my parting with Jasper, and I loathed the thought of it; but it had to be; for who could say how much it might mean to Peggy? And as it turned out, I should never have forgiven myself if I had failed her. I had looked for a rather dull, social call flavoured with porcelain. But it was quite otherwise. Miss Tallboy-Smith had at length heard of Peggy's genius and had invited a few specially choice connoisseurs to meet her including Mr Hawkesley – unless he had invited himself. At any rate, there he was, reverential and admiring, but yet with a certain air of proprietorship which I noted with interest and not without approval. It was quite a triumph for Peggy, and she took it very modestly, though with very natural satisfaction. To me, however, there was a fly in the ointment, though quite a small one; for Mr Hawkesley proposed an exploration of the Wallace Collection, which Peggy had never seen and which I felt bound, for her sake, to agree to. But I looked forward with prospective relief to the time – not far distant I suspected – when these two pottery enthusiasts would be intimate enough to dispense with a chaperon.

Then there came a distraction of another kind. One evening after tea, Lilith took me apart and looking at me with some concern, said: "Our Sibyl has not been herself of late. I hope she is not being worried about anything."

"We all have our little troubles, Lilith," I replied, "and sometimes we don't take them so resignedly as we should."

"No," she rejoined. "Resignation is easier when the troubles are someone else's. But we are very concerned to see you looking so sad – not only Margaret and I, but all of us. We are all very fond of you, Sibyl, dear, and any of us would think it a privilege to be of help to you in any way. You know that, don't you?"

"I have good reason to. No woman could have found kinder or more helpful friends than I have in this house."

"Well," she said, "friends are for use as well as for companionship. Don't forget that, if there is any little service that any of us can render you."

I thanked her very warmly, and she then opened a fresh topic.

"Some time ago, Sibyl, we were speaking of psychical experiments, and I suggested that you might like to see some carried out by my friend, Mr Quecks, who is an authority on these subjects. Mr Quecks was away from home at the time, on a lecturing tour in Kent; but he is home again now. I wrote to him about you and have had one or two talks with him, and he has asked me to invite you to a little demonstration that he is giving to some friends next Friday evening. Would you care to come with me?"

I would much rather not have gone, but I knew that a refusal would disappoint Lilith, who had set her heart on converting me. Accordingly, I accepted the invitation, and we were arranging details of the expedition when Peggy joined us. As soon as she heard what was afoot she was all agog.

"Oh, what fun!" she exclaimed. "You'll let me come too, won't you, Lilith? I did so enjoy it last time."

Lilith, however, was by no means eager for her company, for the Titmouse was a rank unbeliever, and made no secret of it.

"What is the use of your coming, Peggy?" said she. "You don't believe in the super-normal. You would only come to scoff."

"Perhaps I should remain to pray," rejoined Peggy. "It is no use preaching to people who are already convinced. And I should just love it. That Quecks man is so *frightfully* amusing. He is the funniest little guffin you ever saw, Sibyl. Won't you let me come, Lilith?"

"Of course you can come if you really want to," Lilith replied with evident reluctance. "But you shouldn't speak of Mr Quecks as if he were a mountebank or a buffoon. He may not be handsome, but he is a very learned man and very sincere."

"I beg your pardon, Lilith" said Peggy. "I won't call him a guffin any more. And thank you ever so much for letting me come."

The arrangements being thus settled, it is only fair to Peggy to say that she endeavoured, as far as possible, to treat the demonstration quite seriously. Even in our private conversations she made no further disparaging references to Mr Quecks, though I did gather that her anxiety to be present at the seance was not unconnected with a desire to keep an eye on him to see that he did not impose on me.

Mr Quecks' house was situated in a quiet street off Cromwell Road, Kensington, and the "demonstration" took place in a large room intermediate in character between a library and a drawing-room, lighted by three electric bulbs, all of which were encased in silk bags, so that the illumination was of a twilight dimness. The visitors were about a dozen in all, and while we were waiting for the late arrivals Mr Quecks made a few observations upon super-normal phenomena in general.

To me he required no disparagement from Peggy or anyone else, his own appearance doing all that was necessary in that respect. The first glance at him impressed me disagreeably; but then he was a manifestly uncomely man, with a large, bald face and long, greasy black hair, which was brushed straight back and accumulated in an untidy bush at the nape of his neck. He spoke unctuously, and his manner was confident, persuasive, didactic and authoritative, and he gave me the impression of a man who was accustomed to dealing chiefly with women – his present audience was composed of them exclusively.

"In interpreting the results of the experiments which we are about to perform," he observed, "we have to bear in mind that psychical and super-normal phenomena, inasmuch as they are not concerned with material things, are not directly appreciable by the senses. We cannot see or touch the subliminal self, either our own or that of others. But neither can we see the electric current or the Hertzian waves. We know of their existence and properties indirectly, through their effects. Electricity can be transformed into heat, light or sound, and these can be perceived by means of the radiator, the electric lamp or the telephone, which act directly on our senses. So it is with the hidden subconscious self. Invisible itself, it can be made to produce effects which are perceptible to the conscious mind through the senses, and through those effects its own existence is revealed."

This sounds reasonable enough; but the experiments themselves were rather disappointing on the whole. Perhaps I expected too much; or perhaps the preoccupied state of my mind did not allow me to bring to them sufficient interest or attention. Moreover, Mr Quecks had an assistant (I had almost said "confederate") whose appearance pleased me no more than his own; a wall-eyed, taciturn woman of about thirty-five, of the name of Morgan who acted as the "percipient" – the word "medium," I noticed, was not used – and helped to prejudice me against the experiments.

We began with a demonstration of thought-transference, which I found dull, tiresome and unconvincing. Probably I was unreasonable; but the apparent triviality of the proceedings, which resembled a solemn and unspeakably dull, drawing-room game, influenced my judgment. The percipient, Miss Morgan, being seated, blindfolded, in the middle of the room, a pack of playing cards and another pack of cards, each of which bore a single capital letter, were produced. A card was drawn out at random and held up behind the percipient and in view of everyone else, including Mr Quecks, who held the percipient's hand. Miss Morgan then guessed the card or the letter. Sometimes she guessed correctly, sometimes nearly correctly, sometimes quite incorrectly. The proportion of correct guesses, Mr Quecks informed us, was vastly greater than could be accounted for on the law of probabilities. And I dare say it was. But the exhibition left me cold, as did those of table-tilting and planchette writing which followed. Even the *"pendule explorateur,"* which had so impressed me on a previous occasion, fell flat on this. For, since that rather startling experience, I had given some thought to the magic pendulum, and believed that I had found at least a partial explanation of its powers. Accordingly, when my turn came to try the "autoscope," I took the string in my fingers and shut my eyes; and when Mr Quecks objected to this I gazed fixedly at the opposite wall, seeing neither the pendulum nor the clockwise alphabet. Under these conditions the pendulum was a complete failure; it would spell nothing. But when I looked steadily at the pendulum and the letters, the swinging ball spelled out clearly the word that I chose – Lilith.

I was thus in a decidedly sceptical frame of mind when the next set of experiments began; and even these produced, at first, no effect on me other than a slight tendency to yawn. Their object was to demonstrate the existence of a "psychometric" power or faculty; that is to say, a power to detect in certain material objects a permanent impression left by contact with some particular person. Such a faculty, Mr Quecks explained to us, was possessed by certain exceptionally sensitive persons. He had it to some extent himself, but in Miss Morgan it was developed in a really remarkable degree, as the experiments which were to follow would convince us.

Hereupon Miss Morgan was once more blindfolded, all the lights but one were switched off, so that the room was almost in darkness, and the demonstration began. One of the visitors, at Mr Quecks' whispered request, slipped a ring from her finger and passed it to him. By him it was handed to Miss Morgan who solemnly applied it to her forehead. Then followed an interval of expectant silence, in which I thought I heard a faint giggle from Peggy Finch, who sat in the row in front of me.

At length Miss Morgan opened her mouth and spake. It seemed that she was seeing visions, and these she described in detail. Naturally I was unable to check them, nor could I judge whether they had any relation to the ring. The owner of that article stated, at the close of the experiment, that the visions, as described, corresponded closely to certain places and events which were known to her and to no one else. Which seemed conclusive enough; but yet it left me only with a feeling that the whole proceeding was ridiculous and trivial.

The next experiment was performed with a glove from the hand of another visitor, and when this was concluded, Mr Quecks whispered to a lady in the front row, who whispered to Peggy, who turned to me.

"He wants your handkerchief, Sibyl," she said in a low whisper.

I took my handkerchief from my pocket and gave it to Peggy, who squeezed it up into a ball and passed it to the lady in front, who passed it to Mr Quecks, who handed it to Miss Morgan; who, in her turn, applied it to her forehead as if it had been an ice-bag, and assumed an attitude of intense mental concentration. And again the sound of a suppressed giggle came from the neighbourhood of the Titmouse.

Then Miss Morgan began to speak.

"I seem to be passing through the country – swiftly – very swiftly; past great, wide fields and woods. They are, strange-looking woods. The trees are all in lines – in straight lines... But wait! Are they trees? No, they can't be; they are too small. No – they are plants growing up poles – they must be vines. It is a vineyard – and yet they don't look quite like vines. No, no! Of course, I see now; they are hops. It is a hop-garden. And now I am passing another. Now I have come out on to a road on the top of a hill. There are hills all round, and in the hollow there seems to be a town... and I seem to see water in the town... yes, it is water. It is a river... But I don't see any ships... only some red things... Oh, yes! I see; the red things are sails – red sails. I thought sails were always white."

She paused; and in the intense silence I leaned forward listening eagerly. All my indifference and boredom had vanished. This was quite a different affair from the card-guessing and planchette-reading. She had described Maidstone vividly, accurately – or at least so it seemed to me; Maidstone as it would appear to one approaching the bridge from the west. Of course it might be mere guessing; but –

"I seem," Miss Morgan resumed, "to be descending a hill by a broad street... What is that in front of me? Is it – yes, I see; it is a bridge. Yes, I see it plainly now. I am coming towards it. But what on earth is this thing on my left hand? It seems to be a mass of gold... and yet... and yet it looks like an elephant. That's ridiculous, of course. It can't be... But it certainly looks like gold... and yet it... it really does look like an elephant! Well, I can make nothing of it. And now it is gone and I am on the bridge."

Again she paused, and I sat gazing at her in blank astonishment. There could now be no question as to the reality of the visions, unless the whole exhibition was a fraud. The idea of skilful guessing could not be entertained for a moment. The description did not merely fit Maidstone; the detail of the golden elephant on the brewery by the bridge fixed the identity of the place beyond the possibility of doubt. It was either a genuine – and most amazing – psychical phenomenon or an outrageous imposture. But an imposture, to which Lilith must have been a party, was more incredible than the "super-normal" itself.

As these thoughts passed swiftly through my mind, Miss Morgan resumed her description.

"I am standing on the bridge, but it is beginning to grow indistinct. By the riverside I can just see a great house, an old, old house, which seems to stand by the water's edge, and beyond it trees and a church tower. Now it is gone and I can see nothing. Is this all?... No; I see, very, very faintly, a small crowd of people. They seem to be in a field. And I make out a number of white objects in the field. They look rather like sheep, but they are very still. Oh! they are not sheep at all; they are tombstones. And I see now that the people are all in black and that they are standing round an open grave. It must be a funeral... Yes; there is the clergyman in his surplice... But it is beginning to fade... Now I can only just see the dark shapes of the people...and now they are gone too. This must be all, I think." She paused for a few moments and then exclaimed: "No, it isn't. Something else is coming. It is very dim, but it looks like a man sitting at a table. Yes... But I can't see what he is doing. He is not writing... He has something in his right hand, and keeps moving it up and down. Oh, I see now: it is a hammer. He seems to be hammering some bright object – a piece of metal, I think... Yes, it is quite clear now. But it isn't a man at all; it is a woman. I saw her distinctly for a moment, but she has grown dim again... Now she has gone and I can see nothing... I think that is all. Yes, that is all. Nothing else seems to come."

She removed the handkerchief from her forehead and held it out towards Mr Quecks, who took it from her and tiptoed round to where I was sitting.

"Thank you, Mrs Otway," he whispered. "It seemed a very successful experiment; but you can judge better than I can."

"It was, indeed, most successful," I replied, as he gave me back my handkerchief. "I am positively amazed at the detailed accuracy of the description."

"You think the correspondence is closer than could be accounted for by coincidence or chance guessing?" he asked.

"There can be no question of chance," I replied. "The descriptions were much too detailed and circumstantial."

"That is most interesting," said he. "For there can be no other explanation but that of genuine psychometric faculty. Miss Morgan is a stranger to you, and moreover, she did not know whose handkerchief it was. The remarkable success of this experiment seems to support Miss Blake's estimate of your unusual psychic gifts. You evidently have the power of imprinting your personality on inanimate objects in an exceptional degree. I should almost think it likely that you would be a successful scryer. Have you made any experiments with the crystal?"

"Yes. But they are all complete failures. I could see nothing."

"That is not unusual in early experiments," said he. "There is a difficulty in concentrating. I wonder if you would care to make a trial now under my guidance. I think I could help you to visualise some simple scene. Will you try?"

The astonishing success of Miss Morgan's experiment had revived all my former curiosity, and I assented readily. Much to Mr Quecks' satisfaction. The nature of the new experiment was explained to the company, and the necessary preparations made. An easy chair was placed for me in the middle of the room, and the chairs for the others arranged behind it, so that I should not have my attention distracted by seeing them. As I passed Lilith on my way to the chair I greeted her with a smile, and was a little surprised at the lack of response on her part. I thought she would be gratified to see me taking so active a part in the proceedings; but apparently she was not; indeed, I had never seen her look so ungenial.

When I had taken my seat, Mr Quecks directed me to lean back and adopt a position of complete physical rest. A black, velvet cushion was then placed in my lap and on the cushion was laid the crystal globe, itself almost black in the dim twilight save for a single spark where it reflected the light of the one electric lamp.

"You will look fixedly at the bright spot of light," said Mr Quecks, who had seated himself beside me; "concentrate your attention on it and think of nothing else. Don't let your mind wander and don't move your eyes. Think of the bright spot and look at it. Soon a mist will come before your eyes; then you will feel a sort of drowsiness. You will grow more and more drowsy, but your eyes will keep open and you will still see the mist. You are seeing it now" (this was quite correct); "it grows denser; now you are beginning to feel drowsy – just a little drowsy – but your eyes are wide open; still you are getting drowsy – rather more drowsy – "

He seemed to repeat these words over and over and over again like a sort of chant; and his voice, which had been at first soft and confidential, took on a peculiar sing-song quality, and at the same time began to grow more and more distant until it came to me thin and small like the voices that are borne from faraway ships on a calm day across the water of a quiet anchorage. And, meanwhile, a strange somnolence fell upon me. I felt as if I were in a dream. Yet my eyes were wide open, and before them floated the mist, out of which shone the single spark of light. And the little, thin voice went on chanting far away, but I could no longer make out what it said. Nor was I attending to it. I was gazing into the mist at the tiny spark – gazing fixedly, unwinkingly, without effort.

Presently the mist seemed to clear a little and the spot of light began to grow larger. Now it looked like a hole in the shutter of a dark room; and now it was as though I were looking through an opera glass or a telescope; but I could make out nothing save a confused blur of light, in the middle of which was a vague, dark shape. But still the area of light grew larger, and now I could see that there were other shapes, all dim, vague and shadowy. Then in an instant it cleared up, as a magic-lantern picture sharpens when the lens is focused. The dark shape was Mr Otway. He stood; stooping forward, gazing at something on the floor – something that lay by the fireplace, motionless with upturned waxen face. It was horribly distinct. I could see my father's face settling into the rigidity of death; I could see the crimson streak on his temple; I could even see the sparkle of the silver knob on the stick that Mr Otway grasped.

The vision lasted, as it seemed, but for a few seconds. Then it grew dim and confused and quickly faded away into blank darkness; and I found myself sitting up in the chair, wide awake, but bewildered and a little frightened. The lights were full on, and the visitors were all gathered around my chair gazing at me with a very odd intentness.

"Did you see anything in the crystal?" Mr Quecks asked suavely.

"Yes," I answered, not quite so suavely. "How long have I been asleep?"

Mr Quecks looked at his watch. "Just five and twenty minutes," he replied.

I got up from the chair, and, addressing Peggy who was looking at me a little anxiously, asked: "What, has been happening Peggy? Have I been talking nonsense?"

"No," she answered. "You've been asleep, and you've been guessing cards and doing most extraordinary sums – multiplying and dividing fractions and all sorts of things. That's all. But," she added in a lower tone, "he'd no business to hypnotise you without your permission. You didn't give him permission, did you?"

"No, I didn't," I replied.

At this moment Lilith came up to us and put the same question.

"No," I answered. "I didn't understand that I was to be hypnotised."

"I thought not," said she in a tone of evident vexation. "It doesn't happen to matter as things have turned out, but it was quite improper. I shall speak to Mr Quecks about it when you are gone."

"Aren't you coming with us, then?" asked Peggy.

"No," replied Lilith. "I have some matters to talk over with him, so I must stay a little while; but I shall follow you in about half an hour."

Shortly after this the meeting broke up and Peggy and I took our departure. As we sat in the train, I tried to extract from my companion some details of what had happened, but I found her curiously unwilling to pursue the topic. I gathered, however, that, as soon as the hypnotic trance was completely established, Mr Quecks suggested to me that I should have a distinct vision of some scene that I had witnessed "in the old town that Miss Morgan had seen and shortly before the funeral that she had described." Then, after an interval he had put a number of problems in multiplication and division of large numbers and fractions, which I had solved with extraordinary ease and rapidity. As to the nature of my vision, Peggy displayed no interest, but turned the conversation on to subjects quite unconnected with Mr Quecks or psychical science.

When we arrived home she followed me to my room and suggested that we should wait there for Lilith, which was what I had intended to do. And here again she showed a marked tendency to avoid the subject of Mr Quecks and his experiments. But, as she sat in my chair gossiping, I caught her eye from time to time, travelling almost furtively towards the clock on the mantelpiece, and I wondered if she was feeling anxious about Lilith, who had to make her way alone through the rather unsavoury neighbourhood of Ratcliff. Whatever she was feeling, however, she kept up a flow of conversation – which was, itself, a rather unusual phenomenon – and presently grew quite confidential about herself – which was more unusual still. It was clear that her friendship with Mr Hawkesley was now quite firmly established and they evidently saw a good deal of one another – but this I knew already. And it was clear that their sympathy in tastes was running parallel to a very strong liking of a more personal kind.

After a pause in this confidential gossip, Peggy suddenly looked down a little shyly, and, turning very pink, asked, hesitatingly: "Sibyl, dear, you haven't quarrelled with Mr Davenant, have you?"

"Quarrelled, Peggy!" I exclaimed; "of course I haven't. Have we ever struck you as quarrelsome people?"

"No, indeed" she replied. "But you don't seem to have seen much of one another lately."

"No; I haven't seen Mr Davenant for quite a long time," I said.

She was silent for a while, and I noticed that her cheeks were growing more and more pink.

"What is my little chameleon turning that colour for?" I asked.

She looked up at me with a shy smile. "Sibyl," she said, "don't think me inquisitive or impertinent. I am your friend, you know, and we are fond of one another, aren't we?"

"We are the very best of friends, Peggy, dear, so you needn't mind asking me anything that you want to know."

"Well, then, Sibyl; why don't you and Mr Davenant marry? Anyone can see how fond he is of you, and I'm sure you care for him an awful lot, don't you, now?"

"My Titmouse is becoming an expert authority on these matters," said I, thereby converting poor Peggy to the semblance of a corn-poppy.

"Perhaps I am," she admitted, defiantly. "But why don't you marry him, Sibyl?"

"My dear Peggy," said I, "there is a very substantial reason. Its name is Mr Otway."

"Sibyl!" gasped Peggy. "I thought you were a widow!"

I shook my head. "No, Peggy. I am a widow in effect but a married woman by law. I have a husband who is no husband; whom I married in error, whom I have never lived with and could never think of living with, but whom I can never get rid of. That is the position."

She flung her arms around my neck, and laid her cheek to mine.

"My poor, dear Sibyl," she exclaimed. "How dreadful for you! I am so frightfully sorry, dear. And is there no end to this?"

"There is death," said I. "That is all. And that is why I am not seeing much of Mr Davenant nowadays."

"It is an awful thing, Sibyl," said she. "You and Mr Davenant could make one another so perfectly happy. And I don't see why you shouldn't, for that matter."

"Why, how could we, Peggy?"

Again she blushed scarlet, and with a defiant glance at me, replied: "I wouldn't have my whole life wrecked. I should just go off with him, husband or no husband."

"You dreadful little reprobate. And what do you suppose the world would say about you?"

"It could say what it liked so long as I'd got the man I wanted. But it wouldn't really say anything. No one with any sense would think a penny the worse of me. Nor would they of you. Everyone would say that you had done the right thing, seeing that you had no choice. You couldn't be expected to be bound for life to a dummy husband."

At this moment I rose from my chair, and going over to the dressing-table, lit a candle. Then I put my hand in my pocket and drew out an unaddressed envelope and a piece of pencil. With the latter I wrote on the envelope my signature and the words "ten minutes to eleven." The whole proceeding seemed quite automatic. I did not know why I was doing it. I had not known that either the envelope or the pencil was in my pocket, for I had not put them there. But I carried out the train of action almost unconsciously and quite without surprise.

When I had written on the envelope, I opened it and drew out a piece of paper. On the paper was some writing in an unfamiliar hand. I held the paper near the candle and read as follows:

"At ten minutes to eleven you will light a candle, take this envelope and a pencil from your pocket; you will write on the envelope your signature and the time. Then you will open the envelope and read this message."

I stood for some seconds gazing at the paper in utter amazement. Then I looked round quickly at the clock. It was ten minutes to eleven. From the clock my glance turned to Peggy, who was sitting watching me with a very uncomfortable expression.

"Do you know anything about this, Peggy?" I asked.

"Yes," she replied. "That Quecks man told you to do it. He wrote the message and put the envelope and pencil in your pocket when you were in a deep sleep. He spoke the message into your ear, and, after about a minute, told you to wake up, and you woke up immediately. It was like his impudence to perform his beastly experiments without getting your permission first."

"It was. But the thing is rather uncanny. I don't like it at all."

"There's nothing in it," said Peggy, though she too was evidently not pleasantly impressed. "It's what they call post-hypnotic suggestion. It isn't in any way supernatural. The doctors know all about it."

"Still," said I, "it is a very strange affair. There is something extremely eerie in finding oneself turned into an unthinking automaton worked by somebody else's will. And some of the other experiments were rather startling: Miss Morgan's visions for instance."

"Mightn't they have been just clever guesses?"

"No, Peggy. That is quite impossible. Her descriptions applied to my case in detail and were correct every time. You heard her describe the view from Maidstone Bridge?"

"Yes. And I recognised it from that water-colour over your mantelpiece."

"Well, don't you think it very wonderful and incomprehensible?"

"No, I don't," said Peggy. "How do you suppose she did it?"

"I can only imagine that some influence that I don't understand passed to her from my handkerchief."

"Then you imagine wrong," said the Titmouse. "Your handkerchief was in my pocket all the time. It was my handkerchief that she was smelling at. And her descriptions didn't fit me the least little bit. I don't hammer my pottery, you know."

"But I don't understand. You passed her my handkerchief, didn't you?"

"No; I passed her mine. You see, I'd seen this handkerchief trick before and I had mine ready, rolled up into a ball in my hand. So it was quite easy to make the exchange. But we may as well change back now."

She took a handkerchief from her pocket and handed it to me; and when I had identified it as my own, I produced hers and restored it to her.

"You are a wicked little baggage, Peggy," said I, "though I must admit that the ruse was quite a fair one. But still, I don't quite see how it was done? It was evidently an imposture. But how was it worked? How did she get the information?"

"Why, she got it from Mr Quecks, and he got it from Lilith."

"You surely don't suggest that Lilith was a party to this fraud?"

"Of course I don't" she replied, indignantly. "Lilith is a lady to the tips of her fingers. That's just where it is. She would never suspect. But we know that she wrote to Quecks about you, and she has talked to him about you, and no doubt he has pumped out all that she knows about you. Then you will remember that he has just come back from a tour in Kent – he is almost certain to have been to Maidstone – and there are such things as picture postcards. There is no mystery as to how it was done; but I do wonder that he was such a fool as to do it before Lilith. I suspect she stayed behind to tell him what she thought of him."

As we were speaking, Lilith came up the stairs, and I ran out to intercept her and bring her in.

"You needn't have waited up for me," said she, "though I am glad you have, for I want to apologise for Mr Quecks' very improper behaviour."

"Don't think any more about it, Lilith," said I. "It didn't do any harm, and it has enabled Peggy and me to have a little private seance to ourselves."

"Did the post-hypnotic experiment work correctly?"

"Perfectly – and most uncannily."

"Then," said Lilith, "you have gained by that amount of experience. As to the rest of Mr Quecks' experiments – well, Sibyl, I am afraid we must consider them on the plane of public entertainment rather than on that of genuine research. But it is getting late. We had better go to bed now and talk things over tomorrow."

This advice was forthwith acted on, as to its first half; and if I owed Mr Quecks a grudge for trying to impose on me, I should have been grateful to him for giving me something to think about other than my own griefs and entanglements.

CHAPTER TWENTY

Cloud and Sunshine

Reviewing on the morrow my experiences at Mr Quecks' house, I was conscious of a rather definite change of outlook. Those experiences had made a very deep impression. The vision that I had seen was something outside ordinary, normal experience, and it still haunted me. And then, even more uncanny, there was that strange automatic action which I had carried out with such perfect unconsciousness and yet so exactly and punctually. It was all very well for Peggy to put it aside with the easy explanation that it was merely post-hypnotic suggestion, and that the doctors knew all about it. That explanation explained nothing. The fact remained that I had suddenly become aware that things which I had been accustomed to dismiss as delusions – as the mere superstitions of credulous people – were actual realities. And this discovery created for me a new standard of possibility and truth. Even Miss Morgan's visions, though I knew them to be a rank imposture, had left an impression that was not to be completely effaced. The shock of amazement that they had produced at the time left a vague after-effect, due, no doubt, to the more real and equally mysterious experiences.

Concerning these latter I was somewhat puzzled. It was not quite clear to me how I had come to be hypnotised at all, and I took an early opportunity of questioning Lilith on the subject.

"There is no mystery about that," she replied. "The orthodox method of producing the hypnotic trance is to cause the 'subject' to gaze steadily at some bright object – a metal button, a crystal, or even a small piece of white paper. He is told to gaze fixedly at this object, to concentrate his attention on it, and to think of nothing else. The purpose of this is to get rid, as far as possible, of the conscious self and to allow the subconscious self to act without disturbance. When this state of mental abstraction has been established, the 'subject' is ready to receive suggestions. If the operator suggests to him that he is drowsy, he becomes somnolent; and at the same time he becomes much more susceptible to suggestion. Now, if the operator suggests to him that he feels certain sensations, he feels those sensations. If it is suggested that he performs certain actions, he performs them. This is what happened to you. Mr Quecks induced you to gaze steadily at the crystal, and when you were in the proper state of mental abstraction, he suggested the hypnotic trance. Then he suggested that you would see a vision of some scene that you had looked on shortly before the funeral, and I understand that you did see such a vision."

"Yes, I did; and most astonishingly vivid it was. But, Lilith, when I lit that candle in my room I was not in the hypnotic trance."

"No; that was a post-hypnotic phenomenon, and really a most interesting one. To understand it you must think of the two personalities, the conscious self and the subconscious, or subliminal self. Now the suggestions are made to the subconscious self, while the conscious is dormant or in abeyance. But when the conscious self returns or awakens, the subconscious mind continues to work, although unperceived by the conscious mind. If the suggestion refers, as in your case, to some action to be performed at an appointed time, the subconscious keeps account of the passing time and at the appointed moment sets the machinery in motion. The action itself is perceived by the conscious mind, but the train of subconscious thought has been unperceived, though it has really been quite continuous. It is very curious, though not particularly mysterious."

"And it is only in the hypnotic trance that these suggestions take effect?"

"That," replied Lilith, "is not quite clear. It seems that in ordinary sleep suggestions of the kind may sometimes take effect. And for the same reason. In sleep, the conscious self is in abeyance – is out of action; but the subconscious is active, as we see in the case of dreams and still more strikingly in the case of somnambulism. But the postponed effects of suggestions made during normal sleep need more investigation. I believe that sleep produced by drugs is much more like the hypnotic trance than natural sleep."

"Well," I said, "it is all rather weird and uncanny" and so the subject dropped. But, as I have said, the influence of these strange experiences remained. My former scepticism of the occult and mystical gave place to a state of mind in which I was prepared to admit the possibility of things that I had once regarded as wildly incredible.

Nevertheless, I was but faintly interested in the wonders of psychical research. Indeed, I was not much interested in anything connected with my daily life. I had endeavoured to revive my enthusiasm for my work by setting myself an ambitious task – a silver candlestick of a semi-ecclesiastical design, worked in repoussé with enrichments in enamel. But all the pleasure in the work was gone. The various processes – skilfully enough executed, as I noticed with tepid satisfaction – which should have been a joy, were but the routine of industry; and through them all the never-ending heartache, the sense of loss, of bereavement, the feeling that the light had gone out of my life for ever. The passing time seemed to bring no mitigation. Rather did it seem to me that every day I missed my dear companion more.

Perhaps if my loss had been more final – if for instance, Jasper had been taken from me by Death – I might have striven more determinedly to shape my life anew. But there was a certain inconclusiveness in our separation. Not that I ever, for a moment, considered the possibility of re-opening the question. But still I think there lurked in my mind the feeling that the door was not finally closed. Jasper's words, "Remember that I am still wanting you, that I am still asking you," would come to me unbidden, again and yet again, reminding me that the way was still open, that I could end the separation if and when I chose. And then Peggy's outspoken declaration was not without its effect. For the Titmouse was a very paragon of modesty and maidenly propriety; and when I recalled her robust contempt of conventional points of view I could not help asking myself sometimes if I had not been too prudish. All of which was very disturbing. It left me with my resolution unchanged, and yet without that sense of finality that would have set me reconstructing my scheme of life.

So the weeks dragged by till the time for the first monthly letter drew nigh; and the passionate yearning with which I looked forward to it told me that that letter was a mistake. It ought never to have been. The chapter should have been ended and the volume shut irrevocably.

As the time for the letter approached, my unrest took me abroad more than usual, and one day, forsaking the sordid east, I took the train to South Kensington and made my way to the Museum though with no special object in my mind. I had ascended the steps to the main entrance, and was approaching the doorway, when I came face to face with Miss Tallboy-Smith who was just emerging. At the sight of me she halted with a dramatic gesture of astonishment.

"Well!" she exclaimed, "so you are *really* alive! I thought I was never going to see you again. Where *have* you been? It's ages – centuries – since I have seen you. And dear Miss Finch, too; whatever has become of her? Were you going into the Museum? I have just been wallowing in the Salting Collection. Delightful, isn't it? The very kernel of the Museum. Don't you think so?"

"I don't think I have ever seen the Salting Collection," said I.

"Never seen the Salting Collection!" she gasped. "My *dear* Mrs Otway! How *dreadful*! And you a connoisseur, too. Why, it's a Paradise; the collectors' Heaven. Do you believe that people come back after death and frequent their old haunts? I hope it's true. If it is, I shall come to the Salting Collection. I shall divide my ghosthood between that and the Wallace. It will really be very jolly. Unlimited leisure, with all eternity at one's disposal. And no silly restrictions; no closing hours or students' days. So convenient, too! You just pass in through the closed door or the wall and float up the stairs. Why, you could even get inside the glass cases! I'm afraid you'll think me an awful, old heathen; but I'm not really. And how are you? And how is Miss Finch? And why haven't you been to the club for such an age. And isn't it *dreadful* about poor Mr Davenant?"

My heart seemed to stand still, and I think I must have turned pale, for Miss Tallboy-Smith said hastily: "I'm afraid I have startled you, Mrs Otway; but surely – surely – do you mean to tell me that you haven't even heard about it?"

"I have heard nothing," I said, faintly. "Is he – tell me what has happened."

"I haven't had very full particulars," said she, "but it seems that a cart – or was it a wagon? No, I think it was a cart – and yet I'm not quite sure that it wasn't – but there! I'm not very clear as to the difference between a cart and a wagon. What is the difference?"

"It doesn't matter," I said impatiently. "Tell me what happened."

"No," she agreed, "I suppose it doesn't matter. Well, it seems that this wagon – but I think it was really a cart – yes, I'm sure it was – at least, I think so – but at any rate it appears that the wagon had run away – that is, of course, it was the horse that had run away, but as he was tied to the cart, it comes to the same thing. And he got on to the pavement – it was in the Strand, somewhere near that shop where they sell those absurd – now what *do* they call those things? I am getting so silly about names, and it's quite a common name, too – "

"Never mind what they are called," I entreated. "Do tell me what happened to Mr Davenant."

"Well, what happened was this. When the wagon got on the pavement all the people scattered to get out of the way – all except a messenger boy, and he fell down right in front of the cart. Then Mr Davenant ran out and tried to drag the boy clear of the wagon; and, in fact, he did drag him out of the way, but he wasn't quick enough to save himself, for the horse swerved and knocked him down violently on to some stone steps."

"Was he badly hurt?" I demanded, breathlessly.

"Hurt!" she repeated. "My dear Mrs Otway, he was battered – absolutely battered. He fell with his side on the stone steps and I understand that his ribs were simply smashed to matchwood."

"And where is he now? Is he in a hospital?"

"He was. They took him to Charing Cross Hospital, but he wouldn't stay there. He insisted on going home directly they put on the splints or whatever the things were. And will you believe me, Mrs Otway, when I tell you that he has been living alone in those wretched chambers ever since! He wouldn't even have a nurse. Isn't that just like a man?"

"But who looks after him?"

"Nobody. Of course there is the charwoman, or laundress as they call them – though why they should be called laundresses I can't imagine. They look more like dustwomen – and the man from the office downstairs looks in sometimes. It's a perfectly scandalous state of affairs. I wish, Mrs Otway, you would go and see him and make him have a nurse."

"I will certainly go and see him," said I. "I will go now," and I held out my hand to bring the interview to an end.

"How sweet of you, dear Mrs Otway!" she explained, keeping a firm hold of my hand, which I endeavoured unobtrusively to withdraw. "I felt sure you would go to the rescue. And you will insist on his having a nurse, won't you? He will listen to you, but you will have to be firm. Promise me you will, now."

"I will see that he is properly looked after," I replied.

"Yes, but he must have a nurse you know – a properly trained and certificated nurse. You can get excellent nurses at that place –

now, what is its name? Cavendish – Cavendish something. I am getting so silly about names. Let me see, I did have a card m my purse; perhaps it is there still –" Here she released my hand to open her wrist-bag, and I took the opportunity to retreat down the steps.

"Don't trouble, please," I urged. "I shall manage quite well. Goodbye!" and with this I hurried away, somewhat unceremoniously, across the wide road, and, as soon as I had turned the corner, broke into a run. A couple of minutes later I arrived at the station, breathless, just in time to see a Circle train move out. I could have wept with vexation. It was but a few minutes before the next one would be due, but those minutes dragged like hours. With swift strides I paced up and down the platform in an agony of impatience, turning over and over again Miss Tallboy-Smith's confused account of the accident and trying to construct by its aid some intelligible picture of Jasper's condition.

Even when I was in the train its progress seemed intolerably slow and the succession of stations interminable. It was an agony to sit still and passively await the leisurely arrival at my destination, and an unspeakable relief when, at last, I reached the Temple Station, to spring from the train, dash up the stairs and hurry along the embankment. My progress on foot might be slower, but I had the physical sensation of speed.

At the top of Middle Temple Lane I emerged into Fleet Street, and, crossing the road, entered Clifford's Inn Passage. I had never been there before, and, though I knew the number of Jasper's house, I thought it best to enquire as to its whereabouts. As I passed through the archway I saw a somewhat clerical-looking man standing at the door of the porter's lodge, and from him learned that No. 54 was in the inner court on the east side of the garden; with which direction I hurried on again. Clearly there came back to me the impressions that seemed so dim at the time; a sense of quiet and repose, of aloofness from the bustle of the city, an old-world, dignified shabbiness that was yet homely and pleasant withal. I crossed a little court, passed through a second archway and came out into a second, larger court, where the gay foliage of plane trees found a foil in the dingy, red brick of the venerable houses. A glance showed me the narrow alley by the garden, and a dozen paces along its roughly-flagged pavement brought me to the entry of No. 54, on the side of which was painted "Mr J. Davenant, Architect." and below, in smaller lettering, "Jonathan Weeble, Law Writer."

I stepped into the entry, and tapping on a door which, by its painted description, appeared to appertain to Mr Weeble's premises, was bidden to "come in." Accordingly, I entered and was confronted by a somewhat unkempt, young man who was apparently engaged in engrossing a large document which was secured to a sort of evergrown lectern by means of a band of tape.

"I have called," I said, "to enquire about Mr Davenant. Is he in a very serious condition?"

"He wasn't when I saw him about an hour ago," was the reply.

"Do you think he would be well enough to see me?"

The young man, whom I assumed to be Mr Weeble, inspected me critically, and then replied: "I should say most emphatically that he would. But we needn't leave it at that. I can soon find out. Won't you sit down?"

He rose briskly and hurried out of the office, and it was only when I heard him ascending the uncovered stairs, two or three at a time, that I remembered that I had given no name.

Mr Weeble's confident manner had lifted a load of anxiety from my mind, but my agitation was little abated. My fears were relieved, indeed, for evidently Jasper's condition was not such as to occasion alarm; but, as my anxiety subsided, other emotions made themselves felt. I was actually going to see him. Within a couple of minutes we should be together. The intolerable separation would be at an end. And the ecstasy of this thought – the almost painful joy of anticipation – brought home to me the intensity of my yearning to look on him again.

The sound of Mr Weeble's footsteps descending the stairs set my heart throbbing, and as he bustled into the office I stood up, trembling with excitement.

"It's all right" said he. "Mr Davenant will see you, if you'll go up. First floor, right hand side of the landing. I've left the door open, and you'll see his name above it."

I did not go up the stairs at Mr Weeble's pace, but I went as rapidly as the trembling of my knees would let me. On the first floor I saw a forbidding, iron-bound door standing ajar, and above it the well-beloved name, painted in white letters. I drew back the heavy door disclosing a lighter one, also ajar, which I pushed open as I closed the massive "oak" after me. For a moment I stood on the threshold looking into the quaint old-world room, with its panelled walls and the soft green light from the plane trees shimmering through the windows. He was reclining by the fire on a low, wooden settle, and held a book in his hand; and even in that instantaneous glance I could see how changed he was – how pale and thin and weary-looking. But as I stepped out from the shadow the worn face lighted up; the book fell to the floor, and he flung his arms out towards me.

"Helen!"

"Jasper!"

In a moment I was on my knees by his side. His arms were around me and my cheek lay against his. And so for a while we rested with never a word spoken and no sound in the room but the ticking of the clock and the soft rustle of a swaying branch on the window panes. And so I could have rested for ever; for at last my heart was at peace.

"Jasper, dear," I said, at length, "how is it with you? Are you badly hurt?"

"Not a bit," he replied. "It is just a matter of a cracked rib and a few bruises; and I've nearly recovered from those."

"But why did you never send me a word? That wasn't friendly of you Jasper."

"How could I, dearest?" he protested. "A bargain is a bargain. The month wasn't up."

"Jasper!" I exclaimed; "how could you be so silly? Of course you ought to have sent me a message, and I would have come to you instantly."

"I am sure you would, Helen," said he, "which was an additional reason for my keeping to our covenant. It would have seemed a shabby thing to do; for badly as I wanted you, I was never really in any danger. By the way, how did you hear of my little mishap?"

I told him of my meeting with Miss Tallboy-Smith, and he chuckled softly. "She was an old goose to frighten you with those lurid stories, but I'm very grateful to her, all the same. I *have* wanted you, Helen."

He drew me closer to him and stroked my hair fondly; and again we were silent for a while. The clock ticked on impassively, the plane tree rustled gently on the window, and I was filled with a quiet, restful happiness that I was unwilling to interrupt even by speaking.

Presently Jasper bent down to my ear and whispered: "Helen, darling, you haven't anything to tell me, have you?"

I knew what he meant, of course; and the strange thing is that, though the question came unexpectedly, and though I had not consciously given the subject a moment's thought, I found my mind completely and finally made up.

"Yes," I replied, "I have. Jasper, dear, I am your own. I can't live without you. The world must say what it will. I can do without the world, but I can't exist without you."

He drew me yet closer to him and kissed me reverently.

"Dear heart" he said softly, "sweet wife, I would try to thank you if words could tell you what your precious gift means to me. But life is before us, and mine shall be one, long thanksgiving. You have given me my heart's desire; if love and worship and faithful service can in any degree repay you, they shall be yours as long as our lives endure."

Thus in a few moments were the long weeks of misery and despair blotted out. We were reinstated, and, indeed, much more than reinstated; we were admitted and accepted lovers. And, just as my mind had, so to speak, made itself up without conscious thought on my part, so now that I had entered into this new covenant it seemed quite inevitable and satisfying. Its nonconformity with social conventions left me completely undisturbed.

Presently Jasper made me draw up a low, rush-bottomed chair that I might sit comfortably by his side while we talked. But, in fact, we talked little; for there is a sort of telepathy born of perfect sympathy that makes speech superfluous. We were both very happy and very deeply moved; and it seemed more companionable to sit, hand clasped in hand, and let our thoughts run on undisturbed by speech, knowing that the thoughts of each were but a reflection of the other's.

Anon came Mr Weeble, stamping slowly up the stairs like an infirm coal-porter and making such a prolonged to-do about inserting the latchkey into the outer door that we both laughed. A very discreet man was Mr Weeble.

"I've just come to see if I can do anything," said he, when Jasper had introduced me. "I generally make his tea and straighten out his bandages. Shall I make the tea now or are you taking charge, Mrs Otway?"

"I will make the tea," said I, "but while you are tidying up the bandages I will run out and get some fresh cakes."

"Yes," said Mr Weeble, "that would be a good idea. Our stock is rather low and a trifle old and fruity. And talking of cakes, that reminds me that an old rooster called a day or two ago and left one. I put it in a spare deed-box and forgot all about it. I'll go and fetch it up."

"A rooster, you say, Weeble," said Jasper. "May we assume that you are speaking figuratively?"

"Yes," replied Mr Weeble. "Elderly party with an automatic smile and the rummiest name I ever heard. Now what was her name? Something double-barrelled – Bigboy-Jones, was it?"

"Tallboy-Smith, I expect," said Jasper.

"That was it. I sent her a letter of thanks the same day in your handwriting and signed it with your name. Are you starting now, Mrs Otway? You'll find a very good cake-shop in Fetter Lane near the top on the left-hand side."

I took a brief bag of Jasper's and his latchkey and sallied forth into Fetter Lane by the postern gate; and as I walked up the quaint, old street I found myself looking into the homely shops and inspecting the ancient timber houses with a queer sort of proprietary air, as if I belonged to the neighbourhood.

I found the cake-shop — it was really an old-fashioned baker's shop, such as one might find in a country town — and as I made a selection of the wares based on experience of Jasper's tastes, I found myself almost unconsciously considering the merits of the establishment as a source of supply for a family of two. If the change in my mental state was sudden, it was certainly complete; as I sauntered back down Fetter Lane with my bag of provisions, carefree and filled with a delightful sense of emancipation, loitering to look into shop windows or to peer up strange courts and alleys that I might not return prematurely; I could not but contrast my condition with that in which I had set forth in the morning, hopeless, heart-weary, despondent.

When I arrived at Jasper's chambers, Mr Weeble had already gone; but he had filled the kettle and set it to boil on the gas-stove in the kitchen, where I found it murmuring placidly and breathing out little clouds of steam.

That kitchen was a delightful absurdity. About the magnitude of a good-sized china cupboard, it suggested, with its ranges of shelves and little chemical sink, a doctor's dispensary or a chemist's laboratory. Yet it was very orderly and quite convenient, and it had the advantage that, while I was engaged in the preparations for the meal my heart singing in unison with the kettle's song, I could look out of a tiny window on the moss-grown garden, or through the open door see Jasper watching me with a smile of ecstasy, and receive his instructions as to where the various articles were to be found.

It was all very pleasant and intimate, and every little, homely detail helped to bring home to me the reality of my happiness.

During the very leisurely tea we gradually approached the subject of our future arrangements, which had evidently been very carefully thought out by Jasper.

"I'm not quite such a graven image as I look," said he. "I don't believe it's necessary for me to keep so immovable. But that is the doctor's business. I just do as I'm told. However, my bandages are coming off in a few days, and I understand that I shall be practically well in a fortnight. Until I am well, we had better let things remain as they are; and I think it would be better for you not to come and see me again in the interval."

"Do you mean that I am to leave you, a helpless invalid, all alone and no one to look after you?"

"Yes," he replied. "Of course, I shall want you dreadfully, but as to my being alone and helpless, that is merely a sentimental view of the case. You can see for yourself that I am quite comfortable and well cared-for. Weeble never forgets me for an instant. And I think it most necessary that, until we are definitely married, we should have the most scrupulous regard for the conventions.

"We can't get the sanction either of the Law or the Church to our marriage; therefore, it is the more necessary for us to treat it ourselves with the utmost respect and seriousness. We are not going to enter into a casual and irresponsible relationship. We are going to contract a marriage; and I propose that we do so publicly and with proper formalities suited to the dignity and importance of the transaction."

"But," I asked, "what formalities are possible?"

"My proposal," he replied, "is this: we shall appoint a day and a time to meet here, and have two witnesses in attendance. Weeble could be one and the Inn porter, Mr Duskin, the other. In the presence of those witnesses we shall formally agree to take one another as husband and wife. Each of us shall make a written declaration to the same effect, reciting the circumstances which render the unusual procedure necessary, and, in your case, denouncing and repudiating your marriage with Otway. These declarations we shall respectively read to the witnesses – who will also read them – and we shall each sign our declaration in the presence of the witnesses.

"I am not quite clear whether it would be legal for them to counter-sign as witnesses. If not, we shall add a note stating that the signatures were made in their presence. Then we shall exchange declarations and we shall notify Mr Otway and whosoever else may be concerned, or whom we wish to inform, of what has taken place. Does that meet with your approval, Helen?"

"Entirely," I replied, "excepting the sentence of banishment. Don't you think I might just look in on you now and again to see if you want anything?"

"It is only a fortnight, dearest," said he, "and we can write as often as we please. Until we are married we can't be too careful to avoid provoking criticism."

I made no further objections, for I felt that he was right; and, moreover, I could not but perceive that this rather excessive primness, like the formalities which he had proposed, was simply an unconscious expression of chivalrous respect, a protest in advance against any unfavourable criticisms of me.

And in accordance with what I felt he would consider prudent, I took leave of him comparatively early, so as to avoid a second meeting with Mr Weeble, who, I learned, came in every night between eight and nine to help him to get to bed.

"I shall write to you every day," I said as I drew on my gloves, "and you must promise that, if there is anything that I can do for you, you will let me know and never mind about Mrs Grundy. Is that agreed?"

He gave the required promise, and when I had handed him back his latchkey, I stooped and kissed him; and as I looked back at him before closing the iron-bound door, I could not but contrast this parting with the miserable farewell of less than a month ago.

CHAPTER TWENTY-ONE

A Dreadful Inheritance

It has always been and still is, somewhat of a puzzle to me to account for the sudden and complete change in my point of view in regard to my union with Jasper. Lilith would doubtless have explained it as a case of subconscious reflection, and probably she would have been right. My impression is that Peggy's matter-of-fact attitude towards marriage unsanctioned by law had a more profound effect than I was aware of; that her words – which I had certainly recalled from time to time – had remained in my mind subconsciously exercising a continuous influence. Or it may be that I had found a life of separation impossible, and had realised it consciously only when I found myself once more in Jasper's presence.

But, however it may have happened, the fact remains that I accepted the new order without a qualm. The conditions that I had scouted as unthinkable now seemed entirely reasonable and acceptable. The only twinge of misgiving that I ever had, was produced by the draft of the declaration that Jasper sent for my approval and criticism. For that well-meant document, with its half-defiant, half-protesting phrases, did certainly bring home to me with uncomfortable vividness the fact that this marriage was not like any other marriage, and that I was not as other married women were. But I sent it back approved and tried to forget it, and quietly went on with my preparations for the new life.

Outwardly, however, I made no change in my habits, and even tried to suppress the gaiety and buoyancy of spirit that I felt, lest the sudden change from my recent depressed condition should attract notice. I still lived my life apart, only too happy in my solitude and spent most of my time in the workshop conning over Jasper's letters, or meditating on the happy days that were drawing so near. For a time the candlestick was sadly neglected, until I had the sudden inspiration of finishing it as a wedding-gift to Jasper. And then all the joy of work revived and blossomed into unsuspected skill. Tracer and punch seemed to travel along their appointed paths unguided; the spindle-shanked chasing hammer became a familiar demon and appeared to develop a volition of its own, and the little enamel furnace roared with glee.

So the days sped by, each bringing me nearer to the golden gate of my enchanted garden, and each so filled with quiet happiness that I could not wish it shorter. About the end of the first week came a letter from Jasper saying that the bandages had been discarded, and that he had taken a walk and had appeared quite well and strong. Then, a day or two later, came another fixing the date and time of our meeting. It was to be on the following Thursday – only five days ahead – at six o'clock in the evening. The formalities were to be carried out immediately on my arrival; we should then dine quietly at the club, spend the evening at a concert or the theatre, and take the boat train either to Flushing or Calais, whichever I preferred.

The arrival of this letter, though I had been daily expecting it, came as quite a shock, and turned my tranquil happiness into feverish excitement which I had some difficulty in concealing. The fixing of an actual date and the selection of a definite region in which to spend the honeymoon (I chose the north of France) gave a reality to this Great Adventure and brought it out of the undefined future into the present. For now I had to carry out the final preparations. Lightly as I might travel, I must take some luggage, and this would entail a conveyance; and this in its turn involved something in the nature of a public departure, so that, if

I had desired to disappear secretly – which I did not – the thing would have been impossible. Yet I was, naturally, loath to say much about my immediate intentions, preparing to make my explanations by letter after the event; and this the prevailing good manners of the little community rendered quite easy. I notified Miss Polton and my more intimate friends that I was going away on a visit of uncertain duration, and, whatever curiosity they may have felt, no further particulars were asked for. I went about my immediate preparations – the packing of those few things that I must needs take away with me – unnoticed, or at least uncommented on, and then began unobtrusively to arrange the rest of my possessions for the final removal.

On Wednesday – the day before that of my departure – a letter arrived from Mr Otway. It reached me just after lunch, and I glanced at it before rising from the table. The subject was the same as that of previous ones, but it was evident that something in the nature of a crisis was approaching. The extreme agitation of the writer was shown not only in the matter and the impassioned, rather incoherent manner but even in the handwriting; which was ill-formed and slovenly, in great contrast to Mr Otway's usual businesslike neatness.

"My dear Helen," it began, "I have not troubled you for quite a long time with my miserable affairs – which are to some extent your affairs too. But they are going from bad to worse, and now I feel that I am coming to the limits of endurance. I cannot bear this much longer. My health is shattered, my peace of mind is wrecked, and my brain threatens to give way. Death would be a boon, a relief, and I feel that it is not far off. I cannot go on like this. Those wretches leave me no peace. Hardly a week passes but I get some new menace; and now – but I can't tell you in a letter. It is too horrible. Come to me, Helen, for the love of God! I am in torment. Have pity on me, even though you have never forgiven me. I cannot come to you, for I am now unable to leave my bed. I am a wreck, a ruin. Come to me just this once, and if you cannot help me, at least give the comfort of your sympathy. You will not be troubled by me much longer.

"Your distracted husband,

"Lewis Otway."

The emotions that this letter aroused were mixed and rather conflicting. Never had I felt a deeper loathing of Mr Otway than now that I was being forced to accept what I knew in my heart to be but a counterfeit of marriage. I had been robbed of my birthright, and he had robbed me. Never was I less in a mood to offer him sympathy in the troubles that he had created for himself and me by his callous selfishness. And yet I decided to go to him. Whether the decision was due to some sort of compunction for the blow that I was going to strike on the morrow; or whether to curiosity, or to a desire to verify his foreboding of approaching death, I cannot say. Certainly the last consideration entered into the mixture of motives, and probably was the determining factor. At any rate, I decided to go. Dimly, I perceived that I ought to have consulted Jasper, though I was unaware of the possible legal significance that my visit might acquire. I formed my decision at once, and early in the afternoon set forth westward with the letter in my pocket.

I did not go direct to Mr Otway's chambers. Promptly as I had made up my mind I felt the necessity of thinking over the circumstances and forecasting the possibilities. On my way westward I made a halt at a tea-shop and while I awaited the leisurely service I drew out the letter and read it through again. Clearly the blackmailers were becoming more urgent and possibly more definite. It seemed as though they had adopted some new tactics. But it was not the blackmailers who interested me. I found my eye travelling again and again to those two sentences that hinted at the possibility of Mr Otway's death.

"I feel that it is not far off." And again, "You will not be troubled by me much longer." Had he any solid grounds for these forebodings? Or were they merely the offspring of abiding terror, or perchance simply rhetorical flourishes designed to arouse my sympathy? These were questions of no small moment to me, for Mr Otway's death would set me free and in an instant unravel the tangled skein of my relations with Jasper.

As I drank my tea with reflective deliberation I turned these questions over in my mind, not disguising from myself the cool, impassive, egoism of my attitude. My feeling in respect of Mr Otway was devoid of any trace of sentimentalism. I viewed him as the insurance director views interested in his decease, not in his survival. I loathed him, the generalised "proposer," – but inversely; for I was but I did not hate him. I did not wish him ill. If I could have saved him from suffering I would have done so, even at the cost of some considerable effort. But if he had stood in the peril of instant death, and I could have averted that peril by moving a finger, I would not have moved a finger.

That was my position. As I rose from the table and returned the letter to my pocket, what was in my mind was that Mr Otway seemed to think that he was going to die and I hoped that he was right.

When I reached Lyon's Inn Chambers the sun was already low and the gloom of the evening was beginning to settle on the closed-in block of buildings. I ascended the ill-lit stone stairs to the second floor where the light on the landing was so dim that I had difficulty in deciphering Mr Otway's name above the door of his "set"; and as I did so I noted with surprise that the inscription was faded and obscure, and had the appearance of having been in existence for many years whereas Mr Otway had, as I believed but recently entered on his tenancy.

The door was opened by Mrs Gregg, who stood in the gloom of the entry confronting me without a word.

"Good evening, Mrs Gregg," I said. "Mr Otway has asked me to call on him – "

"Ye need make no excuses," she interrupted, "for coming to see your lawful husband."

"Thank you, Mrs Gregg," I replied. "Is Mr Otway disengaged?"

"No," she answered; "he is expecting a visitor."

"How very unfortunate," said I. "He wanted particularly to see me, I know."

"Perhaps you could look in some time tomorrow?" she suggested.

"No, I am afraid I can't. If Mr Otway is unable to see me this evening I must write to him. I shall not have another opportunity to call for some considerable time."

She reflected for a few moments, and I gathered that she was unwilling to take the responsibility of cancelling the interview.

"Could you call again a little later?" she asked, at length. "He will have finished with his visitor by about half past seven, or say a quarter to eight. Could you look in again at eight?"

I had not wanted to be out as late as this would make me, but if I was to see Mr Otway at all, it would have to be tonight. Eventually I accepted the arrangement, somewhat, I think, to Mrs Gregg's relief.

As I descended the stairs I heard the footsteps of two persons – apparently a man and a woman – ascending. On the first-floor landing I met the man, who turned out to be the lamplighter. Just as I had passed him he lit the landing lamp, and its light, which came from behind me, fell full on the woman who was coming up. It was only a momentary glimpse that I caught as she passed me on the stairs, but I recognised her instantly. She was Mrs Campbell, the wife of the Wardour Street dealer.

It was an odd meeting, and it gave me the material for a good deal of thought and speculation. Mr Otway's chambers were the only ones on the second floor; from which it seemed probable that Mrs Campbell was the visitor whom he was expecting. This was a rather queer coincidence; but it was not the only one. That sudden recognition of the face, thrown into strong relief against the dark background by the bright lamplight, had set my memory working. I remembered how, when I had seen Mrs Campbell in the shop and had heard her speak, her face had seemed to suggest something familiar, and her accent and the intonation of her voice had called up some accent and tone that I had heard before. It had been but a vague impression at the time; but now, in the new setting and aided by association, the impression became quite definite. The face that hers had suggested was Mr Otway's face; but the really odd thing was that her voice and accent suggested not Mr Otway's but Mrs Gregg's. And this very queer resemblance was made yet more queer by a singular discrepancy. Mrs Gregg spoke with a distinct Scottish accent. It was a peculiar one, different from that of any other Scots person whom I had ever heard speak; but it was quite pronounced. Mrs Campbell, on the other hand, had no trace whatever of a Scottish accent; of that I was quite sure. But I was equally sure of the resemblance between the two, subtle and elusive as it was.

Here, then, was a problem the consideration of which gave me quite a considerable amount of occupation, and helped me to while away the hour and a half that I had to wait. The almost fantastic oddity of the coincidence might have made me reject my impressions as mere delusions; but, on the one hand, there was Mrs Campbell evidently making for Mr Otway's chambers, and, on the other, was the fact that it was Mr Otway who had introduced me to the shop in Wardour Street. However, I could get no farther than speculation; and, as speculation tends rapidly to exhaust its limited material, I presently dismissed the problem and returned to the consideration of Mr Otway's health and its bearing on my own future.

The hour and a half I spent in a leisurely survey of Lincoln's Inn and the Temple. My perambulations with Jasper had brought home to me that London is an entertainment in itself; that no observant person need be dull who has access to its historic streets and picturesque backwaters. And now it was very pleasant to revisit the scenes of former rambles – to be repeated often in the future – and meanwhile to reflect on the happenings of the present and let my thoughts stray to the new life that was about to open; and the time slipped away so agreeably that when the three-quarter chime was struck in a polite undertone by the genteel clock in the Inner Temple, it came to me as quite a surprise.

On the stroke of eight I rang the bell of Mr Otway's chambers, and was forthwith admitted by the taciturn Mrs Gregg. In silence she conducted me along a narrow corridor that led from the entrance lobby, across a largish room furnished partly as a library, partly as a dining-room, and by a communicating door into the bedroom, when – still without uttering a word – she departed, shutting the door after her.

Mr Otway half rose in bed as I entered, and made a vague gesture of welcome, finally extending his hand, which I shook formally.

"This is really good of you, Helen," said he, "to come and see me, and to come so promptly. I am sorry Mrs Gregg sent you away. There was no need. My other visitor could have been put off."

"It is of no consequence," said I. "My time was my own tonight. What is the new trouble – for I infer from your letter that there is some new development. Is there any definite threat?"

Again he half rose in bed, and looking at me with anxious intensity said, in a low, suppressed tone: "Helen, just see that the door is properly shut."

I did so, and he then begged me to draw the chair, which had been placed for me closer to him. This I also did, and, having seated myself, looked at him expectantly.

Still half raised in bed, he bent his head as near to me as he could, and in a whisper said, "Helen, I want to ask you a question. What became of your father's stick?"

The question, whispered with such strange secrecy, and accompanied by a singular look compounded of eagerness, fear and suspicion, somewhat startled me; for I remembered, even as he spoke, that the same question had been asked by Dr Thorndyke.

"I haven't the least idea," I replied. "Haven't you got it?"

"No. I never had it. I have never seen it since the – ah – the occasion when – ah – you remember – "

"Of course I remember. I have good reason to."

"Ah – no doubt. Yes. But are you quite sure – thought you might have taken it away with you."

"But, Mr Otway, you let me out of the house yourself. You saw me go, and you must have seen that I was not taking it. And you know that I never came to the house again."

He sank back on his pillow with a gesture of despair.

"Yes," he murmured, "that seems to be so. It must be so, I suppose."

"It is so," I said. "There is no question about it. When I went away that morning the stick was in your house. But why are you asking me about it? Is it of any importance?"

He turned towards a table that stood by the opposite side of the bed, and taking up a bunch of keys, unlocked a deed-box that was on the table, and took from it a sheet of paper.

"Read that," said he, handing me the paper.

The document was a typewritten letter of a similar character to the previous ones, and of about the same length. It ran thus:

"Mr Lewis Otway,

"Some funny questions are being asked. What about Mr Vardon's stick – the loaded stick with the silver knob to hide the lead loading? Where is it? Somebody says they know where it is and who's got it. And they say there is a bruise on the silver top, and they say something about a smear of blood and a grey hair sticking to it. Do you know anything about it? If you don't, you'd better find out. Because I think you'll hear from that somebody before you are many weeks older or else from the police.

"A well-wisher."

As I came to the end of this document I raised my eyes and met Mr Otway's fixed on me with a very singular expression. But he quickly averted his gaze, possibly embarrassed by the steady intensity of my own. For this letter, together with Mr Otway's agitated questionings, had revived the old doubts in my mind. Could there be any truth in this veiled accusation? Was it possible that I had really made a hideous mistake in shielding this man? As these doubts flashed through my mind, some reflection of them may have appeared in my expression as I steadily looked Mr Otway in the face. At any rate, he looked away as I have said; and when I handed him back the letter, he took it in a hand that shook like a dipsomaniac's, and replaced it in the deed-box without a word.

For a space we were both silent, and I sat looking at him and his surroundings with profound distaste. The close, stuffy air of the room aroused a faint disgust; the objects on the bedside table – the cigarette box – the large spirit decanter and siphon and a bottle of veronal tablets – conveyed a disagreeable impression of drinking and drug-taking. And the man himself, with his pasty face, his baggy eyelids, creased with multitudinous wrinkles, his drooping tremulous underlip, was distinctly repellent. The whole atmosphere of the place and its occupant was unwholesome, sordid and abnormal.

Yet, unwholesome and unhealthy as he looked, there was no striking change in Mr Otway's appearance; nothing new to justify so far as I could judge his alarming account of himself. His aspect supported the suggestions of the spirit-bottle, the cigarettes and the veronal; he looked distracted, terrified, nerve-shaken; but he did not, to my eye, look like a dying man. I inspected him critically during that interval of silence, and arrived, almost regretfully, I fear, at the conclusion that his forebodings were merely the result of a chronic state of fear – if they were real and not deliberately assumed to excite my sympathy.

I think he must have had a feeling that I was regarding him with disfavour, for presently he turned towards me with a deprecating air and sighed wearily.

"I am afraid Helen," said he, "that you are very tired of me and my troubles. But you must try to be patient. It may not be for long."

"Why do you say that?" I asked. "Is your health really bad, apart from the worry of these letters?"

"My health gets worse from week to week," he replied. "Not that I am suffering from any definite disease. But the constant alarm and anxiety, the shocks which keep coming one on top of another, are breaking me up. I get no interval of peace in which to recover. I am in a constant state of worry and depression by day, which leads to that," and he pointed to the spirit-decanter, "and it is even worse at night unless I secure a little rest by those things" pointing to the veronal bottle; "and cigarettes, whisky and veronal don't make for a long life or robust health."

"Still," I said, "you mustn't exaggerate or alarm yourself unnecessarily. You are not in very good condition, I can see; but there is no reason to suppose that you are in a dangerous state. Couldn't you cut off these drugs and the whisky and go away for a change?"

"He shook his head. I couldn't go away," he said. "They would find me out and follow me. And as to cutting off the stimulants and the sedatives that is impossible. Bad as they are, they are the last bulwark against something worse."

"What do you mean?" I asked.

He did not answer immediately, but seemed to be considering my question and debating whether he should make any further confidences. At length he turned to me somewhat abruptly with an expression which I had never seen on his face before: a wild expression strangely unlike his usual, heavy stolidity, suggesting excitement and terror, with yet a curious dash of exultation.

"Helen," he said with a singular intensity of voice and manner, "there are men who are born into this world under sentence of death. The black cap hangs over their cradles. Throughout their lives they have continually to watch – to evade the execution of the sentence if they can. But the time comes when they can escape no longer. They are tired of evasion, of the struggle to escape; and then they give themselves up; and that is the end.

"I am one of those men, Helen. My mother put an end to her own life. My only brother put an end to his life. My mother's father made away with himself. It is in the blood. My mother was found hanging from a tree in an orchard. My brother disappeared and was found a month later hanging from a peg in a disused wardrobe. My grandfather hanged himself from a beam in the loft. Perhaps there were others. At any rate, there it is. The fathers have eaten sour grapes and the children's teeth are set on edge."

He paused, and I sat looking with uneasy surprise at the unwonted animation in his face: the faint flush, the awakening light in his eyes, the suppressed eagerness of his manner. There was something weirdly unpleasant about this new phase.

"You mustn't allow these fancies to disturb you," I said feebly.

"They are not fancies," he retorted. "They are weighty realities. I thought for a long time that the inheritance had passed me by. But when the first of those letters came, I knew that the legacy had fallen in. And every new menace sets the impulse working. Whenever one of those letters comes I feel it; I find myself thinking of my mother and my brother, and wondering if they felt the same. Then I take a stiff whisky, and the feeling goes off. But I don't care, nowadays, to go to bed until I have taken a dose of veronal."

"Why not?" I asked.

He drew himself to the edge of the bed, and, thrusting his head out, peered into a shadowy corner of the room with a sort of half-terrified, half-exultant leer that seemed to stir the very marrow of my bones.

"What is it, Mr Otway?" I asked, staring into the corner but seeing nothing.

"Do you see it, Helen?" he said, rolling his eyes at me and then looking back into the corner, which was in a line with the bed-head; "that great hook, or bent peg. I can't imagine what it was put there for; but there it is, like a great metal finger, beckoning – beckoning."

I looked at the object that he indicated – a massive curved peg or hook fixed to the wall about seven feet from the floor – and shivered slightly. Its appearance was horribly suggestive.

"When I used to lie awake," Mr Otway continued, still gazing into the corner, "after the first letters came, I could lie on my left side, because then it was behind me and I seemed to feel it drawing me. I had to turn so that I could see it; and whenever I looked at it, it seemed to beckon. And so it does now."

"I should have it unscrewed and taken away," said I.

"Yes," he replied, reflectively, "perhaps it might be — and yet I don't know. Perhaps I might be more restless if it were not there. It is, in a way, a satisfaction to know that — ah — that I hold a trump card that I can play if — ah — if all the other cards are against me."

As he spoke, he looked at me with that same curious half-frightened, half-exultant expression that made me wonder whether perhaps his inheritance included a dash of insanity. Then he rolled back to the middle of the bed and lay staring at the ceiling; and by degrees the excitement faded out of his face and he recovered his usual stolid gravity of expression.

Presently he glanced at the little carriage clock that stood on the table, and, turning to me, said: "I usually take my veronal about this time. Would you mind giving me a glass of water and the tablets?"

I rose from my chair, and as I did so my little wrist-bag, which had been reposing, forgotten, on my lap, slipped to the floor. I picked it up and hung it on the knob of the chair-back, and then fetched the water-bottle and tumbler from the wash-stand. Having filled the tumbler and handed it to Mr Otway, I picked up the veronal bottle, and seeing that it was a new one, broke the seal, withdrew the cork and pulled out the cotton-wool packing.

"Three tablets please," said Mr Otway.

I handed him the bottle and as he took it and shook out the three tablets he smiled grimly.

"You are the most cautious woman I have ever met," he remarked. "But you are quite right to make me responsible for my own poison."

He took the tablets one at a time, crunching each between his teeth very thoroughly before washing it down with water. Then he mixed what looked to me a very stiff allowance of whisky with a very little soda water, and swallowed it at a draught.

"I find that the stimulant makes the veronal act more rapidly," he explained. "I shall be asleep in about half an hour. Do you mind staying with me until I drop off?"

I agreed to this, although it was getting late; but, conscious that it was probably the last service I should ever render him, I did not feel that I could refuse. So I sat down again in the chair and watched him, noting that already – probably as a result of the stimulant – he was quieter in manner and more peaceful in appearance. Even when he reverted to the subject that had occasioned my visit his manner was quite calm.

"There is something very mysterious about that stick," he remarked. "Recalling the circumstances, I remember putting it down in the corner by the writing-table. I never saw it again, and never gave its whereabouts a thought. I assumed that you had taken it, but I now realise that I was mistaken. Apparently it has got into undesirable hands and we haven't heard the last of it, I fear."

"You had better not think any more about it, Mr Otway," I said. "There is nothing to be done, and the less you worry the less harm these people will be able to do you."

"Yes," he agreed; "that is good advice, and I can follow it now. But if I should wake up in the small hours of the morning it will be very different. That is the worst time, Helen. Then this persecution seems beyond bearing. The horror of it makes me sweat with fear. I seem to hear the police on the stairs. I find myself listening for the sound of the bell. It is horrible – horrible! And then I think of that wardrobe, unnoticed all those weeks, and the figure inside in the dark. And then – "

He made a motion of his eyes towards the shadowy corner, and involuntarily I glanced at the great peg high up on the wall.

He did not speak again for some time, and I sat silently watching him and thinking – thinking of his dreadful heritage and all that it might mean. Was it a reality, this legacy of death that he saw coming to him? Was it true that even now the black cap hung over his bed? Supposing it were? Supposing that this very night, in the chilly middle watch, he should wake with all his terrors clutching at his heart! Should creep out of his bed and – Here my glance stole into the shadowy corner, and, as I looked, my mind seemed to picture a dim shape filling the wall space below the big, massive peg. There were no details and hardly any form; it was just a shape, vague and rather horrible. I shivered slightly, but I did not try to blot out the mental picture. It was a gruesome thing, that dim, elongated shape, but it did not disturb me much; for it set going other associated trains of thought. There was the ceremony tomorrow evening, the witnesses with their doubtful rights of attestation, protesting that all was in order – and protesting in vain. There were two Ishmaelites going forth hand-in-hand into the wilderness, ready to meet scorn with defiance – but still Ishmaelites. And at the thought, the shape upon the wall space below the peg seemed to grow less dim, to loom out more distinctly. That shape was Mr Otway – dead. The late Mr Otway. No longer a legal impediment, but just a fiction that had ceased to exist.

From the dark corner I turned my eyes on to the living man as he lay motionless, breathing softly with an occasional faint snore, and now and again puffing out his cheeks. He was not asleep, for I could see his eyes open and close at intervals; but he was evidently growing somnolent. I watched him with deep interest, almost with fascination, as one might look on a condemned man making his last journey in the hangman's cart. This was a condemned man, too: a potential suicide. At any moment he might set forth on his last journey; and his arrival at his destination would set the Ishmaelites free. He was ready to go; but he awaited the determining influence that would start him on his journey. What form would that final cause take? Would it be some sudden shock of alarm? Or the cumulative effect of prolonged, abiding fear?

I leaned forward and spoke softly to him.

"Do you know, Mr Otway, what caused your brother – "

He opened his eyes and looked at me, dully. "What did you say, Helen?" he asked.

"I was wondering if you knew – if there was anything in particular that caused your brother to take his life."

He cogitated sleepily for a while before replying. At length he answered, in a drowsy voice: "I am not very clear about it. He had had a good deal of worry of one kind and another, financial and domestic. I don't know that anything unusual had occurred; but he had been in a nervous, depressed state for some time."

Having made this reply, Mr Otway closed his eyes and took a deep breath; and I reflected on the significance of his answer. There had apparently been no specific cause of his brother's suicide, but just the accumulating effects of nervousness and depression, which exploded when they reached a certain degree of intensity. His condition, in fact, seemed to have been almost identical with Mr Otway's present condition.

Once more my eyes wandered away to the shadowy corner; and again the wall space below the great hook-like peg became occupied by that elongated shape. Now I seemed to visualise it more completely. It was no longer a mere shape. It had parts – recognisable members. There were the limp-dangling arms, the downward-pointing toes, the shadowy head lolling sideways. It was very horrible, yet I found myself viewing it without horror, but rather with a certain detached interest. I was getting used to it, and was disposed to consider it in terms of its significance.

It was not a person. It was a thing which had replaced a person who had ceased to exist. That person had had a wife. But the wife had ceased to exist, too. In her place was a widow – a free, unattached woman in whom were vested all the rights and liberties of spinsterhood, including the power to contract a valid and regular marriage. The shape was an ugly and forbidding thing; but it held precious and desirable gifts.

From the shape projected by my own imagination my eyes turned to the actual man – the man who was convertible into such a shape. He was fast asleep now; lying on his back, breathing a little stertorously and blowing out his cheeks at each breath. He was an unpleasant spectacle, and the sound of his breathing was disagreeable. He ought not to be lying on his back; for sleepers who lie on their backs are apt to dream, and dreams are not good for men with a tendency to suicide. And sleepers who breathe stertorously are apt to dream ugly dreams.

This consideration set my thoughts working afresh. Supposing this man should have a dream presenting his waking terrors with all the added intensity and vividness of a nightmare; the heavy footfalls of the police upon the stairs, the hands groping in the darkness of the landing for the bell-pull! Or if his dream should show him that wardrobe with its dreadful occupant! What would happen? And even as I put the question to myself my imagination supplied with startling vividness the answering picture. I saw the affrighted sleeper suddenly awaken in uncontrollable panic, scramble from his bed and shuffle hurriedly towards the corner under the peg.

The mental construction of the scene was singularly complete and orderly. I even found myself filling in the details of the means. There, indeed, was the peg. But a man cannot hang himself without some means of suspension. And these must be immediately available or the impulse might die away before they were found. I glanced around the room to see what means were to hand; and at once my eye lighted on an old-fashioned bell-rope that hung beside the head of the bed. Its perfect suitability was evident at a glance – provided that it could be detached without ringing the bell. But the necessity for cutting it rather than pulling it down would be obvious, even to a suicide.

The means, then, were all ready to hand. And there was the man, charged with this self-destructive tendency, sleeping in the very posture calculated to start it into action.

I sat still, watching him with absorbing interest, and as these thoughts shaped themselves with more and more distinctness, an impulse of which I was barely conscious formed itself and steadily grew in intensity. At length I leaned forward and spoke in a low voice.

"Mr Otway, you should not lie in that position."

There was no answer and he made no sign. The heavy breathing went on with uninterrupted regularity, the eyes remained closed. Again I spoke, this time more loudly, clearly and distinctly.

"Mr Otway can you hear me? If you lie as you are lying, you will probably dream. You may have bad, dangerous dreams. You may dream of your mother and your brother. You may dream that the peg on the wall is beckoning to you. And then you may wake in a panic and think that the peg is still beckoning. And then – "

I stopped suddenly. What was this that I was doing? Was it a warning to avert disaster? So the words were framed. But I knew it was nothing of the kind. It was suggestion, pure and almost undisguised. The dreadful truth struck me like a blow and seemed to turn me into stone. I sat rigid as a statue, still leaning forward with my lips parted as if to complete that awful sentence, every moment more appalled by this frightful thing that I had done. There came to me in a flash a vision of my own automatism after the seance; I heard Lilith telling me how the sleep of the drugged resembles the hypnotic trance; and again it came to me how I had been sitting looking at that terrible peg on the wall and – without conscious intention – creating by my will the awful shape beneath it.

How long I should have sat, bent forward as if frozen into rigid immobility by the horror of this hideous thing, it is impossible to say. The realisation of what I had done, that had fallen on me like a thunderbolt, had petrified me in a posture of arrested action. It seemed to have deprived me of the power of movement.

The place was intensely silent. The monotonous breathing of the sleeping man – the snoring intake alternating with the soft blowing expiration – made no impression on the profound quiet and the rapid ticking of the little carriage clock on the table seemed only to make it more intense.

Suddenly something stirred in the outer room. I sprang to my feet with a gasp that had almost been a shriek. Probably it was only Mrs Gregg, but in my overwrought state the sound was vaguely alarming. I stood for a few moments, my heart thumping and my breath coming short and fast; then I stole on tiptoe across the room and softly opening the door, peered into the outer room. It was in darkness except that a bright beam of moonlight poured in at the window; but this gave enough light to show that there was nobody in the room.

Still fearful of I knew not what, I stepped softly through the doorway and looked about me suspiciously. The moonlight struck on a large cupboard or wardrobe, which instantly suggested the lurking-place of some eavesdropper and at the same time aroused horrible associations connected with Mr Otway's brother; so that, in spite of my alarm, I was impelled to pluck at the handle to satisfy myself that no figure was hidden within. But the cupboard was locked, or, at any rate, would not open.

Then I looked under the table and peered into the darker corners of the room, growing – naturally – more and more nervous every moment, and pausing from time to time to listen, or to look back through the doorway into the bedroom, where I could see Mr Otway lying motionless like a sepulchral effigy.

Suddenly something stirred softly quite near to me – the sound seemed to come from the cupboard. I could have screamed with terror. The last vestige of my self-possession was gone, and in sheer panic I fled across the room and down the corridor to the entrance lobby. This place was in utter darkness, and as I frantically groped for the latch, I felt my skin creep and break out into a chilly sweat. At last I found the latch, dragged the door open and darted out; and as the clang of the closing door filled the building with hollow echoes, I ran swiftly down the stairs.

Once out in the inhabited streets, my alarm subsided somewhat; but still the image of that motionless figure in the bedroom, the sinister-looking peg on the wall and the recollection of those dreadful words that I had spoken into the sleeper's ears pursued me with an abiding horror. I walked quickly out into the Strand and I was in the act of hailing a cab when I remembered that I had left my wrist-bag hanging on the chair-back by Mr Otway's bedside. My purse was in that bag. But if it had contained my entire worldly possessions I could not have summoned up courage enough to go back for it.

The cab drew up by the kerb. I hesitated a moment, but reflecting that it was yet hardly ten o'clock, and that someone would be waiting up from whom I could borrow the fare, I gave the cabman the address, with the necessary explanations, entered the cab and shut the door. But as the crazy vehicle – it was an ancient four-wheeler – rattled over the uneven roadways of the side streets, the scene in that warm and stuffy bedroom was re-enacted again and again. And yet again I looked on that ill-omened cupboard in the ghostly moonlight; speculated on the mysterious sounds in the living-room; wondered uncomfortably if there had been a watcher or a listener, and if so, whether that eavesdropper knew the meaning of silent willing and suggestion.

CHAPTER TWENTY-TWO

The Catastrophe

Viewed by the cheerful light of the morning sun as it streamed in through my bedroom window, the phantoms of the previous night dwindled to mere scarecrows. On the panic-stricken state in which I had fled from Mr Otway's chambers I was now disposed to look back with faint amusement. Even the words which I had spoken into Mr Otway's ears as he slept had no longer any terrifying significance, though I had to admit that they were not susceptible of any satisfactory interpretation. They had been spoken under the influence of an impulse which I could not account for, and did not care to examine too closely, but which I vaguely connected with my excursions into psychical research – a subject which I decided to avoid as far as possible in the future.

As to Mr Otway, if his account of his family was correct, it seemed quite probable that, sooner or later, he would make away with himself, though, seeing that he was now well past middle life, the propensity could hardly be as strong as he had represented it. On the other hand, he was now being subjected to a very excessive nervous strain, and was undoubtedly letting his mind run on the subject of suicide. If the blackmailers continued to keep up an increasing pressure, as they seemed inclined to do, the breaking-point might be reached quite soon. And I could not disguise from myself that the catastrophe, if and when it occurred, would not present itself to me as a personal misfortune.

With this I dismissed Mr Otway and his affairs, and let my thoughts roam into more attractive regions. For this was the day of days. In a matter of a few hours my separation from Jasper would be at an end. We should be united, never again to part.

As I rose and dressed, this was the burden of my thoughts. The weeks of separation and loneliness were gone and the hours that lay between the present and that final meeting were running out apace like the grains of sand in an hourglass that is nearly spent. I hurried over breakfast that I might the sooner escape to be alone with my happiness; and most of the morning I spent in the workshop, arranging my apparatus so that it might easily be packed, in case I should not come back to superintend the removal myself. The candlestick, which was finished and successful beyond my expectations, I took upstairs to place in my trunk that I might give it to Jasper this very day. And then I paid a visit to my friend Peggy, whom I found in her workshop chirruping gaily and very busy making a complicated set of plaster moulds from the dissected wax model of her masterpiece. But I did not stay long with her, for the making of piece-moulds is an engrossing occupation and one better followed in solitude.

As I entered the house from the garden I encountered our little housemaid with a telegram in her hand.

"This has just come for you, ma'am," said she, holding it out towards me. "The boy is waiting to see if there is any answer."

I suppose that to most persons unaccustomed to receiving telegrams, the appearance of the peremptory, orange-tinted envelope is a little portentous. Especially so was it to me at that moment, with the crisis of my life so near at hand; and my heart beat tumultuously as I tore open the envelope and unfolded the flimsy paper. It bore but a brief message; but when I had read that message, the joy of life, the half-timorous happiness that had come to me with the morning sunlight, went out in a moment, like a wind-blown taper, and left me desolate.

"Cancel appointment for today and do not come to the club. Letter follows. Jasper."

That was all. There was really nothing very alarming in it. But to me it came as a dreadful anticlimax, strung up, as I was, to the highest pitch of nervous tension. With a trembling hand I refolded the paper, and, having told the maid that there was no answer, ran up to my room and bolted myself in.

It was a terrible blow. Only now, by the bitterness of the disappointment, did I realise the heart-hunger that I had endured, the intense yearning for the moment in which my beloved companion would be restored to me. And then, beyond this sudden collapse of my happiness, almost in the moment of its realisation, was the mystery, the suspense, the uncertainty. What could it be that had happened? Had Jasper's condition suddenly grown worse? That could hardly be, for he was practically well – at least, he had so regarded himself – and moreover there was that cryptic reference to the club. Why must I not go to the club?

There was something very mysterious in that prohibition.

The more I reflected on the matter the more puzzling did it appear. On the other hand, the very mystery in which the affair was shrouded was itself a relief. For, of course, I never for one moment had the faintest doubt of Jasper's loyalty, nor could I entertain the possibility of his having changed his views on the subject of our marriage. Something had occurred to hinder it; but Jasper was my own and I was his, and that being so, the hindrance, whatever it might be, could be but temporary.

So I comforted myself and made believe that all was well though when by chance my eye lighted on the trunk, packed and even provided with a blank label, I could hardly keep back the tears. At lunch I let Miss Polton know that my visit was postponed, and immediately after the meal I prepared to go out and seek relief in a long, sharp walk. By the time I returned, the letter from Jasper would probably have arrived and I should know how matters stood.

I had put on my outdoor clothes and was just about to start, when, opening the drawer in which I kept my wrist-bag, I suddenly remembered my loss of the night before. The bag contained, not only my purse but my card-case and one or two other things I could not conveniently do without. The prohibition to go to the club could hardly, I reflected, extend to Lyon's Inn Chambers, though they were in the same neighbourhood. At any rate I wanted the bag, and in my restless state a journey with a defined purpose offered more relief than an aimless walk through the streets.

During the short journey from Mark Lane to the Temple I turned over and over again the words of the telegram without obtaining any glimmer of enlightenment. If I had been less sure of Jasper, I should have been intensely wretched; but now, as the shock subsided, my optimism revived and I found myself looking forward to Jasper's letter with a confident expectation of reassuring news.

Emerging from the Temple Station, I walked up Arundel Street, and, crossing the Strand, presently passed through Half-Moon Alley and cast a glance of friendly recognition at the old gilded sign, so pleasantly associated with the scarlet parasol that hung outside the umbrella-maker's shop in Bookseller's Row. The two signs recalled the old delightful explorations with Jasper, and put me in quite a cheerful frame of mind, which lasted until I found myself once more ascending the bare and rather sordid stone stairs of Lyon's Inn Chambers. Then there came a marked change. As I walked up the cold, gloomy staircase a feeling of depression settled on me. I passed the grimy lantern that had looked on my headlong, terror-stricken flight, and some of the forgotten qualms came back. I breathed again the close air of that unpleasant bedroom; I saw again the unwieldy figure in the bed, with its pasty face and puffy eyelids; and even the sinister-looking peg on the wall came forth with uncomfortable vividness from the recesses of memory. By the time I reached the landing, my distaste for the place had grown so strong that I was half inclined to turn back and complete the transaction by means of a letter.

This weakness, however, I overcame by an effort of will and resolutely rang the bell. There was a short interval and then the door opened, revealing the figure of Mrs Gregg, who, according to her custom, stood and stared stonily at me without uttering a word.

"Good afternoon, Mrs Gregg," said I. "When I went away last night I left my wrist-bag behind."

"Ye did," she answered; "and ye left the bedroom door open and the gas full on. I found it so this morning."

"I am very sorry," I said.

" 'Tis no matter," she rejoined, impassively, and continued to stare at me in a most singular and embarrassing fashion.

"Could I have my bag, please, Mrs Gregg?" I asked.

"Ye could," she replied; but still she made no move, nor any suggestion that I should enter; and still she continued to look at me with the strangest, most enigmatical expression.

"I hope," said I, by way of relieving the extraordinarily uncomfortable situation, "that Mr Otway is better today."

"Do ye?" said she; and then, after a pause, "Maybe ye'd wish to see him?"

"I don't think I will disturb him, thank you," I replied.

"Ye need have no fear," said she. "Ye'll no disturb him."

"Well, I don't think I have time to see him today. I just called to get my bag."

"And is that all ye've come for?" she demanded glowering at me in the most astonishing manner.

"What else should I have come for?" I asked.

She thrust her head forward and replied in a low, mysterious tone: "I thought maybe ye'd come to ask where your husband is."

"I don't understand you, Mrs Gregg. Is Mr Otway not at home?"

"He is not," she replied; and as I made no comment, she asked: "Shall I tell you where he is?"

"It really isn't any business of mine, Mrs Gregg," said I.

"Is it not?" she demanded. "Will it no interest ye if I tell ye that your husband is in St Clement's Mortuary?"

"In the mortuary!" I gasped.

"Aye, in the mortuary." She glared at me in silence for a few moments, and then, suddenly grasping my arm, exclaimed: "Woman! do ye ken yon peg on the bedroom wall? Aye, ye may well turn pale. Ye'd ha' turned paler if ye'd seen what I saw by the gaslight this morn hangin' from yon peg."

I gazed at her for a few moments in speechless horror, until she seemed to sway and shimmer before my eyes. Then, for the first and only time in my life, I must have fainted, for I remember no more until I found myself lying on the floor of the lobby, with Mrs Gregg kneeling beside me slapping my face with a wet towel.

I rose with difficulty, feeling very weak and shaken. Mrs Gregg silently handed me my bag and preceded me towards the door, where, with her hand on the latch, she turned and faced me.

"Weel, mistress," said she, " 'tis a fit ending, seeing how it began. Ye've been a poor wife, but ye'll make a bonny widow, though I doubt it will stay long at that."

To this insolent and brutal speech I made no reply. I was completely broken, physically and mentally. I tottered out on to the landing and slowly descended the stairs, holding on to the iron hand-rail, my horror of the place urging me to hasten away, my trembling limbs and lingering faintness bidding me go warily. As I walked unsteadily up Holywell Street, a newspaper boy, running down the narrow thoroughfare, halted and held out a paper.

"Here y'are, Miss, sooicide in Lyon's Inn. The housekeeper's story."

I hurried past him with averted face, but out in the Strand there were others, shouting aloud the dreadful tidings or displaying posters on which the hideous fact was set forth in enormous type. And it seemed as if each and all of them were specially addressing themselves to me. I returned down Arundel Street, instinctively making for the station, but as I approached it a fresh group of newsboys made me swerve to the left and pursue my way along the Embankment on foot.

As I walked on, and the air and exercise helped me to recover physically from the shock, I began to collect my faculties. At first I had been utterly bewildered and overborne by a sense of horror and guilt. I had sent this wretched man to his death. I had ordained the means, the manner and the time of his death, and it had duly befallen according to my directions. Morally – and perhaps even legally – it amounted to murder. I had willed, I had suggested; and that which I had willed and suggested had come to pass. That was what had flashed into my mind in the very moment in which Mrs Gregg had made her dreadful communication.

But now, as I walked on, I began to argue the case in my own favour. In the first place, I told myself, it was not certain that the act of the dead man had any connection with the willing or the suggestion. It might have been a mere coincidence. I tried to dwell on this view; but it would not do. The coincidence was too complete to be explained away by any such casuistry. I could not in this way escape the responsibility for Mr Otway's death.

Then I considered the question of intention. I told myself – truthfully enough – that I had not consciously willed that Mr Otway should kill himself. I had not even been conscious of any intention to suggest to him that he should kill himself. But though I did make some sort of point in my own defence, it was extremely unconvincing. I had allowed my mind to dwell with hardly-disguised satisfaction on the possibility of his suicide (in a particular manner at a particular time), and between that and actual willing the distinction was not very obvious. And then there were those words, spoken to him in his sleep. It was not conscious, deliberate suggestion; but what was it? The impulse to speak those words was apparently evolved from the subconscious. But does no moral responsibility attach to subconscious intentions?

So I argued, back and forth, round and about; but always came back to the same conclusion. Mr Otway was dead; and it was my act that sent him to his death. Locked up in my own breast this dreadful secret might remain; but it was my companion for life. There was no escape from it.

But would it remain locked up in my own breast? That was another question that began to loom up with a very real menace.

How much did Mrs Gregg know? She might easily have overheard our conversation and even those final, fatal words. And if she had, would she understand their significance? Now that I came to consider the circumstances, there was something rather alarming in the manner of this inscrutable woman; something threatening and accusatory which I had vaguely felt at the time. And as I reflected on this and the possibilities that it suggested, a fear of something more substantial than my own accusing conscience began to creep around my heart.

When I arrived home, Jasper's letter was awaiting me. But it contained nothing new. He had seen the posters had bought an early paper and had immediately sent off the telegram. His tone was that of matter-of-fact satisfaction. The legal impediment to our marriage had now been removed. No declarations were necessary now. We could marry like other people. We were free.

That was the burden of the letter. All our troubles were at an end. Until everything was settled, we had better avoid meeting. But when the chapter was closed with all due formalities we could sing "*Nunc dimittis*," and thenceforth live only for one another.

I laid the letter down. All that it said was true. The picture that my imagination had drawn under the guidance of desire as I had sat looking into the shadowy corner of the bedroom in Lyon's Inn had become a reality. The fetters that I had forged and put on that fatal morning in the little church at Maidstone, had fallen off and given me back my freedom.

And even as I told myself this, some voice from within seemed to whisper a *caveat*, and my heart was sensible of a chill of fear.

BOOK THREE
CRIME

CHAPTER TWENTY-THREE

The Dead Hand

The entry of Mr Otway into my life inaugurated a long succession of disasters. The very first words that I heard him speak shattered the peace of a lifetime. Thenceforward, like the Ancient Mariner, I was haunted by a malign influence which seemed to exhale continuously from his ill-omened personality. And even now that he was dead that malignant spirit was not at rest. His very corpse, lying in the mortuary, was a centre whence radiated sinister influences that crept into my secret soul and enveloped me from without. During his life Mr Otway had been my evil genius; and death had but transformed him into a malicious poltergeist.

His first, tentative appearance in this character was made on the very evening of my second visit to Lyon's Inn Chambers, when the coroner's officer called at Wellclose Square to serve the subpoena for the inquest. The announcement of his arrival caused me some qualms of vague alarm, which I knew in my heart to be nothing but the stirring of my own conscience. For the purpose of this inquest was to find an answer to the question, "How did Lewis Otway come by his death?" And that question I could have answered in four words – Silent Willing and Suggestion. But I had no intention of answering that question; and hence, as I entered the room into which the officer had been shown, I was consciously on the defensive.

I had, however, no occasion to be. The officer was a civil, fatherly man in a constable's uniform, sympathetic, deferential and not at all inquisitive.

"I have called, ma'am," he began, "on a very sad errand. I don't know whether you have heard the dreadful news – "

"Of Mr Otway's death?" said I.

"Ah! then you have heard. That is a relief. Well, I have called to let you know that the inquest is arranged for the day after tomorrow, at 3 p.m. in the room adjoining the mortuary." He gave me a few explicit directions as to how to find the latter and then added: "If there is any information that you could give us that would guide us in starting the inquiry, we should be glad. Or the names of any witnesses that we ought to subpoena."

I reflected. The threatening letters must necessarily be referred to at the inquest. I should have to mention them myself, even if Mrs Gregg knew nothing of them.

"I happen to know," I replied "that Mr Otway had received a number of anonymous, letters and that he was greatly worried about them."

"Blackmailing letters?" he asked.

"I don't think any demands for money were made," I replied.

"Do you know what was their nature? Were they threatening letters?"

"Yes, indirectly. The two or three that I saw had reference to the death of my father, who died very suddenly and who was alone with Mr Otway at the time. They suggested a suspicion that Mr Otway was responsible for my father's death."

The officer looked at me quickly and then became deeply reflective.

"Will it be possible to produce those letters at the inquest?" he asked, after a cogitative pause.

"They are not in my possession" I answered; "but if the coroner will make an order for their production I will endeavour to have it carried out."

"Thank you, ma'am," said he; and then, as an afterthought, added: "If you could make it convenient to call at the coroner's office tomorrow, say at about two o'clock, I could give you the order and perhaps help you to carry it out."

The latter suggestion appealed to me strongly and I fell in with it at once. Thereupon the officer picked up his helmet with an air of satisfaction, and, having handed me the subpoena, moved towards the door. I accompanied him along the hall and let him out; and as I wished him good evening and launched him down the steps, another figure emerged from the darkness and passed him on the way up.

"Does Mrs Otway live here?" the newcomer enquired. I glanced at him with faint suspicion, for the exact coincidence in time of his arrival with the officer's departure suggested a connection between the two events.

"I am Mrs Otway," said I.

"Oh, indeed! Could I have a few words with you on a matter of some importance? I will not detain you more than a few minutes."

I hesitated, eyeing my new visitor dubiously. But there were no reasonable grounds for a refusal; and I eventually ushered him into the little parlour that the officer had just left, and indicated the vacant chair.

"The matter concerning which I have taken the liberty of calling on you, Mrs Otway," said he, "is connected with – er – with the painful occurrence – er – at Lyon's Inn Chambers. A most deplorable affair. Most distressing for you – most distressing! Pray accept my sincere sympathy."

"Thank you, Mr – "

"Hyams is my name – you may have heard your late husband speak of me. We have been acquainted a good many years."

"He has never spoken of you to me, Mr Hyams. But what can I do for you?"

"Well, I can put my business in a nutshell. Your husband, at the time of his death, had certain valuable property of mine in his possession. I should like to get that property back without delay."

He had certainly wasted no time. Unsentimental as was my own attitude I felt this haste to be almost indecent.

"I should think you will have no difficulty," said I, "if you apply in the proper quarter."

"That is what I am doing," he retorted. "You are his widow. His property is in your hands."

"Not at all," I replied. "Pending probate of the will, the property is vested in his executors."

He looked at me in not unnatural astonishment. I suppose the phraseology that I had acquired from my father was unusual for a woman.

"Who are the executors?" he asked.

"I don't know," I replied.

"But," said he, "I suppose you have seen the will."

"No, I don't know that there is a will. I am only assuming the existence of one from my knowledge of Mr Otway's businesslike habits."

"But this is very unsatisfactory," said Mr Hyams. "There is portable property of mine worth several thousand pounds lying in his chambers for anyone to pick up and those chambers in charge of a woman who probably has access to his keys. It really isn't business, you know."

"What is the nature of the property?" I asked.

"It is a collection of very valuable stones, the whole lot contained in a little box that anyone could carry away in his pocket."

"Then," said I, "the probability is that he has deposited the box with his bankers."

"Who are his bankers?" he asked.

"I really don't know."

"You don't know!" he exclaimed. "But you must have seen his cheques. I presume he made you an allowance?"

"I accepted no allowance from him and I have never seen one of his cheques."

Mr Hyams looked at me with undisguised incredulity. "A most extraordinary state of affairs," he commented. "Can you give me the address of his lawyers?"

"I am sorry, Mr Hyams, that I cannot. I don't even know if he has a lawyer. I know nothing whatever about Mr Otway's affairs."

Mr Hyams' countenance took on an expression that was very much the reverse of pleasant. "I suppose, Mrs Otway," said he, "you realise that you are talking to a man of business and that you are telling a rather unlikely story."

"I realise it very clearly, Mr Hyams," I replied "and I realise also the difficulty of your position. What I recommend you to do is to go to Lyon's Inn and see the housekeeper, Mrs Gregg. She has been with Mr Otway many years and can probably tell you all that you want to know."

Mr Hyams shut his mouth tightly, rose deliberately and picked up his hat.

"Then," said he, "the position, as I understand it, is this: You don't know whether there is or is not a will; you don't know the name of your husband's bankers; you don't know who his lawyer is; you don't know anything about his affairs; and you disclaim any responsibility in regard to property that was in his custody when he died."

"Yes," I agreed, "that is the position; a very unsatisfactory one for you, I must admit. Perhaps I may be able to help you later, when I know more about Mr Otway's affairs. Will you leave me your address?"

He was on the point of refusing, but prudence triumphed over anger and he laid on the table a card on which I read the name, "David Hyams, Dealer in precious stones," and the address, "501, Hatton Garden."

"If I learn anything fresh I will write to you," I said; whereupon he thanked me curtly and gruffly and walked towards the door with pursed-up lips and a lowering, truculent expression and took his departure without another word.

When he was gone I reflected at some length on the significance of his visit. The interview had brought home to me very vividly my anomalous position. Mr Otway had been a total stranger to me. Of his past, of his recent habits and mode of life, his friends, his occupation – if he had any – his family and social status, I knew nothing. My father had referred to him as a retired solicitor and as a collector of, or dealer in, precious stones. Vaguely, I had conceived him as a man of some means – perhaps a rich man. But I knew nothing of him and had given him and his affairs barely a thought. He was a stranger who had come into my life for but a moment, and had straightway gone out again, leaving a trail of desolation to show where he had been.

That was the real position. But to strangers, to the world at large, it would seem incredible. I was Mr Otway's widow. I had been his wife – in law if not in fact. And the world would hold me to the legal relationship. The dead man, lying in the mortuary, seemed about to make good the claims that the living man had been forced to abandon. My status as a wife had been a mere fiction: my status as a widow was an undeniable reality.

The clear perception of the extent to which I was involved in the dead man's affairs gave my visit to the coroner's office a new importance. For now, while seeking information for official use at the inquest, I must gather what knowledge I could for my own guidance under cover of the coroner's order. The address of the office – in Blackmoor Street, Drury Lane – was printed on the subpoena, and there, after a few enquiries, I made my appearance punctually on the following day.

My friend of the previous evening – whose name I discovered to be Smallwood – was in the office, looking over some documents with the aid of a pair of spectacles, which gave him a curiously unconstabulary aspect. He rose when I entered, and, opening a drawer, took out a sheet of paper.

"This is what you asked for, Mrs Otway." said he (upon which a young man at a desk looked up quickly), "the coroner's request for the production of the letters that you told me about. Can I give you any other assistance?"

"If you could accompany me to the chambers and be present during the search for the letters, I should be glad," I replied. "You see," I added, seeing that he looked somewhat surprised, "I am almost a stranger to the housekeeper, I know nothing about the household or Mr Otway's arrangements, and I shall be accountable to the executors, if there are any, for any interference with the papers or their removal. I should very much prefer to have a reliable witness."

He saw the position at once, and, greatly to my relief, agreed to come with me, or rather to follow me in a few minutes. Thereupon I left the office and walking at a leisurely pace into Drury Lane presently made my way into the Strand by way of May-pole Alley and turned eastward towards Lyon's Inn Chambers.

At the entrance I lingered for a minute or two and then slowly ascended the stairs to Mr Otway's landing, growing more and more uncomfortable with every step. For the bare stone staircase set my memory working very unpleasantly, recalling again my headlong flight and the terrible episode that had preceded it – that episode that I would so gladly have sponged out of my recollection for ever.

I stood at the door with my hand on the bell, listening for Mr Smallwood's steps on the stair, and so might have remained until he arrived; but suddenly the door opened and Mrs Gregg confronted me. Apparently she had some means of observing a visitor from within.

"What are ye standing there for?" she demanded. "Why did ye not ring?"

"I was just about to ring when you opened the door," I replied.

She smiled sourly and looked at me in that strange, inscrutable fashion of hers that I found so disconcerting.

"And what might your business be?" she demanded. "I have come about some letters of Mr Otway's – some anonymous letters that he has received from time to time. Perhaps you know about them?"

"You mean perhaps I have been in the habit of reading his letters. Weel, mistress, I have not. I know nothing about his letters."

"Perhaps you can show me where his letters were kept."

"Indeed, I'll do no such thing. What! Do you think I'll have you scratching up in his chambers and pawing over his letters and papers and him not under-ground yet?"

At this moment I caught the welcome sound of footsteps on the stairs. Mrs Gregg listened suspiciously, and as Mr Smallwood came into sight there was a visible change in her demeanour.

"What does he want, I wonder?" she said.

"He has come to receive the letters and to be present at the search for them," I replied, producing the coroner's order. She glanced at the paper, and, as Mr Smallwood stepped up to the door, she motioned us to enter.

"Come in," she said, gruffly. " 'Tis no affair of mine, but I'll no hinder ye."

We were just about to enter when footsteps were again audible on the stairs, and we waited to see who this other visitor might be. Somewhat to my surprise it turned out to be Mr Hyams, who certainly seemed to have a genius for coincidences.

"Now this is quite a lucky chance," said he doing himself, as I suspected less than justice. "I didn't expect to find you here, Mrs Otway. I presume you are just having a look round."

"I have come to search for some documents that have to be put in evidence," said I. "The coroner has asked for them."

"Well," said Mr Hyams, "you might, at the same time, see if you can find any trace of my property."

"What property is that?" demanded Mrs Gregg.

"A parcel of stones – a very valuable collection – that Mr Otway had from me on approval."

Mrs Gregg snorted. "Man," said she, "ye're talkin' like a fool. Do you suppose Lewis Otway would have left a valuable parcel of stones lying about in his rooms like a packet of snuff? Ye'll find, no stones here."

"That may or may not be" said Mr Hyams. "At any rate, I'll stay and see if anything turns up."

During this dialogue we had gradually moved from the lobby down the corridor and now entered the living-room. As we crossed it I looked curiously at the large cupboard and wondered idly what I could have found so alarming in its appearance on the night of my visit. But if the living-room had, by the light of day, lost its disturbing qualities, it was otherwise with the bedroom. I opened the door with trepidation, and as I did so and was confronted by the disordered bed the horror of the place began to come back to me. Nevertheless, I entered the room with a firm step and with my eyes on the bedside table, which appeared to be in the same condition as when I had last seen it. I had just noted this when I felt my arm grasped, and turning quickly found Mrs Gregg at my side. Her eyes were fixed on me and with her disengaged hand she was pointing towards the corner by the bed-head. Involuntarily my gaze followed the direction in which she was pointing and lighted on the fatal peg, which now bore a loop of the red bell-rope with two free ends. Of course I had known it was there, but yet the sight of it made me turn sick and faint, and I must have shown this in the sudden pallor of my face; for when controlling myself by an intense effort, I turned to speak to her she was looking at me with a leer of triumph.

"Can we have Mr Otway's keys?" I asked.

"Ye'll find them in the right dressing-table drawer," she answered. "I'm no party to this, but I'll no hinder ye."

Mr Smallwood opened the drawer and produced a bunch of keys which he handed to me. I looked them over and selecting the most likely-looking ones, tried them, one after the other, on the deed-box. The fourth key fitted the lock, and when I had turned it and raised the lid of the box, the letter which Mr Otway had shown me lay in full view. I took it out and laid it on the table and then proceeded to lift out the remaining contents of the box. There was not much to remove: a chequebook, a passbook, a small journal, a memorandum-book, a bundle of share-certificates, a canvas bag containing money, and at the bottom of the box, a foolscap envelope endorsed, "Anonymous Letters."

I opened the unsealed envelope and drew out the letters which I glanced through one by one. There were seven in all, of which I had already seen three. When I had looked at them I returned them to the envelope, adding the last letter, and then began to replace the other things in the box.

"I see a chequebook there, Mrs Otway," said Mr Hyams, who had followed my proceedings with intense interest. "May I make a note of the banker's address?"

I handed him the chequebook and continued to replace the contents of the box. When I had finished I paused with the box open, waiting for him to return the chequebook; and at this moment I became aware, with a start of surprise, that an addition had been made to our party.

The newcomer was a short, stout, middle-aged man, obviously a Jew of the swarthy, aquiline type, with a very large nose and rather prominent dark eyes. He stood in the open doorway of the bedroom watching us with a slightly unpleasant smile. As he noted my surprised look, his smile became broader and more unpleasant.

"Make yourselves at home, ladies and gentlemen," said he. "These are public premises – at least I assume they are as I found the door open."

Mr Hyams looked round with a start – as, indeed, did the others.

"May I ask who you are, sir?" he enquired.

"You may," was the suave reply. "My name is Isaacs – of the firm of Isaacs and Cohen, solicitors. I am one of the executors of Mr Lewis Otway's will. And having regard to my responsibilities in that capacity, I may, perhaps, venture to enquire as to the nature of these proceedings. You, sir, appear to be in possession of the testator's cheque-book. Did you happen to require the loan of a fountain pen?"

Mr Hyams turned very red and hastily laid down the cheque-book.

"That," he exclaimed angrily, "is perfectly unwarranted. I was simply making a note of the banker's address."

"With what object?"

"With the object of enquiring whether certain property of mine, which was in Mr Otway's custody, had been deposited in the bank."

"What is the nature and value of this property?" asked Mr Isaacs.

"It is a collection of precious stones of the approximate value of four thousand pounds."

"Then," said Mr Isaacs, "I can give you the information you want. No property, other than documents, has been deposited at the bank."

"In that case," said Mr Hyams, "the stones must be in these rooms."

"It is quite probable," Mr Isaacs agreed.

"Is there any objection to ascertaining, now, whether they are here?"

"Yes, there is," replied Mr Isaacs. "The will has not been proved and no letters of administration have been issued. Pending probate of the will I propose to take possession of these premises and seal all receptacles that may contain valuable property. I shall interfere with nothing until I have letters of administration."

"And how soon will that be?" asked Mr Hyams.

"Seven days must elapse before the will can be proved. Under the circumstances there may be some further delay. And now I should like to know what has been taking place. You for instance, madam – "

"I am Mrs Lewis Otway," said I, "and I have come here by the coroner's direction, to look for some letters that are to be put in evidence."

"Have you found them?"

"Yes," I answered, "they are here; and, as you are an executor, I had better hand them to you and you can deliver them to the coroner's officer if you think fit."

I handed him the envelope and the coroner's letter, which he read, and then asked: "Did you have to make a very extensive search?"

"No, she didn't," said Mrs Gregg. "She kenned fine where to look for them and she found them at the first cast."

On this I noticed that Mr Hyams cast a quick, suspicious glance at me and I thought it wise to explain.

"I looked first in this box because I had seen Mr Otway put one of these letters into it."

"Quite so," said Mr Isaacs. "Very natural." But obvious as the explanation was, I could see that it had left Mr Hyams unconvinced.

I now returned the chequebook to the deed-box, locked the latter and handed the keys to Mr Isaacs; who delivered the anonymous letters to the coroner's officer and took his receipt for them on a slip of paper. My business being now at an end, I offered my card to Mr Isaacs, took his in return, and departed in company with Mr Smallwood.

"A queer business, this, ma'am," the officer remarked as we descended the stairs. "Regular mix up. Seem to be a lot of Sheenies in it."

"Sheenies?" I repeated, interrogatively. "What are Sheenies?"

"Jews, ma'am," he replied, apparently a little surprised at my ignorance. "It's just a popular name, you know."

I reflected on Mr Smallwood's remark, which seemed hardly justified by the facts – two Jews only having appeared in the case, so far as I knew. And yet I seemed to be aware of a sort of Semitic atmosphere surrounding Mr Otway. There were for instance, the

Campbells; and then Mrs Gregg, although a Scotswoman, might easily, but for her strong Scottish accent, have passed for a Jewess; while Mr Otway, himself, had been distinctly Semitic in appearance.

At the entry, where we separated, Mr Smallwood halted to give me a final injunction.

"You had better be in good time tomorrow, ma'am," said he, "because it will be necessary for you to view the body so that you can give evidence as to the identity of the deceased."

I thanked him for the reminder, but would much rather have been without it. For the prospect filled me with a vague alarm, and now the mental picture of the sleeping man, which had haunted me by night and by day, began to be replaced by one more dreadful, and one which I felt that my visit to the mortuary would attach to me for ever.

CHAPTER TWENTY-FOUR

The Gathering Clouds

The distaste which I felt for my errand did not prevent me from following Mr Smallwood's advice on the subject of punctuality. It was some minutes short of half past two when I turned into the mean, little street off Drury Lane in which the mortuary was situated. I had found the place without much difficulty and had still less in finding the mortuary itself, for, as I entered the street I observed a procession of about a dozen men passing in through a narrow gateway, watched attentively by a small crowd of loiterers. Assuming the former to be the jury, I walked slowly past on the opposite side and continued for the length of the short street. I had just turned to retrace my steps when the men filed out of the gateway and proceeded to enter a building a few yards up the street, and immediately afterwards Mr Smallwood appeared at the gate. He saw me at once and waited for me to approach.

"I am glad you have come in good time, ma'am," said he. "The jury have just been in to view the body and the coroner will like to open the inquest punctually. This is the way."

He preceded me down a narrow passage, at the end of which he pushed open a door. Following him I entered the mortuary, a bare, stone-floored hall containing two large slate-topped tables, one of which was occupied by a recumbent figure covered by a sheet. Mr Smallwood removed his helmet and together we advanced slowly towards the awesome, shrouded form, lying so still and lonely in its grim surroundings. Very quietly, the officer picked up the two upper corners of the sheet and drew it back, retiring then a couple of paces as if to avoid intruding on my meeting with the dead.

Strung up as I was the first impression was less dreadful than I had anticipated. The face was pale and waxen, but it was placid in expression and more peaceful than I had ever seen it in life. The hunted, terrified look was gone and had given place to an air of repose, almost of dignity. For a few moments I was sensible of a feeling of relief; but then my glance fell upon a contorted length of crimson rope that lay on the slate table and instinctively my eye turned to the uncovered throat. And as I noted the shallow groove under the chin, faintly marked with an impression of the strands of the rope, the shocking reality came home to me with overwhelming horror. Before my eyes arose that awful shape upon the bedroom wall and the hardly less dreadful image of the sleeping man unconsciously receiving the message of his doom.

With a new horror – an incredulous horror of myself – I looked on the pale, placid face and seemed to read in it a gentle reproach. He had gone to his death at my bidding. He had stood unsteadily on the brink of the abyss, and I had pushed him over.

It seemed incredible. There had been no conscious intention; no guilty premeditation. I would have told myself that there was no connection other than mere coincidence. But there the plain, undeniable facts, were. Unconsciously – or subconsciously – my will had created that premonitory shape upon the wall; the terrible words had formed themselves and issued from my lips. And straightway the thing that my thoughts and words had fore-shadowed had come to pass. This waxen-faced effigy that lay on the stone table, as its living counterpart had lain that night in the bed, was its fulfilment, its realisation.

"Better not stay too long, ma'am," said Mr Smallwood. And as he spoke I became suddenly aware that I had reached the limits of endurance. My knees began to tremble and I breathed the tainted air with difficulty.

"Better come away now," continued Mr Smallwood. "It's been rather too much for you. Good afternoon, Mrs Gregg."

I looked up quickly and perceived Mrs Gregg, who must have come in without making a sound, standing at the foot of the table watching me intently. That penetrating stare and the singular, enigmatical expression would have been disturbing at any time. But now I was conscious of actual fear. As I tottered unsteadily along the passage to the street, the menace of that watchful, inscrutable gaze followed me. How much did this woman know? What had she heard? And if she had overheard those last words of mine, how much had she understood of their import? These were weighty questions, the answers to which I should doubtless hear within an hour or two.

When I was ushered by Mr Smallwood into the room in which the inquest was to be held, the court was already assembled and ready to begin. The jurymen sat along one side of a long table and one or two reporters occupied a part of the other, while a row of chairs accommodated the witnesses and persons interested in the case, including Mr Isaacs, Mr Hyams, Mr and Mrs Campbell, and a youngish man of a markedly Jewish type whom I did not recognise. I took my seat at the end of the row, and Mrs Gregg, who had followed us in, seated herself near the middle.

As I took my seat the coroner addressed one of the reporters: "Let me see, what paper do you represent?"

"I am not a pressman, sir," was the reply. "I am commissioned to make a report for Dr Thorndyke."

"Dr Thorndyke! But what is his connection with the case? I know nothing about him."

"I only know that he has asked me to make a verbatim report of the evidence."

"Hm," grunted the coroner. "I'm not sure that it is quite in order for private individuals to send their reporters to an inquest."

"It is an open court, sir," the reporter observed.

"I know. But still – however, I suppose it doesn't matter. Well, gentlemen, I think we are ready to begin. The witnesses are all present and it is on the stroke of three. I need not occupy your time with any preliminary statement. It seems quite a straightforward case and you will get the facts from the evidence of the witnesses. We are here, as you know, to inquire into the circumstances of the death of Lewis Otway, whose body you have just viewed, which occurred either on the night of the 18th instant or the morning of the 19th. The body was found hanging from a peg in his bedroom by his housekeeper, Mrs Gregg, and it will be best to take her evidence first."

Mrs Gregg was accordingly called and having taken a position near the head of the table, was sworn and proceeded to give her evidence.

"My name is Rachel Gregg, age 51. I was housekeeper to the deceased, Lewis Otway."

"How long," asked the coroner, "had you known the deceased?"

"Thirty-three years."

"What was deceased's occupation?"

"He was a retired solicitor; but he was a connoisseur in precious stones, and, I think, dealt in them to some extent."

"Was he in financial difficulties of any kind, so far as you know?"

"No. I believe he was quite a well-to-do man."

"Had you any reason to suspect him of an intention to take his life?"

"Yes. He used to say that he expected, if ever he had any trouble, that he would hang himself. The tendency to suicide was in the family. His only brother hanged himself, his mother hanged herself and his mother's father hanged himself."

"But that was only a tendency that might not have affected him. Had any reason to expect that he actually might commit suicide? Was there anything in his manner, in the state of his mind or in his circumstances that led you to believe that he might take his life?"

"Not until recently, He always used to be quite cheerful in a quiet way until he got married. After that he was never the same. His marriage seemed to bring all sorts of trouble into his life."

"Tell us exactly how this change came about."

"His marriage took place about eight months ago – on the 25th of last April when he was living at Maidstone. It was quite sudden. I knew nothing of it until the day before, when he told me he was going to marry a Miss Helen Vardon, and that the marriage was to take place secretly because the lady's father had refused his consent. On the morning of the marriage I saw Mr Otway go out, and soon afterwards I went out myself to do some shopping. When I came back I found the new Mrs Otway in the study and her father, Mr Vardon, lying dead on the floor. Mr Otway had gone to fetch a doctor. It appeared that Mr Vardon had called directly after the newly-married couple had arrived home from the church and that there had been a quarrel and Mr Vardon had fallen down dead. I understand that Mr Vardon was alone with Mr Otway at the time.

"Soon after I arrived, Mrs Otway left the house and went back to her own home, and Mr Otway told me that she refused to live with him. At any rate, she never did live with him, and she never came near him until the night of his death."

"Do you know if the deceased agreed to this separation?"

"Apparently she made him agree. But it was a great trouble to him, and I know that he tried more than once to get her to live with him."

"Do you know what was the cause of the separation?"

"No. Mr Otway never mentioned it to me."

"You say that the separation was a great trouble to the deceased. Did it obviously affect his spirits?"

"Yes; he was very depressed after his wife went away, and he never recovered. He seemed to get more and more low-spirited."

"Do you know of any other reasons than the separation from his wife why he should have been depressed in spirits?"

"Yes. Mr Vardon's sudden death was a great shock to him. He felt that he had been partly the cause of it, by quarrelling with Mr Vardon. Then there was a great deal of talk in Maidstone about the affair and people blamed Mr Otway for what had happened; and later rumours began to get about that there had been foul play – that Mr Otway had actually killed Mr Vardon. These rumours got on his nerves so badly that he gave up his house at Maidstone and moved to London."

"You have spoken of a quarrel between deceased and Mr Vardon. Do you know what the quarrel was about?"

"I believe it was about the secret marriage, but I was not in the house at the time."

"Were there any other causes for the mental depression which you say the deceased suffered from?"

"I think so, but I can't say for certain. There were some letters that came about once a month which seemed to worry him a good deal. I used to see him reading them and looking very anxious and depressed; and after a time he began to get very nervous and fidgety and couldn't sleep at nights unless he took a dose of veronal. And I noticed that he was smoking much more than he used to, and taking much more whisky."

"Did you ever see any of the letters that you have spoken of?"

"I never read one, but I saw the outsides and I noticed that they all bore the postmark of East London."

Here the coroner drew from the large envelope six of the letters which I had found in the deed-box, and handed them, in their envelopes, to Mrs Gregg.

"Do you recognise any of these letters?"

Mrs Gregg turned the envelopes over in her hand, looked closely at the postmarks and replied, as she returned them: "Yes; these look like the letters that I spoke of."

The coroner laid the letters on the table, and after a few moment's reflection said: "Now, Mrs Gregg, we want you to tell us what you know of the circumstances of Mr Otway's death. You spoke of a visit from Mrs Otway."

"Yes. She came to Lyon's Inn Chambers on Wednesday night, about half past six and told me that Mr Otway had written to her asking her to come. As Mr Otway was then expecting another visitor, I asked her to call again about eight, which she agreed to do. Mr Otway had been rather poorly for the last few days – very nervous and despondent, and had been sleeping badly – and for three days had kept to his bed. I told him that Mrs Otway was coming at eight o'clock and he then said that he had some private business to talk over with her and that I need not sit up. I gave him his supper at half past seven and just after I had cleared it away Mrs Otway came. I showed her into the bedroom and went to the kitchen to finish up my work. At half past nine I went to bed – a little earlier than usual because I thought they would like the place quiet for their talk. At

a quarter to seven on Thursday morning I got up, and as soon as I was dressed, went into the living-room to tidy it up. Then, to my great surprise, I saw that the door of the bedroom, which opens out of the living-room, was wide open and that the gas in the bedroom was full on.

"Thinking that Mr Otway might be worse, I called out to him to ask if he wanted anything; but there was no answer. I could see the bed from where I was and could see that he was not in it; so I called to him again, and as there was still no answer, I went into the bedroom. At first I thought he was not there; but suddenly I saw him in a corner of the room that was in deep shadow. He seemed to be standing against the wall, with his arms hanging down straight and his head on one side; but when I went nearer I saw that he was hanging from a large peg and that his feet were three or four inches off the floor. He had hanged himself with a length of bell-rope that he had cut off with his razor – at least that was what it looked like, for the razor was lying open on the bed. I picked up the razor and ran to him and cut the loop of rope, and as he fell, I let him down on the floor as gently as I could. He seemed to be quite dead and his skin felt cold, so I ran out to fetch a doctor. Just outside the buildings I met a policeman and told him what had happened, and he told me to go back to the chambers and wait, which I did. A few minutes later he arrived at the chambers with a doctor, who examined the body and said that Mr Otway had been dead some hours."

"Did you see any means by which deceased could have raised himself to the peg from which he was hanging?"

"Yes. There was an overturned chair lying on the floor nearly underneath him. It looked as if he had stood on it to fix the loop of rope and then kicked it away. Mrs Otway's bag was lying on the floor by the side of the chair."

"Mrs Otway's bag! What bag was that?"

"A little wrist-bag such as ladies use to carry their purses and handkerchiefs. She called for it the same day and I gave it to her. She had not heard what had happened, and when I told her she fell down in a dead faint."

The coroner reflected for a while with wrinkled brows, and I caught the eyes of one or two of the jurymen regarding me furtively. After a somewhat lengthy pause, the coroner asked: "Do you know what time Mrs Otway left the chambers?"

"I heard the outer door slam about half an hour after I had gone to bed. That would be about ten o'clock."

"Did you see Mrs Otway or deceased after you let her in?"

"No. I did not go into the bedroom again. I went into the living-room twice and could hear them talking."

"Could you hear what they were talking about?"

"I could hear a few words now and then. When I went into the living-room the first time they seemed to be talking about suicide. I heard Mr Otway say something about a peg on the wall."

"And when you went in the second time?"

"They seemed still to be talking about suicide. I heard Mrs Otway ask deceased what drove his brother to hang himself."

"You heard nothing suggesting a quarrel or disagreement?"

"No. They seemed to be talking in quite a friendly way."

"Do you know what kind of terms they were on?"

"No. I never saw them together before except for a few minutes on the wedding day."

"You spoke of a visitor who came to deceased earlier in the evening. Who was that visitor?"

"A Mrs Campbell. Her husband is a jeweller and curio-dealer whom deceased had known for a good many years, and used to have business dealings with. I understand she came on business and she only stayed about ten minutes."

"Is that all you know about the case?"

"Yes, I think I have told you all I know about it."

The coroner glanced at the jury. "Do any of you, gentlemen, wish to ask the witness any questions?" he enquired.

Apparently none of them did, and when the coroner had complimented Mrs Gregg on the clear manner in which she had given her evidence, she was dismissed.

There was a short interval in which the coroner read over his notes and the jury conferred together in low undertones. Then the coroner observed: "We had better dispose of the police and medical evidence as they are merely formal and will not take much time. We will begin with the constable."

The policeman was then called and briefly corroborated Mrs Gregg's evidence. When he had finished, the doctor, whom he had brought to the chambers, took his place, and having been duly sworn deposed as follows:

"My name is John Shelburn. I am a member of the Royal College of Surgeons and a Licentiate of the Royal College of Physicians, and am acting as *locum tenens* for the police surgeon of Saint Clement Danes. At seven twenty-eight a.m., on Thursday, the 19th of October, I was summoned by the last witness to accompany him to Lyon's Inn Chambers, where a man was reported to have hanged himself. I went with the constable to a set of chambers, over the door of which was painted the name of Mr Lewis Otway. I went into the bedroom where the gas was alight, the blinds down and the curtains drawn. There, lying on the floor near the wall, I found the dead body of a tall, heavily built man, about fifty or fifty-five years of age, dressed in a suit of pyjamas. The surface of the body was cold and *rigor mortis* was well established. I should say the man had been dead about eight hours. Around the neck was a double loop of red bell-rope and a portion of the same was hanging from a large peg on the wall about seven feet from the floor. The rope had apparently been cut down for the purpose as a portion was still attached to the bell-wire and the severed tassel lay on the bed, on which were impressions of feet, as if someone had stood on the bed to cut it off. The length of rope had been joined at the ends with the kind of knot known as a 'granny' and formed into what is known as a weaver's loop, which had been passed over the head and the standing part of the rope hitched over the peg. This would form a running loop, like this" – here the witness produced a piece of thick string and demonstrated the arrangement on his thumb and the knob of a chair-back.

"I released the double loop from the neck and found a shallow groove on the throat corresponding to the rope. The countenance of the deceased was calm – as it usually is in cases of hanging – and there were no signs of violence or anything remarkable about the body. A chair, on which the deceased had apparently stood to adjust the rope on the peg, was lying close by and near to it on the floor was a lady's hand-bag. The rope had been cut with some sharp instrument – probably a razor, as I was informed by the housekeeper. I looked round the room but saw nothing of any significance excepting a half-empty whisky decanter and a nearly-full bottle of veronal tablets on a table by the bed."

"Can you tell us at what time death took place?"

"Only approximately. I have said that the man appeared to have been dead about eight hours. That would give us eleven o'clock on the night of the 18th as the time at which death occurred. But I will not bind myself to that time exactly. It might have been an hour earlier or later."

"After hearing your evidence and that of the other witnesses which you have also heard, it is a mere formality to ask your opinion as to the cause of death."

"Yes. The cause of death was obviously suicidal hanging."

This concluded the surgeon's evidence and when he had been dismissed, the coroner turned to the jury.

"We have now, gentlemen," said he, "established the fact of death and its immediate cause. Our next investigation will seek to establish the contributory circumstances – the more remote causes. We have ascertained that this unfortunate man committed suicide. The question that we now have to consider is, Why did he commit suicide? Possibly the evidence of his widow may help us to answer that question. Helen Otway."

As I rose to take my place at the table I was dimly aware of a certain ill-defined movement on the part of the jury and the spectators such as one may notice in a church at the conclusion of a sermon. But in the present case the cause was evidently a concentration rather than a relaxation of attention. Clearly, my evidence was anticipated with considerable interest.

"Your name is – ?"

"Helen Otway. My age is twenty-four and I live at 69, Wellclose Square."

"Have you viewed and do you identify the body now lying in St Clement's mortuary?"

"Yes; it is the body of Lewis Otway my late husband."

"When did you last see the deceased alive?"

"On the night of Wednesday, the 18th of October."

"Tell us, please, what took place on that occasion."

"I went to see deceased in consequence of a letter that I had received from him asking me to do so. I arrived at about half past six and was informed by Mrs Gregg that deceased was expecting another visitor."

"Did you know who that other visitor was?"

"No; but as I went down the stairs I met Mrs Campbell coming up and assumed that she was the visitor."

"You know Mrs Campbell, then?"

"Only by sight. I have seen her in her husband's shop. Mrs Gregg asked me to call again at eight and I agreed to do so, and did so. I was then admitted by Mrs Gregg, who conducted me to the bedroom and left me there, shutting the door as she went out. I did not see her again that night. Deceased was in bed and had by his side a table on which were a spirit decanter, a siphon of soda water, a box of cigarettes, a bottle of veronal tablets and a deed-box."

"Did you notice anything peculiar in his appearance?"

"No. He was not looking well, but he seemed less ill than I had expected from his letter; which conveyed the impression that he was in a dangerous condition."

"Have you got that letter?"

"Yes," I replied, "I have it here." As I spoke, I drew the letter from my pocket and handed it to the coroner, who glanced through it and then laid it down with some other papers.

"We will consider this letter," said he, "with the others that you have handed to me, later. Will you now tell us what passed between you and the deceased?"

"At first we talked about an anonymous letter that he had received a day or two previously. He showed me the letter, and when I had read it, he locked it in the deed-box."

"We will deal with the anonymous letters presently. What else did you talk about?"

"Deceased repeated the statement that he had made in the letter, that he did not expect to live much longer. I asked him if he had any reason for saying this and he then told me that there was a strong family predisposition to suicide; that his brother, his mother and his mother's father had all hanged themselves, and that since he had received the anonymous letters he had been conscious of an impulse to make away with himself in the same manner."

"Had you not known previously of this family tendency?"

"No. He had never mentioned it before, and I knew nothing of his family."

"Did deceased speak as if he actually intended to make away with himself?"

"No, but he spoke of an impulse which he found it difficult to resist; and he mentioned that a large peg on the bedroom wall seemed to fascinate him and to make the impulse stronger. I advised him to have it taken away."

"Previous to this conversation, had you ever thought it possible that the deceased might commit suicide?"

"No; the possibility never entered my mind."

The coroner considered these replies and made a few further notes; then he proceeded to open a fresh subject.

"Now, Mrs Otway, with regard to your relations with deceased. Were you on friendly terms with him?"

"Not particularly. We were practically strangers."

"A witness has stated that you refused to live with deceased and that you never had lived with him. Is that true?"

"Yes, it is quite true."

"Had you quarrelled with deceased?"

"No, there was no quarrel. Our marriage was a business trans-action and immediately after the ceremony I discovered that my consent had been obtained, as I considered, by misrepresentation."

"We don't want to be inquisitive Mrs Otway, but we wish to understand the position. Could you give us a few more particulars?"

"Do you wish me to describe the circumstances of my marriage and the separation from my husband?"

"If you please."

"My marriage with Mr Lewis Otway took place under the following circumstances: I accidentally overheard a portion of a conversation between Mr Otway and my father from which I gathered that Mr Otway claimed the immediate payment of five thousand pounds held by my father – who was a solicitor – in trust. It appeared from the conversation that my father was unable immediately to produce the money, and Mr Otway threatened to take criminal proceedings for misappropriation of trust funds. To this my father made no very definite reply. Then Mr Otway offered to abstain from any proceedings and to allow the claim to remain in abeyance on condition that a marriage should take place between him and me. This my father refused very emphatically and angrily, and Mr Otway left our house.

"Being greatly alarmed on my father's account, I communicated with Mr Otway and informed him that I was prepared to accept his offer on the terms stated − namely, that he should release my father from the immediate claim and secure him from any proceedings in connection with it. Mr Otway accepted the conditions, and as it was certain that my father would strongly object, we agreed not to inform him until after the marriage had taken place.

"In accordance with this arrangement we were married privately on the 25th April of the present year and we went together from the church to Mr Otway's house. I had left a letter for my father informing him of what had been done, and very shortly after our return from the church he came to the house. From an upper window I saw him enter the garden and I was very much alarmed at his appearance. I had heard that he suffered from a complaint of the heart and had been warned against undue excitement and exertion, and I could see that he was extremely excited and was looking very ill. Mr Otway let him in and, in answer to a question, admitted that the marriage had taken place. Then I heard my father ask Mr Otway if he had told me about a letter that he − my father − had sent, and when Mr Otway gave an evasive reply my father called him a scoundrel and accused him of having tricked and swindled me.

"I heard no more of what was said, as the two men went into the study and shut the door; but a minute or two later I heard a heavy fall, and, running down to the study, found my father lying on the floor and already dead. There was a small wound on his temple and Mr Otway, who was stooping over the body, held my father's walking-stick − a thick Malacca cane with a loaded silver knob − in his hand. He stated that my father had threatened him with the stick and that he had taken it away from him and that during the struggle my father had fallen insensible, striking his head on the corner of the mantel-piece as he fell."

"Did you believe him?"

"I think, at the moment, I did not. But on reflection, remembering how ill my father had looked, I had no doubt he was speaking the truth."

"Was there an inquest on your father's death?"

"Yes. The jury found, in accordance with the medical evidence, that death was due to heart failure caused by excitement and anger."

"And after this you refused to live with deceased?"

"Yes. I asked him about my father's letter and he said he had not seen it. I went with him to the letter box and there we found it. The postmark showed that it had come by the first post and my father's address was on the outside of the envelope. There were no other letters in the box. I had no doubt that Mr Otway had seen the letter and put it back in the box."

"Was that why you refused to live with him?"

"Partly. The letter stated that my father was able to meet his liabilities and gave a date on which payment would be made. Consequently the threatened proceedings against my father were impossible and Mr Otway had obtained my consent by false pretences. But further, Mr Otway's action had been the cause of my father's death, and this alone would have made it impossible for me to live with him as his wife."

"Did deceased agree to the separation?"

"Yes. He saw that the position was impossible; but he hoped that the separation might be only temporary – that we might become reconciled at some future time."

"Did you consider this possible?"

"No. I held him accountable for my father's death and could never have overcome my repugnance to him."

The coroner noted down this answer and having glanced over his notes reflectively, looked up at the jury.

"Do any of you, gentlemen, wish to put any questions on this subject?" he asked.

The jurymen looked at one another and looked at me; and one of them remarked that, "This young lady seems to have rather easy-going ideas about the responsibilities of marriage."

"That," said the Coroner, "is hardly our concern. The next matter that we have to consider is that of certain letters received by the deceased from some unknown person or persons. There are seven of them and they seem by the postmarks to have been sent at intervals of about three weeks and to have been posted somewhere in the East end of London. We will begin with the first." He handed a letter to me and asked: "Have you seen that letter before?"

"Yes," I replied. "Deceased showed it to me one day last June when I met him by appointment at his request. He seemed to be extremely worried about it."

The coroner took the letter from me and read it aloud.

" 'Mr Lewis Otway,

" 'The undersigned is writing to put you on your guard because Somebody knows something about how Mr Vardon came by his death and that somebody is not a friend, so you had better keep a sharp lookout for your enemy and see what they mean to do. I can't tell you any more at present.

" 'A well wisher.' "

"Do you know," the coroner asked, "who wrote that letter?"

"No, I do not?"

"Have you no idea at all? Is there no one whom you suspect?"

"I have not the least idea who sent that letter."

"You say that deceased was extremely worried about it. Do you know why he was worried?"

"I understand that there had been rumours in Maidstone that Mr Otway had killed my father. Those rumours seemed to have preyed upon his mind and made him unreasonably nervous."

The coroner nodded gravely and opened another letter: and as he read aloud the well-remembered phrases I realised that I should need all the courage and self-possession at my command.

" 'The writer of this warns you once more,' " the letter ran, " 'to look for trouble. The person that I spoke of knows that something was held back at the inquest at least they say so and that they know why your wife won't live with you and that she knows all about it too and that someone knows more than you think anybody knows. This is a friendly warning.

" 'From a well wisher.' "

The coroner looked keenly at me as he finished reading.

"Can you explain the meaning of this letter?" he asked. "It refers to something that was held back at the inquest. Was anything held back, so far as you know?"

"I remember that there was one omission in the evidence. Mr Otway made no mention of my father's stick."

"Was it not mentioned at the inquest at all?"

"No."

"Did you not give evidence?"

"Yes; but I was merely asked if I confirmed Mr Otway's evidence, which I did."

"You confirmed Mr Otway's evidence! But that evidence was not correct. The duty of a witness is to state the whole truth; whereas Mr Otway had withheld a highly material fact. How was it that you did not supply this very important fact?"

"It did not appear to me to be of any importance. The medical evidence showed that death was due to heart failure."

"Medical evidence!" the coroner exclaimed, testily. "There is too much of this medical evidence superstition in these courts. People speak as if doctors were infallible. It was your duty as a witness to state
all that you knew, not to decide what was or was not of importance. And I cannot understand how you came to hold such an opinion. You found your father lying dead with a wound on his head and

a man standing over him with a loaded stick, and you considered this fact of no consequence?"

"I see now that I ought to have mentioned it."

"What was the verdict?"

"The verdict was in accordance with the medical evidence – Death from natural causes."

"Did the medical witness or witnesses know that Mr Otway had had a loaded stick in his hand?"

"No."

"Did anybody besides yourself and Mr Otway know about the loaded stick?"

"Mrs Gregg came into the room when Mr Otway had gone for a doctor. She saw the stick in a corner and picked it up to examine it. She asked whose it was and remarked on its weight."

"Did she know it had been in Mr Otway's hand at the time of your father's death?"

"I have no reason to suppose that she knew."

"Well," said the coroner, "it is a most extraordinary affair. You heard Mr Otway give his evidence, you knew that that evidence was incomplete, and yet, though the dead man was your own father and you have declared an unconquerable repugnance to Mr Otway, you allowed this garbled evidence to pass unchallenged. It is an amazing affair. However," he continued turning to the jury, "that is not our concern. But what is our concern, for the purposes of this inquiry is that we now begin to see daylight. We can now understand the extraordinary effect these letters seem to have had on the man whose death we are investigating. Lewis Otway, when he gave his evidence at the inquest suppressed a most important and damaging fact, which he believed to be known only to himself and his wife. Thereby he obtained a verdict of Death from Natural Causes, which exonerated him from all blame. Had all the facts been known, the verdict might have been very different.

"Now the receipt of these letters must have destroyed his sense of security. Apparently someone else – and that someone evidently an enemy – knew of this damaging fact, and knew of the further damaging fact that it had been suppressed at the inquest. In effect, these letters held out a threat of a charge of murder, or at least, manslaughter. It is no wonder that they alarmed him. But we had better take the rest of the evidence. There is this letter of deceased to his wife, which I will read. It is dated the 17th of October, and this is what it says:

" 'My dear Helen,

" 'I have not troubled you for quite a long time with my miserable affairs – which are to some extent your affairs too. But they are going from bad to worse, and now I feel that I am coming to the limits of endurance. I cannot bear this much longer. My health is shattered, my peace of mind is wrecked and my brain threatens to give way. Death would be a boon, a relief, and I feel that it is not far off. I cannot go on like this. Those wretches leave me no peace. Hardly a week passes but I get some new menace; and now – but I can't tell you in a letter. It is too horrible. Come to me, Helen, for the love of God! I am in torment. Have pity on me, even though you have never forgiven me. I cannot come to you, for I am now unable to leave my bed. I am a wreck, a ruin. Come to me just this once, and if you cannot help me, at least give me the comfort of your sympathy. You will not be troubled by me much longer.

" 'Your distracted husband,

" 'Lewis Otway.' "

When the coroner finished reading the letter (which evidently made a deep impression on the jury) he looked at me gravely.

"Before passing to the next letter I must ask one or two questions about this one. What did you understand from the phrases 'I feel that it (death) is not far off. I cannot go on like this. You will not be troubled by me much longer.' Did they not suggest to you an intention to commit suicide?"

"No. I understood them as referring to his state of health."

"If you had known of the family tendency to suicide, how would you have understood these passages?"

"I should have suspected that he contemplated suicide."

"But you say you were not aware of this tendency?"

"No, I was not."

"He refers to his 'miserable affairs – which are to some extent your affairs too.' What did you understand him to mean by that?"

"I understood him to refer to the fact that I was partly responsible for the omission of certain details in the evidence at the inquest."

"When you received this pitiful letter, what did you do?"

"I went to him the same day to find out what the trouble was. He then showed me an anonymous letter that he had received."

"Is this the one?" the coroner asked, handing it to me; and when I had glanced at it and identified it, he proceeded to read it to the jury.

" 'Mr Lewis Otway.

" 'Some funny questions are being asked. What about Mr Vardon's stick? – the loaded stick with the silver knob to hide the lead loading? Where is it? Somebody says they know where it is and who's got it. And they say there is a bruise on the silver-top, and they say something about a smear of blood and a grey hair sticking to it. Do you know anything about that? If you don't you'd better find out. Because I think you will hear from that somebody before you are many weeks older or else from the police.

" 'A well wisher.' "

As he laid down the letter, the coroner looked at me curiously.

"There are one or two important questions, Mrs Otway," said he, "that arise out of this letter. The first is, What has become of this stick?"

"I don't know what has become of it. I saw Mrs Gregg replace it in the corner by the writing table and I never saw it again. The deceased asked me the same question when he showed me the letter; but I reminded him that I did not take the stick with me when I left his house, and that I never went to the house again."

"It never occurred to you to ask what had become of your father's stick?"

"No. I always assumed that it was in Mr Otway's possession."

"You have told us that Mrs Gregg had seen the stick in Mr Otway's house. Had anyone else seen it there?"

"I don't know of anyone else having seen it; but, of course, it may have been seen there by other persons. I know nothing of what went on in that house. I never entered it after my father's death."

"With the exception of Mr Otway and yourself, did anyone know that you had seen that stick in Mr Otway's hand on the occasion of your father's death?"

"So far as I am aware, no one else knew."

"There is a statement in that letter referring to a bruise on the silver knob and a smear of blood with a grey hair sticking to it. Is it possible, so far as you know, that that statement might be true?"

"I cannot say that it is impossible."

"After your father's death, did you examine the stick?"

"No. I saw it in Mrs Gregg's hands, but I did not look at it closely."

At this point a police superintendent who had been sitting near to the coroner's table, rose, and, approaching the table, stooped over it and spoke to the coroner in a low voice. The latter listened attentively and nodded once or twice, and when the superintendent had returned to his seat he addressed me.

"I think that will do, Mrs Otway – for the present, at any rate. We may have to ask you one or two questions later. Do any of the jury wish to ask anything before the witness sits down?"

As none of the jury responded, I returned to my seat, and the coroner then recalled Mrs Gregg.

"You have heard the last witness state that she saw you take up Mr Vardon's stick. What made you examine that stick?"

"I did not examine it. I noticed it standing in the corner and saw that it was a strange stick – that it was not Mr Otway's. I took it out of the corner to look at it and then noticed that it was heavily loaded at the top."

"Can you say whether there was or was not a bruise or a blood smear on the knob?"

"I cannot. I did not look closely at the knob. I just picked the stick up, felt its weight and put it back in the corner."

"Did you know that Mr Otway had had that stick in his hand when Mr Vardon fell dead?"

"No. I never heard of that until today."

"Could anyone other than Mrs Otway have known, so far as you are able to say?"

"I can't say. I should think not. I did not get back to the house until it was all over. But I thought, and believe, that there was no one in the house but those three – Mrs Otway and her husband and her father."

"Do you know what became of that stick?"

"I do not. I put it back in the corner and never saw it again. It was not in the corner when I tidied up the room the next day."

"Thank you, Mrs Gregg. That will do."

Having dismissed the witness, the coroner turned to the jury.

"I had hoped, gentlemen," said he, "to finish the case today, but, as you have seen, its apparent simplicity was rather illusory. Some rather curious issues have arisen which will have to be considered in detail. Moreover, there appears to be a suspicion that property of very great value has been removed from the premises – at least, it seems to be missing. Under these circumstances, the police authorities ask for an adjournment to enable them to make some enquiries; and I am sure you will agree with me that this, and certain other matters, should be cleared up before a verdict is returned. I therefore propose to adjourn this enquiry for fourteen days."

The court rose, and I rose with it. As I stood up and turned towards the door I saw Jasper standing at the back of the hall. He made no sign, nor did I; and as soon as our eyes had met, he turned and walked out. I did not attempt to follow, for I understood at once that he did not consider it desirable that we should recognise one another in that place. Moreover, I was detained for a minute or two by the coroner, who informed me, with a curious dry civility, that he wished me to attend at the adjourned meeting of the court, as further evidence from me might be required; and after him, by Mr Isaacs, who, as executor, was responsible for the funeral arrangements and who promised to inform me when the date had been fixed.

As I emerged from the gateway I glanced up the street with a wistfulness which I would hardly acknowledge to myself. But, of course, Jasper was already out of sight. Feeling very lonely, weary and exhausted, I walked slowly down Drury Lane considering what I should do next. And suddenly there came on me a longing for the quiet and comfort of the club. It was quite near; and once there I could wash, refresh and rest in peace, alone, or at least among civilised people. And it was even possible that Jasper might be there.

At this thought I must have unconsciously quickened my pace, for a few minutes later found me passing through the entrance hall, telling myself that, of course, Jasper would not have come there. Nevertheless as I opened the door of the large room my eye instantly sought the familiar table in the corner; and when I saw Jasper sitting by it with a watchful gaze fixed on the door, my weariness and loneliness seemed to drop from me like a garment.

CHAPTER TWENTY-FIVE

Suspense: and a Discovery

"I had hoped," said Jasper, as we met by the table, "that you would come on here. I had to take the chance. I suppose you understood why I made myself scarce as soon as you had seen me?"

"I assumed that you thought it better that we should not be seen together just at present."

"It is more than unadvisable," said he. "It is vitally important. We will talk about that letter – but not here. There is a lot that I have to say to you, but we had better have our talk where we cannot be seen, or possibly overheard. I propose that I run off now – nobody has seen us here yet – and wait for you at my chambers. You just have a wash to freshen you up and come along at once. Don't stop for tea; I will have some ready for you. And you had better come by the least frequented way. Go down to the Embankment, up Middle Temple Lane, along Crown Office Row, cross King's Bench Walk to Mitre Court, come out into Fleet Street by Mitre Court Passage, cross to Fetter Lane and into Clifford's Inn by the postern gate."

"All this sounds very secret and mysterious," said I.

"It is necessary," he replied. "We mustn't be seen together if we can help it. Remember the jury and other interested parties are local men, and might easily run against us in the public thoroughfares. So I will run off now and you will come along as soon as you can."

To this arrangement I agreed, although the precautions seemed to me somewhat excessive, and he hurried away while I went in quest of hot water and the other means of ablution.

The process of purification did not take long, for the temptation to linger luxuriously over the ceremonial of the toilet was combated by curiosity and anxiety to rejoin Jasper. In a few minutes I emerged, greatly refreshed and sensible of a very healthy appetite, and set forth by the prescribed route towards Clifford's Inn, reflecting earnestly as I went on Jasper's rather mysterious attitude. I did not have to ply the knocker, for as I reached the landing I found Jasper standing at his open door.

"Now," said he, when I had entered and he had softly closed both the massive "oak" and the inner door, "we are secure from observers and eavesdroppers, and we can pow-wow at any length we please."

"You are very secret and portentous," I remarked. "What is it all about?"

"The secrecy and portentosity," he replied, "are possibly by-products of a legal training. We will discuss that presently. Meanwhile, the need of the moment is to provide nourishment for a starving angel."

He placed an easy chair for me by the fire, and then retired to the little kitchen, from which issued a gentle clink of crockery very grateful to my ear. Presently he emerged with a tray on which were a teapot and two covers, and having deposited it on a small table, placed the latter by my chair and removed the covers with a flourish.

"There is only one cup and one plate," said I, noting that the "nourishment" had been provided on a scale of opulence appropriate to masculine conceptions of appetite.

"Dear me!" exclaimed Jasper. "How many cups and plates do you generally use?"

"Go and get another plate and cup and saucer," I commanded, severely.

When he had made the necessary addition to the table appointments, he drew up a second armchair, and, as he poured out the tea he said, gravely: "We have had a long probation, Helen, dearest – at least, it seems so to me; and it is not over yet. But this little interlude should hearten us for what remains. To me it is a glimpse into a future of perfect happiness and comradeship. Do you realise, Helen, that we are now a normal, engaged couple, free to marry when we choose?"

Of course I had realised that we were free; but as I thought of the shrouded figure that even now reposed under its sheet in the mortuary, I doubted whether the word "normal" was fully applicable.

"It is perfect peace and happiness to be here with you, Jasper," I replied; "but I think I shall feel more normal when we can meet without all this secrecy. And even now I don't quite understand it. Why is it so important that we should not be seen together?"

"That is fairly obvious, I think," he replied. "I am going to be very frank with you, Helen, because I have complete confidence in your courage and strength of character. There is no use in blinking the fact that you are in a difficult position. That coroner man thinks you wrote those anonymous letters; and he suspects that you knew about Otway's suicidal tendencies."

"But I distinctly said I did not."

"Yes, but, you see, the person who wrote those letters is not a person whose statements would carry any weight; and he thinks you are that person. He thinks you have tried deliberately to drive Otway to suicide, and he will be looking for a motive. There is a fairly obvious motive already, as you were encumbered with a husband whom you didn't want; but if you add another husband whom you did and do want, the motive for getting rid of the unwanted one becomes much more definite. That is the kind of motive he will be on the lookout for. Hence the necessity for the utmost caution on our part. If a witness could be produced who could depose to having seen us together, it might be possible for him to put some inconvenient questions."

"Could he not question me on the subject apart from any such witness?"

"I don't think it would be admissible for the coroner to suggest the existence of a lover if he had no facts. And that brings us to the point that I was going to raise. You ought to be represented either by counsel or by a solicitor; preferably by counsel, as a barrister is more agile – more accustomed to deal with the sudden exigencies that arise in court."

"You seem to suggest that I am charged with having brought about Mr Otway's death."

"I wouldn't use the word 'charged' as I don't know that there is any such offence recognised by law. Morally, to cause a man to commit suicide would be much the same as to murder him, but I can't say off-hand what the legal position would be. My impression is that it would not be an offence that could be dealt with by law unless the causation were direct, as in the case where two persons agree to commit suicide together and one of them survives."

I listened to this exposition with a sinking heart. Jasper's intention was to reassure me. But if only he had known what I knew! If only he could have looked into my heart and seen the secret guilt that was hidden there! And, after all, was it so secret? Was it so securely hidden? Was the still, small voice of my own conscience the only accusing voice that I should hear? As I asked myself the question, uncomfortable memories of the mysterious sounds that had seemed to issue from the locked cupboard arose and whispered a new menace.

"I am putting the matter bluntly," Jasper continued, "as the position has to be faced, and I am confident that you have the courage and resolution to face it The coroner holds you accountable for Otway's death. He thinks you made a deliberate plan and carried it out to the bitter end. That is his line, and we have got to show that he is wrong, if we can, and in any case prevent him from misdirecting the jury. You must certainly be represented by counsel."

"What could my counsel do?" I asked.

"His principal function would be to prevent the coroner or the jury from putting improper questions – questions that do not properly arise out of the evidence, such as the one we spoke of just now. Of course, I could represent you, but it would not be advisable under the circumstances; and besides, I have had no experience of actual practice. Do you know any barrister whom you could ask?"

"The only barrister I know is Dr Thorndyke, but I couldn't ask him to attend a coroner's court."

"I don't know that you couldn't. Of course, he is a great man. But the case is quite in his line, and I know that he doesn't mind where he appears if the case interests him."

"You know him then, too?"

"Only by repute. All lawyers know him as the leading authority on medical evidence. His position is unique, for he is a first-class criminal lawyer and a first-class medical specialist. You couldn't have a better man for your representative. I advise you to see him or write to him without delay. Does he know anything about your affairs?"

"Yes, I consulted him a month or two ago, about these very letters and told him about my reservations at the inquest. He promised to make a few inquiries but I have not heard from him on the subject, so I suppose his inquiries led to no result."

"You can't be sure of that," said Jasper. "At any rate, as he knows something of the case, and is by far the best counsel you could get, the obvious thing is to communicate with him at once."

Of course, Jasper was quite right – in so far as he knew the facts. For he was assuming that I had nothing to conceal excepting my bargain with Mr Otway and my relations with himself. He knew nothing of the dreadful events that befell on the night preceding Mr Otway's death; of the silent willing and suggestion that my own conscience called murder, and that any jury would have called murder if they had known of it. But it was vivid enough in my mind; and I had hardly spoken Dr Thorndyke's name before I realised that I dare not ask for his help. My own experience fully endorsed my father's estimate of his powers. He missed nothing. Hidden significances that no one else guessed at were to him as the writing of an open book. With no knowledge of the facts, he had instantly perceived that Mr Otway's evidence was false, and that I was withholding something of importance. And so I felt it would be now. If he came into the case, my hideous secret would be a secret no longer. I dare not run the risk.

"I must think it over," said I. "It seems rather a liberty to ask a man of his position to watch the evidence at an inquest."

"He can but refuse," said Jasper; "and don't think it over for too long, or you may miss your chance. He is a busy man."

I made some sort of non-committal reply and changed the subject. Full as we were of the events of the moment, there were other matters that were more pleasant to discuss. For Mr Otway's death had made a radical change in our prospects and plans for the future, and these we talked over with interest and pleasure but little dimmed by the dark clouds that hung overhead at the moment, until the chimes of St Dunstan's, hard by, announced that it was nine o'clock and time for me to go.

"I suppose," said Jasper, as he bade me farewell, "we had better not meet again until this affair is over. It is only a fortnight, and after that we shall be free. Meanwhile, we can write as often as we please."

I agreed to this the more readily as I saw that another meeting with Jasper would make it difficult for me to escape from his demand that I should invoke Dr Thorndyke's help. Nevertheless, as I took my way through Clifford's Inn Passage into Fleet Street, I found myself looking forward somewhat gloomily to the lonely and anxious fortnight that lay ahead.

For several days nothing out of the ordinary occurred. My friends at Wellclose Square, who knew approximately what my position was, were quietly sympathetic, but never referred to the matter; excepting the incorrigible Titmouse, who frankly congratulated me on my newly-acquired freedom.

"It's horrid for you, Sibyl," said she, "but still it is all for the best; though he might have managed it a little more decently – level crossing, you know, or 'found drowned,' or something of that sort."

"You are a callous little wretch, Peggy," said I.

"I don't care" she replied, defiantly. "You know it's true. I am awfully sorry for you now. It must be perfectly beastly to have to answer all those impertinent questions and have your answers printed in the newspapers. But it will soon be over, and then you can forget it and have a good time. I shall dance at your wedding before I am six months older."

I had to pretend to be shocked, but the Titmouse's optimism did me good. For there *was* a bright side to the picture, and it was just as well to gather encouragement by an occasional glance at it.

About ten days after the first sitting of the inquest I received a letter from Mr Isaacs. He had already written to me briefly to inform me that the funeral had been postponed by the coroner's direction until after the adjourned inquest, but had then said nothing about the will. The present letter supplied the omission, and its contents surprised me very much. It appeared that the will had been proved and that I was the principal beneficiary. "The testator," said Mr Isaacs, "has bequeathed to you the bulk of his personality – upwards of eight thousand pounds – and the lease of the premises in Lyon's Inn Chambers, together with the furniture and effects contained therein. You are also constituted the residuary legatee. The chambers have now been evacuated by Mrs Gregg, and are at your disposal. They are at present locked up, and the keys are in my possession pending your instructions and advice as to whether you intend to occupy the premises, to let them or to dispose of the lease. A copy of the will can be seen at my office, and, of course, the original can be examined at Somerset House."

The provisions of this will caused me, as I have said, considerable surprise. I had regarded myself as having no pecuniary claim on Mr Otway, and had not considered myself as concerned in his will at all. Now it was evident that, selfish as he had been during his life, he had been anxious at least to make some atonement after his death for the injury he had done me; and the fact did not tend to make my sense of guilt less acute.

Before I had replied to Mr Isaacs' letter I received two other communications. One was from Jasper; and though it was written in a tone of quiet cheerfulness, its contents filled me with alarm. It appeared that Jasper, becoming uneasy at my continued neglect to take any measures to secure a counsel to represent me, had called on Dr Thorndyke with the object of retaining him. "We have had rather bad luck," he continued, "though I don't suppose it will matter. Dr Thorndyke would have been pleased to represent you, but unfortunately he has been commissioned at the last moment by the Home Office to make an independent investigation of the case. He gave me the name of a suitable counsel – a rising junior named Cawley – with whom I have made the necessary arrangements. So your interests will be looked after, and we can trust Thorndyke to clear up the obscurities of the case."

The other letter was from Dr Thorndyke himself, and confirmed Jasper's account. "Your friend, Mr Davenant," it said, "called on me today to ask me to watch the proceedings of the inquest on your behalf, which I would have done with great pleasure if I had been at liberty. But I had just received instructions from the Home Office to look into the case and give evidence at the adjourned inquest; so I referred your friend to Mr Cawley, who is an excellent counsel and will be able to do all that is necessary.

"Mr Davenant expressed great disappointment that I should be, as he expressed it, 'retained by the other side.' But I pointed out to him that there is no 'other side.' I am not a 'witness advocate.' My evidence would be the same whichever side employed me. I never undertake to represent a particular interest, but merely to obtain what facts I can and give those facts impartially in my evidence; and I always make it clear to clients that they employ me at their own risk – at the risk that the facts elicited may be unfavourable to them. So, although I am not retained by you, I shall act precisely as if I were. I shall find out all I can, and tell the court all I know. This will, presumably, be entirely in your interest.

"And now I am going to ask a favour of you. I wish to examine and make a plan of the premises at Lyon's Inn Chambers, and I understand that the tenancy of the Chambers is now vested in you. Will you be so kind as to lend me the keys and authorise me to make this survey? If you will, I shall be able to make my evidence more complete."

If Jasper's letter had alarmed me, Dr Thorndyke's positively terrified me. The cool, relentless impartiality, the unhuman indifference to everything but the actual truth that the letter conveyed appalled me; and I even seemed to read a direct menace in its tone. If I had employed him, I should have done so at my own risk; so he seemed to hint. His intention was to "find out all he could and tell the court all he knew." How much would he find out? How much did he know already? He had a verbatim report of the evidence so far. He had Mrs Gregg's statement that "they seemed to be talking about suicide." He would know all about suggestion and silent willing. Was it possible that he already knew that I had sent that wretched man on his last journey? When I recalled all that my father had said of his amazing powers of inference; when I remembered how unerringly he had detected the reservations in Mr Otway's evidence and mine; I could not but feel that my chance of keeping my guilty secret was infinitesimal. The probability was that it was discovered already.

As to his request, obviously I had no choice but to grant it; and I was on the point of writing to Mr Isaacs to instruct him to hand the keys to Dr Thorndyke when it occurred to me that it might be well to avoid unnecessarily taking the former gentleman into my confidence. I knew nothing about Mr Isaacs, and was not particularly prepossessed by him; nor did I know the object of the proposed survey of the premises; concerning which indeed I was somewhat mystified and rather uncomfortable. Eventually I decided to call at Mr Isaacs' office for the keys and deliver them myself to Dr Thorndyke.

Accordingly I wrote a short note to the latter informing him of my intentions, and on the following morning betook myself to Mr Isaacs' office, which was situate in New Inn. I could see that my visit was somewhat unexpected, and evidently aroused the solicitor's curiosity.

"You will see," said he, "that the keys are all labelled, and I have made a rough inventory of the furniture and effects. Perhaps you would like me to come with you and check it."

"Thank you," said I "but I don't think I will check the inventory today. We will postpone that until I take formal possession. At present I am merely going to take a look at the premises."

When I said this, I had, of course, no intention of going to the chambers at all, but as I walked down Wych Street with the keys in my bag, I reflected that, as I had said I was going, I had better go. Moreover, it was possible that the arrangement of the place had been disturbed and that some things might need to be replaced; for I assumed that Dr Thorndyke would wish to see the premises as they were on the night of the tragedy. And then I was not without some curiosity concerning this place which had been the scene of events so momentous to me.

At the bottom of Wych Street I turned round by the "Rising Sun" and walked along Holywell Street to the entrance of Lyon's Inn Chambers; and as I once again ascended the gloomy stone stairs the sinister atmosphere of the place enveloped me as it had done on previous occasions, and induced a vague sensation of fear. When I reached the landing and stood at the ill-omened portal, the feeling had grown so pronounced that I hesitated for a while to enter the chambers. At length I summoned up courage to insert the key and as the massive door swung open I stepped into the lobby.

But my nervousness by no means wore off. Leaving the outer door ajar, I walked quickly down the corridor, peered into the kitchen and the little, empty room that had presumably been occupied by Mrs Gregg – apparently the furniture had belonged to her – crossed the living-room and entered the bedroom. Here nothing seemed to have been changed. Even the great peg – on which, of course, my eye lit instantly – still bore the end of crimson rope; the bed had been stripped, but the bedside table stood intact even to the bottle of veronal tablets. I looked about me quickly and nervously, noting the arrangement of the furniture and comparing it with my recollections of that unforgettable night; and when I had decided that it was unaltered, I turned to go.

As I crossed the living-room, the large, wardrobe-like cupboard attracted my attention, and I recalled the mysterious sounds that had seemed to issue from it. Was it possible, I wondered, that Mrs Gregg could have been concealed in it that night and have overheard those last incriminating words of mine. She had not referred to them in her evidence but the inquiry was not finished yet. I resolved to settle the question whether it was physically possible for her to have been concealed in the cupboard, and having tried the door and found it locked I turned the keys over one by one until I found one labelled "cupboard in living room." It was a rather unusual type of key, with a solid stem instead of the more usual barrel, and when I had inserted it and opened the door, I noticed that the key-hole passed right through the lock, so that the door could be locked from the inside as well as the outside. The cupboard itself was fitted like a wardrobe with a single shelf just above my eye level, beneath which a short woman like Mrs Gregg could have easily stood upright. Thus the construction of the cupboard and the peculiar form of the lock made it at least possible that an eavesdropper might have been concealed that night; and that was all that I could say.

Before shutting the door I stood on tiptoe to see if there was anything on the shelf. In the semi-darkness of the interior I could see some kind of metallic object, and reaching in, took hold of it. As I drew it into the light of day I gave a gasp of astonishment. It was my father's stick.

I took it down and turned it over curiously in my hands, marvelling how it should have got into this receptacle; and as I turned it over, there came into view a flattened dent on the silver knob covered by a thick smear of blood to which two hairs had stuck. I looked at the hairs closely, but could come to no opinion as to whether or not they were my father's. One of these was white and the other a brownish grey. My father's hair had been iron grey as a whole, but I could not judge what the appearance of individual hairs might have been. If these were really his, then the man who had gone to his account was my father's murderer. It was a dreadful thought, but yet not without a certain compensation. As I looked at this relic of that day of wrath I felt my heart hardening. If the message that it bore was a true message, then I need have no more compunction for what I had done. If I had known with certainty that Mr Otway had killed my father, those words which had slipped from me subconsciously would have been consciously uttered with full and deliberate intent and without a qualm.

I stood for a while with the stick in my hand considering what I should do with it. That its mysterious reappearance would create a complication I plainly foresaw, but to take it away and conceal it would be not only dishonest but very unsafe; for it was almost certain that someone knew of its existence. It must have been seen when the inventory was taken. Eventually I replaced it on the shelf and locked the cupboard; and having put the keys back in my bag made my way to the door, which had been standing ajar all this time.

As I walked slowly to the Temple, I turned over in my mind the significance of this strange discovery. Someone must have known of the presence of this stick in the chambers, and that someone was either Mr Otway or Mrs Gregg. But both had declared positively that they had never seen it; and it was difficult to imagine why either of them should have kept it hidden away and disclaimed all knowledge of it. I could make nothing of the problem. Only one thing was clear to me. I must let Dr Thorndyke know of my discovery; for it did not incriminate me in any way and might give him a clue to some of the elements of the mystery, the unravelment of which would be to my advantage.

The door of Dr Thorndyke's chambers was opened by Mr Polton, who greeted me with a friendly smile, all creases and wrinkles.

"I'm sorry to say that the Doctor is not at home, ma'am," said he; "and he will be sorry, too. He would have liked to see you, I am sure."

"It doesn't matter, Mr Polton," said I. "I have only called to leave these keys. But I should like to leave a message. Will you ask him not to disturb things more than he can help, as the inventory has not been checked yet; and will you tell him that the stick is in the large cupboard in the living-room? You won't forget, will you?"

"I shan't *forget*," he replied, with a slight emphasis on the last word, "but I never trust my memory in important matters. Would you mind writing the Doctor a little note?"

He produced writing materials and placed a chair by the table, and I sat down and briefly put my message into writing. When I had given him the note – which he set in a conspicuous place on the mantel-piece – he looked at me as if he had something to say, and I waited to hear what it was.

"I've got an old verge watch to pieces upstairs," he said at length. "I don't know whether you would care to have a look at the movement. It's worth looking at. If you want to know what workmanship is, you should look at the inside of a good, old watch."

I was not, at the moment, much interested in watches or workmanship, but I could not resist his companionable enthusiasm – to say nothing of the implied compliment. So we went up together to the workshop, where he exhibited with a craftsman's delight the delicate wheels, the engraved plates and the little chased pillars, and even brought out a microscope that I might appreciate the finish bestowed on the links of a fuse-chain that was hardly thicker than a horse-hair.

As the day of the adjourned inquest drew near, my anxiety – intensified by the consciousness of my guilty secret – grew more acute. My position was, as Jasper had said, a difficult one in any case. But the really alarming element in it was the introduction of Dr Thorndyke into the case. The suggestion factor in the suicide would probably remain unsuspected by the coroner and the jury. But would it escape Dr Thorndyke's almost superhuman penetration. I could not believe that it would, for the hint of it was plain in Mrs Gregg's evidence. And if it were detected, it would be revealed. Of that I had not the shadow of a doubt. Dr Thorndyke was a kindly, even a genial man; but he was Justice personified. He would investigate the case with relentless accuracy and completeness; and he would tell the truth to the last word. Of that I felt certain. If he held my fate in his hands I was lost.

Of the view of the case taken by outsiders I had an unpleasant illustration the day before the adjourned sitting. It was furnished by an article in an evening paper that I had taken up to my room to read. Glancing over its pages my eyes was caught by the words "Lyon's Inn," and I read as follows:

"The new Lyon's Inn seems to be emulating the reputation of the old. Within that ancient precinct occurred the famous Weare murder, forgotten of the present generation, but immortalised in those rather brutal verses of Tom Hood's:

> " 'They cut his throat from ear to ear,
>   His brains they battered in;
>   His name was Mr William Weare,
>   He lived in Lyon's Inn.'

"The drama of Lyon's Inn Chambers, however, is not a murder – at least we hope not. It is at present regarded as a suicide. But there are some queer features in the case. There is, for instance, a handsome young wife, who, it seems, flatly refused to live with her elderly husband from the very wedding day; there is a series of unaccountable anonymous letters; and there is a rumour of a hoard of precious gems spirited away from the chambers, apparently on the very night when Mr Lewis Otway hanged himself from a peg on his bedroom wall. So the adjourned inquest, which opens at 11 a.m. tomorrow, may elicit some curious revelations."

As I laid the paper down, a cold hand seemed to settle on my heart. The writer had exaggerated nothing. He had not even stated all the accusing facts. But even so, put quite impartially, the article exhibited me as the central figure of the tragedy, as the visible agent of the sinister events that had befallen in those ill-omened chambers. And could I say that it misstated the case? Of the anonymous letters, indeed, and the stolen gems – if stolen they were – I knew nothing. But the central fact of the case was Mr Otway's death. For that the coroner held me accountable. And though he misjudged the evidence as to the means, I could not but admit that the coroner was right. The coming inquiry was, in effect, the trial of Helen Otway.

CHAPTER TWENTY-SIX

The Adjourned Inquiry

The second sitting of the inquest was a much more portentous affair than the first. The large room, or hall, in which it was held was nearly full when I entered, and it was evident that a considerable proportion of the occupants were spectators, attracted hither, no doubt, by the picturesque comments of the newspapers. But besides these were a number of persons connected with the inquiry. Behind the coroner's chair sat a group of police officers. Mr Isaacs and Mr Hyams were again present; the witnesses now included Mr and Mrs Campbell and a youngish man of a pronouncedly Hebrew type, who sat next to them. The side of the long table allotted to the press was filled by reporters – among whom I noticed the gentleman employed by Dr Thorndyke, and there were one or two men whom I judged to be lawyers representing the various parties interested.

My own counsel, Mr Cawley, a shrewd-looking man of about thirty-five, introduced himself to me as I took the seat reserved for me, and gave me a few words of advice.

"I think," said he "I have had all the necessary instructions from Mr Davenant, who, I see, is here." (I had had an instantaneous glimpse of him as I entered the room.) "His impression is that the coroner is disposed to put a certain amount of blame on you for your husband's death. If that is so, you will have to be rather careful about answering questions, especially any questions that the jury may put. Don't be in a hurry to answer any doubtful questions. Give me time to object if they seem inclined to go beyond the evidence."

I promised to bear his advice in mind, and then asked: "Do you know if Dr Thorndyke is giving evidence today?"

"I presume he is," was the reply; "but I notice that he is not present and that his reporter is."

At this point the coroner laid down the papers which he had been looking over, and opened the proceedings with a short address to the jury.

"The adjournment of this inquiry, gentlemen," said he, "which was decided upon a fortnight ago, is amply justified by the mass of new facts which are now available. These new facts bear chiefly on the property which, as you heard at the last sitting, was believed to be missing; but in other directions they throw a very curious light on the case. The first witness will be Superintendent Miller, of the Criminal Investigation Department."

As his name was spoken, the officer rose and took his place by the table. He took the oath, and disposed of the preliminaries with professional facility, and then waited gravely for the coroner's next question.

"You had some knowledge of the deceased, Lewis Otway, and his affairs, I understand?" said the coroner.

"Yes. I have known of his existence for more than twenty years."

"Will you tell us what you know of him?"

"I first made his acquaintance about twenty-three years ago. He was then practising as a solicitor – chiefly as a police-court advocate – and was known by his real name, Lewis Levy, which he subsequently changed to Otway. After a time, he began to engage in business as a money-lender, and it was at this time that he took the name of Otway. Presently he began to combine with money-lending a certain amount of trafficking in precious stones, and it was then that the police began to keep a somewhat close watch on him, with the idea that he might be also acting as a receiver. We never really had anything against him, but we always had the impression that he did some business as a middleman, or disposer of stolen jewels.

"When I first knew him, he had living with him a young woman, named Rachel Goldstein. She was nominally his housekeeper, but there were two children – a boy named Morris, and a girl named Judith – whom he admitted to be his. When he changed his name to Otway, Rachel Goldstein took the name of Gregg, and used to pass as a Scotchwoman. The children lived with their parents until they grew up, when Otway (or Levy) provided for them in a way that made the police watch still more closely. Judith married a David Samuels, who traded under the name of Campbell as a dealer in works of art, especially goldsmith's work and jewellery; and Morris Goldstein started as a dealer in antiques, with a shop in Hand Court, and some workshops in Mansell Street, Whitechapel, where most of the antiques were made.

"Now both these men were practical working jewellers. It was believed that Otway financed them both, and it was known that he was the lessee of the premises that they occupied. Moreover, as soon as they were established in business, Otway gradually abandoned the money-lending, and occupied himself almost exclusively in dealing in gem stones. He was an exceedingly good judge of stones, and was quite successful as a legitimate dealer; but the police had an impression that he did a considerable amount of business that was not legitimate. I want it to be quite clear that I am not making any accusations; I am referring merely to an impression that the police had; it may have been quite a mistaken impression, but I mention it because the matter bears directly on this inquiry.

"The idea of the police, then, was that Otway dealt to a considerable extent in stolen property. We supposed that he obtained this property – precious stones, without the mounts – not from the thieves, but from the receivers, and that he disposed of them with the aid of his son and son-in-law. Both those men did a fairly large trade in high-class jewellery. They did not touch commercial goods but dealt exclusively in work produced individually by skilled goldsmiths and jewellers, some of whom they kept regularly employed. They also did a good deal of repairing and re-setting, and their transactions were always with private customers, not with the trade.

"Our idea of the way it was worked was this: We thought that when Otway had got a collection of stolen stones he would pass on some of them to these two men. They would then commission their craftsmen to make some articles of jewellery, and would provide them with stones which had been bought from the regular dealers, and the purchase of which could be proved if necessary. Then, when the jewels were delivered – or even after they had been sold to a private buyer – Campbell or Goldstein would take the purchased stones out of their settings and replace them by stolen stones. And a similar method could have been employed when jewels were brought for alteration, repair or re-setting. This kind of substitution would be very difficult to trace, for it is not easy to identify particular stones and prove that they are not the ones referred to in the dealers' receipts. As a matter of fact we never did trace any stolen gems excepting on a single occasion; and then the evidence was not good enough for us to risk a prosecution.

"And now we come to the case that concerns this inquiry. About a year ago there was a burglary at the premises of Messrs Middleburg, of New Bond Street, the well-known jewellers, and, among other things, a collection of valuable stones, worth about five thousand pounds, was carried off. It was a small collection, but all the stones were individually of considerable value, and several of them were remarkable, either in respect of size or other peculiarities. The collection has never been traced, and none of the stones has reappeared either here or abroad; and the police have reason to believe that the whole collection is still in this country.

"When these stones disappeared so completely, the police formed the opinion that they had passed into the possession of Otway, and that he was holding them up until an opportunity occurred to issue them one by one. At this time he was living at

Maidstone – he had been there a year or two, but he had kept his old chambers at Lyon's Inn, and often stayed in them for a week or more at a time. Last May or June he left Maidstone and came back to his old chambers, and we then began to keep a closer watch on him.

"About a couple of months ago he bought – or rather took on approval – from Mr Hyams, of Hatton Garden, a collection of stones of which I have seen the list. These stones were carefully selected by Otway, and the remarkable thing about them is that, taken as a whole, they are singularly like the stolen collection. Among the stolen stones, for instance, there were two large tourmalines, one green and one deep blue, both table stones with step-cut backs; four emeralds, two step-cut and two cut *en cabochon*; two large chrysoberyls, one brilliant-cut green and one *en cabochon*, yellow; one pale-blue diamond; and one pale-pink. Now, the collection taken from Mr Hyams' includes tourmalines emeralds, chrysoberyls, and diamonds, of almost exactly the same size, colour and cutting; and there are many other passable duplicates of the stolen stones.

"When I became aware of this transaction I inferred that Otway was making arrangements to release the stolen stones, and I caused a still closer watch to be kept on him; but up to the present not one of the missing stones has been discovered. Now I understand that the Hyams collection has disappeared; and if that is so, it seems probable that the person who has taken it is also in possession of the stolen collection. But that, of course, is only a guess."

"Quite so!" said the coroner, "and it is a matter that is more in your province than in ours. Is there anything more that you have to tell us that is relevant to the inquiry?"

"No, I think that is all."

"You will be remaining here, in case we want to refer to you again?"

"Yes; I want to hear Dr Thorndyke's evidence, and, of course, I want to hear the verdict."

"I am afraid you may have a long time to wait, for I have had a telegram from Dr Thorndyke saying that he has been detained at Maidstone, and has missed his train. It is a great nuisance for us all. However, we will go on with the evidence. The next witness will be Mr Samuel Isaacs."

As the superintendent retired to his seat and Mr Isaacs approached the table, I reflected rapidly on what I had just heard. Dr Thorndyke had apparently been down to Maidstone. Was his visit connected with the present inquiry? And if so, what was it that he had been investigating? The locality suggested some kind of research in which I was concerned, but at the nature of that research I could make no guess whatever. However, there was no time to speculate on the subject, for Mr Isaacs had been sworn, and was ready to begin his evidence.

"You were solicitor to the deceased, I understand, Mr Isaacs?"

"Yes; I am one of the executors of his will."

"In that capacity have you heard of any property said to be missing from the chambers which he occupied?"

"I have. Mr Hyams has made a claim to have restored to him a parcel of precious stones, valued at about four thousand pounds, which, he states, was his property, and which he asserts the deceased had in his possession."

"Have you examined the premises with a view to discovering that property?"

"Yes, I have examined the premises very thoroughly, and have made a complete inventory of all the effects of the deceased. I have gone through the contents of the safe and all other receptacles, and have checked the property which he had deposited at his bank. I have made a most exhaustive search, but have failed to find any trace of the parcel referred to, or of any precious stones whatever."

"Is it possible that you may have overlooked the parcel?"

"I should say it is impossible. My opinion is that the parcel is not on the premises, and it certainly is not at the bank."

The coroner and a legal-looking gentleman at the table both noted down this reply. Then the former said: "You are, no doubt, in a position to tell us what was the state of the deceased man's affairs. Was there any kind of financial embarrassment?"

"I should say, certainly not. The gross value of the estate – which is entirely personal – is a little over seventeen thousand pounds; and the liabilities, so far as they are known to me, are quite trivial."

"Can you tell us roughly, what are the main provisions of the will, that is, if it has been proved?"

"It has been proved. The principal beneficiary is the widow, who receives eight thousand pounds, and the lease of the chambers in Lyon's Inn, with the furniture and effects, and is made residuary legatee. Rachel Gregg – or Goldstein – receives one thousand, and Morris and Judith, each, two thousand pounds, and the lease of the premises in which they respectively carry on their business. There are a few small legacies – less than a thousand pounds in the aggregate; so that there will probably be a residue of about three thousand pounds, which will go to the widow."

"What is the date of this will?"

"It is dated the 10th June last."

"Do you know whether the provisions of the will were known to the widow, or the other beneficiaries?"

"I do not know. They were not disclosed by me until probate had been granted."

"Thank you," said the coroner. "I think we need not trouble you any further, unless the jury wish to ask any questions."

The jury did not; but the legal-looking gentleman at the table did, and springing up like a Jack-in-the-box, he addressed the coroner.

"As representing Mr Hyams, sir" said he, "I should like to ask the witness whether, in the event of the missing gems not coming to light, their loss would be chargeable to the estate?"

The countenance of Mr Isaacs hereupon assumed that peculiar expression known to students of sculpture as "the archaic smile."

"You are asking me to admit liability," he replied; "I can't do that, you know. There is a recognised procedure in these cases, with which I have no doubt you are acquainted."

The questioner sat down with a jerk, and Mr Cawley stood up.

"May I ask the witness, sir, whether, in the event of this loss being adjudged to be chargeable to the estate, that loss would affect equally all the beneficiaries?"

"No," replied Mr Isaacs, "it would not. It would fall, in the first place, on the residuary legatee. It would only affect the estate as a whole in so far as the amount of the charge exceeded that of the residue."

"Thank you," said Mr Cawley. "There is one other question that I should like to ask. The present will is dated the 10th of last June. Did the execution of that will involve the revocation of a previously-existing will?"

"Yes, it did. After his marriage deceased re-acknowledged the existing will by a fresh signature and attestation, but he revoked this will when he made the new one."

"Could you tell us who were the beneficiaries under that will?"

Mr Isaacs fixed a thoughtful (and somewhat beady) eye on the coroner's pewter ink-pot, and cogitated for a few moments.

"Is it necessary, sir, for me to answer that question," he asked at length, looking up at the coroner.

"Is the point material?" the latter asked, looking at Mr Cawley.

"I submit, sir, that it may become highly important," was the reply.

The coroner reflected with his eyes fixed on Mr Cawley. Then he nodded. "Yes," he said, "I think you are right. We must ask you to answer the question, Mr Isaacs."

Mr Isaacs bowed. "The beneficiaries under that will were Rachel Goldstein, Morris Goldstein, and Judith Samuels."

"In what proportions was the property devised?"

"The bulk of the personalty was divided between Morris and Judith. Rachel Goldstein – or Gregg – received two thousand pounds, but she was also the residuary legatee."

"And the value of the estate?"

"I can't tell you that. I only know what it is now."

Mr Cawley sat down, and Mr Isaacs retired to his seat. Then the coroner pronounced the name of Mr Hyams, and its owner took his place by the table.

"We have heard, Mr Hyams," said the coroner, "of certain property of yours which was in the deceased man's custody. Will you give us a few particulars of the transaction. When, for instance, did it come into the possession of the deceased?"

"Two months ago – on the tenth of August, when the deceased called at my office, and asked me to let him have a selection of stones for a special purpose. He said that he had an opportunity of disposing of a number of pieces of jewellery to a wealthy American gentleman, and that he had discovered an extremely clever artist whom he proposed to commission to make them. They were to be important pieces, chiefly pendants, brooches, and bracelets. The stones were to be exceptional in size and quality, and he wanted an assortment for Mr Campbell – who was conducting the transaction – to show the intending purchaser. He had a list in his pocket-book, which he referred to as he made his selection from my stock. The stones which he selected were rather unusual – the sort of stones that appeal to collectors and connoisseurs, rather than ordinary wearers of jewels. And some of them were very valuable; one ruby alone that he took was worth fifteen hundred pounds. The total value of the parcel that he carried away with him was four thousand two hundred pounds."

"I understand that he did not pay you for them?"

"No; he was not proposing to keep them all. They were a selection to show to the customer. I made out a full list, and he signed a receipt at the foot of it. I had known deceased for many years, and had often had similar dealings with him."

"And did he never return these stones, or any part of the collection?"

"No. From the time that he left my office with the stones in his pocket I never saw him or heard from him again."

This was the sum of Mr Hyams' evidence; and when he had retired the name of Judith Samuels was called. The new witness took her place at the table, and, after the usual preliminaries, proceeded to give her evidence.

"I am the wife of David Samuels who trades under the name of Donald Campbell. He is a dealer in works of art, principally goldsmiths' work and jewellery. He is a practical jeweller himself, but most of the alterations and repairs are put out. The new work that he sells, or which is commissioned by customers, is executed for him by independent goldsmiths, not by workmen employed by him."

"You visited the deceased on the night preceding his death, I understand, is that so?"

"Yes. I came to his chambers about half past six, and left about seven o'clock."

"Did you notice anything unusual in his manner or appearance?"

"He was not looking very well, and he seemed rather depressed but he brightened up as we talked. He was very much interested in the business which I had come to discuss."

"What was the nature of that business?"

"It was connected with a collection of stones that he had got on approval from Mr Hyams to carry out a commission that he expected to get from a very wealthy American gentleman, to whom he had an introduction. He did not disclose the name of the gentleman, but it was understood that if he secured the commission, my husband should conduct the negotiations, and get the work executed."

"Did you gather that he had the stones in his possession?"

"Yes; he showed them to me. They were in a small wooden box, the different kinds of stones wrapped up separately in little paper packets. He took the box from a deed-box on the table by his bed-side, and put it back there when he had shown me the stones."

"Did you make any arrangements as to the disposal of these stones?"

"No final arrangements. He advised that we should get some of our artist goldsmiths to submit designs for the customer to see; and he suggested that my husband should ask Mrs Otway to design and execute a pendant to take some of the finest stones."

"Mrs Otway!" exclaimed the coroner. "What Mrs Otway do you refer to?"

"I mean Helen Otway, the wife of the deceased."

"Are we to understand that Mrs Otway is a designer of jewellery?"

"She is not only a designer; she is a practical goldsmith, and a very clever one too. My husband admires her work exceedingly and has paid her some very high prices. He paid her, for instance, twenty-five guineas for a set of silver teaspoons."

The looks of astonishment that the coroner, the jury, and the press-men bestowed on me might, in other circumstances, have flattered my vanity. Now, I could see that Mrs Campbell, without (so far as I knew) departing one single jot from the truth, was enveloping me in the most hideous entanglements.

After a pause – filled in with strenuous note-taking – the coroner again addressed the witness. "It has been given in evidence that the deceased had received a number of anonymous letters. Do you know anything about these letters?"

"I know nothing beyond what I heard when the evidence was given."

"Have you any means of judging who wrote these letters?"

"I have heard the evidence, and I can make a pretty good guess who wrote them."

"That is not quite what I mean. Have you any information about them other than what you gathered from the evidence?"

"No; I never heard of them until then."

This concluded Mrs Campbell's evidence. When she had retired Mrs Gregg was recalled and questioned concerning the missing stones.

"Did you know that deceased had these stones in his possession?"

"Yes. He showed them to me on one occasion, and I often saw him looking at them. He was very fond of precious stones. He used to set them out on a small square of black velvet, and try them in different lights, and look at them through a magnifying glass."

"When did you last see these stones?"

"After Mrs Campbell – that is the last witness – had left, and just before Mrs Otway arrived. Deceased was then sitting up in bed looking at a large green stone. I reminded him that Mrs Otway, was due at eight, and he then put the stones back in their box, and put the box away in the deed-box that was on the table."

"When did you first learn that the stones were missing?"

"The day after the discovery that the deceased had committed suicide, when Mrs Otway came to the chambers with Mr Hyams and the coroner's officer. She came to search for the anonymous letters, and she went straight to the deed-box, and there they were. But the stones were not there. I saw her take all the things out of the deed-box for Mr Hyams to see and there were no stones there."

"Thank you," said the coroner. "That will do. We must now, gentlemen, see if Mrs Otway can give us any further information."

I once more took my place at the table and was again sensible of a generally heightened curiosity on the part of the jury and the spectators."

"We may as well dispose of the question of the missing stones," said the coroner; "for though it does not affect our inquiry directly but is rather the business of the police, it seems to have an important, indirect bearing. You have heard, Mrs Otway, the evidence of Judith Samuels, and Rachel Goldstein – or Gregg. Can you throw any light on the disappearance of these stones?"

"No, I cannot."

"Did you know that deceased had these valuable stones in his possession?"

"No; I never heard of the stones until Mr Hyams called on me on the evening of the day on which Mr Otway's death was discovered."

"Do you know, or have you any idea, where those stones are now?"

"I do not know, and I have no idea where they are."

"Did you know that deceased was a dealer in precious stones?"

"No; my father told me that deceased collected gem-stones, and that he sometimes had dealings in them. But I supposed that he was merely a collector, not a professional dealer."

"How long had you known deceased when you married him?"

"I had known of his existence about a year, but I had hardly ever spoken to him. He was virtually a stranger to me."

"Had you never heard of the suicidal tendency in his family?"

"Never until the night preceding his death, when he told me."

"It has been stated that you are a practical goldsmith, and that you have executed work for Mr Samuels, or Campbell. Is that true?"

"I work as a goldsmith and I have sold some of my productions to Mr Campbell; but I have never been employed by him. I work as an independent artist."

"Has he ever supplied you with precious stones?"

"No. I purchase my own materials."

"Have you ever done any alterations or resettings for him?"

"No. I have done no work of any kind for him, or anyone else. I work on my own account, and sell what I make."

The coroner nodded, and glanced over his notes. After a pause he asked: "At what time on the night of your visit to deceased did you leave his chambers?"

"A little before ten o'clock."

"What was the condition of deceased when you left? Did he seem particularly depressed or worried?"

"He was asleep when I left."

"Asleep!" exclaimed the coroner, "How long had he been asleep?"

"Not very long; perhaps a quarter of an hour. When he took his usual dose of veronal he asked me to stay with him until he went to sleep, and I did so."

"I see that the housekeeper states that when she entered the living-room in the morning, the bedroom door was wide open, and the gas full on. What was the condition of affairs when you left?"

"The gas was full on, and I did not shut the bedroom door. I was not aware that the housekeeper had gone to bed and assumed that she would look in on deceased and make what arrangements were usual for the night."

"But if you had turned down the gas, and shut the bedroom door, that would have prevented the housekeeper from going to deceased."

"No. It did not appear to matter either way."

"When you went away, did you leave your hand-bag behind?"

"Yes, I had hung it on the back of my chair, and when I got up to go, I forgot about it."

"When did you discover that you had left it behind?"

"I first remembered it when I hailed a cab at the corner of Holywell Street to take me home."

"Why did you not then go back for it?"

"I did not like to disturb Mrs Gregg and deceased, as it was so late."

"Was your purse in the bag?"

347

"Yes; but that was of no consequence. I knew there would be someone sitting up who could pay the cabman."

"The housekeeper has told us that you came to fetch the bag on the following day."

"Yes, in the afternoon, about three. It was then that I first heard of Mr Otway's death."

"The housekeeper states that, when she told you what had happened, you fell down in a dead faint. Is that so?"

"Yes. It gave me a great shock, especially as Mrs Gregg told me the bad news so very abruptly."

"Were you expecting to hear that the deceased had committed suicide?"

"No; the subject was not in my mind."

"Is that not rather remarkable, having regard to your conversation with deceased on the previous night?"

"I don't think so. That conversation had certainly given me the impression that there was a danger that deceased might be driven to suicide if this persecution were continued. But I had not supposed that the danger was immediate."

"And that pitiful letter that you received from deceased? Did that convey no note of warning?"

"At the time when I received it I was not aware of any predisposition to suicide on the part of deceased. What he told me caused me some alarm, but he became so much calmer after our talk that I thought the danger was past, so far as the immediate future was concerned."

"And when you went to his chambers on the following day, you felt no uneasiness as to what might have happened?"

"No, the possibility that anything unusual might have happened was not in my mind at all."

"Well," said the coroner, "it seems to me rather remarkable that the possibility did not even occur to you. However, we are dealing with the facts, and if those are the facts, there is no more to be said. We will now pass on to the consideration of the will. When did you first learn that deceased had made a fresh will?"

"Four days ago, when I received a letter from Mr Isaacs informing me of the fact that I was one of the beneficiaries."

"Had deceased never mentioned to you that he had made a will in your favour?"

"No."

"Was there no stipulation on your part at the time of the marriage that he should make such a will?"

"No. Nothing ever passed between us on the subject."

"And had you no knowledge or belief that a will affecting you had been executed?"

"I had no knowledge or belief that such a will had been executed nor any expectation that it would be. I did not consider myself as having any pecuniary claim on deceased."

"Did you not receive an allowance from deceased?"

"No. He wished to make me an allowance, but I declined to accept it."

"But you were entitled to an allowance for maintenance. Why did you refuse to accept it?"

"I did not consider that I had any claim on deceased so long as I insisted on living apart."

"Then do we understand that you subsist entirely on your own means or earnings?"

"Yes, entirely."

"Would you kindly tell us what those means and earnings respectively amount to? And what are their sources?"

"I have a small private income – about sixty pounds a year – derived from the realisation of my father's estate. I cannot estimate my earnings very exactly, as I have been working only a few months. Probably I shall be able to earn from a hundred and fifty to two hundred pounds a year, when I am established. Up to the present I have sold all my work to Mr Campbell."

"How did you first become acquainted with Mr Campbell – or Samuels, to give him his correct name?"

"Deceased recommended him to me when I first came to London. He stated that he had known him for many years."

"Did you know that Mr Campbell was related to deceased?"

"Not until I heard it here today."

The coroner considered awhile, turning over his notes reflectively. At length he said, "Before you sit down, Mrs Otway I should like to ask you again about those anonymous letters. You have stated that you have no idea who wrote them."

"That is so," I replied.

"When you discussed them with deceased, did neither of you arrive at any conclusion as to who might have written them?"

"Deceased assured me that he could make no guess as to who had sent them. Naturally, I could not, since all his acquaintances, whether friends or enemies, were unknown to me."

"And you adhere to your statement that you know nothing about these letters?"

"I know nothing about them whatever, excepting that deceased received them; and that I have only known by his telling me."

"And with regard to your father's stick? You have stated that you have no knowledge as to what became of it, or where it is now. Do you adhere to that statement too?"

"That statement was correct when I made it; but the stick has since come to light."

"Indeed!" exclaimed the coroner. "When and how did that happen?"

"It occurred three days ago, when I went to look over the chambers in Lyon's Inn. I chanced to open a large cupboard in the living room, and there, on the single shelf at the top, I saw the stick lying at the back, and hardly visible in the deep shadow."

"In-deed!" said the coroner, with a strong emphasis on the second syllable. It was perfectly evident that he did not believe me, and he made no secret of it. Nor were the jury any better impressed. In the silence that followed my statement they whispered together eagerly, and disbelief was writ large on the faces of them all.

"Had you any particular occasion to look over the chambers?" the coroner asked after an interval.

"Yes; I had received a letter from Dr Thorndyke saying that he wished to make a survey of the premises and asking me to give him permission, and the necessary facilities to do so. I accordingly went, on the following day, and fetched the keys from Mr Isaacs to leave them at Dr Thorndyke's chambers. On the way I called in at Lyon's Inn to see what condition the chambers were in."

"And to plant the stick for Dr Thorndyke to find, eh?" said one of the jurors, with a truculent leer.

Mr Cawley rose instantly to protest, but he was anticipated by the coroner, who said severely: "That sir, is quite out of order. Members of the jury must not suggest motives or actions on the part of witnesses which are not given in evidence. They may have their opinions, but those opinions must not be expressed until all the evidence has been heard and the verdict has to be considered." Having administered this reproof, he again turned to me.

"When you looked over the chambers, did you examine the other furniture and receptacles. Did you, for instance, look in the other cupboards and drawers?"

"No."

"Only this one cupboard? Now what made you look into this cupboard in particular?"

I saw the awkwardness of the question; but I also saw that a complete explanation of my motives would land me on much more dangerous ground. My immediate motive had been to ascertain what the inside of the cupboard was like, and this was as much as I dared tell.

"I wished to see what kind of a cupboard it was – whether it had shelves, drawers, or simply an open space."

"Did you take the stick out of the cupboard?"

"Yes, I took it out to examine it and see if the statement in the letter as to the bruise, the blood-smear, and the hairs was correct."

"And was the statement correct?"

"Yes; there was a bruise on the silver knob, and a thick smear of what looked like dried blood, to which two hairs had stuck."

"Did those hairs look to you like hairs from your father's head?"

"I could not say. They might have been. They were short and looked as if they had come from the head of a grey-haired man. My father's hair was grey."

"What did you do with the stick?"

"I put it back in the cupboard."

"Why did you not bring it here?"

"I thought it best to leave it where I found it."

"Are the keys of the chambers in your possession now?"

"No; I left them at Dr Thorndyke's chambers, and he has not yet returned them. I left a note informing him that the stick was in the cupboard."

"May I ask why you did that?"

"Dr Thorndyke mentioned in his letter that he was investigating the case on instructions from the Home Office, and I wished to give him any assistance that I could."

"But," the coroner exclaimed irritably, "don't you understand that this court is investigating the case? That a coroner's court is the proper authority to carry out such investigations? I don't know why this medical specialist has been brought into the case at all. I have not asked for his assistance. It is quite irregular and most unnecessary. And how did this gentleman come to write to you?"

"He wanted to survey the premises, and someone − I don't know who − had told him that I was the present lessee."

The coroner grunted in evident displeasure. The importation of Dr Thorndyke into the case was clearly a sore point, for he rejoined: "The whole affair is highly unsatisfactory. I am not clear that you had any right to give permission to any unofficial person to survey these premises without obtaining my consent; or that he had any right to ask you. The jury have surveyed the premises, and that ought to be enough. However, we shall see what comes of these mysterious investigations. Meanwhile, I think that is all we have to ask you, Mrs Otway, unless the jury have any questions to put."

The jury, warned, perhaps, by the result of the last question put by a juryman, had no question to ask; and I returned to my seat by Mr Cawley, in time to hear Mr Isaacs recalled.

"You have heard," said the coroner, "the very remarkable evidence given by the last witness concerning the finding of a stick in a large cupboard in the living-room of the chambers in Lyon's Inn?"

"I have."

"In your previous evidence you stated that you had made a minute search of those chambers, and drawn up an inventory of their contents. Do you remember whether, when you made that search, you examined that particular cupboard?"

"Yes, I remember quite clearly that I examined it, and found it empty. I have marked it 'empty' in the inventory."

"Are you sure that it was really empty? Is it not possible that this stick lying in the shade on the shelf, might have been overlooked?"

"It is quite impossible. I made a most exhaustive search, and I used an electric torch for examining dark interiors. Moreover, the object that I was looking for – a little parcel of precious stones – was much smaller, and less conspicuous than a walking stick. I could not have missed a large object like that. And I have quite a clear recollection of looking on that shelf – it was the only shelf in the cupboard – and throwing the light of the torch along it. I had to stand on tiptoe to see in distinctly, and so, I suppose, had Mrs Otway."

"Do you swear that the cupboard was empty when you examined it?"

"I swear that it was absolutely empty."

The coroner entered the reply in his notes, and then asked: "Did you receive any communication from Dr Thorndyke respecting his proposed survey of the chambers at Lyon's Inn?"

"He called to enquire in whom the tenancy of the chambers was vested, but did not state why he wanted to know. I told him that the widow was the lessee. I don't know how he got her address. I didn't give it to him. I may say that when I had finished the inventory I locked up the chambers, and kept the keys until I delivered them up to Mrs Otway."

"Thank you," said the coroner. "That is all I wanted you to tell us. And that, gentlemen," he continued, turning to the jury, "appears to be the whole of the evidence, with the exception of Dr Thorndyke's; and the question now arises, what are we to do? Let me explain the position, and then you can decide on our procedure.

"This inquiry was adjourned to enable the police to make some investigations in connection with it. On their application, Dr John Thorndyke, who, I may inform you, is an eminent medico-legal expert, was instructed by the Home Office to proceed to Maidstone to conduct an exhumation of the body of the late John Vardon, the father of Mrs Otway. He was to make an examination of the body, and ascertain if possible, whether the cause of the said John Vardon's death was as stated at the inquest, or whether, as is hinted in these anonymous letters, he died from the effects of violence. The question is an important one, but it is more important to the police than to us. Then, it seems that the Home Office further instructed this gentleman to carry out an independent investigation into the facts of this case which we, in our humble and inefficient way, are trying to investigate. It is an extraordinary proceeding, and one that I do not in the least understand; but then I am not a medico-legal specialist. I am only a mere coroner, and you are only a mere coroner's jury. It is just as well that we should know our place.

"Well, I understand that Dr Thorndyke has made an examination of the body of Lewis Otway, and, as you have heard, he has made a survey of the deceased man's chambers. We, also, have surveyed these chambers, but apparently our survey doesn't count; and Dr Shelburn, whose evidence you have heard, examined the body within a few hours of death. It would seem as if medical evidence were the last thing we want. Meanwhile I have had a telegram from Dr Thorndyke saying that he has been detained at Maidstone, and has missed his train. I don't know when he will arrive here. He may be here in a few minutes or he may arrive in an hour or two. It is for you to decide what is to be done. We have a great deal of evidence to consider. We do not seem to need any more medical evidence, and the question of Mr Vardon's death is not of vital importance to this inquiry.

"The question is shall we wait to hear Dr Thorndyke's evidence or shall we proceed to consider the great mass of evidence that we already have? It is for you to decide, gentlemen."

The jury conferred for a couple of minutes, and then the foreman announced their decision. "The jury say, sir, that we are inquiring into the death of Lewis Otway, not John Vardon. They would like to proceed with the consideration of the evidence without waiting for Dr Thorndyke."

"I am entirely with you, gentlemen," said the coroner. "I think that the evidence that we have heard will prove amply sufficient to guide us to our verdict; and we can still revise our opinions if the expert witness should have something fresh to tell us."

CHAPTER TWENTY-SEVEN

The Indictment

During the short interval, in which the coroner took a final glance over his notes, there was a general stirring among the occupants and a suggestion of preparation for the next act. Jurymen re-settled themselves in their seats, reporters straightened their backs, and looked about them, the police officers and the spectators conversed in low undertones. At length the coroner laid on the table before him a single sheet of paper – probably an abstract of the evidence – sat back in his chair, and looked towards the jury; whereupon a deep silence fell upon the court, and he began his address:

"It is hardly necessary to remind you, gentlemen, that we are assembled for the purpose of ascertaining how, when, and by what means Lewis Otway came by his death; but it may be necessary to remark that our inquiry is not entirely concerned with the immediate causes of that death, but is also – and in fact, principally – concerned with the more remote contributory circumstances. For in this case, the 'How, when, and by what means' are simple enough. We have the testimony of an eye-witness who saw the deceased hanging dead, from a peg on the wall, under conditions strongly suggestive – in fact characteristic – of suicide; and we have the testimony of the deputy-police surgeon that all the appearances were those of suicide, and we have his expert opinion that the cause of death was undoubtedly suicidal hanging. Indeed, we may say that the immediate cause of death is self-evident, and that the whole of our inquiry is concerned with the remote causes. We are not asking 'Did this man commit suicide?' for the evidence of the first two witnesses settled that question. We are asking ourselves, Why did he commit suicide? The questions that we have to answer are, Was that suicide the spontaneous act of the deceased, for which he alone is responsible? Or was deceased driven to suicide by the deliberate, purposive, and malicious acts of some other person, or persons? And if the latter appears to be the case, Who is, or are, that person or persons, and what degree of criminal responsibility attaches to such acts?

"Now we have at our disposal a considerable mass of rather miscellaneous evidence, and, I think the best way to deal with it will be to sketch out lightly the general course of events, and fill in the details later. The deceased, Lewis Otway, is the central figure of our picture, and the history that we have to trace, is his history. As to what we may call his past, that does not much concern us. Among the Ancient Egyptians the deceased was conceived as being brought before the tribunal of Osiris to answer for his conduct during his earthly life. We are not a tribunal of that kind. We are not trying Lewis Otway. If, as the police suspect, he had feathered his nest with a certain amount of illicit plumage, that is not our concern. Our interest in him is mainly confined to his connection with a particular series of events which began with his marriage and ended with his death. Let us now trace that succession of events, at first in outline, and then in more detail.

"Lewis Otway first comes into our view on the occasion of his marriage. As presented in the evidence of his widow, Helen Otway, that marriage offers us the spectacle of an act of the most amazing folly. We see an elderly man – and an unattractive one at that, as you must have observed – marrying by compulsion, under threats, and greatly against her wishes, a young woman, of very unusual physical attractions, of great talent, and of exceptional mental gifts, and strength of character. You have seen this lady, and have heard her give her evidence, and you can confirm my description of her.

"It was, I repeat, an act of amazing folly. For she must, in any case, have detested him. His conduct towards her was cruel and unscrupulous to the last degree, and in marrying her he could not fail to introduce a bitter enemy into his household. But there were added causes for that repugnance to him which she has freely admitted. In the first place, she believed that her consent had been secured by actual fraud. And in the second place, Otway's action was the undoubted cause – whether directly or indirectly, we need not enquire at this stage – of John Vardon's death. So that our history opens with the tableau of an elderly man who has married a young beautiful, and clever wife, who loathes him, and has abundant reason for loathing him.

"And now we pass on to the second scene – a scene almost more amazing than the first. Within an hour or two of the marriage ceremony, the young wife has repudiated the marriage, and demanded a separation for an indefinite period – practically a permanent separation. But it is not the demand that is so astonishing. The really astounding thing is that the husband seems to have agreed to this demand without demur. Consider the extraordinary inconsistency of his conduct. On the one hand we see this man, in his eagerness to possess this beautiful girl, trampling without scruple on her happiness, and her father's, oblivious of everything but his own desires; on the other, we see him meekly submitting to a demand which – natural as it may have been – the law would not have supported.

"Whence this sudden compliance? Why did he consent? He need not have consented. The marriage was quite regular. No suit for nullity could have been sustained, whereas he could have sued at once for restitution. Why did he agree in this incomprehensible manner to surrender his unquestionable rights?

"But this is not the only inconsistency. The conduct of the wife is even more inexplicable. When Otway gave evidence at the inquest on Mr Vardon he omitted all reference to the loaded stick; which is not unnatural, seeing that it was a highly incriminating circumstance. But that suppression of a material fact made his evidence, in effect, false evidence. For the truth is, according to the terms of the witnesses oath, the whole truth. Yet Helen Otway, when she gave evidence, confirmed this virtually false testimony; and she also suppressed – or, at least, omitted – the facts relating to the loaded stick. Her explanation is that feeling convinced that her father died from a heart attack, she did not consider the stick incident of any importance. In estimating the credibility of that explanation you will bear in mind that the verdict was 'Death from natural causes,' but that the jury were not in possession of the facts. You will also bear in mind that this woman had seen her father lying dead, with a wound on his head, and this man, whom she loathed, and detested, standing over the body, grasping a formidable weapon. But whatever view you take of the explanation, the fact remains that at the inquest she not only refrained from accusing him, but she withheld a material fact which, if it had been disclosed, might have put Otway in the dock on a charge of murder.

"Here; then, are two cases of incomprehensible inconsistency of conduct. But they are only incomprehensible so long as they are considered separately. Consider them together and a perfectly intelligible suggestion emerges. The husband had the power to compel his wife to live with him – and he did not exercise it. The wife had the power to expose the husband to a suspicion of having committed a capital crime – and she did not exercise it. The appearance is that of a surrender by each of the power to injure the other; in short, of a bargain or agreement, involving collusion to suppress evidence.

"But this suggestion of collusion raises another question, which we shall consider later, but which we may note in passing. What was really the cause of Mr Vardon's death? Did he die from natural causes as the coroner's jury believed and affirmed? Or was his death due to violence inflicted by Otway? It is by no means clear that Otway did not kill him, either inadvertently or with malice. And supposing Otway to have killed Mr Vardon, was the fact known to Helen Otway? If it was Otway's easy compliance is the more readily understood; for he would be absolutely in his wife's power. But we shall consider these points at more length presently, and perhaps we may get further light on them from the evidence of Dr Thorndyke – if he should arrive before the verdict is agreed on.

"The next phase of this drama opens about two months after the marriage. On the 21st of June, the deceased received an anonymous letter, the first of a series of seven, which were sent thereafter at fairly regular intervals of about a fortnight. Now, let us consider those letters from various points of view in relation to their probable authorship. You have heard them read, and know their general purport. They all contain veiled threats to make certain exposures. Some are vague and some are more explicit, but there is a general crescendo note, culminating in the last letter, which pretty openly makes an accusation of murder and threatens criminal proceedings.

"First, what is the purpose of these letters? It is clearly not to levy blackmail. They hold out menaces, but there is no suggestion of an attempt to extort money. Those menaces are incomprehensible until we supply an explanatory fact. The man to whom these letters were sent suffered from a strong inherited predisposition to suicide. The very obvious inference to which we are forced, in the absence of any other explanation, is that the purpose of these letters was to convert that latent tendency into action – to produce a state of mind in which the deceased would be likely to take his own life.

"But that purpose implies knowledge on the part of the writer that this inherited tendency existed, and consequently limits the possible authorship to persons possessing such knowledge. The only persons known by us to possess such knowledge are deceased's own family. His widow has sworn that she had no knowledge of this tendency, and if you believe her statement to be true, you will tend to exclude her from the possible authorship of these letters.

"Next we have to consider the characters of the letters themselves. They all bear the East-London postmark, but there is not much in that. Anonymous letter-writers commonly post their letters in districts remote from their own residences. Still, we must take it into consideration. The two persons known to us who occupy premises in East London are Morris Goldstein and Helen Otway.

"Then as to the style of the letters. They are rather markedly uneducated in manner. The composition is ungrammatical and the phraseology vulgar. But that does not help us much; for, on the one hand, none of the persons known to us is grossly uneducated, and on the other it is usual for anonymous letter-writers to disguise their personality. Obviously, it is easy enough for an educated person to write an apparently illiterate letter.

"The next point is a much more important one. We have decided that the purpose of these letters was to produce in the deceased a state of mind which would render his suicide probable. Now, what was the motive behind that purpose? Who could have wished deceased to commit suicide, and why should that person have wished it?

"The possible motives in this case are, in effect, the usual motives of murder, with full premeditation, viz: Revenge, or hatred; direct profit; and indirect profit by the elimination of an undesired person. Let us consider each of these motives in relation to the known facts of this case.

"First as to hatred or revenge. The only persons known to us are the family of deceased and his wife. His family certainly had a grievance against him, for the children were illegitimate, and the mother was unmarried. But it was an old grievance, and the family appeared to be on quite amicable terms. The children were quite well provided for, and their mother continued to live with deceased. There was, indeed, a new factor of possible discord. The deceased had married, and that marriage was manifestly to the disadvantage of his family; a fact of which it is necessary to take due account.

"When, however, we turn to the consideration of the wife, the facts are much more striking. She had suffered grievous injuries from deceased. He had ruined her life. He had virtually condemned her to perpetual spinsterhood, since she would not live with him and she could not marry anyone else. He had caused the death of her father; and she has admitted that she had an unconquerable repugnance to him. That is actually known to us; and there is a further possibility that he was actually her father's murderer, though we must leave that out of consideration in the absence of positive evidence. But on the evidence which is before us, you will see that the motive of personal animosity is much more evident in the case of the wife than in that of the family.

"We now come to the motive of direct profit, and the question that we ask ourselves is, Who stood to benefit by the death of Lewis Otway? And as soon as we ask that question, a very striking fact comes into view. The first letter is dated by the postmark, the 21st of June. But on the 10th of that month – only eleven days previously – deceased had made a new will. By the provisions of that will Helen Otway stood to gain from eight to twelve thousand pounds by the death of her husband.

"But did anyone else stand to gain by Lewis Otway's death? Observe that we are still dealing with the same group of persons – the only persons known to us in connection with the case. Well, the family of deceased stood to gain by his death, though to a much smaller extent. But the fact that must instantly impress us is the opposite effects of the new will on the family, and the wife respectively. The execution of the new will involved the revocation of a previous will, which had left the bulk of the estate to the family. The position of affairs is consequently this: up to the 10th of June, the family, jointly, stood to benefit by Lewis Otway's death to the extent of the bulk of his estate and the wife did not stand to benefit at all; after the 10th of June the wife stood to benefit by Otway's death to the extent of the bulk of his estate, and the family to a relatively small extent.

"But the first of the anonymous letters was sent almost immediately after the 10th of June. That is to say, it was sent almost immediately after the family had ceased to be and the wife had become the principal beneficiary."

"From the motive of direct profit we turn to that of indirect profit, by the elimination of a person whose existence was a hindrance, a danger, or an inconvenience. Is there anyone known to us who could have regarded deceased in that light? We cannot attribute any such view to his family, for, as I have said, they appear to have been on quite amicable terms, and deceased seems to have maintained an interest in his children's welfare to the last. But what are we to say with regard to the wife? She was married, against her wishes, to a man unsuitable in age, uncomely in appearance; a man whom she loathed – and had good reason to loathe; who, while she repudiated him as a husband, yet held her chained to him for life; who stood inexorably between her, and any marriage which she might wish to contract; whose existence condemned her for life to the dubious position of a married woman who is not living with her husband. Think, gentlemen, of this woman – young, handsome, clever, accomplished, capable; think of what life might have been to her, and what it was with this millstone hung round her neck! And then ask yourselves whether – apart from all pecuniary considerations – she did not stand to gain incalculably by his death; whether his elimination from her life would not have opened to her the gates of a world of happiness, and freedom.

"And it is here that the importance of that further evidence, which we unfortunately have not yet heard, appears. For if it should now transpire that Otway did actually kill John Vardon and that Helen Otway was privy to the homicide, then there would be yet another powerful reason why she should desire to be rid of him. But this evidence is not in our possession and we must, therefore, leave this aspect of the case out of our consideration. Nor is it essential. The facts within our knowledge are amply sufficient to enable us to answer the question whether Helen Otway's position would or would not have been improved by the death of her husband.

"And now we come to something much more definite. Hitherto we have been dealing with the question: 'Who *might* have written these letters?' We shall now consider the more specific question, 'Who *could* have written them?'

"There seems to be only one possible answer. The writer of those letters had knowledge that was possessed by only two persons – the deceased and his wife. One letter refers to something that was held back at the inquest. But who knew that anything had been held back at the inquest? No one, according to the evidence, but these two persons. Of course, it is possible that there may have been some watcher secreted in that house at Maidstone who knew that Lewis Otway had stood over the body of John Vardon with a loaded stick in his hand. But the evidence before us is to the effect that there was no one in the house but John Vardon, Lewis Otway, and Helen Otway. Consequently, unless Lewis Otway wrote these letters to himself, there is nobody, so far as we know, who could have written them but Helen Otway.

"The last letter refers explicitly to the loaded stick, and even describes its condition minutely and, as it appears, correctly. The writer had, therefore, presumably seen the stick and very probably had possession of it. But where was that stick? Deceased certainly did not know where it was; the housekeeper states that she had never seen it since that fatal morning, and Helen Otway has denied all knowledge of its whereabouts. No one knew what had become of it.

"But if its disappearance was a mystery, its reappearance is a greater mystery still. The account given by Helen Otway is obviously unsatisfactory. She went to the chambers, for no very apparent reason. When there she did not examine the various cupboards, drawers, and other receptacles; but she went direct to this particular cupboard, unlocked it, stood on tiptoe and looked on the shelf. And behold! there was the missing stick. She took it out, examined it, and put it back. And she not only put it back, but she went out of her way to inform a person who is to give evidence on this inquiry that the stick was to be found in that cupboard.

"Now, how did that stick get into that cupboard, and when was it put there? You have heard Mr Isaacs swear that it was not there when he made out the inventory, and you will probably agree that he could hardly be mistaken. A stick is a fairly large and conspicuous object, whereas he was searching for a small and inconspicuous one. Clearly the stick was put into the cupboard after his search was made. But when he had finished, the chambers were locked up, and the keys remained in his possession until he delivered them up to Helen Otway. Bearing these facts in mind, you have to consider whether you can accept Mrs Otway's statement, or whether it is more probable that she took the stick to the chambers, and put it into the cupboard herself.

"We now come to the incidents of that terrible night. What really happened in those chambers on that occasion will probably never be known. But the accounts that we have are full of sinister suggestions. We cannot, for instance, but note the fact that after this, the first and only visit from his wife, Lewis Otway made away with himself. Why he did the dreadful deed on this particular occasion, and at this particular time, is not clear. According to his wife's account he was much calmer, and more cheerful after their talk and she left him peacefully asleep. That is what she has told us. But what are the facts? Within an hour or two hours after she had left, his dead body was hanging from that peg. Nay! There is even a more dreadful possibility. The medical witness has told us that death took place about eleven, 'But it might have been an hour later or earlier.' So that it is physically possible – since Mrs Otway left the chambers about ten – that the suicide may have actually taken place before she left. It is a horrible suggestion, and I should not have made it but for the fact that there are certain appearances which seem to support it.

"You must have been struck by the singular circumstance that when Mrs Otway took her departure she left the gas full on, and he beroom door open. You have heard her explanation, but we are not concerned with that for the moment. The remarkable thing is that in the morning, the gas was still full on, and the bedroom door still open. Now how could that have been? If deceased was asleep when his wife left, then he must have arisen, made his preparations, and finally hanged himself, not only with the gas full on – which might easily have been the case – but with the door open, which is improbable in the extreme. Men do not usually commit suicide *coram publico*. Commonly suicides lock themselves in their rooms or otherwise seek security from interruption. Yet this man, whose bedroom opened directly into the living-room and whose housekeeper might still have been about, cuts down the bell-rope, arranges the chair and hangs himself, all in a brightly-lighted room with the door open. It is certainly against common probabilities.

"But there are other suggestions of a similar tendency. If the fully-lighted gas and the open door suggest a hurried and agitated departure, so does the forgotten hand-bag containing the purse. And you will have noted that Mrs Otway remembered that she had left her purse behind when she hailed a cab at the corner of Holywell Street. Now why did she not go back for it? She was quite near Lyon's Inn. She could have left the cab waiting, or brought it to the gate. She says she did not like to disturb Mrs Gregg. But she has also said that she thought that Mrs Gregg was still up and about. The explanation is not convincing, but on the other hand there is a strong suggestion of dislike to the idea of going back – a dislike which we can understand well enough if we believe that the tragedy had already been enacted, and that the body was even then hanging on the wall.

"Then, too, the disappearance of the precious stones points in the same direction. They might have been taken when the deceased was asleep; but the theft would have been far easier if he was dead. But, of course, we cannot say with certainty that Helen Otway took the stones. We can only consider the evidence. That evidence, however, is almost overwhelmingly strong. It goes to show that the stones were in the deed-box within half-an-hour of Helen Otway's arrival. There is no reason to suppose they were then removed. It is practically certain that they were there when she arrived, and they were never seen there or anywhere else after she left. And there is a further corroborative circumstance. To ordinary persons un-mounted precious stones illicitly obtained are difficult to dispose of. But this woman is not an ordinary person; she is a working goldsmith and jeweller who buys her own materials and sells the finished works to individual buyers. She could easily dispose of stolen gems in a manner that would render them untraceable.

"The theft of these stones is not directly our business. It is that of the police. But indirectly it is of great importance. For it furnishes strong support to the suggestion that deceased was already dead when Helen Otway took her hurried departure. But what is the importance of that suggestion? The answer to that question will be found in the consideration of certain further facts and certain points of criminal law.

"First, we must notice that if deceased committed suicide while Helen Otway was in the chambers, he must have done so with her consent and connivance. But was it only a matter of consent? Is there not a suggestion that some direct means may have been employed to induce or compel him to commit suicide? On this point we have very little information. But we have the evidence of Rachel Goldstein or Gregg that she overheard the conversation between Helen Otway and deceased on two separate occasions; and that on both occasions they seemed to be talking about suicide. There seems to be a strong suggestion that some active, direct, means were employed: persuasion, threats, or perhaps the mysterious agency of suggestion. We cannot say that it was so; but it would be in close agreement with the known circumstances and quite consistent with the course of action exhibited by the anonymous letters.

"Supposing such active, direct means to have been employed, what degree of criminal responsibility would their employment entail? With regard to the letters though the moral responsibility for their effect is beyond question, I should hesitate to give an opinion as to the exact legal position. But in the case of direct means there is no doubt at all. The law on the subject is quite clear. Let us consider it for a moment.

"First as to the legal nature of suicide. In law, suicide is murder. It has been expressly laid down that a person cannot commit manslaughter on himself. But since suicide is necessarily murder, it follows that any person who is accessory to suicide is accessory to murder. If such person aids or abets any other person in so killing himself, that person is an accessory before the fact, or a principal in the second degree in the murder so committed; an accessory before the fact being defined as one who directly or indirectly counsels, procures, or commands any person to commit any felony or piracy which is committed in consequence of such counselling, procuring, or commandment.

"Here, then, is the importance of the matter. The criminal responsibility attaching to the anonymous letters may be involved in some obscurity; but if it can be proved that any person counselled, procured, or commanded the deceased to kill himself, that person can be dealt with as a principal in the second degree in the murder of deceased. It is for you to say whether, in your judgment, such action can be proved in the case of any person, and if so, who that person is.

"There is only one more item of evidence that I shall refer to, and that I shall touch upon only lightly. You have heard the witness Rachel Goldstein state that when she informed Helen Otway that deceased had hanged himself, Mrs Otway fell down in a dead faint. You have heard the explanation that Mrs Otway gave and you must decide what weight you attach to it; whether you can regard this fainting as due to the shock of an unexpected tragedy, or as the culminating effect of prolonged and extreme nervous tension. In any case, its evidential value is but small.

"And now, as our expert witness has still not arrived, let us take a last look over the evidence to see what material we have for our verdict." Here the coroner paused, and laying a number of sheets of paper in a row before him glanced rapidly through them.

I watched him with a dreadful fascination, even as a bird might watch the stealthy approach of a snake, terrified, but despairing of any hope of escape. So I had listened to this terrible summing-up – all false and erroneous in detail, but so horribly true in regard to the central fact. Through that dense fog of error and false appearances the coroner had seen the essential truth; that Lewis Otway had gone to his death at my bidding. Like some great spider he had wound around me a network of horrid entanglements; and now he was about to wind up the final turns.

At length he looked up, and laid his hand on one of the papers. Then he turned once more towards the jury and began his summary of the evidence. And at that moment, unnoticed, apparently, by anyone save myself, Dr Thorndyke entered silently by a side door, and seated himself on a vacant chair.

CHAPTER TWENTY-EIGHT

The Verdict

The arrival of Dr Thorndyke seemed to me to close the last avenue of escape. The coroner had guessed at my guilty secret, but he only offered his guess as a speculative possibility on which no decisive opinion could be founded. But Dr Thorndyke was not a guesser. If he had penetrated to that secret he would offer no speculative probabilities, but definite evidence, which would reduce the matter to certainty.

It was a terrible thought. Self-accusation – the denunciations of a guilty conscience – had been dreadful enough. But there is a world of difference between self-accusation in secret and a public criminal indictment; between calling oneself a murderess, and standing in the dock to answer the charge.

During the coroner's address I furtively watched Dr Thorndyke. But I could gather nothing from his face. As he sat motionless, with his eyes steadily bent on the coroner, his expression denoted nothing but a grave and concentrated attention. After the first quick glance round the court, he never looked at me. What was in his mind I could not guess, though I felt that he held my fate in the hollow of his hand.

"There is no need, gentlemen," the coroner began, "for us to go through the mass of evidence again. We have looked over it as a whole, and we have seen that certain striking suggestions emerge from it. In our last glance we have to bring those suggestions to a definite focus. Our inquiry deals with a man who committed suicide, but the appearances suggest that that suicide was not a voluntary, spontaneous act, but was the effect of a compelling force exerted by some other person.

"Who was that other person? The compelling force seems to have been exerted by means of certain menacing letters. The person who procured the suicide of deceased was therefore the writer of those letters. Now who was the writer of those letters? The question is best answered by asking certain other questions.

"First: Had deceased any enemies? Well, we know of one, and one only. His wife, Helen Otway, has confessed to a deep repugnance to him. She had suffered grievous injuries at his hands, and she resented those injuries profoundly.

"Second: Who gained most, financially, by his death? Again the answer is his wife, Helen Otway.

"Third: Did anyone stand to gain in any other way by his death? The answer again is yes; and the person who stood to gain – by liberation from an intolerable bondage – was Helen Otway.

"Fourth: Who could have written those letters? who possessed the secret knowledge that those letters exhibit? Only one such person is known to us besides deceased himself. That person is Helen Otway.

"Fifth: Who was the last person who was with him before his death? Again the answer is, Helen Otway.

"Sixth: Is there any evidence of the use of more direct means to procure or compel this act of suicide? And if so, by whom do those means appear to have been employed? The answer is that there is such evidence, and that the person who appears to have used those means is Helen Otway. There is evidence suggesting that she was actually present when the suicide took place; there is evidence of a hurried flight and unwillingness to return for the purse that she had left behind; there is the open door, the lighted gas, and the missing jewels, which were in the chambers when she arrived, and which were never seen after she left. And then there is the mysterious stick which had vanished, and which reappeared so strangely after her unexplained visit to the chambers.

"That, gentlemen, is in brief the whole of the evidence with the exception of that relating to John Vardon's death. That evidence is important to this inquiry; for if it should be proved that John Vardon was killed by Lewis Otway, and that Helen Otway was privy to the homicide, that would furnish a further motive for procuring the suicide of deceased – the motive of the removal of the sole accomplice in a serious crime. But that evidence is not vitally important, and it is for you to decide whether you will still await the arrival of Dr Thorndyke, or whether you will proceed to consider your verdict on the evidence that you have heard."

As the coroner concluded, Dr Thorndyke rose and advanced to the table, placing on an empty chair a small green-covered suitcase. The coroner looked up at him sharply and with somewhat definitely unfriendly recognition.

"How long have you been here, sir?" the former demanded.

"About seven minutes," Dr Thorndyke replied, glancing at his watch. "You were just beginning your summary when I entered."

"You should have announced your arrival immediately," said the coroner. "However, as you are here, you had better take the oath, and give your evidence without further delay."

The coroner's brusque, and even rude manner, did not appear to disturb Dr Thorndyke in the smallest degree. With the same impassive expression and quiet, composed demeanour, he took the oath and disposed of the usual preliminaries.

"We understand," said the coroner, "that you have made an examination of the body of the late John Vardon."

"Yes, I proceeded to Maidstone on instructions from the Home Office and conducted an exhumation of the body of John Vardon, of which I then made an examination. The object of the proceeding was to ascertain whether the cause of death had been correctly stated at the inquest."

"And what was the result of your examination – I don't, think we want minute details."

"I found that the cause of death was, as stated at the inquest by the medical witnesses, failure of an extremely dilated heart. There was a small wound on the right side of the forehead adjoining the temple, which I examined very thoroughly. It was a glancing wound caused by a very oblique impact, and was such a wound as might have been produced in the manner described – by striking the corner of the mantelpiece in falling. There was no injury to the bone nor to the brain or its membranes. It was quite a trivial wound, and was not either wholly or partially the cause of death."

"Could that wound have been caused by a blow with a loaded stick?"

"I should say not. It was an oblique tear in the scalp and was apparently produced by some object more angular than the knob of a stick."

"Well," said the coroner, "that seems to dispose of the question of Mr Vardon's death. It is a thousand pities that it was not cleared up more completely at the time. However, it is cleared up now; and that, really, is all, I think, that we want you to tell us, unless you have some other information. I understand that you had a sort of roving commission to investigate the matter of this inquiry?"

"I received instructions to make certain investigations with a view to my giving evidence at this inquest, and I have made such investigations as seemed to me to be necessary."

"Yes, you have, in fact, held a sort of one-man inquest on your own account. Well, the question is, do you suppose that you are in a position to tell us anything that we do not know already?"

"I am quite sure that I am. If you will allow me to present a summary of the facts in my possession – "

"I shall allow nothing of the kind. You will be good enough to answer questions like any other witness."

Dr Thorndyke bowed with the same immovable serenity, and the coroner proceeded with his examination.

"Have you had much experience of cases of suicide?"

"I have."

"Have you had personal experience of any cases in which the suicidal act was procured, or brought about, by acts of persons other than the suicide, performed by them with deliberate intent?"

"Yes, I have had experience of several such cases."

"In those cases, what methods were used to procure the other person to commit suicide?"

"The majority were cases in which two persons agreed mutually to commit suicide together. In the less common cases in which the procurer did not propose to commit suicide, the method employed was usually some form of suggestion."

"Can you give us an instance of the employment of suggestion?"

"A very typical case occurred in my practice some years ago. A young man, who had a strong inherited predisposition to suicide, was caused by certain persons, who stood to benefit very considerably by his death, to make away with himself. The method adopted was this: The victim was made to believe that a certain Chinese jewel in his possession carried a curse; that all previous owners of it had hanged themselves, and that the appointed time for the suicide was made known by the apparition of a dead mandarin. When by frequent repetitions of this story the suitable state of mind had been produced, one of these persons dressed himself in a mandarin's costume and presented himself to the victim, with the result that, within an hour or two, the latter hanged himself."

"In that case," observed the coroner, "the suggestion seems to have been in two stages. Is that usual?"

"One could hardly call it usual, as the cases are so rare. But it is the most obvious and effective method – to produce a suicidal state of mind by preparatory suggestion, and then, as it were, to explode the mine by a definite determining suggestion."

"Are you acquainted with the evidence which has been given in this inquiry?"

"I have read a verbatim report of the first proceedings, and I have heard your summary of the whole I case."

"You have, then, read the evidence relating to the anonymous letters. What opinion did you form as to the purpose of those letters?"

"I formed the opinion that their purpose was to impel deceased to commit suicide."

"Do you consider that, in the case of a person predisposed to suicide, they would be likely to produce that effect?"

"I should say that they would have a tendency to induce a suicidal state of mind."

"And suppose such a person, having received a series of such letters, and being greatly depressed by them, should be engaged – in his bedroom, the last thing at night – in a conversation on suicide, his own suicide, and that of relatives who had killed themselves, what would you expect to be the effect of such conversation?"

"It would not be possible to predict the effect, but the tendency would be to reinforce the influence of the letters."

"And what would be the condition of such a person in regard to his susceptibility to further suggestion?"

"His susceptibility to further suggestion would probably be increased."

"Looking at this case as a whole, by the light of your experience of suicide, do you regard the death of deceased as the result of his own spontaneous act or as due in part to the acts of some other person or persons?"

"I regard his death as due entirely to the acts of some other person or persons."

At these terrible words my heart seemed to stand still. There was a fearful certainty and confidence in Dr Thorndyke's tone that chilled my very blood. He did not guess. He knew. In the short pause that followed, I set my teeth and waited for my condemnation.

"You consider that the suggestion conveyed in the letters and in that conversation and by other possible means operated so as to convert deceased into an automaton? Is that what you mean?"

"No. I do not consider that the letters or the conversation had any effect in causing his death."

The coroner frowned, perplexedly. "I don't think I quite understand," said he. "There seems to be – if you will pardon me – some self-contradiction. You state that the letters and the conversation would tend to produce a suicidal state of mind; but yet, though the letters were actually received and the conversation occurred, neither had any effect in causing the death which followed them. Do I state the case correctly?"

"Yes; quite correctly."

"Then I do not understand you in the least. You appear to be flatly contradicting yourself. I think you will agree that we are not making much progress."

"We are not making any progress at all. The examination has not elicited a single, relevant fact."

"Indeed, sir!" exclaimed the coroner. "And, pray, whose fault is that?"

"I suggest," Dr Thorndyke replied, suavely, "that it is due to the method of examination."

The coroner turned purple. "This is insufferable!" he exclaimed; "that a witness should presume to instruct an experienced officer of justice in the duties of his office! But I suppose we must be humble in the presence of an expert. May I ask, sir, what you object to in my method of examination?"

"The lack of result," Dr Thorndyke replied, "is due to the fact that your examination has been conducted to support a particular theory; and that theory happens to be the wrong theory."

"Again, I don't understand you," the coroner said, angrily. "No theory has been advanced by me. Will you be good enough to explain what theory you are alluding to?"

"I allude to the theory, which you seem to have adopted, that the deceased Lewis Otway committed suicide by hanging himself from a peg on the bedroom wall. That theory is erroneous. It is practically certain that Lewis Otway did not commit suicide; and it is quite certain that he never hung from that peg on the bedroom wall."

"But," exclaimed the coroner, "we have the evidence of a witness who saw deceased hanging from that peg; and not only saw him, but cut him down and found him to be dead."

"As a witness," said Dr Thorndyke, "I am not concerned with the testimony of other witnesses, but only with the facts as ascertained by me."

"No doubt," retorted the coroner. "But we are concerned with the testimony of all the witnesses; and the statement of this witness that she saw the body hanging from the peg, and that she cut it down from the peg, is a clear statement on a question of fact. If that statement is true, deceased hung from that peg. If he did not hang from that peg the statement is false. You say that he never hung from that peg. On what facts do you base that statement?"

"On the strength of the peg and the weight of the body of deceased. The strength of the peg – that is, the maximum weight it was capable of supporting – was under 175 pounds. But the body of deceased weighed 231 pounds – more that half a hundredweight in excess of the greatest weight that the peg was capable of supporting."

"What method did you employ to measure the strength of the peg."

"I used simple weights, which I thought preferable to a dynamometer for purposes of evidence. These weights I had conveyed to the chambers, and I carried out the experiment in the presence of Mr Anstey, K.C., and my assistant, Francis Polton. I hung from the peg a wooden tray, slung by a chain, the total weight of which was ten pounds. On this tray I placed – with great care to avoid shocks – two half-hundredweights. I then added weights, five pounds at a time, until the total weight, including that of the tray and chain, reached 170 pounds. This was evidently very near the limit of what the peg would bear, for it was bending

Nathaniel

noticeably under the weight; and when I added another five pounds the peg doubled under, breaking halfway through. I have brought it with me for your inspection." He opened the green suitcase and produced the peg, which he handed to the coroner.

"You see," he said, "that, in spite of its massive appearance, it had very little strength. It is merely a piece of thinnish, brass tube."

The coroner was impressed, but puzzled. "You consider," said he, as he handed the peg to the foreman of the jury, "that the test is conclusive?"

"Quite," replied Dr Thorndyke. "Clearly, a peg which breaks under a weight of 175 pounds could not have supported a body weighing 231 pounds."

"Yes," agreed the coroner, "that appears to be undeniable." He again reflected for a few moments, and then said: "I notice that you went to the chambers provided with this apparatus. The suggestion is that you had already a definite suspicion in your mind. Is that the case?"

"Yes; I had already come to the conclusion that deceased had never hung from that peg."

"Will you tell us what led you to that conclusion?"

"When I received instructions to investigate the case, I proceeded to make an inspection of the body, and it struck me, at once, that the appearances were not quite in agreement with the alleged facts, which I had learned from a verbatim report of the evidence. The amount of injury to the structures of the neck was much less than I should have expected in the case of so heavy a man, and the characteristic signs of death by hanging were absent. It is my invariable rule, in all cases of suspicious death, no matter what the apparent cause of the death may be, to examine the contents of the stomach and the secretions. In this case the procedure appeared to be necessary, and I made a careful examination of the contents of the stomach. The examination disclosed the presence of small quantities of veronal and alcohol, but when I tested for alkaloids, I obtained from the stomach and its contents no less than twenty-three minims of nicotine, the alkaloid of tobacco. Now nicotine – which differs from all other alkaloids but conein, the alkaloid of hemlock, in being a liquid – is an intensely poisonous substance. The fatal dose has not been exactly ascertained, but it may be stated at not more than five minims; that is, roughly, five drops. So that the quantity of this virulent poison actually obtained from the stomach of deceased was about four times the fatal dose. But this was only a part of the quantity that had been swallowed, for the examination was made ten days after death, by which time an appreciable amount of the poison would have been lost by post-mortem diffusion. I also examined the liver and other organs and the secretions, and in these I detected minute quantities of nicotine. The evidence afforded by these minute quantities is very important. Nicotine is a poison that acts with great rapidity – in fact, with the exception of hydrocyanic acid (prussic acid) it is probably the most rapidly-acting poison known. The importance, therefore, of these minute traces of the poison in remote organs is this: their existence proves that the poison entered the stomach during life – while the blood was still circulating; and the minuteness of the quantity absorbed proves that death occurred very rapidly – practically instantaneously.

"But the very large quantity of the poison and the evidence of its almost instantaneous effect created this dilemma: a witness had stated that she saw deceased hanging from the peg; but since death was practically instantaneous, he could not have hanged himself after taking the poison; and obviously he could not have taken the poison after he had hanged himself. This discrepancy, coupled with the absence of appreciable injury to the neck, raised a doubt as to whether deceased had ever hung from the peg at all. That doubt was increased by certain other circumstances. There were, for instance, post-mortem lacerations of the hamstring muscles and other muscles of the thighs, which could not be accounted for in the case of a body which had hung vertically, fully extended. There were faint impressions below the knees of some coarse-textured fabric, not part of his clothing, and there was the condition of a length of red, worsted rope by which deceased was said to have been suspended. Both ends of this rope – which had formed part of a loop – had been cut through with a very sharp instrument; and both ends were cut cleanly right through. But this could not possibly have happened in the alleged circumstances. If a body of this great weight had been suspended by two thicknesses of a flimsy, woollen rope, and an attempt had been made to cut that rope, the cutting instrument would not have passed right through, but would have divided the rope until the remaining portion was too weak to sustain the weight, and then that portion would have broken, leaving a ragged end. Having regard to the great evidential importance of the question, I decided to clear up the doubt, if possible by examining the peg itself. There are not many pegs which could carry this great weight without either bending, breaking or pulling out of the woodwork, and I thought it probable that an actual test with weights would settle the question. I accordingly obtained the keys from Mrs Otway, went to the chambers and applied the tests as I have stated."

"If the deceased was not suspended at all," the coroner objected, "how do you account for the marks of the rope on his neck?"

"He *was* suspended – or rather partially suspended. I looked about the chambers for the probable means of suspension, and decided that this was the knob of the bedpost at the right-hand side of the head of the bed. On this side of the bed was a hard jute matting, the texture of which corresponded exactly with the impressions on the knees, the faintness of which is accounted for by the partial protection furnished by the pyjamas. The procedure seems to have been this: the rope was secured to the neck of deceased immediately after death, while he was lying on the bed. It was then hitched over the knob of the bedpost and the body drawn off the bed so that it was supported against the bedpost in a kneeling position. This would account for the shallowness of the marks on the neck, the impressions of the matting on the knees, and the post-mortem lacerations of the muscles. With regard to these latter, it is evident that the body was left suspended in an approximately kneeling position for a good many hours – probably for the purpose of producing as deep an indentation as possible on the neck – and that during that time cadaveric rigidity became well established; so that when the rope was cut and the body allowed to fall to the floor, the legs were found to have stiffened and to be firmly set in the kneeling posture. As deceased was to be represented as having hanged himself from the peg, it would be necessary to straighten out the legs by force; but as the muscles were already rigid, the forcible extension would tend to produce such lacerations as were found. These lacerations were, of course, under the skin and would not be noticeable excepting on close examination."

"Is that the whole of your evidence?" the coroner asked as Dr Thorndyke paused.

"It is the whole of my evidence concerning the immediate circumstances of the death of Lewis Otway. I have certain other information, but you will probably not consider it of much importance to the inquiry. I have examined the two hairs that were found adhering to Mr Vardon's stick. They were not his hairs. As a matter of fact, the wound on his head was on a part in which there was no hair; but in any case, these were not his hairs. One of these was apparently a hair of Lewis Otway's – probably taken from his hair brush. His hair was white, but was dyed with a stain containing sulphide of lead. This hair was of a similar character and stained with the same material. The other was white and appeared to be a woman's hair. It was cut at both ends, and was evidently part of a much longer hair. I have also made some enquiries concerning the anonymous letters. Mrs Otway consulted me about them a month or two back, and I promised her to look into the matter, and did so. I collected very few facts, but if I may look at the letters I can tell you at once whether those facts throw any light on the authorship of these letters."

"It really is not of much importance to us," said the coroner, "though it may be important evidence in another place. Still, you may as well look at the letters." He handed the bundle of letters to

Dr Thorndyke, who examined each of them closely, holding them up to the light to inspect the watermark and comparing them with some other letters which he produced from his pocket.

"I think," said he, as he returned the letters to the coroner, "there is no doubt that all these letters were written by Morris Goldstein. I have several letters which were received from and signed by him, which are identically similar in character. All are typed on the same foreign paper – made in Sweden – with an old Calligraph machine which had three type-bars slightly bent – the lower-case 'g' and 's' and the capital 'O.' I have further evidence on the subject, if you care to hear it."

The foreman of the jury interposed at this point. "We don't want to hear any more about those letters. If deceased did not commit suicide, the letters don't matter."

"They will matter a good deal in another court," said the coroner, "but I agree with you that they do not affect our probable verdict; but there is one question to which we may as well have a definite answer, and then we need not detain Dr Thorndyke any longer. You have told us, sir, that the immediate cause of Lewis Otway's death was nicotine poisoning. Can you say whether the poison was taken by deceased himself, or whether it was administered by some other person?"

"The medical evidence proper furnishes no answer to that question, but from the attendant circumstances I infer that the poison was administered by some other person – probably while deceased was asleep. But that is only an opinion, based on the circumstantial evidence."

"Exactly. It is really a question for the jury. And now I don't think we need trouble you any further." The coroner bowed, a little stiffly, and as Dr Thorndyke walked back to his chair, he once more faced the jury.

"Well gentlemen," said he, "you have heard Dr Thorndyke's very remarkable evidence, and you will see that it compels us completely to revise our views of the case. The suicide by hanging, which we have been considering at such length, is seen to be an illusion, carefully, elaborately and ingeniously prepared. The question now is, was there a suicide at all? The cause of death was poisoning by nicotine, and death was almost instantaneous. Is this, then, a case of suicidal poisoning or of homicide?

"It is unnecessary for me to dwell on the suggested probabilities. You have heard a witness swear, in the most circumstantial manner, that she saw deceased hanging from a peg, and that she cut the body down. You now know that deceased could never have hung from that peg. That statement was false. But what was the object of that false statement? Its object must be considered in conjunction with the illusory appearances produced by an elaborate set of preparations – the cord-marks on the neck, the overturned chair, the end of the rope fastened to the peg – a set of preparations, the only intelligible object of which seems to be the concealment of the real cause of death. And then there is a further series of preparations revealed by the anonymous letters. These we now have reason to believe were written and sent by Morris Goldstein. Our reason for connecting Mrs Otway with those letters was based on Rachel Goldstein's statement that no one was in the house at Maidstone but Mrs Otway, and her husband and father. But we can no longer accept that statement. The suggested probability is that she was in the house, and that she either saw, or heard enough to gather what had taken place. In that case we seem to detect a carefully-laid plan to procure the suicide of the deceased, and throw suspicion on his wife; and when the suicide failed to occur the alternative of poison would seem to have been adopted.

"I must draw your attention to the circumstances existing at the time of the tragedy. In deceased's chambers were precious stones to the value of over four thousand pounds. Possibly there were stolen gems of a somewhat greater aggregate value. It is highly probable that Rachel Goldstein knew of the deceased's letter to his wife, for as he was bed-ridden at the time, the letter would have been posted by her, and could easily have been opened and read. The time of the interview was arranged by her so that Mrs Otway should be the last visitor.

"Here then is a group of circumstances furnishing a perfect opportunity for the carrying out of the plan. The gems were within reach, and a visitor was expected on whom could be thrown the suspicion of the theft, and the responsibility of the apparent suicide.

"As to the motive, apart from the theft of the gems we must remember that here was an illegitimate Jewish family into which had been introduced a legitimate Gentile wife. Her arrival had affected the interests of the family injuriously, and if a reconciliation between husband and wife should have occurred, those interests would have been still more unfavourably affected.

"But we are not called on to go deeply into the question of motive. This is a coroner's inquest, and our business is to decide how and by what means deceased met with his death. That decision is with you, gentlemen. You have heard the evidence, and I shall now leave you to consider your verdict."

As the coroner ceased speaking and silence fell upon the court I allowed myself, for the first time, to think of my own position. Previously I had not dared; for when Dr Thorndyke had made his dramatic statement, the revulsion of feeling had been so great that I had much ado to restrain myself from bursting into hysterical tears or laughter. But now I was more calm, and could think upon the change that a few magic words had wrought in my condition. I was free – free in body and soul. My imagined guilt had been a delusion; the silent willing and suggestion, a myth. I had never had any conscious intention to procure Lewis Otway's suicide; and no suicide had been procured. The death of that wretched man – my evil genius – had been brought about by no act of mine, conscious or unconscious. I was guiltless, I was free.

The jury took but a short time to consider their verdict. In a few minutes the foreman intimated that they had come to a unanimous decision. The coroner then formally put the question.

"Have you considered the evidence, gentlemen, and are you agreed upon your verdict?"

"We are," replied the foreman. "Our verdict is that the deceased Lewis Otway, met his death as the result of a poisonous dose of nicotine administered to him by Rachel Goldstein."

"Do you say that the poison was administered inadvertently or with malice?"

The foreman consulted his colleagues, and then replied, "With malice."

"That," said the coroner, "amounts to a verdict of wilful murder against Rachel Goldstein; and I may say that I am entirely in agreement with you."

As the coroner concluded, I looked at Mrs Gregg. Her face was set, and had turned a horrible, livid grey. Presently she rose slowly from her chair, and looked furtively over her shoulder; and as she did so she looked into the face of Superintendent Miller.

Epilogue

The history that I have set forth in the foregoing pages is the history of an episode. That episode opened with instantaneous abruptness; and in an instant it came to an abrupt end. The fatal words that I had overheard in my father's house had been as an incantation that had cast over me a malign spell. In the moment in which they were spoken the sinister shadow of Lewis Otway had fallen upon my life: and in the long months that followed it had never lifted. Even the death of the unhappy wizard had left the spell still working, the shadow deepening from hour to hour, until Dr Thorndyke, like a benevolent magician, had spoken the counter-charm. Then, in an instant, the spell was broken: the shadow lifted and lifted for ever.

And with the breaking of the spell and the lifting of the shadow, the episode is at an end, and my tale is told. Yet I am loth to lay down my pen until the reader who has followed my pilgrimage through the valley of the shadow, has been given at least one glimpse of me straying in the sunshine, "along the meads of asphodel." I would crave his attendance at the sombre, old church of St Clement Danes, where, on a bright May morning, was spoken another incantation that opened to four faithful hearts the gates of a Paradise of lifelong happiness and love. I would bid him admire sweet Peggy, tripping forth, all smiles and blushes, beside her stalwart husband to foregather with Jasper and me and our friends from Wellclose Square and the Temple in the ancient rooms in Clifford's Inn.

But my tale is told. The curtain is rung down; and I may not linger before it, babbling over the extinguished footlights on an empty stage – perchance to an empty house.

R Austin Freeman

The D'Arblay Mystery
A Dr Thorndyke Mystery

When a man is found floating beneath the skin of a green-skimmed pond one morning, Dr Thorndyke becomes embroiled in an astonishing case. This wickedly entertaining detective fiction reveals that the victim was murdered through a lethal injection and someone out there is trying a cover-up.

Dr Thorndyke Intervenes
A Dr Thorndyke Mystery

What would you do if you opened a package to find a man's head? What would you do if the headless corpse had been swapped for a case of bullion? What would you do if you knew a brutal murderer was out there, somewhere, and waiting for you? Some people would run. Dr Thorndyke intervenes.

R Austin Freeman

Felo De Se
A Dr Thorndyke Mystery

John Gillam was a gambler. John Gillam faced financial ruin and was the victim of a sinister blackmail attempt. John Gillam is now dead. In this exceptional mystery, Dr Thorndyke is brought in to untangle the secrecy surrounding the death of John Gillam, a man not known for insanity and thoughts of suicide.

Flighty Phyllis

Chronicling the adventures and misadventures of Phyllis Dudley, Richard Austin Freeman brings to life a charming character always getting into scrapes. From impersonating a man to discovering mysterious trapdoors, *Flighty Phyllis* is an entertaining glimpse at the times and trials of a wayward woman.

R Austin Freeman

Mr Pottermack's Oversight

Mr Pottermack is a law-abiding, settled homebody who has nothing to hide until the appearance of the shadowy Lewison, a gambler and blackmailer with an incredible story. It appears that Pottermack is in fact a runaway prisoner, convicted of fraud, and Lewison is about to spill the beans unless he receives a large bribe in return for his silence. But Pottermack protests his innocence, and resolves to shut Lewison up once and for all. Will he do it? And if he does, will he get away with it?

The Mystery of Angelina Frood
A Dr Thorndyke Mystery

A beautiful young woman is in shock. She calls John Strangeways, a medical lawyer who must piece together the strange disparate facts of her case and, in turn, becomes fearful for his life. Only Dr Thorndyke, a master of detection, may be able to solve the baffling mystery of Angelina Frood.

'Bright, ingenious and amusing' - *The Times Literary Supplement*

6495642R00220

Printed in Great Britain
by Amazon.co.uk, Ltd.,
Marston Gate.